Sarah Lefebve

Sarah Lefebve is a former journalist who after 6 years writing for local and regional newspapers decided that making up stories must surely be much more fun than sticking to the facts.

The Park Bench Test is the result.

She lives in Hampshire with her husband and two young children, now works in event management, and currently spends any miniscule bit of spare time she can find building pretty Lego houses for her daughter, crafting interesting Mr Potato Heads for her son and adding a few words here and there to her second novel. In a good year she even makes it to the gym once or twice.

*For Ruth, my oldest friend, who found her Mr Right.
And for Tom, my brother-in-law, who always wanted to
know when this book would be published.
Well here it is!*

PROLOGUE

Love flies, runs and rejoices; it is free and nothing can hold it back.

Thomas À Kempis (1379-1471)

When I was eight years old Ken asked Barbie to marry him.

Barbie said yes.

I wanted to know why.

I wanted to know everything when I was eight. I wanted to know why I had two eyes and two ears, but only one nose and only one mouth. I wanted to know why grass was green and why sky was blue. I wanted to know why my eyebrows didn't grow to be as long as my hair.

And I wanted to know why Barbie loved Ken.

It was the first day of the summer holidays and my best friend Emma and I had laid on a lavish wedding for our bride and groom – in a marquee made out of four plastic tent poles and a pink lacy pillowcase from Laura Ashley. It was *the* place to be that Saturday afternoon, with an enviable guest list that included four other Barbie dolls, My Little Pony – who'd plaited her mane for the occasion, Paddington Bear – minus one wellington boot which Emma had dropped out of the window while she was showing

1

my mum the flower we'd forced into his buttonhole, and a naked Tiny Tears, all of whom were treated to a wedding breakfast of chocolate digestives and Love Heart sweets.

It wasn't the first time they'd got married but it *was* the first time we ever questioned why Barbie *wanted* to marry Ken. Not that we thought there was anything wrong with Ken – he was quite cool really, particularly in the white sparkly trousers we had made for him out of one of my dad's old handkerchiefs, some Pritt Stick glue and a pot of blue glitter.

My mum was helping out at the village plant sale, so it was my dad who had drawn the short straw.

"Daddy," I said, my tone giving away the fact that I was about to ask a question he'd rather I had saved for my mum.

"Yes Rebs," he replied hesitantly, over the top of his newspaper. My dad still calls me Rebs. Everyone else calls me Becky – or B. He likes to be different.

"Barbie loves Ken, doesn't she?" I asked, pulling off the bride's luminous green swimsuit, which probably convinced my dad he was about to have to deliver his "birds and bees" speech a little earlier than expected.

"Yes that's right, love."

"Why does she?"

"Why does she what, love?" he said, half listening, half reading his newspaper.

"Why does she love Ken? Why does she want to marry him?"

Of course, the answer was obvious – Barbie was marrying Ken so that Emma and I could get our hands on enough chocolate digestives and Love Heart sweets to make ourselves sick. But my dad chose to overlook this minor detail.

"What makes you ask that sweetheart?" he asked instead, buying himself a bit of time to come up with a plausible answer, no doubt, while simultaneously breathing a sigh of relief that he wasn't going

2

to have to explain where babies came from.

"I just wondered."

"Well," he ventured, both Emma and I now hanging off his every word.

"Well…he's her Mr Right, I suppose."

Hello?

We were only eight years old, dad.

"What's a misterite?" Emma asked, trying to flick a bit of glitter off her finger.

My dad thought about it for a moment.

"Mr Right is the man a lady loves and wants to spend the rest of her life with. He's the man she wants to marry. Because he makes her happy. Because they're sort of meant to be together, sort of, I guess…"

You had to hand it to him – it was a damn good try.

"Does that mean you're mummy's misterite, then daddy?" I asked, still intrigued, while Emma, clearly less than impressed with this explanation, had returned to the task of making Ken a sparkly vest to go with his trousers.

"That's right darling," dad said, beaming – maybe because he *was* my mum's Mr Right, maybe because he'd managed to answer the question without her help, probably a bit of both.

I may have only been eight years old, but I am pretty sure that was the very moment I decided I believed in Mr Right. And that one day I would find him.

I suspect it was also the moment that Emma decided it was absolute bollocks. That there was no such thing as Mr Right. And that the best she could ever hope for was to find someone who'd stick around longer than her dad did.

"But why?" I asked my dad for the third time, buttoning up Barbie's wedding dress while Ken waited nervously in the marquee. "Why are you mummy's misterite?"

My dad looked up from his newspaper and pondered the question for a second.

"Because, Rebs. Just because."

CHAPTER ONE

Somewhere there waiteth in this world of ours
For one lone soul another lonely soul,
Each choosing each through all the weary hours
And meeting strangely at one sudden goal.

'Destiny', Sir Edwin Arnold (1832-1904)

"Sorry, sorry," I shout, running down Pretty Street where Emma and Katie are both waiting for me outside the shop.

I look at my watch. I'm 30 minutes late. Damn.

"Sorry," I say again, trying to catch my breath. I really should work on my fitness.

I hug them both.

"The train was delayed leaving Leeds," I explain. "And then we had to stop in Grantham to replenish the buffet car. I blame the fat git in coach D – every time I went past him to get to the loos he was scoffing another king size Mars Bar. And then I had to wait 20 minutes for a bloody tube. The underground was packed. Whose idea was it to go wedding dress shopping in London on the first day of the January sales?" I ask. "Oh yes – yours!" I say, grinning at Katie.

"Let's have another look then. I've forgotten what it looks like already."

She waves her left hand in my face and I throw my head back, pretending to be blinded by the sparkle.

"Gorgeous," I say, and she beams – which is pretty much all she's been doing for the last ten days, I suspect.

"Right then. Let's get this show on the road," I say, pushing open the door to Maid in Heaven.

"I'm sorry," a lady with half-moon glasses perched on the end of her nose and a tape measure wrapped around her neck tells us when we explain we've come in search of a wedding dress for Katie – a little pointless really, given that we are stood in a shop full of the bloody things.

"We're fully booked," she says. "You really should have made an appointment."

I don't like the way she's looking at us – like she would look at something sticky on the bottom of her shoe. Lips turned down, nose tilted slightly in the air. I'm tempted to pull that tape measure a little tighter...

"What about this afternoon?" Katie asks.

The woman shakes her head.

"Fully booked," she repeats. "All day."

She reaches for a big leather diary from a desk and flicks nonchalantly through the pages until she stops at the first one that isn't completely obliterated with brides' names, telephone numbers and dress sizes. She taps the page decisively.

"April the third," she says, ever so slightly sarcastically. Anyone would think she's trying to make a point. "I can fit you in on April the third."

"APRIL THE THIRD?" Katie shrieks. "That's..." – she counts on

6

her fingers quickly – "…four months away. I want to get married on September the eighteenth. I can't wait four months!"

"SEPTEMBER EIGHTEENTH?!" the woman shrieks, obviously now in competition with my friend as to who can inject the most alarm into three simple words. "September the eighteenth, *this year*? In that case you *really* should have made an appointment."

Katie looks at Emma and me.

If I didn't know better, I'd say she's going to cry.

But of course I do know better. I've known Katie for nearly ten years. Katie would never let a nasty woman like this make her cry.

"I'm sorry," she tells her, instead, "I'm used to shopping in Marks and Spencer and Next, where you don't have to make an appointment to use a cubicle." And then she glances over to the rails of dresses on display at the back of the shop, and grimaces.

"In any case," she says, "I really don't think you have what it is I'm looking for."

Emma and I grimace too – just for good measure. And then the three of us leave the shop and leg it back up the road laughing.

The woman at the next shop is not quite so nasty. But she does laugh at us. How rude.

"Have you any idea how many men propose over Christmas and New Year?" she asks.

Katie looks crestfallen. I think she thought it was just Matt – that it was just the best day of his and hers lives – not every Tom, Dick and Harry's.

"We filled three months of the diary in one week," she explains.

"Okay. Thanks anyway," Katie says.

And so we leave shop number two.

Katie looks at her list.

Old New Borrowed Blue is next. But it's a tube ride away. I'm not sure I can face the underground again just yet. I've only just

7

got over the ordeal of being pressed up against Worzel Gummidge all the way from Kings Cross to Knightsbridge. I don't think I've ever held my breath for so long. I almost held the Metro paper between us as a makeshift barrier until I discovered someone had already used it to scrape a bit of chewing gum off the bottom of their shoe.

"Let's go grab a coffee," I suggest. I'm a tea drinker actually, but nobody says that do they? – 'Let's go grab a cup of tea' – unless they're over sixty five and planning on ordering a fruit scone to go with it.

"Good idea," Emma and Katie both agree.

"So, Emma. Have you changed your mind yet?" Katie asks, before shovelling a huge forkful of chocolate fudge cake into her mouth. She's as skinny as a rake too. There's no justice.

"I can't, Katie," she says, offering her a piece of double chocolate chip cookie with extra chocolate – presumably in the hope that it will help soften the blow.

Emma is refusing to be a bridesmaid – on account of the fact that it will jeopardise her own chances of ever walking down the aisle.

What can I say? My friends are a little odd.

"Three times a bridesmaid, never a bride," she told Katie the moment she blinded us for the first time with her newly acquired diamond ring on Boxing Day, when we met at my parents house in Sussex for leftover turkey and recycled Christmas cracker hats.

"You were only five when your godmother got married!" Katie had argued. "And Alison and Paul are already divorced, so that doesn't count either."

"Age is irrelevant. And the only way to reverse the curse is to be a bridesmaid another four times. And even if Becky does get off her arse and marry Alex," Emma had said, looking pointedly at me, "that still leaves me three times short, and I don't know anybody who's even remotely close to getting that ring on their finger. Sorry Katie, I can't do it."

Personally I think she's just trying to avoid the humiliation of wearing a peach dress in front of all of Katie and Matt's friends and family. Not that Katie is planning on dressing us in peach. At least I hope she's not. It's every bridesmaid's worst fear, isn't it – being made to look like a giant helping of peach cobbler? Or worse still, being forced into some floral number that looks like it has come straight from your Auntie Mabel's living room curtain pole.

Anyway – a battle ensued, involving a minor strop on both parts and an in-depth discussion on every possible superstition from the importance of good manners when coming face to face with a lone magpie, to the day-long good fortune to be had from seeing a penny and picking it up (frankly I'd be much happier to see a £20 note and slip that into my pocket – but maybe that's just me).

Katie relented, eventually, and agreed that Emma could do a reading instead – on the proviso that she comes on every shopping trip that involves the wedding in any way, shape or form. Starting today.

She's not quite given up trying to persuade her yet though.

"I can't afford to risk it," Emma explains, for the umpteenth time. "I have such shit luck with men."

She's right. She does.

She has no trouble meeting men. And getting them, for that matter. Emma is stunning – with legs up to her armpits, and perky boobs. And the blonde hair. And the blue eyes. And she's a lovely person too. Makes you sick, doesn't it?

Men, for Emma, are a bit like buses. Buses which turn up in the most unexpected places. In the baggage claim area at Gatwick Airport following a teachers' conference in Glasgow, for example. Or the frozen vegetable section of her local Tesco Express. Or the back row of a karate class (the one and only class she ever made it to, I hasten to add, being too busy, as she inevitably was, loved up with the guy from the back row).

Yes – Emma can get the men.

It's just the keeping them that she tends to have a problem with. Before long, either they lose interest – or she does.

Either she's about to add her toothbrush to the pot on their bathroom sink and a spare pair of knickers to their bottom drawer when they give her the elbow or she decides she doesn't want them anymore, in which case they tend to hang around like a bad smell.

Emma's last four boyfriends, in no particular order, were:

Greg – who told her he loved her on their third date. He sent her 12 bunches of flowers, 37 voicemail messages and 52 text messages in six days. On the seventh day she dumped him. Good decision, I think.

Dean – who couldn't get it up. But she really liked him and was prepared to help him through it – and would have done, had she not discovered that he had told all his mates she couldn't keep her hands off him, that they were at it like rabbits and that they had virtually cleared the local branch of Boots of their entire supply of Fetherlite Durex. She dumped him after six weeks and promptly told his mates exactly why they weren't at it like rabbits.

Barry – who most certainly could get it up – and did so on a regular basis. Just not exclusively for Emma, as she discovered when she let herself into his apartment to surprise him on his birthday after fibbing that she was busy – only to discover he had already put on his birthday suit for someone else.

And Peter – who dumped *her* after she discovered he was growing marijuana in his bathtub and suggested he might like to take up a more law-abiding hobby – like draughts or ping-pong.

Emma doesn't believe in Mr Right. She just wants to meet someone she likes – or loves – enough to want to stick around.

When she was seven her dad left her mum for his secretary and moved to the South of France. Maybe that's why. I don't think she's ever got over it.

"So have you made any other plans yet?" I ask Katie, blowing on my tea.

She nods and waves her hand to signal she intends to give details. But her mouth is still full of chocolate fudge cake.

"You don't have to eat it all in one go," I tell her. "We've got all day, you know. My train doesn't leave until eight."

I normally stay the night with Katie and Matt. It's a long way to come from Leeds just for the day – but I have to go home tonight as Alex and I have a christening to go to tomorrow.

"Well, we've set the date, obviously."

They're getting married on the anniversary of the day they met – six years ago. September the eighteenth. Nine months from now. She's assures us that's coincidental. I'm assuming she's telling the truth. I'm guessing she wouldn't choose to give birth whilst walking up the aisle.

"And we've booked the venue - a lovely little church in Beaulieu in the New Forest followed by a reception at the Montagu Arms Hotel."

Matt took Katie to Beaulieu for the weekend when they had been together for a year. Katie fell in love with the place and told him when they got married that was where she'd like them to do it. Even back then she knew she'd met the one.

"You'll love it," she says, draining her coffee cup as we get ready to leave. "It's so beautiful. I couldn't believe it when they said it was available on the date we wanted. They'd had a cancellation, I think. Obviously someone decided not to get hitched after all," she grins, pleased that someone else's misfortune has turned into her own good luck.

It's also due to a cancellation that we are finally able to make it all the way into a wedding dress shop without being laughed straight back out again. *Old New Borrowed Blue* has had a cancellation.

"You're a lucky girl," the owner tells Katie in a very teachery voice, as if she's telling her off for colouring outside the lines.

"We've just this minute had a cancellation. The bride is sick, apparently." From the tone of her voice I'd say she doesn't believe the bride for one minute. I'd say she hears this excuse all the time. I'd say she thinks the bride has actually been dumped but doesn't want to admit it.

"Great," Katie says, before realising how that sounds.

"What I mean is, great that you've had a cancellation, not great that the bride is sick, obviously..."

She takes our coats and shows us upstairs to a waiting area next to numerous racks of dresses. There are big comfy sofas, wedding photographs all over the walls, and piles and piles of wedding magazines stacked up on a large glass coffee table.

"Catriona will be with you shortly," she says. "Feel free to browse."

We are about to start rifling through the magazines when Catriona arrives.

She introduces herself, before asking: "Which one's the bride?"

I quickly push Katie forward, before she gets any ideas that it might be me.

"I am," Katie says, at the same time as Emma says "not me". You can tell by her tone that what she really means is "not bloody me!"

"Wonderful," Catriona says.

I like her. She isn't nasty and she hasn't laughed at us. Yet. She's in her mid forties, I'd say. She's small, and smartly dressed in a navy trouser suit and white top. She looks like she knows what she's doing. And she's smiling too. For now.

"When's the big day?"

"September eighteenth," Katie volunteers.

"Oh good. That gives us plenty of time then. That's twelve, thirteen, fourteen... twenty one months," she says, flicking through the months in her diary.

"No, September the eighteenth this year," Katie says.

"SEPTEMBER THE EIGHTEENTH THIS YEAR?!" Catriona gasps. "But that's nine months away!" she says, verging upon becoming hysterical.

"Yes?" Katie says, panic beginning to sound in her own voice, although she is not entirely sure why.

"Nine months?" Catriona repeats, this time as a question, presumably to check she has heard right.

"I'm not pregnant," Katie says, defensively.

"I didn't think for a moment that you were, dear. But nine months is really not very long at all to plan a wedding. A wedding is the best day of a girl's life, after all." She looks like she might actually be about to have a nervous breakdown. Anybody would think we'd just told her Katie was getting married tomorrow and needed a dress making from scratch.

"They want to get married on the anniversary of the day they met," Emma explains, helpfully.

"So what about next year?" Catriona suggests, in a deadly serious tone. "I mean, for starters you won't be able to have any of these dresses here, because we'd never get them in time," she says, sweeping her arms dramatically across a rail of dresses. It's no great pity, frankly – a good ninety per cent of them are hideous meringues and would therefore fall at Katie's first test – 'will they make me look remotely like Katie Price when she married Peter Andre?'

"Or here. Or here," she continues, on a roll.

"What about these?" Emma asks, pointing out what appears to be the only rail that has not yet been waved at dramatically.

"Well, yes, those would be okay," she says, almost begrudgingly.

13

"But you'd have to order it pretty soon. We wouldn't have much time to play with. Especially if you needed it altering at all. Which you probably will. What sort of thing are you looking for?" she asks Katie, who has already started rifling through the rail.

"I don't want a meringue," she says decisively. "I don't like fussy things. No lace. No frills. No bows. No fuss. I want something white, but not too white. And I'd prefer it to be strapless.

"But I would happily try straps," she adds hastily, registering the look on Catriona's face, who appears to be mentally narrowing down the list of options by the second.

"I can spend whatever I need to," Katie tells her, silently thanking her dad who is paying for the wedding, "but I'd rather not spend a fortune," she continues, because she is not the sort to abuse her dad's generosity.

At the mention of sort-of-unlimited cash Catriona's mood perks up considerably and she takes over the rifling.

"You go in there and strip off while I get some dresses ready for you to try on," she tells Katie, who obediently dumps her bag and coat on my lap and disappears behind a white linen curtain into a cubicle.

Moments later Catriona hangs three dresses on a rail outside the cubicle and pokes her head around the curtain.

"Take your bra off too, love," she instructs Katie, inviting herself into the cubicle and pulling the curtain across behind her. I look at Emma and grin.

"How are you doing?" I call out several minutes later when they still haven't reappeared.

It's hard to tell but the loud guffaw from the other side of the curtain may well be a clue.

"Almost there," Catriona shouts.

Emma and I flick through the magazines while we are waiting.

"Blimey! Guess how much this one is," I say to Emma, holding

14

up *Bride Be Beautiful* and pointing to the dress at the top of the page. I quickly cover the price with my finger.

"Dunno. Twenty pence," she says, glancing up from *White White Weddings*.

"No, seriously, guess."

"I want to say about eight hundred quid but judging by your reaction it's probably more like five grand?"

"Twenty-five grand!" I tell her, bringing the magazine right up to my face. I must have misread it. "That's ridiculous!" I say, having established there is nothing wrong with my eyesight and that, yes, this wedding dress really does cost almost as much as my annual salary.

"That's a deposit on a house, for heaven's sake."

"If I ever get married, I'll be doing it on a beach somewhere in my bikini," Emma says. She would too.

"Why waste all that money on a dress that's only going to be worn for a few hours – and on a day when all your new husband can think about is getting you out of it?"

Catriona pokes her head outside the curtain – to check we are still here probably – there's a fabulous cake shop around the corner which I'm sure must be an incredible temptation when you are on the tenth or eleventh dress and the bride still hasn't found one she likes.

"She's ready girls," she announces, before sweeping back the curtain and waiting for Katie to emerge.

"So. What do you think?"

"I don't like it," Emma says, screwing her nose up.

"You don't get a say," Katie tells her.

"What have you made me come for then?"

"Consider it your punishment."

Emma says nothing – just rolls her eyes at me.

"What do *you* think Becky?" Katie asks me, not before giving

15

Emma one more moody glance for good measure.

"Well, it's okay... But there's probably something out there that is more you," I confirm, before she promptly disappears back behind the curtain.

"I am NEVER going to find a dress," Katie says, despondently shoving a prawn cracker in her mouth.

We've come to China Palace for dinner before I head home. And we've ordered enough to feed an army, after Katie complained she had 'not eaten a thing all day'. I did point out that this wasn't strictly true – that she had in fact wolfed down an extra large helping of chocolate fudge cake as well as an entire king size bag of giant chocolate buttons between 2:12pm and 2:18pm. Single-handedly. The chocolate fudge cake she conceded, but the chocolate buttons didn't count, apparently, since 'chocolate buttons are an addiction, not a source of sustenance'.

Life is not fair. Katie can eat chocolate all day every day and never put on an ounce, whereas I only have to sniff the empty packet and I put on five pounds. And it's not even as if I can just say 'to hell with it' and sod the five pounds. I have a bridesmaid dress to squeeze into. Or will do, anyway, if we ever get Katie sorted out first.

"You've tried on five dresses," Emma laughs. "I don't think you need to panic just yet, hun."

"Yes, but I hated them all. Hated," she repeats, slopping a spoon of sweet and sour chicken onto her plate. "And so did you two. God I hope it's easier finding you a bridesmaid dress Becks. Unless you just want to get a wedding dress and have a double wedding?" she asks hopefully, eager for someone to share her frustration.

I shake my head as I help myself to some chicken with cashew nuts.

"Sorry hun, you're on your own. But don't worry. You've got

16

plenty of time, despite what any of these wedding shop witches tell you. They're bound to tell you to hurry – they want you to buy one of their dresses. They don't want you to take your time and look elsewhere."

"Yeah, I guess you're right. So, anyway, enough wedding talk. Tell us how it's going with Jim, Emma."

Jim is Emma's current man. She met him at the chip shop after a drunken night out in Brighton and offered to let him dip his chips in her curry sauce. She's a classy chick, our Em. And despite her inexcusable opening line, it appears to be going well. I think it's been about two months now, which is something of a record for her.

"It's going really well, actually," she grins.

I think she really likes this one because she goes all mushy whenever you mention his name – a bit like a lovesick teenager.

"We're going away in a few weeks - to this posh hotel in Hampshire. Jim won this spa weekend at his work's Christmas do. Two nights' bed and breakfast with spa treatments for two. Let's just say I think we might be missing out on the breakfast – and the spa treatments!" She licks her lips and smiles sweetly – like butter wouldn't melt in her mouth, when in actual fact she's planning the dirty weekend to end all dirty weekends.

"So when are we going to meet him?" I ask. "You don't want to let it go too far. You might have to dump him if Katie and I don't approve."

"Oh you'll approve," she assures us. "He's gorgeous. And totally fabulous in bed!"

"Excellent," Katie says, helping herself to more egg-fried rice. She's got hollow legs, I'm sure.

"So?" I ask.

"So what?"

"So when are we going to meet him? It's not often you go this

17

gooey over someone. It's time we met the guy."

"I'll sort something out soon, I promise. But you'll definitely love him.

"You know what…" she says, biting into a prawn cracker – a pause for thought. "He might just be Mr Right."

"You don't believe in Mr Right," I remind her.

"I know I don't. But someone this good in bed has to be as close as I'm gonna get to him, damn it!"

18

CHAPTER TWO

*A soul mate is someone who has locks that fit our keys, and
keys that fit our locks.*

Excerpt from 'The Bridge Across Forever', Richard Bach

I've thought more than once since that little 'chat' with my dad
that I might have found Mr Right.

When I was nine I thought it might be Jonathan Jamieson
because he gave me a bit of his Sherbet Dib Dab after I fell over
in the school playground and grazed my knee.

When I was thirteen I thought it might be Andrew Bradley. We
'went out' for two whole weeks, which basically means we held
hands on the school bus and passed love letters to each other
during maths classes when we were supposed to be working out
simultaneous equations.

And when I was sixteen I thought it might be Stephen Clarkson
– my first proper boyfriend. But that didn't mean anything because
at sixteen I was also convinced that Brad Pitt, Tom Cruise and
Johnny Depp could all be Mr Right.

I'm not sure I've ever thought Alex is Mr Right.

Alex is there to meet me when I arrive back in Leeds station on

19

Sunday night. I have been instructed to warn him that weekends in London are the norm from now on. "We have a wedding to prepare for," I keep being told. I'm not sure who this 'we' is she's talking about. I was under the impression it was Matt she was marrying.

He takes it well, and rather than moaning about how we'll hardly see each other, points out that it will mean more time for football and nights out with the lads without having to feel guilty. There's nothing quite like feeling appreciated, is there? But Alex's easy-going nature is one of the things I love about him – that and his lovely bum.

"I thought we'd pick up a bottle of wine and a DVD on the way home," he says.

"Lovely," I say, squeezing his thigh appreciatively as he changes gear.

All you really need to know about Alex is this – he's lovely.

But to elaborate – he's gorgeous, he's funny, he's incredibly generous, he can cook – and bake – which is a definite bonus since I can do neither. He makes the best banoffee pie I've ever tasted, which just happens to be my all-time favourite dessert. And he has the best bum in the world. No, really, he does. It's perfect. Dead pert, but soft as a baby's bum. I can't keep my hands off it. Well, I didn't use to be able to anyway. Alex used to joke that if we ever split up I'd want custody of his bum. He's right, I would.

So why haven't I ever thought Alex is Mr Right – especially after all those lovely things I've told you about him (did I mention his lovely bum)?

I wish I could tell you. I really do.

But I don't know.

I love him, of course I do. I love him a lot. But if he was Mr Right I wouldn't question it, would I? Just like you wouldn't question whether a banana was a banana, or whether a bowl of cornflakes was a bowl of cornflakes. You know it's a bowl of cornflakes, so you don't need to ask.

So if Alex was Mr Right, I wouldn't need to ask myself the question, right?

But I do need to ask.

I *am* asking.

I met Alex in my final year at university, at the Student Union Christmas ball. He was stood next to me at the bar, but despite looking particularly scrummy in his tuxedo and bow tie, he couldn't get himself noticed by the male bar staff who were more interested in serving all the gorgeous girls in their skimpy dresses. I like to include myself among their number but I suspect my being served was more down to the fact that I was leaning so far over the bar I was practically poking one of the barmen in the eye with my reindeer antlers.

Out of pity I offered to get Alex's drink for him and, well, to cut a short story even shorter, we basically spent the rest of the evening snogging in a corner. Admittedly, pity no longer played any role. I can only blame my actions on a combination of seven gin and tonics and Alex's gorgeousness, which – by sheer luck rather than good judgement I'm sure – still existed the following night when I left my beer goggles at home for the evening and met him for a post-snog drink.

Fast forward six years and here we are, both still in Leeds, nothing much changed except for the fact that it's now our jobs that are paying for the drinks and not our overdrafts/student loans/ parents. That, and the fact that we now live together – in a rented house for now, but we are saving for our own place. Well, strictly speaking, it's Alex who is doing the bulk of the saving, earning, as he does, almost twice as much as I do and having considerably fewer pairs of shoes to buy each month.

And I love him.

I absolutely do.

But…

But what?

I don't know.

But isn't the very existence of a 'but' enough? And now I'm not talking about his lovely bum.

How do you know? If someone is the one, I mean? How do any of us know? It was easy for Barbie – Emma and I decided for her that Ken was Mr Right. But who decides for the rest of us? We have to do that for ourselves, which hardly seems fair. It would be so much easier if we all came with a label saying who we belong to.

Maybe Alex *is* my Mr Right. Maybe I just haven't found his label yet?

CHAPTER THREE

Had I the heaven's embroidered cloths,
Enwrought with golden and silver light,
The blue and the dim and the dark cloths
Of night and light and the half-light,
I would spread the cloths under my feet;
But I, being poor, have only my dreams;
I have spread my dreams under your feet;
Tread softly because you tread on my dreams.

'He wishes for the cloths of heaven', W.B. Yeats

Bollocks.

It's Monday morning. Quite how it can be is beyond me. It only feels like five minutes since I switched off my computer and dumped my dirty mug in the office sink.

I contemplate phoning in sick. This is not a first. I contemplate phoning in sick every Monday morning. The possibilities are endless – I could put a peg on my nose and pretend I have the flu. I could tie a scarf tightly around my neck, cut the air supply to my vocal chords and pretend I have tonsillitis. I could come out with complete gibberish and pretend I'm hallucinating – though I tend to come out with complete gibberish a lot of the

23

time, so this probably wouldn't be terribly convincing.

I never actually do phone in sick. Not because my excuses are not entirely plausible, but because I like to think of myself as a conscientious employee, persevering with the rest of the rat race in the face of sheer boredom.

I used to be depressed when I woke up on a Sunday morning because I knew I was going back to work the next day. Now I'm depressed when I wake up on a Saturday morning, because I know that the next time I wake up I will be going back to work the next day. I spend Monday to Friday wishing my life away for the weekend, and Saturday and Sunday depressed that the weekend is almost over. Which, if you think about it, leaves only Friday available for not being miserable, when I'm too stressed out after a whole week in the office to really appreciate it.

I must get out more.

I love my job, I love my job, I love my job.

This is not a statement of fact, by the way, merely a mantra I am trying out.

I'm saying it to myself every morning as I make my way into Penand Inc's head office in the misguided hope that it might eventually come true.

It's not working.

I have a terribly glamorous job, you know.

I sell pencils. No, really, I do. I sell pencils. Okay, so I'm selling myself short. I also sell pens. And pencil sharpeners. And Post-It notes. In fact – take a look around your desk – anything you can see, the chances are I sell it. Or, at least, I work for the people who sell it.

It wasn't meant to be like this. I never intended to sell pencils for a living. No, in actual fact, I was meant to be the next Carrie Bradshaw. Not necessarily being paid to write about sex, but being paid to write at least – being paid to do what I love. It doesn't have to be Carrie, of course. I'd settle for Kate Hudson's character in *How To Lose A Guy In Ten Days*.

How To Give Up Your Dream Job And Sell Pencils Instead.

How To Convince The Bride-To-Be That Peach Only Suits A Peach.

How To Tell Your Boyfriend You're Not Sure He's The One...

The plan was to move back home and look for a journalism job in London after my finals. But then Alex got a great job up here with a high profile law firm. And I wanted to be with him, so I stayed too. I got a temporary job. It was meant to be a short term thing. Just until I had paid off some of my (rather hefty) student debts. Just until I began pursuing my 'real' career by pestering unsuspecting editors of local newspapers to give me a job.

That was five years ago.

I love my job, I love my job, I love my job, I chant as I walk through the automatic doors, smile sweetly at Marie on reception and swipe my ID card to let me through the security door.

I often wonder why they make it so damned difficult to get into this building. We're really not that keen on getting in, after all. It would make far more sense to make it harder for us to get out, if you ask me – getting out is much more popular.

I love my job, I love my job, I love my job, I continue up the stairs to the second floor. It was my New Year's resolution never to take the lift, on account of the fact that I'm supposed to be on a diet. Because I've just been asked to be bridesmaid. And because I ate far more than my fair share of a Christmas kilogram tub of Cadbury's Miniature Heroes.

Not that I'm a fatty or anything. But I could do with losing a pound or two, because I'm sure peach looks even less attractive when you're wearing a spare tyre underneath it.

Anyway, it's the second week in January and I haven't succumbed yet. Apart from the day after the office Christmas party (held on January sixth for reasons I will never understand) when I was feeling particularly hungover. But that doesn't count, because it was a Christmas party, and so technically still December. Okay, so I'm a cheat. I hold my hands up. But everyone knows that New Year's resolutions are made to be broken.

My heart sinks when I see my desk. Plummets, in fact. I don't know why I'm even vaguely surprised. What did I expect – that Mary Poppins would pop in over the weekend, click her fingers and magic everything into its correct folder, drawer and filing tray (not that I actually have any filing trays to speak of)?

I'm surprised I'm not forever being disciplined over the state of my desk. You could actually grow things in the mugs that have, on occasion, been found on my desk. They say mould produces penicillin, don't they? If that's right then I'm pretty sure that the contents of a mug that was (allegedly) found on my desk last week could probably have saved a small community from the bubonic plague.

I don't know what happened really. I was such a tidy child. I would spend hours tidying my already immaculate bedroom. All my cassettes were neatly filed in alphabetical order in their wall-mounted plastic storage cases, my white pants were kept separate from my coloured ones, my socks separate from my tights, and all my games were stacked neatly on top of the wardrobe in size-order – Game of Life and Monopoly at the bottom, Yahtzee at the top. If I ever found a loose playing piece I'd painstakingly slide out the relevant game, open it up and put the piece away in its proper place before returning the game to its correct position.

Now I'd probably just lob the loose playing piece to the top of the wardrobe and hope it didn't bounce back and hit me in the face; my bills are filed in the kitchen drawer, along with old freebie newspapers and menus for a dozen different takeaways; CDs are put away in whichever empty case happens to be close to hand – which is fine, until Alex goes to play his favourite

Stereophonics album when he's driving the lads to a footie match and my favourite Will Young CD blasts out of the car stereo instead; and the *Sex & The City* quiz cards are scooped up and put away back to front and out of order, giving the cheats among us the perfect opportunity for a sneaky glance at the answers while they are being sorted (I remain convinced this is how Katie beat both me and Emma hands down on their last visit).

I'm even worse at work. My desk is an embarrassment, to be honest. It is littered with coloured pens, enough Post-It notes to create my very own roll of Post-It-themed wallpaper and dozens of scraps of paper covered in illegible notes under the scribbled heading 'to do'. Organised chaos, I call it. But there really is no excuse. I work for an office supplies company, after all, with unlimited pen pots, filing trays and notepads at my disposal.

I am one of eight account planners at Penand Inc who set up and manage new accounts after unsuspecting office managers have been hypnotised by our sweet-talking salesmen – and women – and their copies of our two-inch-thick glossy catalogue.

I'm really an admin assistant with a fancy title and a salary to match, which is probably why I have stayed for so long. You get used to earning decent money, don't you? Especially after being a student when you are used to pooling your coppers for a loaf of bread to make cheese on toast after a night in the student union bar.

I work with the biggest bunch of knobs. Dickheads, all of them, except Felicity and Erin, who I share an office with. Between us we look after the big national companies. There were four of us but Hannah, the senior account planner, was sacked last month for stealing a bottle of Tippex. Strictly speaking, it wasn't the Tippex that got her the sack. If they were that petty then I'd have been out on my ear long ago – I could open up my own branch of WHSmiths with all the pens and Post-It notes that have made their way home in my handbag over the years. The Tippex was merely the straw that broke the camel's back, shall we say, because Hannah didn't just nick the odd pen or pencil, or pad of Post-Its, or bottle of Tippex. She nicked an entire office. Well, obviously not an office as such, but everything needed to equip one. Her boyfriend was starting up his own recruitment agency and Hannah thought it would save him a few quid if she got him a few bits from work. Like pens and pencils, and a ream of paper or two, for example. I'm sure she didn't actually intend to put the flat-pack beech-effect corner desk with matching filing cabinet into the boot of her car. Or the traditional executive leather facing manager's chair. Or the Canon C1492X printer scanner. Although, if she had stopped there then she may well have got away with it. But when she was spotted leaving the warehouse with a 12-pack of Tippex – there's only so much Tippex a person can get through, even if your employers are paying for it – suspicions were aroused, and an investigation was launched. In other words, Hannah was summoned to personnel where she 'fessed up and was promptly handed her P45.

Which has left Fliss, Erin and I holding the fort. And for some ludicrous reason the two of them have nominated me to be in charge of the team until a new senior account planner is appointed. Erin says she isn't 'boss material' and Fliss says she's past it.

But I'm a terrible leader. I hate telling other people what to do. I'd rather do something myself than have to ask somebody else to do it.

Fliss and Erin are very sweet though. They never take advantage of my complete inability to delegate. If the roles were reversed, I can't promise I wouldn't completely take the piss – come in late, take extra long lunch hours, leave early...

Come to think of it – I do all that already...

As if to prove my point, they are both already in as I survey the nuclear disaster that is my desk.

"Cup of tea, Becky love?" Fliss asks, illustrating one of the many reasons I totally adore her.

"That'd be fab, Fliss, thanks," I reply, shrugging my coat off and draping it over the back of my chair.

Erin and Fliss are the perfect people to share an office with. Fliss makes a fabulous cup of tea, and Erin, despite being on a permanent diet, always has a well-stocked bucket of Maltesers hidden between the hanging files in her desk drawer.

Fliss is amazing. She has worked for Penand Inc her whole life. Well, almost. Thirty-eight years to be exact. Can you imagine that? Working for the same company for nearly forty years? If I'm still at Penand Inc when I'm forty, never mind sixty, someone please put me out of my misery.

Not that I'm knocking Fliss. It's what you did in her day, isn't it? You joined a company straight from school and stuck with them, getting your carriage clock after thirty years and a big retirement bash a decade or so later. Incidentally, why a carriage clock? Why not something more useful like an iPod, or a Kindle, or a weekend in Paris? A carriage clock, tick-tocking away on your mantelpiece, is surely just a brutal reminder of all the time you wasted working for a company that deems you worthy of nothing more than a carriage clock?

Fliss has had her carriage clock, but she has another few years to go before the big bash. She's thinking about early retirement though. She should. She can afford to. Her husband Derek has just sold his veterinary practice. They're loaded. But she says she'd miss Erin and I too much. She says we keep her young.

Despite that claim, Fliss has been doing her damndest to get rid of me for the last eighteen months. In the nicest possible way, of course.

29

"Don't be like me," she keeps saying. "Still here when you're sixty."

No chance.

"You're wasted here, lovey," she says.

Fliss knows my real goal is to be a writer. I wrote a short piece about her once – and Erin and Hannah – after I realised how much they all made me laugh.

For weeks I kept a little notepad in my desk drawer and every time one of them did or said something funny I would write it down. Like the time Erin laughed so much at a joke I told she did a huge fart in the middle of the office cafeteria. And the time Hannah told us she'd forgotten to take her contact lenses out before she went to bed and woke up the next morning thinking there had been a miracle. And the time Fliss came out of the ladies with her skirt tucked into her knickers.

When I had completely filled the notepad I wrote a short story about them. It was only meant to be for the girls to read, but they loved it so much they made me submit it for the company magazine.

And ever since then, Fliss has been on at me to "chase my dreams."

"Malcolm wants us to split the Leeds accounts between Roger Calvin and Dave Anderson," Fliss tells me, flicking the kettle on and dropping tea bags into three mugs. We're not supposed to have a kettle in our office – we're supposed to use the kitchen on the third floor, but we can't be arsed. We're rebels. And it gives us a little thrill every time we plug it in, knowing there's a chance we might get caught.

"Why, for heaven's sake?" I ask.

Fliss shrugs.

"Does he realise how much time that's going to take us?"

30

"Bill is leaving, apparently. He and his wife are moving to France to run a Bed and Breakfast. He says he's had enough of doing a job he hates."

"I know how he feels," I say, immediately regretting it, as I sense Fliss lifting one foot up onto her soapbox. Three, two, one…

"So leave. I keep telling you that you should."

You don't want to be like me…

"You don't want to be like me…"

Still here when you're sixty…

"Still here when you're sixty…"

You're wasted here, lovey…

"You're wasted here, lovey. Go and use that degree of yours."

Chase your dreams…

"Chase your dreams, Becky."

"Yeah, I will Fliss," I say, getting the milk out of the fridge – another illegal appliance – "just as soon as we've changed these accounts over." I grin at her and she shakes her head, resigned to the fact that she's probably stuck with me.

I switch on my computer and wait for it to whir into action, Fliss's words ringing in my ears.

It would be great to be that brave – to just chuck it all in and 'chase your dreams'. People do it all the time, supposedly. You read about them in magazines, don't you – people who pack in their high-powered city jobs to run a pig farm in the Yorkshire Dales, people who swap their laptops and Blackberries for packets of doilies and recipes for fruit scones and run their own tea rooms, people who give up their six-figure salaries to become aid workers in Rwanda? People who give up something safe and secure, to do something they actually *want* to do.

It happens.

31

CHAPTER FOUR

Alex is out when I get home. He plays five-a-side football on a Monday night with the boys from work.

I unlock the door and trample on a pile of mail on the doormat.

There is more than usual and for a brief moment I imagine that the contents of one of these envelopes is about to change my life. A letter telling me I have been picked at random to win a year off work, for instance, notification that I have won the competition I entered for an all-expenses-paid trip to Australia, or a letter saying that I've been headhunted by *Hello* magazine.

As if...

But as I open the envelopes and stare at the property details for seven different houses for sale, I realise that one of the envelopes really *could* be about to change my life.

Do you think I should be considering buying my first house with a man I'm not sure is Mr Right?

Me neither.

I look at the details just long enough to come out in a cold sweat before putting them down on the coffee table. Upside down. Underneath the newspaper. If I can't see them, I can pretend they are not there, that they don't exist, that I'm not about to have to make one of the biggest decisions of my life.

CHAPTER FIVE

When I get into the office the next morning I phone Katie.

"Hello, *Books!*, Katie Roberts speaking," she answers.

Katie is a publicity manager for a big publishing company in London. She works in the entertainment section, which basically means she gets to swan about the country accompanying celebs on their book tours. Last year she met three film stars, two footballers and a well-known soap-star who has written her autobiography at the ripe old age of twenty four.

It's her ideal job. Not just because she's some maniac celebrity stalker, but because she loves books. When she and Matt started renovating their flat in London, Matt's first job (he's an architect) was to put in a wall-to-wall bookcase in their living room. It's already half-full. It's a wonder the floor hasn't fallen into the flat below under the weight of it. And it's going to get worse. Instead of the traditional wedding gift list of Egyptian cotton bath sheets and Jamie Oliver muffin moulds, they are asking their guests to buy them a copy of their own favourite books. Knowing Katie and Matt's friends they'll end up with eighty nine copies of the Karma Sutra and one copy of Delia Smith's Complete Cookery Course Volumes 1-3 from Katie's Great Auntie Rose.

"It's me," I say. "How's things?"

"Good. You?"

"I'm bored."

"I thought you might be. You don't usually phone this early. Haven't you got enough to do? I've got some press releases you can write if you like?"

"I've got plenty to do. I just can't be bothered to do it!"

"I don't know why you don't just look for something else. You've hated that job for as long as I can remember."

"Is it really that long? Hmm… Maybe I'll just pack it in and move back home…"

"Really?" she asks, excited.

"No, not really," I laugh, though I'm not entirely sure why.

The worst thing about staying up in Leeds with Alex is being away from my friends. Katie moved back to London as soon as we finished our finals and Emma has never been far from the south.

"Katie…"

"Yes?"

"If I ask you something, will you promise to forget all about it when everything's okay again?"

"Yes."

"What do you think about Alex? About him and me, I mean. Do you think Alex is right for me?"

She says nothing for a few seconds.

And then, "I don't know."

It's not what I expected her to say. I mean, I didn't expect her to say yes, or no even, but I guess I expected her to be a bit more surprised that I was asking – a bit more surprised that I am having doubts at all. I forget sometimes how well she knows me.

I take a slurp of lukewarm tea and wait for her to say something else. I know she will. Katie never finishes anything with 'I don't know'.

"Well, personally I think you are perfect for each other," she says. "You have the same values. You find the same things funny. You are both incredibly gorgeous, obviously," she laughs at this one. "You love each other. And you want the same things out of life.

"But whether you want those things with each other is a different matter altogether. And only you can answer that. Only you know if he's the one for you, B."

"Yeah, I know," I sigh.

And I do. I know it's up to me. I think I just want someone else to make the decision for me. But it doesn't work like that, does it? I have to find that damn label myself.

"Let's chat about it at the weekend," Katie says. "Are you still coming? I've made an appointment for 12pm."

"Yes. Alex is going to bring me to work in the morning and Fliss said she'll drop me at the station."

"Excellent. And Emma's going to meet us at the shop. I've got a good feeling about this shop, B. I think it might be the one."

CHAPTER SIX

"I think I might want to split up with Alex," I tell Katie and Emma as we take a well-earned break from wedding fever on Saturday to get some lunch. We've found a lovely little Italian restaurant around the corner from *All Things Bride And Beautiful*, which is very handy as we'll be going back there as soon as we've stuffed our faces. They have loads of dresses that Katie likes and she's only tried on fifteen so far.

"What?" Emma says, as the spaghetti she has just spent the last five minutes twirling onto her fork falls back onto her plate in a heap.

"I think I might want to split up with Alex," I say again.

"That's what I thought you said. Why?"

Katie takes a bite of her pizza while I bring Emma up to date on my love life.

"I am happy," I say. "I'm just not sure Alex is Mr Right." This is the wrong thing to say to Emma, who rolls her eyes at me.

As I've said, Emma doesn't believe in Mr Right. She thinks the whole idea is, and I quote, 'codswallop.' She thinks that the best you can hope for is to meet someone who loves you, who you love ┆ ᵏ. and who doesn't drive you too far up the wall when they ┄ ┄ heir dirty underwear on the bedroom floor, drink the last ┄ ┄ ⸗lk before putting the empty carton back in the fridge, or delete the final part of a three-part drama that you haven't quite got around to watching yet.

"Right, shmite," she says. "You love him, yes? And he loves you?"

I nod.

"Well, there you go then."

"But what if there's someone else out there I'm meant to be with?"

"And what if there isn't? And you throw away what you have with Alex for nothing? You said you're not sure he's Mr Right. But you're not sure he isn't either, right? So what if he is?"

"I don't think she'd be questioning it if he was, Em," Katie says, my fellow follower of the Mr Right religion.

"Well I think you're both bonkers," Emma says, abandoning her spoon and chopping up her spaghetti with a knife and fork instead.

"I know you think it's rubbish but I've always believed in Mr Right," I tell Emma back at *All Things Bride And Beautiful* while we wait for Katie to emerge from the fitting room in dress number sixteen. "Ever since we held that wedding for Barbie and Ken and I asked my dad why Barbie wanted to marry Ken."

"Oh god! Yeah!" she laughs. "When we made ourselves sick on Love Hearts! And made Ken those sparkly trousers out of one of your dad's old hankies and some glitter!"

"Yeah. Well, I'm just not sure Alex is my Ken."

Today we are being looked after by Pippa. And she is looking a little concerned. I guess this is not the sort of conversation you would normally hear in a wedding shop. More like gushings of eternal love and all things fabulous.

"Better I discover it now, before I get to the point where you're getting *me* to strip off and try on wedding dresses," I tell her as she scuttles away to fetch dress number seventeen.

"Maybe you'll get it when you've met someone you're crazy about," I tell Emma.

"Who says I haven't already?" she says, suddenly grinning like the Cheshire Cat.

"So things are still going well with Jim then?"

"Really well, actually. He's cooking me dinner tomorrow night. He says there's something he wants to talk to me about."

"Ooh, what do you think it is?"

"I'm not sure. But I think maybe he's going to ask me to move in with him."

"Wow. That's exciting, Em."

"I know. I really like him, B."

"What's he up to this weekend?"

"He's in London, actually. He was meant to be away for some work thing but it was cancelled."

"Why don't you phone him? Get him to meet us for a drink. Katie and I are dying to meet him. Aren't we Katie?" I shout through the cubicle curtain.

She pokes her head out, looking a little flushed.

"What?"

"Emma's Jim. He's in London this weekend. I said she should call him so we can meet him."

"Absolutely," she says, disappearing back behind the curtain.

"I could, I guess. He's pretty busy, I think, but I can ask."

She takes her phone out of her bag and dials Jim's number.

"It's ringing," she mouths. I hear him answer.

"Hello you," she says. "I was just wondering if you fancy meeting up for a quick drink. I'm in a wedding dress shop with Becky and Katie," she tells him. "They want to meet you. And I've probably kept you to myself for long enough!" She looks over at me and grins. I nod enthusiastically.

"No...Yes...Oh, that's a shame. Oh well, never mind. Another time. Becky's down here all the time at the moment, anyway. Are you still okay to pick me up from the station tomorrow night?

"Great…okay, see you tomorrow."

She switches off her phone and tosses it back in her bag.

"He says he's already made plans to meet up with a mate," she says. She looks disappointed. I think she really likes this guy. I hope it lasts. She deserves a bit of luck on the love front.

Emma and I have been friends our whole lives. Well almost – since we were barely out of nappies. We grew up in the same street in a little village by the sea near Brighton. From the moment she and her family moved in next door, Emma and I were inseparable. She and her brother Sam sat on the curb watching my brother Johnny and I playing hide and seek with the rest of the kids in the street while their parents supervised the removal men. The first time she spoke to me was to tell me where Johnny was hiding when I was 'it,' which I was chuffed to bits about because he had won every single game so far and was being a smug little git about it.

We walked to school together every day with our matching My Little Pony lunchboxes and on weekends we'd spend hours playing with our Barbie dolls – usually at Emma's house because she had the Barbie mansion. It was brilliant – it was four storeys high and had a pulley-operated lift on the side, a kitchen sink with taps that you could get real water to come out of and a four poster bed which though it was very swish was clearly designed without heed to Barbie's enviably long legs.

Every summer my nana and granddad hired a beach hut near their home in Bognor Regis for the holidays and they would take the two of us there as much as we could pester them to. It was our summer treasure trove – filled with buckets and spades, inflatable dinghies and fishing nets that we used to scoop up crabs from the rock pools. My granddad had a greenhouse and we'd spend hours walking up and down the path behind the huts looking for ice-lolly sticks which he'd use to label his plants. We played mini-golf on the green across from the beach and went to the amusement arcades on the seafront and played on the two-pence machines until we'd spent all my granddad's coppers.

I've known Emma so long I don't really know a life without her as my friend. We've grown up together, really,

My friendship with Katie had a far less innocent beginning – evolving primarily from a mutual appreciation for red wine and a mutual aversion to studying. We met at university, where we were both studying English, both of us chronically overworked with our eight hours of lectures a week...

We met in our hall of residence and quickly became friends after it dawned on us that we were, in fact, the only two vaguely normal girls in our block – my immediate neighbours, just to illustrate, being:

To my right – Wendy, the maths student away from home for the first time, who not only still considered it cool to wear Converse trainers with fluorescent socks, but also considered it cool to wear a different coloured Converse trainer and a different coloured fluorescent sock on each foot.
To my left – Heather, the religious Medic who wore hand-knitted jumpers with pictures of elephants on them, and who liked to begin each and every day with a solo rendition of 'I'd like to teach the world to sing.'
And directly opposite, Victoria, the token Goth. Enough said.

We spent the next three years together – two of them in halls, and one in a student house with our goldfish Bob (now sadly in goldfish heaven) – getting pissed, getting as many guys as possible to snog us at the hall balls, and, miraculously, making it to the odd lecture.

Emma and Katie met each other loads of times while I was at uni, but it was at my twenty first that they really hit it off.

It was an elaborate affair – much like Barbie's wedding – with a big marquee in the garden decorated with embarrassing photographs of me, blown up to humiliating proportions and pinned to every available surface – me in a pram, me sitting on the potty, me on my first day of Brownies, me playing a Christmas tree in my primary school play, me and Emma as Perkin and Pootle from The Flumps for the school carnival (Emma was not pleased with my dad for digging out that one)...

We had a pond back then, which my dad had fenced off with some tent poles and a bit of fluorescent ribbon. Whether it was there to stop people falling, jumping in or throwing things in, I never did establish. But I do recall helping my dad drain the pond the following summer and discovering an item or two that had mysteriously gone missing – coincidentally around the night of that party. Namely, a garden gnome, my mum's best whisk, and the remote control for the kitchen television. I don't know where the garden gnome fits in but I do remember Emma and Katie giving the guests an impromptu Karaoke performance of *Girls Just Wanna Have Fun*, both of them hunting frantically for anything that could pass as a microphone.

I also recall, I'm sorry to say, how I went missing just as my dad was about to make a speech in my honour and was spotted through the kitchen window, by absolutely everyone at the party – gathered, as they were, for dad's speech – sat on the kitchen worktop with my legs wrapped tightly around Alex, snogging the face off him.

I'm a much classier chick these days.

Anyway, despite my own mortification at the whole spectacle, Emma and Katie were united in their approval, shouting frankly unrepeatable encouragement through the fanlight window at us. In between stuffing whole profiteroles in their gobs, that is. And so, another great friendship began.

And the three of us have been best mates ever since.

We know it's good from the way Pippa theatrically sweeps back the curtain and practically shoves Katie out of the cubicle at us.

"What do you think?" our friend asks. She's beaming.

And for what must surely be the first time in history, Emma and I are both simultaneously speechless.

Well, almost.

"It's beautiful," I whisper, as if I'm afraid to say it out loud in case the spell is broken and she turns into a pumpkin or something.

"That's the one, Katie," Emma agrees. "You look stunning."

"Turn around," I instruct her. "Let's see the back."

It's an empire line dress. Ivory. Strapless. With tiny little glass beads in the bodice which sparkle in the light. The buttons on the back are similar to the beads – only bigger – and they go virtually all the way to the ground. I make a mental note to allow plenty of time for button-fastening on the day.

"It's fab, isn't it?" Katie asks.

She doesn't need us to tell her.

Standing unobtrusively behind her, Pippa beams too. What a lovely job – witnessing the moment a girl finds the dress that she'll wear on the biggest day of her life.

She's soon business as normal though, when Emma lunges forward to hug Katie.

"Don't touch the fabric," she urges. "It's only a sample dress, but we do like to keep them in pristine condition."

"Oooh," Emma mumbles, jumping back. "Sorry! I'm just so excited!"

After completing the paperwork and putting a significant dent in Katie's dad's bank account, we spend the rest of the day celebrating at a trendy wine bar in Wimbledon called The Hedge. It was only meant to be a pit stop on the way home, but it's one of those places with comfy sofas that once you have collapsed onto you just can't seem to drag yourself off, no matter how hard you try. Which we don't, obviously.

Between us we polish off a couple of bottles of red, two packets of pistachios and a bowl of olives. We then succeed in emptying an entire carriage on the tube – stop by stop – with our rendition of Billy Idol's White Wedding. And when we finally reach Katie's flat we all climb into bed with Matt, waking him up and telling him that when he sees Katie in her dress he will think he has died and gone to heaven.

He rubs his eyes, surveys the three of us cuddled up together next to him and calmly informs us: "I already do!"

CHAPTER SEVEN

It's Monday. *Again*. Bollocks.

And I'm back at work. Again.

Thirty-eight new emails, twelve new accounts to open, nine credit limits to chase, countless arsey salesmen to get right up my arse. So to speak.

I got the train back from London on Sunday morning. I figured I ought to spend at least a few hours with my boyfriend this year.

We cooked – or should I say Alex cooked – roast chicken, and we watched '50 First Dates' on DVD. I asked Alex if he loved me enough to ask me out on a first date every single day for the rest our lives. He said he did.

Maybe Drew Barrymore's character had it good. To be able to feel that first longing for someone in the pit of your stomach every day. To never reach that point where they piss you off by leaving toenail clippings on the bathroom floor. To never reach that moment when you need to ask if something is 'right'. That has to be good, doesn't it?

We went to bed after that. And had sex for the first time in six weeks.

"The milk's off," I tell Fliss and Erin, sniffing the carton I have just pulled out of our illegal fridge. "I'll nip out and get some fresh. Do you want anything?"

"Get us a packet of Hob Nobs," Fliss says, handing me a £1 coin. "My treat."

I'll start my diet tomorrow.

When I return fifteen minutes later, Fliss and Erin are both on the phone and there's a Post-It note in the middle of my computer screen, informing me Alex called – at 9.42am. It's from Fliss. The neat handwriting and the reference to the exact time tell me that. And the Post-It. If Erin had taken the call it would have been a note scribbled on the back of a sweet wrapper saying 'Al phoned'. Either that or she'd have forgotten to tell me altogether.

I move the Post-It to the side of my screen and dial Alex's mobile number while I wait for the kettle to boil.

"I can't talk long, I'm making tea for the girls," I tell him when he answers. Priorities…

"Are you doing anything tonight after work?" he asks me.

"No," I say, immediately regretting it. It's always wise to find out why you are being asked before you give your answer, I find.

"Great. I've arranged for us to look at some of those properties we got details for." He means the ones I hid. On the coffee table. Upside down. Underneath the newspaper.

See what I mean? Clearly what I should have said was "yes, I am going out, and I am going to be out all evening, tonight, tomorrow night and every night from now until next Christmas".

Bugger.

I quickly consider my options. Option 1 – stay at work and tell him I had an urgent can't-possibly-get-out-of-it last-minute meeting. Option 2 – tell him the car wouldn't start and I had to get the AA out, but they got lost on the way. Option 3 – 'forget', and drag Fliss and Erin to the pub. Or option 4 – I could just go. Because I can't put it off forever. Well, I suppose I could, but I suspect that might get a bit tedious before long.

"Great," I say.

I'll just have to say I hate them all instead. That I wouldn't live in those hell holes if you paid me.

Which would have worked like a dream, had they not all been absolutely fabulous. Just what we've been looking for, in fact.

What are the bloody odds? We have viewed some right dumps in the last few months – dry rot, mould, nicotine-stained flock-lined wallpaper, carpets stained with cat pee…

Hence I didn't think I was being unrealistic in thinking this lot would at the very least have a bit of damp or an avocado bathroom suite to speak of.

But no. Each and every one of the four properties we have just been to view were perfect. With a capital P. Our dream homes, you might even say.

They are all in 'nice' safe areas, all within our budget, and the most any of them need is a fresh lick of paint on the walls. One even has a brand new fitted kitchen *and* a brand new bathroom suite – both exactly what we would have chosen ourselves.

Bollocks.

"I think we should make an offer on that one in Maple Road," Alex says when we get home. "That place isn't going to be on the market for long."

"I don't think we should rush into it," I tell him. "We still have plenty more to look at."

"But it's exactly what we're looking for," he laughs. "And we can afford it!"

He's right. It is. We can.

"I don't know," I say, desperately trying to come up with something I didn't absolutely love about it.

"The kitchen could be a bit bigger," I venture.

"Says who?" he laughs. "You're not the one who'll be using it!"

He's right. Again. As I said – I can't cook. I don't cook. Not if I can help it anyway. Not unless beans on toast counts as cooking. And even then I'd probably burn the beans. Or the toast. Or both.

In our last year at university when Katie and I shared a house, she and Alex tried to get me on *Can't Cook, Won't Cook*. I only found out when we got a phone bill with a premium number listed on it over and over again. Katie only admitted what she'd been up to when I accused her of phoning sex lines. I think I was actually a bit disappointed to discover my best friend wasn't a secret sex addict after all.

I never did get on the show. I was probably too bad even for *Can't Cook, Won't Cook*.

"Okay, but let's just wait a day or two and see how we feel then," I say.

"Fine. But don't blame me if someone else gets there first and we lose the house."

"I won't."

I phone Katie on her mobile as soon as I leave the house the next morning.

"We've found a house," I tell her, before I've even said hello.

"Hang on a sec, B, I'm just paying for a coffee…Thanks mate," I hear her say. There's a loud clunking noise as she puts the phone down on the counter. Then the noise of the zip opening on her purse, and coins dropping in…a big slurp of cappuccino froth.

Does she not realise I am in the middle of a crisis that requires immediate attention?

"B? Sorry, what did you say?" Now the sound of heels clicking along the pavement.

"We've found a house. Alex and I. It's perfect it's in a nice area it's five grand under our budget it's got a brand new bathroom

47

and a brand new kitchen and it's got wooden flooring in the living room the good kind not the shit kind what am I going to do?" I'm so desperate for her to tell me, I don't even draw breath.

"What do you want to do, B?" Click, click, slurp…

"I don't know," I admit. "Katie…can I ask you a question?"

"Of course."

"Do you ever think that Matt might not be the one?"

"No. Never…Becks, is this just about Alex?"

"What do you mean?"

"Is there someone else?"

"No!" I shout, a little louder that I'd intended. "God no. I wish it was that simple. No, I just keep wondering if the thoughts I've been having are normal. Maybe everybody questions at some stage whether they are with the right person. Maybe it doesn't mean anything. But then *you* don't question it, do you?"

"No. I know Matt is the one for me. I can't imagine my life without him. I see myself growing old with Matt."

I can see myself growing old with Alex. I can. I can see us sitting in our slippers, holding cups of cocoa, watching Countdown and re-runs of Heartbeat on UK Gold. But that means nothing really. I can see myself growing old with anyone if I look hard enough. Jude Law, for example, or Aidan from *Sex & The City* (lovely guy – can't imagine what Carrie was thinking,) or that cute new doctor in Holby City. But just because you can see it, doesn't mean it's right, or that it's going to happen – Jude might not feel the same way about me, for instance and, well, sadly Aidan isn't even real.

But more importantly – not growing old with Alex – I can see that too.

I suddenly remember Katie on the other end of the phone.

"B?" she is saying. I think I've worried her. The clicking has stopped. So has the slurping.

"Yeah?"

48

"Do you still love Alex?"

"Yes."

"And do you know for sure that he's not the one?"

"Not for sure, no."

"Then you need to find out. You *could* just be having a wobbly moment."

"Yes, but how do I do that?"

"Maybe you should have some time apart? Maybe you could go and stay with Felicity for a few days?"

"But what about the house?" I ask.

"Forget the house. You can't possibly consider buying a house with Alex while you're feeling like this. It would be total madness. You'll have to stall him."

"How?"

"Can't you just tell him you didn't like it?"

"He wouldn't believe me. It's perfect."

"There must be something wrong with it. Why are the owners selling?"

"I'm not sure. They've just had a baby so they're probably looking for somewhere bigger."

"There you go – tell Alex you want to wait and find something bigger."

"But we can't afford anything bigger."

"Exactly. Tell him you want to wait and save up a bit more money so you can get something a bit bigger. So that when you have kids you won't have to move. That'll be enough to put the wind up him!" she laughs.

Now I don't know what frightens me more – the thought of buying a house with someone who might not be Mr Right, or the thought of having children with him.

"It might work, I guess."

CHAPTER EIGHT

Let's fall in love –
In our mid thirties
It's not only
Where the hurt is.
...
We'll make the whole thing
Hard and bright
We'll call it love –
We may be right.

'The Proposal', Tom Vaughan

Great minds think alike.

On reflection, Alex thinks we should save for longer too. He thinks we should spend the money we have saved so far on something else.

On getting married.

They say there comes a point in your life when you know you've met the person you want to spend the rest of your life with.

By the same rule, I can now confirm there comes a point when you know for sure you haven't.

And when your boyfriend is knelt in front of you holding out a sparkling platinum and diamond engagement ring and asking you to marry him is not, you might say, the ideal moment for it to happen.

Alex is not Mr Right.
Why?
I don't know.
I just *know*.

CHAPTER NINE

My true love hath my heart, and I have his.

'The Bargain', Sir Philip Sidney (1554-1586)

Have you ever broken somebody's heart?

It's horrible. I think I'd rather have my own heart broken. I think it would hurt less.

Telling Alex I can't marry him is without a doubt the hardest thing I have ever had to do in my life.

I don't have to say the words. My eyes tell him for me, when they fill with tears. Not the happy kind.

"You don't want to marry me, do you?" he asks quietly, clutching the ring in his hand.

I shake my head.

"But it's not because I don't love you." It seems like such a stupid thing to say. Do I think it will soften the blow somehow? A consolation prize of sorts? Hard luck mate, she won't marry you, but on the plus side, she does love you.

"Then why?"

It's a fair question.

"I don't know. I just can't." As answers go it's inadequate. But it's the only one I have.

Of course, saying yes would have been easier. Because I *do* love Alex. And I know we could have a good life together. And I *am* scared I won't ever meet that person I seem to have convinced myself I'm meant to be with – that person I think I might love more than I love Alex. But I also know if I did marry Alex, then I'd be settling. And we both deserve more than that.

The next day I move out.

CHAPTER TEN

The minute I heard my first love story
I started looking for you, not knowing
How blind that was
Lovers don't finally meet somewhere
They're in each other all along

Jabal ad-Din ar-Rumi (1207 – 1273)

Fliss and Derek have offered me their spare room while I sort my life out. It's quiet where they live. You can hear the slightest noise. The pipes creaking as the central heating cools down. An insect hitting the window outside. My own heart beating.

I can't sleep. I'm not used to being alone in bed. I've spent nights away from Alex, of course, but it's been a long time since I've slept alone because I *am* alone.

I haven't told anyone yet – apart from Katie. I can't face the questions. People who believe in Mr Right will be surprised because they thought I was happy and because they thought Alex *was* Mr Right. And people who don't believe in Mr Right will just think I'm bonkers. And *everyone* will want to know why. But even I don't know that.

At 4.30am, after waking on and off all night, I give up trying to sleep and go in search of the kettle.

I'm pouring water into a mug when Fliss walks into the kitchen.

"Oh I'm sorry Fliss, did I wake you?"

"No, no, I'm not a good sleeper these days," she says. I look at the ungodly time on the clock on the oven.

"It's my age," she laughs. "I always wake up early."

I hold up the hot chocolate. "I hope you don't mind?"

"Don't be silly. You must help yourself to anything you want while you're here, lovey."

"Do you want one?"

"That would be lovely."

We take the drinks through to the living room and Fliss turns on a lamp.

Sitting on the sofa I pull my knees up to my chest and balance my drink on them in my hand, blowing on it gently.

A painting on the wall above the television catches my eye. It's a woman sitting on a deckchair, holding a parasol. I lean forward to confirm what it is I think I'm seeing. The woman in the picture is Fliss, only much younger – about my age.

"Who painted that picture of you in the deckchair, Fliss?" I ask.

"It's one of Derek's" she says. "He did it on our honeymoon. We had such a wonderful time," she smiles, remembering. "We went to Cornwall for the week. Had sunshine the whole time. It was perfect. He painted that picture on our last day. We didn't want to forget."

"I didn't know he could paint. It's fantastic. It looks just like you."

I blow on my drink again and sip it tentatively.

"How are you doing, lovey?" Fliss asks. "Are you okay?"

"Not really," I admit. "But I know it's for the best."

"Are you sure? Is there no way you and Alex can work things out?"

"There isn't really anything to work out – that's the problem. It's not like one of us has cheated or anything – you know, something you can get over if you both really want to. It's more than that."

"Hmm." She sips her drink. She probably doesn't understand. Fliss is of the generation where a guy met a girl, they went out and then they got married. And they stayed together forever – for better or for worse.

I, on the other hand, am from the generation where one in three couples give up on a marriage. Which kind of makes you think twice about doing it in the first place, doesn't it? Or at the very least it makes you more determined to find the right person in the first place – because surely then it can't possibly fail – not if you've found that one person you are *meant* to be with.

Or maybe it doesn't really work like that at all. Maybe there are lots of people out there we could make it work with. But we're so busy looking for that one person that we can't see all the other possibilities.

"I do understand, you know," Fliss says, breaking my thoughts, reading my mind.

"If something isn't meant to be, you won't ever make it work. No matter how much you might want to."

I sip my drink. It's cooling down.

"Fliss…," I say.

"Yes, lovey?"

"How did you know Derek was the one for you? How will *I* know when I *have* met the right person?"

"Honestly?"

"Yes."

"When you don't need to ask that question."

CHAPTER ELEVEN

"Jim's split up with me," Emma tells me the next day, when I phone her during my lunch break.

"He doesn't love me," she sobs down the phone. "He says he thinks the world of me, that I'm one of the loveliest people he's ever met, and that he wishes he could fall in love with me. But that he just hasn't and doesn't think he ever will."

Ouch.

"He says it's not me, it's him," she says, her tone revealing exactly what she thinks of this particular explanation. "He says I am fabulous and that any man would be lucky to have me. Just not him, obviously. Oh B, what am I going to do?"

"You'll meet someone else," I reassure her. "You always do."

"But I don't want anybody else. I want Jim. I love him."

"Really?" I ask. She said she really liked him but she's never mentioned love. "Do you really love him, Em?"

"Yes. No. Oh, I don't know," she says. "I guess I just hoped he was Mr Right."

But Emma doesn't believe in Mr Right…

"But you don't believe in Mr Right…"

"Maybe I do. Oh I don't know. I just really liked him, B. He's lovely. He makes me laugh. He makes me smile. *Made* me smile. And he was so bloody good in bed," she adds, an afterthought that is followed by a fresh wave of sobs.

"Anyway, you rang me," she says, composing herself with a big snort. "Was there a reason or did you just phone for a chat?"

"Alex asked me to marry him," I tell her. "And I said no," I add quickly, before she rushes to congratulate me.

Silence. And then...

"Oh my god B. I can't believe it. And you let me go on and on about Jim!"

"That's okay. You're upset. I understand that."

"But B. Oh my god. Are you okay? I didn't think you were being serious the other day. I thought it was just a phase. I thought you really loved him."

"I did love him. I *do* love him. Just not enough to marry him. Not enough to know I want to spend the rest of my life with him."

"Well if that's how you really feel then I guess you've done the right thing. But blimey, I still can't believe you let me go on about Jim for so long."

CHAPTER TWELVE

When I get to work the following morning Erin says Malcolm wants to see me in his office.

"He has a 9.30am meeting so he says can you go in before you do anything else."

No cup of tea then.

"Did he say what it was about?"

"No. He probably just wants to make sure you're okay."

"Probably wants to make sure my mind is still on the job, more like."

I'm being unfair really. As bosses go we could do a lot worse than Malcolm Hurley – Penand Inc's sales director for as long as anyone can remember, including Fliss. Admittedly he makes our lives a bit difficult sometimes and demands account changes which virtually have us camped out in the office for days on end. And he wears the most shocking ties that require both a strong stomach and dark glasses. And he looks like a slightly better looking version of Shrek – although in fairness you can't really hold that against him. But on the plus side he does give us generous pay rises and bonuses and always makes sure we have a Christmas bash to remember – even if it is for his not-quite-perfected plate spinning demonstration – with a free bar all night, which really shouldn't be scoffed at.

But nonetheless, I'm dreading this. I'm already feeling wobbly. What if he's mean to me and I start sobbing in his office? How embarrassing. Or, even worse, what if he's really nice to me and I start blubbing because of that instead? It happens, doesn't it? A few kind words from an unexpected source and, whoosh, enough tears to make Niagara Falls look like a leaky tap.

I knock lightly on his door. If he doesn't hear me I can slope back to my desk and avoid him for the rest of the day.

"Come in." Damn.

"Ah, Rebecca," he says, pushing his glasses up his nose as I enter his office.

"Thank you for coming to see me. I know how busy you girls are. Take a seat."

I sit in the chair opposite him. I feel like I'm in a job interview.

"Can I get you a cup of coffee?" he asks.

Odd. He doesn't normally offer hot beverages. Maybe this isn't going to be as quick and painless as I was hoping.

"Erm, that would be great," I say nervously, because I *am* a bit parched as it happens. I'm normally slurping my first cup of tea at my desk by now.

Malcolm buzzes through to his secretary and orders two coffees. I decide not to tell him I'm a tea drinker. He looks at me and smiles.

This is all looking very formal.

Maybe I've made some gargantuan cock-up with one of the accounts – given someone too much discount, perhaps, or given a £500,000 credit limit to a dodgy customer who has ordered his maximum and skipped the country with a lorry load of laptops?

Maybe he's going to sack me. Do you think you'd get coffee if you were getting the sack? To soften the blow, maybe?

Hang on... maybe he *is* going to sack me. Excellent. If he sacked me then that would force me to do something else, wouldn't it...?

"How are you feeling Rebecca?" Malcolm asks, interrupting

my fantasy. Damn him. "I gather you're having a few personal problems."

"I'm fine," I say, a little defensively. And then I feel bad because he is only showing concern. I think.

"I'm fine, thank you," I repeat, a little softer this time.

"If you need to take some time off…"

"No, it's okay, I'm fine," I say quickly, hoping that will put an end to all this. Although, I would quite like to have my coffee before I go back to my desk. Malcolm drinks the posh stuff, none of your instant rubbish.

And then he leans back in his chair, takes his glasses off and rubs the bridge of his nose. He looks very serious. He looks like he's about to offer me some words of wisdom on affairs of the heart or something. Oh please no….

Thankfully I am saved by the arrival of the refreshments, complete with a plate of chocolate Hobnobs. My favourite. Actually, that's a fib. Jammy Dodgers are my favourite, but chocolate Hobnobs definitely come in a close second.

What? You hardly expect me to diet when I've just split up with my boyfriend? I need comfort foods. And somehow lettuce and celery sticks just don't quite make the grade. Hobnobs, on the other hand, most definitely do. I take one and put it next to my coffee on the edge of Malcolm's desk.

"So, Rebecca," he says, putting his glasses back on. Back to business then.

I'm a bit nervous. I want to say "So, Malcolm." I pick up my coffee and take a sip instead.

"As you know we had to let Hannah go last month."

"Yes," I confirm.

"For reasons I won't go into," he continues.

Who's he trying to kid? It was the talk of the office.

"Of course," I say, picking up my biscuit and taking a quick bite before it's my turn to speak again.

"You have been acting senior account planner since then haven't you?"

"I have, yes," I confirm, wiping a crumb from my lip with my thumb.

"And have you been enjoying the role?"

"Oh yes, very much so," I say.

Yes, I know it's a big fat lie, but what do you expect me to say? "No, Mr Hurley, I can't stand the bloody job. In fact, you can shove your rotten job up your bum"?

"It's giving me some exciting challenges through which I can develop my skills and enhance my experience," I add for authenticity, before taking another slurp of coffee.

"That's excellent news Rebecca, excellent news, because the reason I've asked you in here today is to offer you the role on a more permanent basis."

Bollocks.

Does coffee stain? And did I just say bollocks out loud?

"There will of course be a pay rise to go with the promotion," Malcolm adds, clearly mistaking my horror for financial intrigue, and apparently overlooking the whole 'bollocks' faux pas.

"As well as a generous bonus structure," he says. "I have prepared a contract so take it away it with you to read and perhaps I could ask you to sign it and have it back to me by…shall we say Monday?"

"Right, sure," I say. "Thank you very much Mr Hurley," I add, because, again, what else could I say?

"It's no more than you deserve Rebecca. You are a hard worker and, if you want to, you can go far in this company."

If I want to. Exactly.

"So?" Erin asks, as soon as I get back to the office.

She can't bear not knowing anything, that girl. She'll have

chewed her finger nails right down to her knuckles in anticipation while I was gone, because she knew as well as I did that Malcolm didn't ask me into his office to express his heartfelt concern for my welfare. I was either being bollocked or rewarded. I'm still not sure which category I'd put it in.

"It seems I'm being promoted," I say, moving the pile of papers that have been dumped on my chair during my brief absence and sitting down. The sales guys are in the office today for their twice-monthly meeting, which means shed loads of work for us. I don't know why they think it will get done any quicker if they put it on my chair, though. It's not as if I ever pick it up and get straight on the case – I just move it onto my desk where it has to draw straws with every other bit of paper marked 'urgent.'

"Wow, that's great," Erin says, rushing over to my desk to hug me.

I look over at Fliss, who isn't saying anything. She doesn't need to. She doesn't want me to take this job; I know that. She wants me to leave. She wants me to do what I really want to do.

"Well done, lovey," she says, eventually. A compromise. "Do you really want it though?" she asks. '*You don't really want it though, do you?*' is what she actually means.

"Not really, no," I admit.

"Why not?" Erin asks, puzzled.

"Wait a minute, Erin love," Fliss says, holding her hand up to stop her from saying anything else.

"So what did you say to Malcolm then?" she asks me, hopeful.

"I said thank you very much."

I phone Katie while Fliss makes the tea.

"*Books!*. Katie Roberts speaking."

"It's me."

"Hi B. How are you doing? How is everything at Felicity's?"

"I'm okay. Fliss and Derek have been fantastic," I say, looking over at Fliss and smiling.

"I need your advice. Again."

"What about? Has Alex phoned you?"

"No, it's nothing like that. It's work. I've been offered a promotion."

"Hey, well done! More money then?"

"Yes, and some sort of bonus structure, although I don't know all the details yet."

"But? I'm sensing a 'but'?"

"But I hate working here," I say. "I hate my job. Do I really want a promotion that's going to keep me here forever?"

"Nothing's forever."

"Well a couple more years at least and a couple more years here would feel like forever."

"So leave."

"And do what?"

"What you've always wanted to do, but never have."

"It's not that easy though is it?"

"Nothing worth doing is ever easy, B. It just depends how much you want to do it. Listen hun, I'll call you back in a few minutes, I've got to take a call from an author."

"No, it's okay. I'll phone you later. I just wanted to tell you."

"Okay. But if you really want my advice, then I don't think you should take the job."

"Really?"

"Yes, really. Leave, B. Come home. There's nothing stopping you now. There's nothing up there for you anymore."

She's right. There isn't.

64

CHAPTER THIRTEEN

I'm making a habit of turning people down, it seems.

I've done it. I've told Malcolm I don't want the promotion. Or to work at Penand Inc at all, thank you very much.

He was ever so understanding, as it happens. In fact, he even congratulated me on an 'excellent decision' and wished me all the best for the future. Until I pointed out that he had misheard me, that is – that I hadn't said "thank you for the offer, I'm going to take it, you won't regret it," and that what I'd actually said was "thank you for the offer, but if I take it I'll regret it". Seems I'd never noticed his hearing impairment before.

"I don't want to look back in ten years and wonder why I never did something I really wanted to do," I explain, once he has recovered from the initial shock. The concept of not wanting to spend your whole life working for Penand Inc is not one with which Malcolm is familiar. Here is a man who has earned his carriage clock, and then some.

"I see," he says, despite, I suspect, not seeing at all. "And you don't want a bit more time to think about it?"

"No. Thank you. I knew as soon as you offered me the job, if I'm honest. But I *have* thought about it – a lot – and I still feel the same. Now just seems like the right time to make the break, what with Alex and I, and…well…you know…"

65

"Okay, Rebecca," he says, getting up from his chair. He's probably worried I'll start pouring my heart out. "You'll be sorely missed, though. You've been a great asset to Penand Inc. And of course, it goes without saying that I'll be happy to give you a glowing reference."

"Thanks Mr Hurley," I say, shaking his hand, before turning and leaving his office.

"And Rebecca," he calls after me. "Do let me know when your leaving do will be, won't you. I should very much like to help give you a good send off."

CHAPTER FOURTEEN

Today is my last day at Penand Inc. Yay!

I wasn't sure how I'd feel when it actually came to leave. Delirious, obviously, but I have been here a long time, so I thought a touch of sadness wasn't completely beyond the realms of possibility.

It's been okay.

For starters, I've done no work whatsoever. All day. I've pretended to do some – I've sat at my desk from time to time and shuffled papers, clicking on my mouse intermittently for added effect (I was playing FreeCell, but no-one needs to know that). But for the rest of the day I have been wandering around the building saying my goodbyes. Which turns out to have been a complete waste of time as at 4pm, everyone who has ever known me at the company – and several, I suspect, who have never even met me (some people will do anything for half an hour away from their desks) all cram into our office to see me off the premises.

They've put "Sorry You're Leaving" banners up on the walls and tied balloons to my chair and thrown sparkly bits all over my desk.

I'm touched.

And they've bought champagne for a toast.

First Malcolm makes a little speech, during which he completely embarrasses me by telling everyone how in my interview he asked me why I wanted the job and I told him it was because I owed the bank £5,000 for all the university partying they had subsidised. He says he gave me the job for my honesty and slaps me on the back. Just as I'm taking a sip of champagne.

Then Fliss says a few words – about how she may be nearly forty years older than me but thinks of me as one of her dearest friends – despite trying to get rid of me for the last year. Which makes me cry. I blame it on the champagne that went up my nose.

And then I get a card – filled with a mixture of both heartfelt and crude sentiments that I'm sure I'll have great fun reading later – and a present. I knew I was getting one. Everyone who leaves Penand Inc gets a present. But even if they didn't, Erin 'sneaking' around the building clutching an A3 envelope with 'Becky's leaving, cough up your cash!' scribbled on it in big black letters, was a dead giveaway. And I know what I'm getting too – or part of it, at least. Everyone who leaves Penand Inc gets a desk tidy filled with goodies. One of those tubular pen pot things that you loved as a child, but can't see the point of as an adult when you have to tip the whole thing upside down just to locate the last paperclip that you are sure is in there somewhere, leaving a heap of pens, pencils, useless clusters of two or three staples and a selection of chewed pen lids scattered all over your desk in the process. Which kind of makes a mockery of the name 'desk tidy', if you ask me. And when I say filled with 'goodies', I do mean that in the loosest possible sense of the word. When you work for a stationery supplier, 'goodies' can really only mean pens and pencils and, well,…pretty much just pens and pencils.

It started years ago when some guy was given one as a leaving present because he had always had the messiest desk in the entire building (before my time, clearly) and could never find a pen when he needed one. And it went down so well (he was so touched he cried – imagine his elation if he'd stuck it out for the carriage clock) that it became tradition.

You do get something else. Unless you're Billy-no-mates, that is, and no-one is really all that bothered to see you go. Or worse still, didn't know you had arrived in the first place – and even then you'd probably get a couple of extra pens or something.

I'm not a Billy-no-mates, it seems, judging by the two gifts in Malcolm's hands – and the number of people fighting for space in our office. My desk has been so untidy for so long I had no idea it could accommodate so many butt cheeks.

I open the desk tidy first. It's pink – my favourite colour. And I'm honoured – as well as the standard blue and black biros and HB pencils, it has a retractable eraser, a miniature stapler and a small cellophane packet of treasury tags.

"Thanks," I say, putting it down on top of the illegal fridge – the only surface free of bums – and looking at the other gift waiting to be opened.

"Let me guess, it's a fountain pen," I joke, relieving Malcolm of the large box-shaped gift. My dad does that every birthday – feels a present that's obviously a new tie or a pair of socks and says 'let me guess – it's a new golf club'.

Blimey, it's heavy, whatever it is. Definitely not a fountain pen.

I rip off the floral wrapping paper (Fliss' choice, I suspect).

Bloody hell. It's a laptop.

"It's a laptop," I say, or rather, shriek, at the top of my voice, staring at the box in my hands. And then I go into a major panic. What if it's just a laptop *box* with something very definitely not a laptop inside – like a very heavy fountain pen, for instance, or a picture frame, or a box of bath bombs from *Lush!* Because everyone knows I love bath bombs from *Lush!*

But no, it really is a laptop.

I know we sell hundreds of them, but even at cost price they

69

aren't cheap and there's no way Malcolm would just give one away. And I really need one too – I let Alex keep the one we bought together.

"You've worked for Penand Inc for a long time and made a lot of friends who all wanted you to have something to help you in your next adventure, Rebecca," he says, reading my mind as the last bit of wrapping paper floats to the floor.

"If you are going to be a writer, then you'll need something decent to write on."

"I don't know what to say. I'm stunned," I say. "Thank you so much everyone."

"Good luck Rebecca," Malcolm shouts, raising his paper cup of champagne in the air.

"Good luck Becky," everyone echoes.

CHAPTER FIFTEEN

I stare at the pieces of plate on the floor and smile nervously at my new boss.

"Oops," I say.

Which is quite fortunate really. I very nearly said "bollocks" instead, remembering just in the nick of time that I am in the company of ten eight-year-old girls in pink sparkly cowgirl hats.

I have a new part-time job. At a coffee shop.

In hindsight, when Katie said that the sister of one of her colleagues was looking for some help at her coffee shop, it might have been an idea to clarify exactly which kind of coffee shop we were talking about.

This is not a quiet little coffee shop where little old ladies come to enjoy a pot of tea with a fruit scone, or where nine-to-fivers take refuge for a few minutes before returning to their offices with tuna baguettes to eat al desko. No, this is a coffee shop where children – and occasionally adults – sit and drink orange squash with malted milk biscuits whilst they ruin perfectly good white plates with pictures of trees and farmyard animals and call it art.

The name Potty Wotty Doodah should have been a bit of a clue.

But, in all honesty, I couldn't afford to be fussy. I wanted something part time and with as little responsibility as possible to maximise the time I have available for composing begging letters to editors of glossy magazines. Which kind of ruled out half the 'situations vacant' pages in the local newspaper. My newly acquired aversion to paperclips and staples ruled out a further twenty per cent – office clerks, administrators, personal assistants, general dogsbodies... And a traumatic experience as a waitress at the tender age of seventeen, when I mistook a vegetable spring roll for a raspberry pancake and served it up with two dollops of vanilla ice cream and a generous helping of raspberry sauce, ruled out the remaining thirty per cent.

I don't think even I could go wrong with a cappuccino machine. But a cappuccino machine and a slice of art on the side...?

Let me make this clear...

I cannot draw.

I cannot draw to save my life.

No, really, if my life actually depended upon my ability to draw, I would, in fact, be dead.

To illustrate (no pun intended), until the age of ten (okay, fourteen) I drew people with square heads, because I couldn't draw circles, and with arms that protruded horizontally out of their bodies, because shoulders and elbows were beyond even comprehension to me.

But I haven't even got to the stage yet where I'm being asked by a five-year-old to draw a giraffe on the side of an eggcup and I'm already a disaster.

Caroline – my new boss – opened Potty Wotty Doodah three years ago, after six years as an art teacher and two years studying business at night school. In other words – she *can* draw.

It's adorable. The walls are covered with rows and rows of shelves filled with every kind of plain white pottery you can imagine – bowls, plates, cups and saucers, salt and pepper pots, cookie jars, money boxes. There are even light switch surrounds, doorknobs and toothbrush holders.

The far wall is half-decorated with a mosaic of tiles painted by customers since the café opened, while the other half is waiting for the next three years' worth.

To the left as you walk in there is a counter where Caroline greets everyone and serves coffee and juice. And in the centre is an island unit – it's the kind you find in big kitchens, but instead of pots and pans and recipe books it's filled with picture books, stencils, rubber stamps and tracing paper, and hundreds of bottles of paint. Inspiration Island – that's what Caroline calls it.

The rest of the room is filled with pine tables and chairs, a different coloured plastic cloth draped over each table, a miniature pinny hanging from the back of every chair.

It's just like Willy Wonka's Chocolate Factory – except you don't eat the decorations, you paint them.

Caroline has a little girl – Molly, who's five, and she's six months pregnant with her second child. She's starting to take things a bit easier now. Her friend Fiona works here too – but she's in the process of setting up her own shop – a children's clothing shop – just a few doors down in the same street, so she isn't able to work any extra hours.

That's where I come in.

So – Caroline is a former art teacher and Fiona stitches pictures of angels on t-shirts and socks, whilst I, it seems, am the token pleb who can't even draw stick-men.

Today, though, stick-men are the least of my problems.

I am learning how to glaze a pot – that's the bit that makes them shiny when they come out of the kiln, apparently. I haven't gone near the kiln yet. I'm not sure I ever will after today's disaster.

I pick up the larger fragments of plate from the floor and apologise to Caroline. Again.

"Don't worry," she says kindly. "That's why we're doing this – so you can get it right before you start handling the proper stuff."

73

By proper stuff she means the pottery with the pretty pictures – straight from the hands of proud little girls and boys – instead of the plain items straight from the shelves. The very thought of touching the 'proper stuff' makes me nervous. The last time I had anything to do with any kind of pottery was in art class at secondary school when I accidentally dropped Emma's cat dish. It was a masterpiece – a bowl in the shape of a cat's face with delicate clay whiskers sticking out of the sides. She cried for the rest of the day. So did I. It was very traumatic. And we were eleven. Imagine what it could do to a toddler...

"Try again," Caroline says, handing me the tongs you use to dip the pottery. They look like a pair of industrial-size barbecue tongs. I hold them awkwardly. I feel like Julia Roberts in the scene from Pretty Woman when she's trying to pick-up snails at that posh restaurant.

I grip a mug like Caroline has shown me, with one half of the tongs at the bottom and the other on the rim, and slowly ease it into the bucket of glaze. It's a thick blue gloopy substance.

"So why doesn't everything come out of the kiln blue?" I ask Caroline.

"The blue disappears in the heat, but there are chemicals in the paints which make them resist the heat," she explains. "Normal paints – poster paints for example – they would burn off."

"Hmm," I say, taking it all in, twisting the tongs gently in the bucket, to make sure the mug is coated all over.

"That should do it," she tells me.

I ease the mug out of the bucket and then watch as it slips out of the tongs and drops back in. It bobs up and down like a bobbing apple at a Halloween party before filling up with glaze and sinking to the bottom of the bucket.

I smile at Caroline. It's a smile of resignation.

I'm not sure I'm cut out for this. Selling pencils was much easier.

CHAPTER SIXTEEN

By the end of the day I have broken one more mug and successfully glazed a dinner plate and a kitten ornament. Keen to leave on a high point I hang up my apron for the day and get the tube back to Katie's.

I'm staying with Katie and Matt while I get myself sorted. They have said I can stay with them as long as I want. Technically that means I can stay forever – I don't want to be on my own. But I won't stay forever. They are getting married soon. They don't want me cramping their style.

They have a lovely flat in Clapham Junction, just two stops on the Overground from Potty Wotty Doodah. They bought it last year after living with Matt's parents for almost eighteen months to save for the deposit – a period Katie affectionately describes as her 'time inside,' so I know how much it means to her to finally have her own place.

Fortunately I left some of my stuff at Fliss and Derek's. Katie and Matt's spare room is tiny – just about big enough to swing a cat. But only just. Any smaller and there would definitely be claw marks on the walls.

It has a single bed, a bedside table with a lamp and a framed photo of Katie and I dressed as witches, and a canvas wardrobe that Katie and I bought the weekend I moved in. I think we both underestimated just how many clothes I own – something we discovered when we hung the last t-shirt on the wooden pole and watched as it popped out of its sockets, spilling the contents onto the floor in a big heap.

"Matt!" we both yelled simultaneously, before collapsing onto the bed in a giggling heap ourselves.

"We'll see you in a couple of hours," Katie tells Matt as soon as I get home, giving him a quick kiss on the lips and throwing her bag over her shoulder.

"A couple of hours?" I ask, horrified.

Katie is dragging me to the gym. As if my day has not already been torturous enough…

Katie loves the gym. She goes at least twice a week – runs a few kilometres, cycles a couple of miles, rows the equivalent of a small river or two, does a few sit ups, a few press ups…

I hate the gym. All that puffing and panting – not to mention all the sweating. I keep telling her – it's ever so unattractive.

And she pays £75 a month for the privilege!

This is the same gym, might I add, where Katie had her under-wear nicked from the changing rooms while she was having a work-out before work one morning. I saw this as an opportunity – attempting to get out of going on the grounds of security.

"No-one would want to steal your knickers, B," she had politely informed me. "They're old and saggy and off-white."

I decided not to waste crucial time being offended – that could wait till later – and attempted to come up with an alternative excuse instead.

"I don't have any gym gear," I said.

"I have spares," she told me.

"I'm not a member," I said.

"I have guest passes," she announced.

I admitted defeat eventually, of course.

But bloody hell – two hours! Anyone would think we were training for the London Marathon.

We get the tube to the gym where Katie signs me in as her guest. Before I am allowed in I have to fill in a form with my name and address, date of birth and vital statistics – so that they can use them to attempt to con me out of £75 a month, no doubt. And I also have to sign a waiver – to say that I won't sue them when I come flying off the end of the treadmill and break both my legs. Or words to that effect.

"You never know B, you might meet a man here," Katie tells me, shoving her bag in the locker and slamming the door shut before it falls back out again.

Katie wants to find me a man. She thinks I need one. She says it's just like falling off a horse – "you have to get straight back on".

"Or what?" I asked her, "I'll forget how to do it?" I'm not quite sure exactly what it was I meant by 'it'.

"I keep telling you – I don't want a man right now," I say, pulling my ponytail tight and digging my knickers out of my backside through Katie's cycling shorts. Her bottom is a bit smaller than mine, evidently.

"Well keep digging your knickers out of your backside in front of everyone in the gym and you'll probably be safe," Katie laughs.

"Where do you want to start?" she asks me.

Nowhere is not an option, I presume.

I look around at the equipment – there are rows and rows of bicycles, treadmills, cross trainers, rowing machines…all with maniacs on them cycling, running, rowing for dear life and getting absolutely bloody nowhere. It all seems ever so tedious. Whatever happened to getting outdoors – on a real bike, on a real road?

"How about the sauna?" I ask.

I have to earn my time in the sauna, apparently. Two miles on the bike and one mile on the treadmill earns me twenty minutes in the sauna, according to Katie's Law. Well, that sounds easy enough.

There are no pairs of bikes together so Katie and I take the bikes on opposite ends of the row and get to work. Or should I say, Katie gets to work while I fiddle about with the earphones trying to find the best channel on the gym's sound system.

I settle on what appears to be a dance album and start cycling whilst simultaneously pressing buttons on the bike – completely at random. I must look like someone who doesn't know what they are doing because the guy on the bike next to me offers to help.

I continue to prod feverishly at the buttons.

"Thanks, I'm fine," I tell him, even though it's abundantly clear I'm really not.

By sheer bad luck I seem to have ended up on the hill climb setting. On level 18. Out of 20.

Bloody hell this is hard work. I suspect I may have gone a shade of puce.

I am being watched. I can tell. I look up and the guy next to me is grinning at me in the mirror. He's quite cute. Actually he's very cute – in a sweaty kind of way.

Now, is it not bad enough that I have been dragged to the gym against my will, in a pair of shorts that are practically cutting my nether regions in half *and* been left to the mercy of a machine I have absolutely no idea how to use, without being subjected to the scrutiny of a frankly rather gorgeous guy too?

I am quite possibly in danger of hyperventilating on my level 18 hill climb when cute guys leans over and gently taps my screen, bringing it down to a more manageable level 10 (okay, 4).

"Thanks," I pant.

How utterly humiliating.

Cute guy has gone and I have clocked up a pretty unimpressive 0.8 miles (okay 0.4 – my only excuse being the cute guy – I was distracted) when Katie comes bounding over 20 minutes later. Where *does* she get her energy?

I quickly cover the screen with my towel.

"How are you doing?" she asks.

"Yeah, great," I lie.

"Shall we have a go on the treadmill?" she asks, though I don't think I actually have a choice.

"Sounds fabulous," I say, hitting 'cancel workout' before she can see the pitiful distance I have cycled.

CHAPTER SEVENTEEN

On my second day at Potty Wotty Doodah, I am astonishingly given responsibility for operating an oven that reaches temperatures of over 900 degrees and in six short hours I am asked by several naive youngsters to draw a cow and a pig on a seesaw, a giraffe and a hippopotamus playing leapfrog, and two spiders holding hands, amongst other things. On a good note I break only one tile and one saucer. I get home, utterly frazzled, to find a note on the fridge.

B, we've popped to see a man about a band. Can you turn the oven on at 6pm. Ta. K&M x

Unlike me, Katie is a veritable Gordon Ramsay in the kitchen. She can make anything out of anything. Literally. While I am on television demonstrating precisely why *Can't Cook Won't Cook* was so named, Katie will be on *Ready Steady Cook* preparing a four-course banquet from a single tomato, a tin of custard and a packet of salted peanuts.

Between us, Matt and I have negotiated what we consider to be a terrific deal. Katie cooks. He washes. I dry. And for the days she can't be bothered we'll get a takeaway. They live a three-minute walk from two Chineses, an Italian, a curry house and a fish and chip shop (yes, we've actually timed it).

They are also a four-stop tube ride from the offices of a zillion magazines, which will come in very handy when the flood of invitations to meet their editors lands on the doormat. Which it inevitably will.

It just hasn't yet, that's all.

Bollocks.

I have written to no less than twenty seven different magazines so far, begging for a job and so far I have heard absolutely nothing. Not a jot. Zip. Nada.

Okay, so I know I have no journalism qualifications to speak of, and absolutely no knowledge of the magazine industry whatsoever, but apart from that I'm an ideal candidate for a job on a magazine.

I read them, after all. All the time. And I watched Ugly Betty. And I've seen How To Lose a Man in 10 Days at least five times. And I learned a great deal from Lois Lane when she worked alongside Clark Kent on the Daily Planet.

And frankly, considering the CV I sent out, I would have expected them to be beating down Katie and Matt's front door to hire me by now.

Of course, it did require the teensiest bit of embellishment and exaggeration. But who doesn't do that these days?

Okay, so I have sold pens for a living, and, correct me if I'm wrong, but writers use pens, do they not? But I guessed that this alone was not going to be quite enough to get me a job.

All it takes is a little imagination and creativity (key characteristics of a good writer, you might say).

So...

1) I was the editor of my secondary school newspaper.
Truth – it was two sides of A4 and we only ever finished one edition, but it did include some quality material – like the interview with Mrs Hayland, the foreign languages teacher who drove the school minibus under a car-park barrier and took the roof off (it was the first and only time I have ever seen a teacher cry).

Therefore CV entry: Editor of award-winning weekly school publication.

2) At university I wrote the odd story for the student union magazine.

Truth – the stories were rarely (okay, never) about something worthy – like the need for more resources in the campus library, for example – and usually (okay, always) about the drunken exploits of my fellow students – including my mate Lucy who fell off the table she'd been dancing on at the Christmas ball, resulting in a trip to casualty and a nomination for the Pisshead of the Year award.

CV entry: Regular contributor to the highly influential University Life Magazine.

And let's not forget 3) the week's work experience at my parents' local newspaper during the summer holidays before my final year at university.

Truth – the only thing I actually had published was a three-paragraph piece for Pets Corner about a hamster called Travis who was looking for a new home. We found him a home, complete with new hamster girlfriend Morag and a fun ferris wheel on which to see out his days.

CV entry: Do you think 'work experience at the Worthing Gazette covering the exclusive story of a homeless man who found love and a new home and turned his life around' is stretching the truth a bit?

No, me neither.

Who did I think I was kidding? Not one reply out of twenty seven letters, not to mention several paper cuts on my tongue from all the envelope-licking and a small fortune spent on stamps.

Maybe I've made a big mistake. I'm twenty seven. I should be married by now, holding down a steady job and thinking about having kids – not single, dossing down in my best friend's spare room, watching kids paint pictures of pigs on plates and waiting for highly-paid editors of hugely successful magazines to take pity and offer me a job.

Damn. I have made a monumental mistake haven't I? I've given up a perfectly good job, not to mention a perfectly good boyfriend, moved two hundred and fifty miles from the place I have called home for the last nine years, moved in to play gooseberry with my best friend and her husband-to-be and taken a job serving coffee and supervising pot-painting children. And for what? To discover I don't even possess the skills required to get me a job on *Cross Stitching with Mother*.

I had no idea there were quite so many magazines out there. Two thousand, nine hundred and thirty-six to be precise. It says so on the Internet. Surely one of them must want to hire me? *Cosmopolitan* – yes I've heard of that. And *Company*. And *Marie Claire*. And even *Take A Break*. But *Concrete Monthly*? What the hell is that all about? Apart from concrete, obviously.

I thought I might fare better with the magazines that only sell seven copies a year (between them, that is), than the *Hellos* and the *Vogues* of this world, which sell seven million zillion. So I've applied to a few. I mean, if I can't get a job on the likes of *Fruit & Veg* or *Mobile Knowhow*, then there's something very wrong. I may not be able to cook, but I do know my carrots from my cauliflowers and my text messaging speed is up there with the best.

But like I said – absolutely nothing. Not one single reply.

I turn the oven on and scribble a message on the bottom of Katie's note telling her I'll be home around 8.30pm and head for the tube.

I've signed up for a writing class. It's every Tuesday night for six weeks, from 6.30pm till 8pm – starting tonight. It could set me up for life. Or it could be the worst £120 quid I ever spent.

It's at a secondary school in Balham, just one stop on the train from Katie and Matt's, or four stops if I go straight from the cafe.

I follow the directions to the school and head for the reception, where I have to sign in and have my bag checked. Times have changed. It's not apples, bananas and pickled onion Monster Munch that students carry in their bags these days – it's flick knives and packets of drugs.

As soon as he has established that the saucer in my bag is not a lethal weapon but a pottery sample from my new place of work, the security guard reluctantly lets me go, with directions to Room 11B.

Room 11B is small. It has just four double desks, one desktop computer on a stand in the corner, a desk for the teacher at the front and what looks like a very old blackboard. This is clearly a classroom where time has stood still.

Judging by the one remaining empty seat, I must be the last to arrive. I sit down next to a middle-aged woman with greying hair and the palest pink lipstick. She's come prepared. In front of her on the desk she has a dictionary, a thesaurus, a combined dictionary and thesaurus and three other reference books. She can barely see over the top of them. She also has a pretty purple pencil case with a cartoon kitten on the front. She probably made a special visit to WH Smith to pick it out. I pull my one reporter's spiral notepad and pen out of my bag (no, I didn't steal them from Penand Inc, I bought them with my own money – all £1.28 of it) and put them on the desk. She smiles at me. I think she feels sorry for me.

"I'm Audrey," she says.

"Becky," I tell her, returning the smile, twizzling my pen in my hands.

And then, before I have the chance to get to know my new classmate any better, our teacher arrives.

"Hello class," she booms, from the back of the room, before putting a bundle of magazines under her arm and her keys between her lips so that she has a hand free to close the door. She has several bags over her shoulders, which she hoists up before they slip off, and then marches determinedly to the front of the room, arriving just as the magazines are about to slip from under her arm.

"My name is Sheila," she says, catching them and putting them on the edge of the desk. "And for the next six weeks I will be teaching you how to write for magazines."

She's wearing a tweed skirt and a matching waistcoat over a long-sleeved floral blouse, and she has mad wiry hair that looks like it needs a good brush. She's in her fifties, I'd say. She definitely looks like a teacher. But I can't imagine for the life of me that she's ever written for anything more exotic than *Crossword Puzzles Monthly* or *Readers Digest*. Maybe *Woman's Weekly* at an absolute push…

Apparently I'm wrong. Apparently she's had articles published in the *Telegraph* magazine, the *Daily Mail* weekend supplement and *Woman's Own*. When I hear this I decide to sit up straight and give her my full attention. You never know – I could learn a thing or two.

We are learning the basics today – The Writer's Tools.

"So. Can anyone tell me what you need to be a writer?" Sheila asks the class, when we have all introduced ourselves and given a brief explanation of what we hope to achieve from the class. (Bearing in mind I have never written anything for a magazine before I am realistic – "I'm Becky," I told my fellow students. "I hope to write for Vogue!")

As I had expected, her question is met with silence. She peers at us all. One by one. Over the top of her half-moon glasses.

She reminds me of my English teacher, Mrs Conagie. She was more than a little eccentric. She used to talk about a pet spider called Cyril that she kept in a jam jar at home and fed dead flies and small pieces of bacon rind. Some people thought it was just a story, but she was certainly mad enough. She would peer at us just like Sheila is peering at us right now, waiting to hear what excuse we were going to come up with for not handing in our homework. I will never forget the day my friend Libby – well known for her creativity (the goldfish jumped out of his bowl onto it and all the ink ran; I was writing so fast my pen spontaneously combusted and set it on fire) – decided to opt for the truth and told her she had not written her essay on Macbeth simply because she 'couldn't be bothered'.

"The shopping list is not as extensive as you might think," Sheila announces, just as I'm about to suggest 'a pen and a piece of paper?' She perches on the edge of one of the front desks and folds her arms dramatically, as if she has just revealed a state secret.

"You need a desk," she says. "But contrary to popular belief, it doesn't have to be an antique leather-topped desk, with matching chair…"

Right, because that's exactly what I was about to ask.

I did tell you about my room at Katie's didn't I? Do the words 'cat' and 'swing' ring any bells? Where exactly does Sheila think I'm going to put a desk?

"It doesn't even have to be a desk at all," she continues. "What is important is that you have some sort of surface on which to write."

I do a quick mental tour of Katie and Matt's flat. They don't have a dining room table, the kitchen work top is covered in cooking gadgets, and the coffee table in the living room is where we put our wine glasses, so that's definitely out.

The ironing board?

I decide not to make this suggestion out loud. Sheila might think I'm not being serious. Which would be a little embarrassing, since I really am.

She presses on.

"And you need a computer."

Well I'm okay in that department, thanks to my friends at Penand Inc.

"We've all heard the idyllic stories of writers who still write in longhand or on an old typewriter," she says. "But if you can possibly afford one, a computer really is worth the investment. And it will save you a lot of time."

Also on the shopping list are a notepad and pen, and The Writers & Artists' Year Book. It's the media writer's Bible, apparently, and a must-have for anyone hoping to get published.

I make a note of it in my pad, and feel just a tiny bit smug when Audrey asks if she could possibly borrow a piece of paper. It seems she missed the notebook section at Borders. I suspect she didn't actually mean borrow – I don't imagine she'll be bringing me a brand new piece of paper to replace it next week.

And finally – a dictionary, a thesaurus, and a book of quotations – which just happens to be one of Audrey's other reference books. So now it's her turn to look smug.

When the class is finished we head to the pub to get acquainted.

On first impressions, they are a nice crowd.

Cathy has just started a new job which involves a lot of report-writing, so she wants to brush up on her skills and this was the only writing class she could find that fitted in with her yoga night, her Czechoslovakian for beginners and her jewellery-making class.

Bev has never written a thing in her life. She's an accountant for a big fizzy drinks manufacturer in West London. But she fancies having a go at writing a book. She thought she'd be better off starting small – I guess a 1000-word feature has got to be easier than a 100,000 word novel.

Jo has just started work as a trainee writer on a supermarket magazine. It's her first job since leaving university and she feels totally out of her depth. Her boss doesn't know she's here.

Stephanie is a primary school teacher. She had a letter published in *Marie Claire* last month and now she thinks she'd quite like to be a writer.

Tara and Georgina work together and fancied taking a class. They chose this one because Spanish for beginners was full. They tend to laugh a lot, and didn't appear to be writing anything down tonight. I suspect Sheila might end up separating them next week.

As for Audrey, I haven't a clue. She didn't actually say anything. She just kept one hand on her reference books and the other on her wine glass, until her husband came to pick her up.

CHAPTER EIGHTEEN

I am sitting with my hand wrapped around a glass of wine, the rest of the bottle between my legs, and the 'situations vacant' pages open on the table in front of me when Katie and Matt walk through the door on Thursday evening.

"Nobody wants me," I announce dramatically as Matt goes into their bedroom to change and Katie throws herself down next to me on the sofa, takes the glass from my hand and has a swig.

Today is not a good day. Today I got my first rejection. First of many, no doubt.

"Correction," she says, scanning the letter she has just prised out of my other hand. "*Frankly Fossil Fuels* don't want you, which is frankly hardly the shame of the century. Would you really want to work for them? And more to the point, have you ever even heard of them?"

"Well, no, but that's not the point."

"Of course it's the point. You've given up a lot to do this, B. You deserve a job on a magazine you actually like – or one you've heard of at the very least."

"Maybe. But how am I supposed to do that? I've written to practically every magazine that you find on the racks at W H Smith – and a lot that you don't too – and none of them want me."

"One magazine. One magazine doesn't want you. That's the only letter you've had back. You've got to be patient."

After dinner Katie enlists my help with wedding invitation-assembling. She is making them herself. Each one is made up of a cream-coloured card casing over a sheet of translucent paper printed with the invitation details, tied together with a thin strip of gold ribbon.

Personally I think she spent far too much of her childhood watching *Art Attack* and *Blue Peter*, and not nearly enough time watching *The Wombles* and *Worzel Gummidge*. It wouldn't have surprised me if she'd decided to make the invites out of toilet rolls, and empty washing up liquid bottles.

As you would expect, owing to my complete lack of artistic talent, Katie has assumed the role of Artistic Director, while I am General Dogsbody, whose job it is to pass the glue sticks, paper and ribbon when instructed.

"Do you think they look alright?" she asks me.

"Yeah, they're lovely."

"I offered to help her myself but she wouldn't let me," Matt says, fiddling with a new pair of football boots.

I'm honoured.

"It's very delicate work and your hands are too big," Katie points out.

"I'm sure you're devastated Matt," I tell him, handing the Artistic Director a piece of ribbon.

Matt is an absolute gem. He and Katie met in our third year at university when she and I were staying in London for the weekend with our friend Harriett.

Katie and Harriett had gone to the toilet and while they were gone I started talking to two blokes – Matt and his mate Tony

– both dressed in flares and flowery shirts and wearing enormous afro wigs.

"Bloody hell, who has she lumbered us with now?" Katie later admitted to thinking as she clocked the 'two pillocks in afros' on her way back from the loos. I make a habit of talking to random people in bars, apparently. I call it being sociable. Katie calls it 'lumbering us with odd-bods' – this occasion being the exception, as she started talking to Matt and decided he was alright after all. Turns out they weren't just nutters in 70s gear, but on their way to a fancy dress party. We ended up joining them, so were there to witness the very moment when they discovered they were the only two nutters who had bothered with the fancy dress!

The next day Matt phoned and asked Katie out for dinner. She told him she was down from Leeds on a girly weekend. So he took all three of us out instead. We knew then that he was a keeper.

He's three years older than Katie, he's an architect, and he loves football. And he's very handsome – the tall, dark variety, with thick dark hair that flops over his face. If I hadn't recently found Alex when I first met Matt, I would probably have fancied him myself.

But Matt was made for Katie. And she was made for him. And ever since the two of them got together Matt has been like another brother to me.

"It's a bit wonky, B," he says, poking me in the ribs with a football boot just as I'm tightening the ribbon, ensuring it becomes even wonkier.

See what I mean?

CHAPTER NINETEEN

Emma's coming out with us tonight – to help celebrate my first week in my new job. And the fact that I have only broken three plates, two mugs, an eggcup, a tile and a saucer – none of them painted. (That's good, by the way.)

Anyway – any excuse for a night out, I say.

But first, there's something I must do. Something I can't put off any longer. Bridesmaid dress shopping.

Emma is meeting us at the shop. I think Katie is planning on a last-ditch effort at persuading her that she will still get married herself one day, even if she *has* been a bridesmaid three times.

I don't fancy her chances. Emma can be very stubborn.

On a personal note, I have told Katie that as long as she doesn't make me look like a peach cobbler (whatever a peach cobbler actually is), then I'm happy to leave it up to her.

But I'm beginning to think I may be being a little too flexible. There are, after all, plenty of other garish-coloured desserts she could have me resembling. Strawberry blancmange or key-lime pie, for example, would both be fairly hideous. Still, it's her big day, so I'll just have to be brave.

We walk to the tube station arm in arm. There's a new shop that's just opened in Oxford Street, apparently, which only sells bridesmaid dresses. It's called *Bridesmaid Revisited* – based on the owner's confidence that you might look elsewhere, but you'll always come back there in the end to buy. I almost want to hate her dresses just to prove her wrong.

"I don't know why you've got it into your head that I want you in peach anyway," Katie says as we step onto the train. "I don't want you spoiling the wedding pictures any more that you're already going to."

"Oi, you cow," I say, digging her in the ribs. The train is packed so we are forced to get up close and personal with an ensemble of dodgy-looking individuals we'd sooner not get up close and anything with. For most of the journey, I am wedged between one of the poles you're supposed to hold onto for safety, a bloke reading the metro who looks like he has the entire contents of his local allotment under his finger nails and another bloke whose mop of straw-like hair may well be home to a small family of birds.

We tumble out with the masses at Oxford Circus and make our way to *Bridesmaid Revisited* where we find Emma leaning against the shop front flicking through a book of wedding readings.

We both hug her.

"I've found the perfect reading," she tells us.

"The perfect reading or the perfect reading to wind me up?" Katie asks, raising her eyebrows.

"The perfect reading, of course."

"In that case I can't wait to hear it."

Fifteen minutes later I am stripped down to my knickers and socks ("you can take the bra off love, we'll find you one with a bit more padding that'll hold the dress up better") and I am having dresses of every style and colour – except peach – flung at me from all directions by Katie, Emma and Cheryl, one of the shop owner's assistants, whose hair is scraped back so severely I'd swear her eyes are a centimetre further apart than they should be. I have to say, it doesn't inspire us with confidence that she will know a good look when she sees one.

"Take that one off and I'll see if we've got it in the lilac," she instructs me, evidently not intending to leave the cubicle as I do so.

"Erm…yeah," I say, sticking my head through the curtain and giving the girls dagger eyes – the kind that I hope convey the message 'get this woman out of here'.

It doesn't take long to choose a dress in the end. None of us like the lilac, which we were all convinced would be our first choice. Instead we all agree on a pale gold-coloured strapless dress which has a line of tiny glass beads across the top of the bodice, like the ones on Katie's dress.

We love it, but we don't buy it. We tell Cheryl that we'll think about it – that we want to check out a few other shops first. It's not called *Bridesmaid Revisited* for nothing, after all.

And we do go into a few other shops – *Beauty and the Bridesmaid*, *Bridal Be Beautiful*, *The Wedding Shop* and we have a half-hearted rifle through the rails. But in the end, of course we do go back to the first shop we went into.

They have to order the dress in, so I try on the twelve in a frightful green version of the same style to check the size. It fits perfectly from the waist down, but even with one of their extra-padded-for-girls-with-no-boobs bras, I will still need the top taking in, so we make an appointment to come back for a fitting and then leave to get some lunch.

"So what's the reading you've found then, Em?" Katie asks, as we wait for our food at *A Pizza Perfect*.

Her last ditch effort at persuading Emma to be bridesmaid has resulted only in us learning that if you throw a hairy black caterpillar over your shoulder you'll have good luck, if you step on the cracks in the pavement you'll have bad luck, and that Katie should just live in sin with Matt instead of marrying him because his surname is Henley and her surname is Harris…

Apparently if a woman's surname after marriage begins with the same letter as her maiden name, she will be unlucky, because:

Change the name, but not the letter

Change for the worse, and not for the better

It was at this point that Katie finally gave up trying to change Emma's mind.

"It's called Ten Milk Bottles," Emma says, pulling the book out of her bag and holding up her spare hand to stop Katie before she can protest.

"It doesn't sound very romantic," I point out, on her behalf.

Emma carries on, undeterred.

"Ten milk bottles standing in the hall,

ten milk bottles up against the wall,

next door neighbour thinks we're dead,

hasn't heard a sound, he said,

doesn't know we've been in bed,

the ten whole days since we wed."

We both laugh.

"I think it's perfect," Emma says.

"I think my Auntie Rose would have heart failure," Katie replies, pulling out the slip of paper Emma has marking the page.

"What about this one then?

Take a lump of clay, wet it, pat it

And make an image of me, and an image of you

Then smash them, crash them, and add a little water

Break them and remake them into an image of you

And an image of me

Then in my clay, there's a little of you

And in your clay, there's a little of me

And nothing ever shall us sever
Living we'll sleep in the same quilt
And dead we'll be buried together."

"I like that," I laugh, leaning back in my seat as the waiter puts my pizza on the table in front of me. "It reminds me of Morph on Take Hart. Do you remember that? The one with the art gallery where you could send your drawings in and Tony Hart would say 'here's an interesting picture of a horse made out of milk bottle tops,' only it would look nothing like a horse, just a bunch of milk bottle tops stuck on a piece of paper."

The waiter looks at me as if I have just tipped a bowl of spaghetti bolognaise over my head.

"Black pepper?" he asks.

"Yes please."

"That was my picture. And it wasn't a horse, it was a cow," Emma says, dead serious.

"You're kidding?"

"Yeah, I am, but you should have seen the look on your face! Don't worry Katie," she says, "I'm going to find a reading that you'll love. I promise. It'll be perfect."

"Okay. I trust you. I think…"

"So, Em, how are things with you?" I ask. "Have you been out on any dates?"

"No," she says, looking depressed suddenly. Maybe it was a bad idea bringing it up when we were all in such a good mood. But she's usually so blasé when she splits up with a bloke. Out with the old, in with the new – that's Emma's philosophy. Well, it used to be, anyway.

"A colleague of mine is trying to set me up with her brother, but I'm not sure…"

"Why not? It could be fun. What's he like?"

"He's a nice guy. I met him at her housewarming party last year. I'm just not sure…"

"It might be just what you need."

"I know. But I don't think I'm ready…"

"It's been a while since you and Jim split up, Em. You need to get back out there," Katie says. "And you too, B," she says, glancing at me cautiously. I pretend not to notice.

"I know, but I just miss him so much," Emma says.

"Have you spoken to him lately?"

"Yes."

"And?"

"And I asked him if he would give it another go. And he said 'no.' And I felt completely pathetic," she says, promptly bursting into tears.

"Oh, Em," Katie says, pulling her chair closer to Emma's and moving her pizza so she doesn't dip her elbow in it as she hugs our friend.

"He's not worth it, Em. He isn't. There's someone much better out there for you, honestly."

"But I don't want anyone else. I want Jim," she mumbles.

I rummage in my bag for a tissue and hand it to her. "You feel like that now. But when you meet someone else, you'll forget all about Jim."

"I don't want to meet someone else. It's too hard – starting all over again all the time."

"But would you rather be with someone you know isn't right for you?" Katie asks.

"Yes. No. Oh, I don't know. I was just happy with Jim. It all felt so easy. Now I have to start all over again. Again."

"But that's the fun part," Katie tells her. "I'm actually a bit envious of you two, you know. I'll never get to do all that again – the first date, the first kiss, the first time you do the deed… Those are the exciting times, when everything is new and fresh. Choosing which colour bog roll to buy at Tesco's is about as exciting as it

97

gets for me and Matt these days!"

With an image of Katie and Matt stood in the household goods aisle at Tesco deliberating over toilet paper, Emma wipes a tear from her cheek and lets out a little giggle. And then she blows her nose into the tissue like a trumpet. And we all tuck into our pizzas before they go cold.

CHAPTER TWENTY

In every town and village,
In every city square,
In crowded places
I searched the faces
Hoping to find
Someone to care.
…
Then you rose into my life
Like a promised sunrise,
Brightening my days with the light in your eyes.
I've never been so strong,
Now I'm where I belong.

'Where We Belong: A Duet', Maya Angelou

"Pass me the phone book, Becky," Emma says, back at Katie's.

I reach across the coffee table where the phone book is sitting under a pile of Katie's books from work.

"What for?" I ask, handing it to her.

"I'm going to phone the nearest convent. Let them know I'll be over in the morning to sign up."

"I'm not sure it works like that, Em," Katie laughs, before

shoving a Doritos into her mouth.

"I'm serious," Emma says. "I'm giving up men. I'm going to be celibate from now on."

"I'll believe that when I see it," Katie and I say, simultaneously.

An hour later Emma, always the last to get ready, finally emerges from the bathroom, which now smells like a polo mint factory, thanks to her mint-scented shower gel, shampoo, *and* conditioner.

"I think you might be over-doing it on the whole mint thing there, Em," I suggest as she runs a comb through her hair. "Anyone who tries to chat you up tonight will think you've been doing kinky things with After Eight mints."

"Ooh goody, that might help me pull," she says, all talk of convents and celibacy clearly forgotten.

Thirty minutes later we are ready to hit the town. I have a brand new pair of skinny jeans on with a bright pink halterneck top that has sparkly bits across the bottom. Katie has lent me her pink shoes so I am very co-ordinated. Emma is wearing a denim skirt and a silver-grey vest top. And Katie is wearing a really cute blue strapless dress. We all look fabulous, even if we do say so ourselves.

We are off to find Emma a man. She doesn't know that yet. I suspect Katie is also planning to find me a man. I won't be letting her. She doesn't know that yet...

After a quick girly photo using the self-timer on Katie's camera ('quick' being a slight exaggeration as it takes us three attempts before we manage to get us all in the picture) we down the last of our champagne and head outside where the taxi is waiting for us.

"Tonic on Barnaby Street, please," Katie tells the driver.

We're drunk.

All of us.

Spirits were doubles for an extra quid in *Tonic*, so we had a couple of those. It would have been rude not to, wouldn't it? And rather pointless, considering we would have ended up having at least two singles each anyway.

Then Emma insisted on buying us all cocktails. Katie said okay, as long as it didn't have rum in it as rum makes her sick (very sick, as I know all too well having held her hair back many a time after she has made a dash for the nearest available toilet) – and I said I didn't really want one. But she bought me one anyway. And so I drank it. Again, it would have been rude not to.

And so now, a little after 10pm, out of sheer politeness alone, we are already three sheets to the wind, as it were.

We are in the mood for a boogie but *Flares* is dead – except for a couple of women with peroxide blonde hair and skirts that barely cover their arses and who should probably be at home minding their grandchildren, not in Flares, shaking their booty to Kylie Minogue.

So we've come to the *Vod Kerr Baa* instead. Not so good for cheesy music, but great for vodka, as you might expect, and it does have a small space at the back that passes as a dance floor – for about five people – if we feel compelled later on.

Emma heads for the loo as soon as we get past the blokes throwing their weight around on the door, all black coats and chests pushed out like pigeons.

"Quick, grab that table," I shout at Katie when I spot two blokes about to get up. "I'll get the drinks."

One of the blokes catches my eye and smiles as Katie dives into his seat – very nearly before he is even out of it, poor guy.

I smile back, apologetically. Mmm… Bit of a dish…

The queue at the bar is mammoth, but I manage to navigate my way to the front with little more than a hair out of place. It's a skill I have honed over the years. It's simply a matter of being ready that split second that a person's attention is diverted, like when they turn around because they've forgotten to ask their mates what they want to drink. Just like I have in fact. Bugger.

I turn around to find Katie, and he's there, right behind me. Mr Dish. I thought he was leaving.

"I hope we didn't pinch your seats," I say. "We thought you were leaving."

"We are. I just…well…I just thought I recognised you."

"Oh right. No, sorry. I don't think we've met. I've only just moved to London."

"Oh well, it was nice to meet you anyway. Sort of!" he grins, before turning and walking away.

And then I realise where he's seen me before. At the gym. On the bike next to him. Completely clueless. Completely puce. Wearing my best friend's cast-offs and absolutely no make-up. Oh my god – and he recognised me – out tonight, hair straightened, beautifully made-up (sort of), in a new outfit purchased especially for the occasion. How the hell could he recognise me?

I should be depressed. But I have other things on my mind. I have vodka to drink. Copious amounts of the stuff.

The bar is filled with bottles – in every flavour you can imagine, and lots you never would – all being served up in little shot glasses with tiny sheep on them…

Of course! Vod Kerr *Baa*. Love it!

"Two strawberry cheesecakes, a chocolate profiterole and three vodka tonics," I say to the barman, feeling ever-so-slightly stupid and a bit like I'm in a patisserie, not a licensed drinking establishment.

"I just had a very strange encounter with a very dishy bloke," I tell Emma and Katie, putting the tray of drinks on the table.

"Ooh, what happened?" Katie asks, excited.

"It was one of the guys we had the table from. We thought

they were leaving, right? But I turned round to find out what you wanted to drink and he was there, right behind me. He said he thought he recognised me."

"That was a chat up line if ever I heard one," Katie laughs.

"You'd think so, wouldn't you? But then I realised he was right – we have sort of met – at the gym, the other night, when he turned down the speed on my bike because I was about to hyperventilate."

The girls find this far funnier than I'd like.

"You've pulled B. Go and talk to him," Katie says.

"No. Don't be daft."

"Why not?"

"Because…"

"Because what?"

"Because he was leaving anyway – he only came back because he thought he knew me. This is a girly night. And, anyway, I'm not up for meeting anyone new yet. It's too soon."

"You two are as bad as each other."

"Yeah, Becky," Emma says, accusingly. "You keep telling me I should get out there and start dating again! What about you?"

"I think you both should," Katie says, before I can answer. "Even if it's for no other reason than that I don't want a couple of old spinsters at my wedding!"

"Well thanks!" we both laugh.

"Besides, you'll upset my table plan if you don't bring guests."

"You haven't even started the table plan yet," I say.

"That's not the point," she laughs, holding up her shot glass. "Are we ready girls?"

"Oh my god that tasted nothing like chocolate profiteroles – more like paint stripper," Emma protests.

"How do you know what paint stripper tastes like?" I laugh.

"I don't. But at a guess I'd say it tastes something like that," she says, pointing to the empty glass in front of her and screwing up her nose in disgust.

The chocolate profiterole and strawberry cheesecakes are followed by vanilla slices and custard tarts, which are followed by rhubarb crumbles and lemon meringue pies. Which are followed by Katie saying: "Let's dance."

So we do. And just for us – because we are the first people on to the dance floor (which proves just how many desserts we have drunk) – the DJ plays a few cheesy songs - *I Should Be So Lucky*, *Love In The First Degree*, and *Saturday Night Fever*, at which point Emma proceeds to throw herself across the dance floor John Travolta-style, while Katie and I pretend she's not with us.

And then a few more bodies join us, clearly drawn in by Emma's dancing – in much the same way motorists slow down to gawp at the scene of an accident.

And then the DJ starts playing thumpy thumpy music, which we can't stand. So Emma and Katie head off to the loos while I go to the bar for some water – and pray that it's not vodka-flavoured.

I have drunk the entire bottle and am beginning to look like a Billy-no-mates when Katie finally returns from the loos with some bad news.

Emma has locked herself in the toilet and she's refusing to come out.

"Emma," I shout through the door. I'm not absolutely sure it's the right door, but given the sniffling noise coming from the other side, I'd say it's a reasonable guess.

"Emma. Open the door," I tell her. But my orders are met only with more sniffling and the sound of toilet paper being pulled from its container.

It's a wonder she's found a toilet with any paper left in it at all. We've reached the point in the evening when you would normally reach for the paper and discover the only bit left to be had is the tiny scrap still stuck to the roll, which frankly just isn't up to the job. So you tap on the wall separating you from the next cubicle and hope there's someone in there who can shove a bit under for you. But then she doesn't have any either, so you just have to drip-dry instead.

Then you come out and discover where all the paper has gone – all over the floor and around the sinks, covered in lipstick where the girls have been blotting all evening.

"Em, come on," I try again.

Still nothing.

"Emma! Open the door!" Katie shouts, opting for the more brutal approach, which is no more successful than my own softly softly method, I notice.

We're getting suspicious looks from the toilet woman. That's probably not her real job title, but you know who I mean – the woman who hands you a paper towel after you have washed your hands for a bit of spare change (because we are, after all, incapable of fetching one for ourselves – though on this occasion such an assumption might be forgiven). No spare change here, lady – it's all been spent on chocolate profiteroles and rhubarb crumbles.

And sometimes, if you are really lucky, you can also choose from a variety of beauty products to use in the rescue mission after you've looked in the mirror expecting to see the goddess you left the house with and see Godzilla staring back at you instead.

This woman has everything – hairbrushes, hairspray, perfume, tampons, disposable razors (presumably in case someone spots you doing the actions to YMCA by the Village People and politely informs you that you're looking a bit overgrown?) even a palette of eye make-up, which could actually come in handy for the panda eye elimination that will inevitably be required if we ever get Emma out of the bloody loo.

Toilet woman catches me looking at her wares and wastes no

time in swooping.

"You need something?" she asks, hopefully.

"Err...no, thanks," I say, feeling a bit tight. "I'm good."

"Unless you've got a screwdriver?" I add, as an afterthought.

"What on earth do you want a screwdriver for?" Katie asks.

"To unscrew the lock on the bloody door, of course! We could still be here this time next week at this rate."

"I do, actually," toilet woman says, reaching inside her bag – and astonishing us both.

And Emma, it seems, who unlocks the door.

When she hasn't emerged a few seconds later we both squeeze into the cubicle where we find her sitting on the toilet lid with a soggy tear-soaked wodge of toilet paper in her hand, looking very sorry for herself.

"Sorry guys," she says, soaking up a fresh wave of tears with the wodge.

"What for?" I ask, kneeling in front of her, forcing Katie up tight against the wall like a policewoman entering a building where a criminal might be lurking.

"For ruining the evening."

"You haven't ruined the evening, you daft cow. We've had a great night. You're just drunk. We all are. Blimey, how many times have I locked myself in the loos over the years after one too many?"

I start mentally totting it up, out of curiosity.

"Don't answer that," I tell Katie, who appears to be doing the very same thing.

"I just miss him."

"I know you do, Em, but you won't miss him forever. You *will* get over him. I promise. It just takes time, that's all."

"But what if he was the one and I never meet anyone else?"

"He wasn't the one, Em," Katie says gently. "If he was the one you would still be together. And you *will* meet someone else. When have you ever *not* met someone else?"

"But I'm just so tired of being on my own," she says quietly.

"What do you mean? You're never on your own. You've got men falling at your feet," Katie says, genuinely confused.

"But they don't stay there, do they? Not like Matt. Or Alex. Alex didn't leave you, B. You left him. He asked you to marry him. If you hadn't left him he would have stayed. Forever. I just want what you two have both had. I want someone to stay."

"Even if it's the wrong person?" Katie asks. "Em, if I didn't love Matt – if I didn't know for sure that I want to spend the rest of my life with him, then I wouldn't be marrying him. I would wait. Until I *did* meet the right person."

"She's right, Em. That's exactly why I couldn't marry Alex. I wasn't sure. Yes, he would have stayed. But in the end I didn't want him to. Come on." I pull her up. "Let's go home. I think we've all had enough."

As we leave the loos I'm dying to ask the toilet woman why on earth she has a screwdriver in her bag, but decide we are probably better off not knowing. Maybe she has just witnessed too many conversations like ours – conducted after one too many banoffee pies, through a locked toilet door.

CHAPTER TWENTY ONE

It's my second week at Potty Wotty Doodah. Caroline has taken the afternoon off to watch Molly in her school play.

She's left Fiona and I to supervise a four-year-old's birthday party.

How thoughtful.

There are eight of the little darlings, all painting plates. That's eight lots of paint-covered hands to dodge, followed by eight lots of birthday-cake-icing-covered hands. What fun.

Fiona has everything under control.

I am grateful. I am not to be trusted. I dropped a moneybox as soon as I arrived today. Pretty soon Caroline is going to start charging me for working here, never mind paying me.

I like Fiona. She's fun. And very patient.

If I do ever get to be a writer, I think I'll be great at interviewing people. In the short time I've know Fiona I've found out that she's 32, married – to Adrian, and has no kids – yet. And she loves pink, and frogs – in equal measure. Which is why she is calling her shop The Pink Frog. All her clothes have a tiny pink frog stitched on them. I'm sure all the girls' clothes would be pink if she had her way. And all the boys' too, for that matter. She wears pink every day – a bright pink t-shirt, a pink bangle, a pink hair slide. Something has to be pink. It's the law – *Fiona's Law*. And

Caroline wonders why she seems to be ordering twice as much pink paint as any other colour...

"I think you're done," she says to the token boy at this birthday party, who has covered his entire plate with black paint. She is showing incredible self-restraint. I know she's dying to add a splash of pink to brighten it up a bit.

"Have you heard from any of your magazines yet?" she asks me, taking two plates into the back room ready for glazing.

"Just one. A rejection. But I'm sure the rest of them will come flooding in any day now. Rejections, that is."

"Nothing like a bit of optimism," she laughs.

"I know. But I think I'd rather be pessimistic then pleasantly surprised, instead of optimistic then suicidal."

"If you want something badly enough you'll make it happen, Becky. That's what I say. Look at me. I knew I wanted my own children's clothes shop ever since my mum made me my first party dress from her sewing machine in the front room. And now I'm doing it."

"Yeah, I guess. It's just hard to be positive sometimes."

Between us we take the rest of the plates into the back room before clearing the tables.

"Right, I want to see everybody's hands up in the air, as high as you can," Fiona tells her little painters. Obediently, they all reach for the ceiling. Desperate to win this game, the birthday girl stands up on her chair for extra height. While her mum lifts her back to safety Fiona and I swipe the paint-covered cloth from the table and in one swift motion replace it with a new one that's covered in Disney characters instead.

And while Fiona distracts them with a quick Disney Princess quiz, I fill the table with *Cinderella* plates of sandwiches, *Pocahontas* bowls of crisps and chocolate fingers and a big jug of orange squash.

After they have demolished the crisps and chocolate fingers and left most of the sandwiches, it's time for pass the parcel.

There is a packet of colouring pencils inside each layer so that no child goes home distraught at not winning a prize. They are revealed one by one after each short burst of *Beauty and the Beast*, the pause button on the CD player expertly controlled by Fiona as she mentally ticks off each child who has had a turn. The adults in the room breathe a sigh of relief when the stop button is finally pressed and the winner removes the final layer of *Little Mermaid* wrapping paper to reveal her prize – a *Cinderella* money box – in her rags on one side, and in her mice-made ball-gown on the other.

The winner is thrilled.

If you'd told me six months ago that one day I'd be being paid to pour orange squash into Disney Princess paper cups and watch four-year-olds paint rainbows on plates, I'd probably have laughed out loud – and no doubt persuaded you to add an extra hole punch or a packet of over-sized bulldog clips to your stationery order.

But today it feels quite normal as I reach behind the counter for my handbag, find my purse and take out a twenty pence piece. I slot it into the Cinderella moneybox and the little girl beams.

I take a mental picture of that smile. That's the smile I will be wearing when I win my prize – a new job as a writer for *Cutlery Weekly* or *Model Aeroplanes Monthly*!

CHAPTER TWENTY TWO

Idea gathering is one of the most important skills for new magazine writers to acquire. And ideas are everywhere, apparently.

"I want to write, but I have no idea what to write about," Sheila tells us when we meet for our second writing class on Tuesday evening. "How many times have I heard that?"

Well, seven this evening, as it happens.

Cathy, Bev, Jo, Stephanie, Tara, Georgina and I have not come up with one idea between us.

Audrey has come up with six. But they don't count. Because they're rubbish. *How to make the perfect finger buffet, How to grow the perfect courgette, How to ensure over-ripe bananas don't go to waste*…Snore, snore.

"Ideas are everywhere," Sheila tells us again. "Once you know how to find them, you won't know what to do with them all."

I'm not convinced.

"All writers should be avid readers," she says.

Do Jackie Collins and Jilly Cooper novels count, I wonder?

"You should be reading newspapers, magazines, books, leaflets, the yellow pages…"

The Yellow Pages?

"Never reject any source of reading material," Sheila says sternly, looking right at me.

I must have smirked. Now I feel like a naughty child.

"Newspapers will tell you what is important in the world today. Magazines will feature articles that you can find a new slant on. The Yellow Pages could lead you to an unusual new business that might be worth writing about. A drive-through nail salon, a pet beauty parlour, a café where you paint your own mug…"

She's looking at me again.

Point taken.

"And take a good look at your own lives," she says. "There's no better place to find ideas – your experiences, your dreams, your interests. Have you done something that might be of interest to others? Lived somewhere a bit out of the ordinary? Had an unusual job?

"And what about your friends? What about their experiences? Do you know anyone who has had a life-altering experience? Anyone who is an expert in their field? Anyone who has an interesting hobby?"

I'm racking my brains, but I'm not getting very far. Clearly I have led a very dull life. My job at Penand Inc wasn't of any interest even to me, let alone anyone else. And I've lived in West Sussex, West Yorkshire and now London. Whoopy doo.

I look around at my fellow students, hoping their lives are as dull as mine. I think they are – apart from Audrey no-one looks remotely inspired.

"Don't move," Sheila tells us. "I'll be right back."

As soon as she leaves the room Tara and Georgina start a game of Hang Man and Audrey starts flicking through her book of quotations, while the rest of us try and convince ourselves this was 120 quid well spent.

When she comes back she is carrying a pile of newspapers and magazines.

She dumps one on each of our desks.

I'm sitting with Jo today. We get lucky. We get a month-old copy of *Woman's Own*, while Audrey and Cathy next to us get *The Dolls' House Magazine*. Audrey looks quite pleased. Cathy doesn't.

"Now, I want you to look through the magazines and newspapers I have given you and come up with five feature ideas per team," Sheila tells us.

Five?

Did she say five?

"I'll give you 15 minutes."

Now I know she's joking.

"And don't worry if you come up with more than five ideas, which I'm sure some of you will – we have plenty of time to hear them all."

No, she's not joking.

It's actually easier than I thought. They're not spectacular, but we have got five, and at least they are not about finger buffets and courgette growing.

There's a cover story about a woman who dropped ten stone in ten months and then put it all back on again, so we come up with *How To Get Out of the Dieting Trap – a look at how to give up dieting and establish healthy eating habits.* I wish someone *would* write this actually, it could come in handy for the make-sure-I-fit-into-my-bridesmaid-dress plan.

And inside there's a piece about the smoking ban, so we come up with the idea *Never Give Up Giving Up – a look at the difficulties of giving up smoking and how to stick with it.*

On top of that we've got *Finding the Right Exercise to Keep You Interested – anyone can join a gym, but is it right for you?, A Mum's Guide to Summer Holidays – how the working and stay-at-home-mum copes with school holidays,* and *Pregnancy Cravings – a look at the regular and bizarre things women crave when they are pregnant.*

I think Sheila is impressed.

And I think she is even more impressed with our ideas when she hears the rubbish some of the others have come up with.

Tara and Georgina got the *Daily Mail*. They spent 14 minutes doing the crossword and one minute coming up with *How to Make a Cigarette Break Last All Day*, which Sheila didn't even dignify with a response.

Bev and Stephanie got *The Financial Times*. Pretty handy, what with Bev being an accountant and all. They did really well. *How To Claim Back Your Bank Charges*, *Tax Tips For The Self-Employed*, *Securing Your Child's Financial Security*, and *Look After The Pennies and The Pounds Will Look After Themselves*. They ran out of time to come up with a fifth idea, but I think Sheila was too impressed to notice.

And Cathy and Audrey?

Poor Cathy.

How can you possibly get *How To Turn Your Flowerbed Into a Herb Garden* from *The Dolls' House Magazine*?

CHAPTER TWENTY THREE

"I need an idea," I tell Katie when I get home. I'm fresh out of them after my fifteen minutes of inspiration. I need her help. Because I have a plan.

"Any idea in particular?" she asks, as I take my coat off and throw it over the sofa.

A few minutes later she dumps a pile of magazines next to me on the sofa.

"So we need to come up with an idea for a feature?" she asks. "One which you can pitch to a bunch of magazine editors? To show them what they would be missing by not employing you?"

I nod, hesitantly. She doesn't sound convinced

In fact she sounds like she's not entirely sure what message it is we're actually aiming for – that I'm crap and they won't be missing much at all, or that I'm fabulous and they'd be missing a heck of a lot.

As her best friend, I'd like to think it's the latter. But you can never be sure.

Just because Katie happens to be one of my two closest friends, does not necessarily mean she thinks I'm a great writer. Besides, how would she really know anyway? She has little more to go on than a couple of postcards and the odd Post-It note left on the fridge at uni telling her I'd pick up some Pralines and Cream

Haagen Daas ice cream on the way home from the pub.

"I read that thing you wrote at Penand Inc about Fliss and everyone," she says, reading my mind. "That was great. You could send that along with your feature idea as an example of your work."

That's not a bad idea actually.

The plan is to send the 'idea' out to loads of magazines and at least one will love it of course, though ideally a war will ensue where they each outbid the other and I end up being offered thousands of pounds to write it. Okay, maybe not thousands, but at least enough to buy the odd Boots Meal Deal for lunch – I'm getting a little bored of my homemade cheese and pickle sarnies.

It's a great plan.

All I have to do now is come up with an amazing idea.

Matt is at the pub with some friends from work, so we spread out in the living room and flick through magazines looking for a good idea to pinch.

Sorry, did I say pinch? Obviously I meant inspire – a good idea to *inspire* us.

"You open the wine and I'll start flicking," Katie says.

"*The Mother-in-law survival guide*," she reads out loud, so I can hear her from the kitchen.

"*How to handle the other woman in your man's life*. Ha! I should read that later. Matt's mum is getting right on my tits at the moment. If she's not trying to take over the bloody wedding, she's dropping hints about grandchildren. I'm not even up the aisle yet, never mind up the duff."

Flick. Flick.

"*Should you really be with your first love? Dig out your little black book and you may just find Mr Right.*"

"As if!" I shout from the kitchen, easing the cork out of the wine bottle. "My first love was Jeremy Hipkiss. Like he'd be my Mr Right!"

"Is he the one that turned out to be gay?"

I put two glasses of wine down on the coffee table and plonk myself down next to her.

"Yes."

"Hmm. Yeah, they probably should have added a paragraph telling you to cross out the ones who turned out to be gay first!

"*How to bounce back after a break-up*," she says, opening up a different magazine and glancing at me cautiously. "*You've got Gloria Gaynor on repeat and a pile of soggy tissues in your lap. But give yourself some time and a bit of TLC and 'you will survive.*'"

"You don't have to worry, you know," I tell her. "Have you noticed any shortage of Kleenex in the flat? Or any Gloria Gaynor CDs? I'm fine. I'm just not ready to go out with anyone else yet. Anyway – we're not getting anywhere. These have all been written already. We need a new idea."

"Right. We need to find something you know a lot about," Katie says.

I'm not sure I like the implication that this 'something' will take some finding. But I let it go. She *is* supplying both the research materials and the refreshments, after all."

"Well, I really know nothing about getting a job on a magazine," I say, the defeatist in me taking over.

"Or how to be sensible and keep the perfectly good job I had in the first place."

Katie shoots me a warning glance before grinning and returning her attention to the magazines in her lap.

I carry on, undeterred.

"I do, however, know quite a bit about getting paint off children's hands, and out of their ears, and nostrils, and hair; how to fit the entire alphabet around the edge of a plate; how to prise a paintbrush out of two warring toddler's hands and how to convince a seven-year-old that I don't watch *Mister Maker* and therefore

117

have no idea how to draw a clown riding a unicycle on the side of a mug. Will any of them do, do you think?

"I know nothing about love," I continue, back onto the list of subjects on which my brain is a gigantic void.

"Don't be ridiculous," Katie laughs.

"I'm serious. All I seem to know is how to mess up every relationship I've ever been in."

I'm exaggerating of course. I didn't mess up my relationship with Jeremy – he did that himself when he invited Mark Ellis over to do some A level revision with us and tried to kiss him while I was busy working out a particularly tricky algebra question (I saw them in the mirror, if you must know). I still don't know who was more shocked – me or Mark. And my boyfriend before Alex – Terry – that wasn't my fault either. I didn't force him to get drunk, run naked around the grounds of the halls of residence and then shag Molly Mind-What-You-Catch Jenkins at the back of the botanical gardens, did I?

"You've just not found Mr Right yet, that's all," Katie says, breaking my thoughts. "But that doesn't make you any different to half the female population, B. You haven't found him *yet*. That doesn't mean you never will.

"Oh my god," she says, a touch dramatically, grabbing my arm and almost sending her own wine – and mine – flying all over the sofa.

"What?"

"I've got it," she says. "I can't believe we didn't think of it earlier."

"What?"

"We had it the other night. When Emma got drunk on custard tarts and locked herself in the loos."

"What? Tell me!"

She sips her wine, pausing for dramatic effect.

"*How do you know when you've met Mr Right?*" she says, looking dead pleased with herself.

She's lost the plot, clearly.

"But I don't know how you know you've met Mr Right," I remind her in the same tone you might use to remind someone where their nose is. "I haven't met him yet."

"No. But other people have. You can interview them, ask them how they knew. And when you're ready, you can go out there and start looking for him yourself. Unless you're planning on staying single for the rest of your life?" she says, before I can protest.

I think for a moment. It could work, I guess. And it would be kind of fun finding out about everyone else's relationships, instead of obsessing over my own love life.

And Katie's right. Even if it's not for a feature, some day I will have to get out there and start dating again.

Katie's looking at me. Waiting for some kind of reaction.

"Okay," I say. "Let's do it."

An hour later we have drafted a proposal letter no editor could possibly turn down.

But we decide to wait until the morning to print it and send it off, just in case in the cold light of day we aren't quite as enthusiastic about assuring the editors at *She*, *Company* and *Cosmopolitan* that although I am a thoroughly lovely person, I wouldn't think twice about making their lives a living hell – should they in fact choose not to hire me – by coming back when I am rich and famous, buying out their magazines one by one and sacking the lot of them.

And, as we anticipated, when the cold light of day does arrive, some considerable editing is required before I am able to send out fifteen copies of the letter, each with a copy of the piece I wrote at Penand Inc.

"If this doesn't work I'm phoning Malcolm and begging him

for my job back," I tell Katie as I drop the envelopes into the post box the following evening.

"And are you going to phone Alex and beg for him back too?" she asks, ever so slightly sarcastically, but with good reason.

"It'll take time to find your feet, B," she reassures me. "But you will. Going back is not the answer. You can stay with Matt and me for as long as you like. And it sounds like you're doing okay at the café."

"Yes, but I can't spend the rest of my life watching kids paint pots all day."

"You won't need to. It'll all work out, I'm sure."

"I know. Thanks Katie. You're a great friend."

"Takes one to know one," she says, linking her arms through mine as we walk back to the flat.

CHAPTER TWENTY FOUR

The postman thinks I fancy him.

He must do.

Why else would I pounce on him wearing my Little Miss Naughty pyjamas and pink fluffy slippers and whisper 'have you got anything for me this morning Mr Postman?' like I did on Saturday morning.

I didn't whisper intentionally, I had a frog in my throat. But the postman doesn't know that, does he?

It gets worse.

When he came yesterday, it wasn't until he had handed me the electricity bill and the free sample of Always Ultra that I realised I was actually holding onto his arm. I swear it was a look of genuine fear that crossed his face.

Today, though, it's a look of pity, as he hands me a bundle of mail held together with an elastic band. At least I'm dressed this morning.

For a brief moment I allow myself a flicker of hope, until I realise that the top four items are cards addressed to Katie and Matt – the latest in a flood of wedding invite replies.

There are four other envelopes – two junk mail, one bank statement – no doubt informing me there has been an unusually meagre amount of money entering my account of late, and one letter

– addressed to me. It's from *Girlfriend* – a magazine for teenage girls – sent from the editor, Patricia London, pp'ed by her assistant Melissa Curtis (I'm obviously not important enough to warrant her own limited-edition signature) explaining that although they don't doubt I was once a teenage girl myself, they just don't feel I have the necessary experience required by a magazine of their calibre. Okay, so it wasn't my best letter, but still... Calibre?! I had never even heard of them a fortnight ago.

Shoving the letter in my jacket pocket and pulling the front door behind me I head for the tube station, telling myself not to be too despondent. After all, this hasty decision was clearly made before the powers that be at *Girlfriend* had had the opportunity to read my magnificent proposal.

CHAPTER TWENTY FIVE

It's parents' evening at the school tonight so we've been booted out of Room 11B. We are in Room 11C instead. Why they couldn't use that room themselves, I don't know, but whatever.

It's a better room actually.

It's got a white board, instead of a black board. And the desks are covered in graffiti, which gives me something to read when Sheila starts waffling on about research. Don't get me wrong, I *am* interested, just not about reference books in libraries, periodicals and legal journals. Yawn.

It's the 21st century, I want to tell Sheila. We can do our research on the Internet. On our new laptops. That our friends at Penand Inc bought us.

I don't, of course.

I jot down a few notes instead. What I need from Tesco on the way home, for example.

I told Sheila about my idea. "It has potential," she said. I think she hated it. Oh well, what does she know?

I am so engrossed in my list of interviewees, that I almost miss the most vital part of the class.

How to Interview Sources.

There are three important stages, apparently. Preparing for the interview, the interview itself, and digesting the information from the interview.

And there was me thinking all I had to do was ask a few questions.

"We are all shy from time to time," Sheila tells us. "We all get nervous occasionally. But an interviewee does not need to know that. It is simply about being prepared and being professional.

"Never go to an interview unprepared," she says, waving her index finger at us like we're naughty children.

"Set up the interview well in advance. Then follow up with a phone call a few days before.

"Prepare your questions. Coming to an interview with a list of questions will help it go well. And whatever you do, don't forget your notepad and pen."

Seems simple enough. I think even I can manage that lot.

"The interview itself is the most important part of the process," Sheila tells us, rummaging in the drawer of her desk as she does so.

She pulls out a dry-wipe marker and scribbles on the white board. It comes out red, which seems to offend her, but it's the only pen there is.

"These are my tips for making it run smoothly," she says.

She looks at us and smiles, pausing for dramatic effect before she writes a number 1 on the board, followed by a full stop.

"Number one – start casually," she says. "Ask how their day has gone. Talk about the weather. Mention something you've seen in the news recently. A casual beginning will put you both at ease."

"Number two," she shouts this time. I think Georgina and Tara are playing rock paper scissors.

"Take notes. You won't be able to catch everything they say, so try and develop some form of shorthand. Develop abbreviations for key words, for example. And if you find a quote particularly interesting, don't be afraid to ask them to repeat what they said.

"When you do take notes, try to do so unobtrusively. Try to

give the impression that you are simply having a chat. Make eye contact, nod your head, then write it down.

"If you tape a conversation, it's a good idea to take notes too. Tape recorders can break. Batteries can run out. And if you are writing notes, you can mark a particularly significant comment in the margin.

"Number three – be observant." She looks at us all closely for this one, as if demonstrating her point. Jo shuffles uncomfortably in her seat next to me. Audrey fiddles with her book of quotations.

"Don't just listen to what they're saying," she says. "Watch their facial expressions, their hand gestures. If you are in their home, look around you. Do they have any pets? Any particular pictures hanging on the walls? Any trophies on the bookshelf? Look out for anything that could tell you something about them.

"And number four – stay in control. Ask the question, get your answer, and then move on to the next one. Don't let them take you off on a tangent.

"Right," she says. "Let's have a go."

I turn my chair so that I'm facing Jo. I want to laugh, but that would be childish. So I cross my legs and try to look professional instead.

We've got three minutes to find out three things about each of our fellow students. And they have to be completely different things about each person.

We've blown tip number one already. We haven't set the interviews up in advance. We haven't phoned our interviewees to remind them several days in advance. And we haven't prepared a list of questions.

I'm okay with number two. I have a notepad. I have a pen.

"Are you married?" I ask Jo.

Bollocks.

Sheila has told us not to ask closed questions – questions that

125

allow a simple yes or no.

"You only have three minutes on each person so you don't want to waste them getting yeses and nos, now do you?"

"No," Jo grins, in answer to my rubbish question.

"Do you have a boyfriend?" I ask.

Damn. If this were a game show I'd be doing very badly.

"Yes," she says.

I look at my watch.

"How did you meet him?" I ask.

"Speed-dating," she says.

"Really?"

"Yes," she laughs.

That closed question doesn't count, by the way. I was just curious.

After three minutes Sheila bangs her pen on the edge of the desk and the interviewer swaps places with the interviewee. And after another three minutes she bangs it again and we move to the next desk to start all over again with someone else. It's a bit like speed-dating, actually, except there's no wine on the tables – and there's definitely no chance of a date at the end of it.

After forty five minutes we all feel like we know each other a little bit better than we did before.

"Who wants to go first?" Sheila asks.

We have to share our information with the rest of the class, apparently. But we'd also quite like to go to the pub, so we've agreed to give one fact about each student.

Audrey puts her hand up. Teacher's pet.

"Bev's favourite vegetable is sprouts," she tells us, reading from her list, "but everyone else in her family hates them." Isn't that two facts?

"Cathy is allergic to mushrooms; Stephanie's husband grows four types of potatoes on his allotment; Jo once ate seventy four sweet corn kernels in under a minute using only a tooth pick; Tara won her school Halloween apple bobbing contest when she was eight; Georgina's favourite fruit is apples, but only if they are served in a pie with custard, and Becky once served up a vegetable spring roll with ice cream and raspberry sauce when she worked as a waitress."

The rest of the class – including Sheila – falls about laughing.

Can you believe it? Jo once ate seventy four sweet corn kernels in under a minute using only a toothpick and it's me that everyone laughs at? I think I should just keep quiet about that little mishap in future.

I'm up last.

I tell the class what they really want to know about each other. I tell them that Stephanie is married – to an Italian man called Paolo; that Cathy is engaged; that Georgina has just bought a house with her boyfriend; that Audrey has been married for thirty six years; that Tara thinks she's far too young to get married right now; that Jo met her boyfriend speed-dating – and he's just asked her to marry him, and that Bev is still waiting for Mr Right to come along and sweep her off her feet.

This information could come in very handy, you know. When I'm looking for interviewees. When all those magazines out there start fighting over my feature idea...

CHAPTER TWENTY SIX

Maybe they have emailed me instead. Although, that's not necessarily a good thing, is it? An email would be more likely to be a rejection, wouldn't it? If they don't want you they're hardly going to want to waste fifty pence on a second-class stamp to tell you so, now are they? Or maybe they would choose to email you to tell you that they want you – because it's quicker, thus allowing less time for you to be snapped up by some other lucky magazine. Hmm…

I force myself to wait a full week and then I take a look.

I have seven unread emails, Google Mail informs me.

One is an advert for a new credit card, which I delete. I don't earn enough to pay off the one I already have.

One is my Nectar Points statement. I have 43 – approximately enough to buy one plastic carrier bag.

One is details of my new subscription to -

What the hell?!

I told Katie categorically last week: "I am not joining an Internet dating site."

"Absolutely not," I said.

To which she replied: "Why not? It'll be fun."

To which I replied: "For you maybe, watching me make a complete tit of myself."

To which she replied: "You won't make a tit of yourself. Loads

128

of people do it these days."

To which I replied: "Would you do it?" Which was a bit daft really – she was bound to say yes, just to make me do it.

"Yes, if I was single," she fibbed, glancing over at Matt to check he wasn't listening.

He wasn't.

He was watching football.

She could have promised to join with me *and* snog-test a few blokes on my behalf while the football was on and Matt wouldn't even blink.

"You big fat fibber," I said. She pretended to look hurt at that, but she knew I was right. Katie would so *not* join an Internet dating site. She would rather be single for the rest of her life than look for a man on the World Wide Web.

"I'd rather be single for the rest of my life than look for a man on the World Wide Web," I told her.

She hadn't listened, clearly.

"What have you done, Katie?" I shout from the living room through to the kitchen where she is cooking spaghetti bolognaise.

"I don't know what you mean," she says, peering around the door licking sauce from a wooden spoon.

"Why have I got four emails from administrator@moredates-foryou.com?

"How should I know?"

"I'm not doing it," I say.

"Whatever," she says, shutting the door. "But I still don't know what you're talking about."

I stare at the screen, scanning the rest of my emails.

I'm told I have messages from Darren, Lee and Jason on the MoreDatesForYou website.

I should just delete them.

They're probably not my type.

129

And besides, like I said, I'm not into Internet dating. As if I'm going to meet Mr Right through a computer.

But then...

What if they're really nice?

But they're probably not. I should just delete them.

But it wouldn't hurt to take a quick look...

No. I won't bother. I minimise the screen and start a game of patience. I make a bad move right away so I re-start the game. I do like to beat the computer.

One of the messages *could* be from my Mr Right, you know.

I can't believe I just said that.

They could though.

Oh, what the hell. I close my game and open one of the emails. It takes me to the MoreDatesForYou homepage. Where I am asked for my username and password to log in.

Well that's that then.

And I'm about to close the laptop altogether when I hear a noise.

It's the sound of paper being pushed under a door.

I slide off the sofa and pick it up. The words beckywriter and firstfeature1 stare up at me in Katie's handwriting.

Sitting back down on the sofa I grin through the closed door and tap the details into the computer.

I have three unread messages.

I open the first and I'm taken to a new screen containing a message from Darren and an empty picture box with the words 'picture not yet uploaded.' Call me cynical, but...

"Hi Becky. I just wanted to say I liked your profile. I think we could be a good match. Daz x"

Daz?! And what profile?

I open his profile.

A good match? Is he kidding? Or should I say, he's got to be kidding! He's 5'1" for starters. And forty five, for heaven's sake.

And the last time I checked I was not an avid train-spotter or a devoted fan of the Thunderbirds (I quote, 'I have every episode ever made on VHS'). I select 'Thanks for your message but I don't think we are a match' from a list of standard replies, and move onto the next message. With trepidation…

It's from Lee, who at thirty one and 5'9" looks more promising. Until I look at his picture and discover he'd have made an excellent stand-in for *Toy Story's* Mr Potato Head.

I feel a bit mean, thinking that. He's probably got a lovely personality. So I read his message.

"Hello sexy lady. Fancy some fun? If so, I'm just the man to give it to you…if you know what I mean…"

Yuck! Gross! I'm not even going to dignify that with a response – standard or otherwise.

Instead I delete it and open the final message.

It's from Jason, who looks normal enough from his profile.

"Hi Becky. I'm new to this, so not really sure what to say, but I just wanted to say hi and that it would be good to get to know you. Your profile sounded normal – and not many of them do!"

I close his message and go to my own profile to see what Katie has written about me.

I'm a twenty seven year old writer, apparently. Well, that's sort of true. I'm tall-ish and slim, with long straight brown hair and brown eyes. And I love hanging out with my friends, eating Jammy Dodgers, watching *Sex & The City* and cheesy chick-flicks, and working out in the gym.

I'll kill her. I do not love working out in the gym. I hate working out in the gym. Particularly when it involves the humiliation of having to be rescued by a tall dark handsome stranger.

The picture is one of me at my 21st birthday – taken right before the whole snogging-on-the-kitchen-worktop episode. I still look the same. A couple of pounds heavier maybe, with a few more grey hairs than I had back then. But not so different that a guy wouldn't recognise me standing outside the bar where we'd arranged to meet.

Ahem…

If I was actually interested, that is.

Which I'm not.

Oh, what the hell. What harm can it do?

I re-open Jason's message and hit reply. And then I stare at the screen for the next five minutes.

This is hard. What are you supposed to say to a complete stranger? Do I tell him about me? Ask him about him? Tell him my friend suggested I use the Internet to find out how you know you've met Mr Right?!

Yeah, right. I might as well throw in the towel now and join Emma at the convent.

"I've put Emma on as well," Katie says, as we slurp our way through spaghetti bolognaise.

"On what?" Matt asks.

"Don't tell him," I shout, at precisely the moment Katie does exactly that.

"MoreDatesForYou," she says, with a huge grin. She's enjoying this.

"Internet dating," she clarifies, noting the confusion of a man who has never had to resort to such humiliating methods to get a date.

Predictably he laughs out loud. So hard that a piece of spaghetti flies out of his mouth and dangles on the end of his chin before landing back on his plate.

He takes a swig of his lager.

"You don't need the Internet to find a man, B," he says. "There are plenty of guys out there who'd love to go out with you."

132

"Thanks. I think. But even if I *did* want to meet someone," I look pointedly at Katie, "the only men I ever meet these days are either two feet tall with paint up their nostrils – or their dads."

"I've got plenty of mates I could set you up with."

"Hey, I paid good money to set them both up on MoreDatesForYou," Katie laughs. "Stop trying to put her off."

"I'd have to be interested in the first place to be put off," I remind her. "Honestly guys, I appreciate your concern. And your efforts," I say, looking at Katie. "But when I'm ready to date again, I'll tell you."

Katie raises her eyebrows at me.

"Honestly," I say. "You'll be the first to know."

CHAPTER TWENTY SEVEN

After another week the rejections are coming in thick and fast – by post and by email.

We're talking journalism rejections, by the way, not those of the Internet dating variety.

Their responses have ranged from 'we are not currently hiring freelancers', to 'we do not commission unpublished writers' (which seems a bit unfair – I mean, how are you ever going to become published if they won't commission you until you are?), to 'we do not feel your idea is suited to our magazine, but wish you well with your endeavours' – all of which amount to the same thing – 'your idea is a load of bollocks and we strongly advise that you phone your ex-boss and beg for your job back'.

And, I have to admit, I'm on the verge of doing exactly that when on Thursday something totally fabulous happens.

I am painting a little girl's lips (with completely harmless paint, and her mother's express permission, I hasten to add) so that she can kiss a plate she's decorating for her daddy's birthday (it also has her handprint and her footprint, and would have had a print of her ponytail too had I not stopped her in the nick of time) when I hear *The Lion Sleeps Tonight* coming from my handbag (it's my new ringtone).

It's Katie.

"Matt just phoned!" she screeches down the phone, almost perforating my eardrum.

"He had to pop home to fetch something and there was a message on the answer phone," she says.

"It was the editor of *Love Life*. Jennifer something-or-other."

"Jennifer Dutton?" I ask, wedging the phone between my ear and my shoulder and gently prising the toddler's face away from the plate before she is completely covered in paint. Her mother has had to make a mad dash to the toilet with her other offspring who has just regurgitated an entire custard cream down his dungarees. Fiona and Caroline have their hands full on the other side of the room supervising a Thomas the Tank Engine birthday party.

"Yes, I think so. Anyway, she got our letter. Your letter, I mean. And she wants to talk to you about your idea. She left a number for you to phone her back on."

"Oh my god!" I say, resorting to removing the plate altogether from the child, who now has green paint all over her forehead.

"What's the number?" I grab a piece of tracing paper from the table and scribble it down as Katie reads it out.

"Let me know how you get on," she says.

"I will. I better go. I have a green face that needs urgent attention."

I fold the piece of paper and push it into my back pocket, surveying the mess now in front of me.

"Look at the state of you, young lady," I laugh – just as her mother is emerging from the toilet.

"I'm sorry, she's a bit of a mess," I confess. "But on a positive note, her plate looks great." I fetch it from the counter to show her.

"Don't worry," she laughs, pulling a packet of baby wipes out of her bag and wiping the artist's face.

"That's lovely Ella," she says. "Aren't you a clever girl? Shall we go home now darling? Take Charlie home for a bath?"

"I painted my face," she tells us both, clearly extremely chuffed with herself.

"I can see that. Daddy will be so pleased with his plate, won't he?"

"It'll be ready by Monday for you to pick up," I say, taking the money she hands me.

"Okay. It might be my husband who collects it. If it is, perhaps you could put it in a box or something so he doesn't see it?"

"That's fine. He just needs to give Ella's name and whoever's in at the time will be able to find it."

"Great. Thanks so much. And sorry for the mess," she says, putting one child in his pushchair and encouraging the other to put her cardigan on.

"Say thank you to the lady," she tells her.

"Thank you lady."

"You're welcome."

When I've cleared the table and wiped it down, I take Ella's plate into the back room and glaze it ready for firing.

Then I empty the kiln. And restock the shelves. And tidy Inspiration Island – sorting the books in alphabetical order, stacking the stencils in order of size and arranging the paints from light to dark. And I mop the floor, because it's looking a bit grubby

"Are you going to make that phone call or not?" Fiona asks, after the last Thomas the Tank Engine fanatic has finally left the building.

"What?" I ask, wiping the mop over a particularly stubborn blob of paint.

"The magazine? The editor? The dream?"

I turn around and find them both – her and Caroline – staring at me, grinning.

I look at my watch. It's 4.30pm. We close in 30 minutes.

136

"Go on. Get out of here," Caroline laughs. "But make sure you phone us with the good news."

"Thanks Caroline." I lean the mop up against the wall and fetch my coat and bag. And then I leave. To find out whether my dream might actually come true after all.

Do you think she was phoning to tell me she likes my idea? Or to offer me a job? Or to invite me for an interview?

Wow, this is so exciting.

Or do you think she's phoning to ask me to stop wasting her time with ridiculous feature ideas that I don't even know how to write, and to tell me that she wouldn't use it in her magazine if it was the last feature idea on earth? Which wouldn't be nearly so exciting, obviously.

There's a café down the road called *A Slice of Naughty*. I go there and order a cappuccino and a slice of chocolate fudge cake – for Dutch courage, you understand. I'd rather have a gin and tonic, obviously, but I don't want to be slurring my words down the phone at Jennifer Dutton when the Dutch courage kicks in.

But I don't eat the cake, or drink the cappuccino. I just sit there, and stare at the telephone number on the table in front of me. I need a few more phone calls like this one – it would do wonders for my diet.

The truth?

I'm scared.

I can't bring myself to dial the number, because as soon as I do, the dream could be over, and I could find myself back at Penand Inc processing discounts for treasury tags and bulldog clips.

I don't think I realised until right now how much I want this. How right Fliss was. And *Love Life*? Well, that would just be amazing.

It's a women's magazine that was launched about a year ago. And it's really popular. Jennifer Dutton, the editor, is American. She was poached from a magazine over there which became the biggest selling women's magazine in the country within nine months of being launched. *Love Life* is looking set to follow suit with her in charge. A feature in this magazine could set me up as a journalist.

"*Love Life*. How may I direct your call?" the voice on the other end of the line asks me when I finally pluck up the courage to dial the number. (Without the help of chocolate fudge cake, I might add.)

"Could I speak to Jennifer Dutton please," I say in my best telephone voice. It sounds nothing like me.

"Certainly. I'll put you through to her secretary."

Of course. That figures. Jennifer Dutton is far too important to speak to me herself.

"Thank you," I say, feeling slightly foolish.

"Hello. Abbie Kingston. How can I help?"

"Oh, hello, this is Rebecca Harper. I have a message to call Jennifer Dutton," I explain, cringing at my telephone voice.

"Ah yes, Rebecca. I'll just see if she's free."

Oh. My. God. My heart is beating so fast I'm afraid it might actually come flying out of my body.

"Hello Rebecca. Thanks for returning my call," she says, in a soft American accent.

"Oh, no problem," I say. Can you tell from someone's voice that their heart is beating at one hundred times its normal speed?

"I was very interested to read your proposal," she says. Very interested? That's got to be good, right?

"And I wanted to discuss it with you." Discuss it? Discussions are not good, are they? Chats – chats are good. Discussions are not good.

"Here at *Love Life* we don't generally take on trainees, Rebecca."

See what I mean? Discussions are not good. Discussions are bad.

"But I was very impressed with the piece you sent me about your colleagues at…, now where was it, Pens & Paper?"

"Penand Inc," I correct her, hesitantly. Impressed? Did she just say impressed?

"Penand Inc, yes. I was very impressed. It was beautifully written for someone with so little writing experience."

"Thank you very much," I say, blushing a bit. She can't see me though – so that's okay.

"So, as I said, I'd like to meet with you to discuss your proposal further. How are you fixed tomorrow?"

I put my phone in my bag and look around for someone to tell. But the place is empty, except for me and a waiter, who's currently wiping an already spotless counter.

I'll tell him.

"I've got an interview," I say, beaming.

"Great," he says, probably wondering who this nutcase is that's talking to him.

"It's at a magazine," I tell him. "I'm going to be a writer."

"Great," he says again, smiling this time.

"Yes it is, isn't it," I agree, before skipping out of the café on a big fluffy cloud.

CHAPTER TWENTY EIGHT

Okay. So, I'm having a bit of a problem deciding what to wear. What do you wear for a 'discussion' with the editor of a huge magazine? A trouser suit? A designer dress straight from the pages of Vogue? Ripped jeans and a DKNY t-shirt?

I have changed my outfit four times already and there is a pile of clothes on my bed that makes the collapsing canvas wardrobe look like the shelves at Gap.

Katie is beginning to lose patience.

"Becky, this woman is not going to *not* give you the commission just because she doesn't like the colour of your suit or the sleeves on your shirt," she tells me from the edge of my bed where she is perched, in between shovelling spoonfuls of muesli into her mouth.

"First impressions count," I say, holding my hair up as I look in the hall mirror and then letting it go again. This outfit looks better with my hair down.

"But you've already made the first impression," she argues.

She should have been a lawyer.

"You've given her a bloody good feature idea that's going to help her sell thousands of copies of her magazine. After all, what girl doesn't want to know how to spot Mr Right?

"Then my outfit could clinch the deal," I say. Case closed.

Thirty minutes later we say goodbye at the tube station, where Katie leaves me with a good luck hug and the threat of eviction if I dare go back and change my outfit again.

"You *look* great. You *are* great. You *will be* great," she assures me.

I board the train and am amazed when I actually find a free seat – a rare phenomenon at 8.30 in the morning. Although, it is Friday, which is the prime time for holiday days and sickies.

I take this month's *Love Life* out of my bag for a final read through before the interview. I bought it on my way home yesterday and was up half the night reading it from cover to cover. There is not a square inch that I haven't read. Features, personal stories, letters, problem pages, adverts for shiny pink lipsticks that stay on your lips for up to 36 hours…

I am halfway through the cover story when I realise I'm not the only person on the tube reading *Smug, Married and Proud*. The woman to my right is reading the same article. Over my shoulder. Normally I find this incredibly irritating, even though I admit to doing it myself all the time – particularly if someone is doing a Sudoku puzzle, in which case I invariably have to sit on my hands to stop myself pointing to an empty box and shouting out 'that's an eight'. Normally I'd take great satisfaction from closing the magazine just before they finished reading the article. But today I don't. Today I want to say: "I write for this magazine." Not strictly true, I know, but hopefully that's just a technicality. But I don't say that, of course. Instead I just smile sweetly and turn the page so we can both finish reading the article.

"I'm here to see Jennifer Dutton," I tell the young girl on the reception at Kingsland House, home to *Love Life* and several other glossy magazines. Her hair has been straightened to within an inch of its life and she has tiny little jewels in the middle of her fake acrylic nails.

"What's your name?" she asks.

"Becky Harper. Rebecca," I correct myself. "Rebecca Harper." I've decided that is going to be my pen name.

She picks up the phone and taps a few numbers, her nails clicking against the buttons.

"I have Rebecca Harper in reception to see Jennifer Dutton," she says to whoever is listening on the other end.

I feel sick.

"If you'd like to take a seat her secretary will be down to meet you shortly," the girl tells me, with what looks suspiciously like a sympathetic look. Which makes me even more nervous than I was already.

Does a meeting with Jennifer Dutton merit sympathy? Or at the very least a sympathetic look?

I sit in one of the leather armchairs in the reception. There are magazines on shelves and in frames on the walls and an assortment neatly arranged on the coffee table in front of me. I go to pick one up but my palms feel all clammy and I'll only spoil the arrangement anyway, so I fiddle with the tassel on my bag instead.

"Help yourself to water," the girl with the nails tells me, indicating a water cooler to the right of her desk.

"Thanks," I say but decide against taking her up on her offer. I'd only spill it, and I don't care what Katie says – the 'I've just peed my pants' look is definitely not going to clinch the deal.

"So, Rebecca, tell me what inspired your feature proposal," Jennifer Dutton asks me twenty minutes later, up in her office, on the top floor of Kingsland House.

It's not what I imagined. The office I'd pictured was big, and plush, with an imposing mahogany desk and leather swivel chair, and a window as big as the wall with amazing views of the capital city, and professionally framed *Love Life* front covers on the walls – not unlike the office of Meryl Streep in *The Devil Wears Prada*, you might say.

Jennifer Dutton's office is nothing like that.

It's small and messy, with a tatty old desk and a chair with foam spilling out of it and *Love Life* front covers hastily hung in what look suspiciously like cheap plastic clip frames from the pound shop – not unlike the broom cupboard from my childhood days of watching CBBC, you might say.

"How do you mean?" I ask.

"Well, I would have thought such a specific idea was inspired by a personal experience of some sort? Something around which you might build your research?"

"I see. Well, yes, I did recently split up with my boyfriend," I tell her.

She doesn't speak. She just waits for me to elaborate.

The door opens, buying me some time.

"Thank you Abbie," Jennifer Sutton says as her secretary puts a tray down on her desk.

"Do you drink coffee Rebecca?" she asks.

"Yes. Thanks."

Abbie pours two cups and then leaves, taking the tray away with her. Jennifer Dutton looks at me expectantly.

She's more normal than I'd pictured in my mind. Less intimidating. She's wearing what looks like an expensive suit and she's very business-like, but there's a softness about her. Her hairstyle maybe? Her subtle makeup? Her short manicured nails? She's missing the harsh features of Meryl Streep in *The Devil Wears Prada* that I'd convinced myself I'd be doing battle with today – the lacquered hair that wouldn't move even in a gale-force wind, the pursed lips, the fake smile that looks more like a grimace.

I take a sip of my coffee and place it back on the desk.

"He asked me to marry him," I tell her. "And I said no."

"I loved him," I say quickly, before she thinks I'm a terrible person who goes around breaking men's hearts. "More than I'd ever loved anyone. But I knew I couldn't marry him. I knew he wasn't the one."

"But I didn't know why," I continue. "And it got me thinking... if I didn't know why Alex wasn't Mr Right, how would I know when I *had* found Mr Right. How do *any* of us know when we have met the one?"

Jennifer Dutton nods.

"And have you come up with any answers?" she asks me.

"Not yet," I admit

She sips her coffee.

"Tell me how you plan to research this feature Rebecca."

I can answer this question. I have prepared for this question.

"Well, I thought I could start with people who *have* found their Mr Right. I'd ask them how they know. And I'd want to get a range of perspectives, so I wouldn't just ask my friends and my friends' friends – I'd ask people of my parents' generation, and my grandparents'."

She nods, encouraging me to go on.

"And I'd ask men too – how they know they've met *Miss* Right, because the readers would probably be interested to know how men define 'the one' too. Women want reassurance, I think, that they could be what some guy out there is looking for."

She smiles at this. Her smile is genuine. She smiles with her eyes.

"Absolutely," she says. "I think you understand our readers very well already, Rebecca."

"And then I thought I would speak to one or two psychologists or relationship therapists, for their views on the subject." I've got no idea where I'd find them, between you and I. But I thought that would be a good thing to throw in. All features seem to have

144

a bit of psychobabble in them these days.

"Anything else?" she asks, leaning back in her chair. I wish she wouldn't. It looks like it might fall apart at any moment.

"Well, I was also thinking you might have letters from readers on the subject that I might be able to incorporate," I suggest.

"Yes. We could certainly forward any letters that might be useful to you. And what about the other side of the argument?" she prompts, clicking the end of her pen on the corner of her desk.

"Well not everyone believes Mr Right even exists, of course," I tell her. "One of my best friends is a perfect example, in fact. She thinks the whole idea that there is one person out there for us is total gobbledygook."

She laughs at this. Though not enough to reveal whether it's an opinion she shares.

And then the questions stop and she just smiles at me again.

The smile is a little unnerving. Is it pity? Confusion? Disappointment disguised?

I settle on indifference.

"What do you think?" I say.

"Oh, I'm not sure," she says. "I'm married. And I love my husband, of course. But is he Mr Right? I'm not sure. I'm not sure I even believe in Mr Right. But if I did then he certainly ticks a few boxes. He's incredibly handsome. Ambitious. Sexy..."

"I didn't - ..." I say

But she's on a roll.

"He makes me laugh," she says. "He does this really funny impression of David Walliams in Little Britain..." She laughs at this, as if imagining her husband wearing a floral dress and declaring 'I am a lady!'

"I meant - ..."

"He's a very good cook," she continues. "He makes the best Beef Wellington. We had a dinner party last weekend and he did

145

all of the catering, bless him.

"And he's pretty good in bed, I must say," she raises her eyebrows and I detect the faintest of blushes.

I decide not to tell her that I meant what did she think of my idea…

"Anyway, it doesn't matter what I think," she says. "It only matters that you can encompass the many opinions that our readers might have."

I nod my agreement and wait.

She looks down at her desk and starts leafing through the pages in her diary

"How does the September issue sound?" she says, after what feels like an eternity.

"Sorry?"

"I know it's quite a while away, but we have a very busy diary during the summer and I would rather give you plenty of time, considering your lack of experience."

"I'm not sure I follow."

"To research and write your feature, Rebecca. I'm assuming you still want to do it?"

Oh my god.

"Yes, definitely. Yes, September sounds perfect," I gush.

"As I'm sure you know, we hit the shops on the 15th of the month, so I shall need it on my desk by the middle of August ideally. It should be between 1800 and 2000 words. You don't need to worry about pictures, we will sort that out. But if you feel it should include photographs of specific interviewees then let us know and we will set that up.

"We pay £175 per 1000 words, which you will be paid upon publication. And make sure you keep any receipts for anything you want to claim as an expense. Travel costs, telephone calls, stationery – that sort of thing.

"I will have Abbie send you all these details along with a contract and our terms and conditions."

"Great. Thanks," I say, a little shell-shocked. "And thank you so much for this opportunity."

"You're welcome, Rebecca," she says standing up. "I think you have definite promise. So let's see how you get on with this and then we may be able to talk about a more permanent arrangement.

"Okay. Thank you."

"If you have any problems then please phone Abbie and we will do whatever we can to help."

She opens the door to her broom cupboard.

"I must apologise for the state of my office, by the way," she laughs. "It's just a temporary measure while my real office is being renovated. But on the plus side, it does give you a taste of the chaotic world of journalism!"

I laugh and shake her hand. "Thank you so much Jennifer."

"You're very welcome Rebecca. Good luck."

And then I get into the lift. Where I try to decide whether or not I have just dreamt the last thirty minutes of my life.

CHAPTER TWENTY NINE

I have decided I didn't dream it. And therefore I am VERY excited.

Eeek!

So here's my plan:

I will ask EVERYONE I know. I'll ask Katie. And Matt. And my mum and dad. And Johnny.

I'll ask the girls at the writing class.

I'll even ask Em. She can be my token sceptic.

I'll ask my granny. I'll ask Caroline. I'll ask Fiona.

I'll ask all the mums who come into Potty Wotty Doodah. And the dads too.

I'll ask Fliss and Derek.

Oh my god. It's going to be great. It's going to be the best feature ever written.

Love Life will sell a zillion copies and magazine editors will be queuing up to employ me.

And everything will be just fabulous.

CHAPTER THIRTY

"What do you mean, you DON'T KNOW?" I ask Katie.

To say I am panic-stricken would be an understatement.

I phoned Katie as soon as I left the interview. And then I phoned Emma and told her to get her arse over here to help us celebrate.

But I'm beginning to think the champagne was a little premature.

"It was your bloody idea. How am I going to write the article if no-one can tell me the answer?" I say. "I've bought a fancy notepad and a new pen and everything," I add, as if a floral notepad and matching pen is going to make her suddenly realise how she knows Matt is Mr Right.

"What the hell am I going to write in it?"

"I would have thought it was obvious," Matt says, coming through from the kitchen with a bottle of champagne and four glasses.

He puts them down on the coffee table. "It's clearly my stunning good looks, my sparkling personality and my six-pack," he says, patting what at the very most – and with a very vivid imagination – could be described as a two-pack.

"Well, obviously, but somehow I don't think Jennifer Dutton's going to go for that," I point out.

"I don't know, B. I just love him. And I can't imagine not being with him. Even though he can be very annoying at times," she adds, sitting on Matt's lap on the sofa and reaching her arms behind her to squeeze his cheeks.

"But you must have *some* idea why," I plead, in between sips of champagne (well, it's open now and it would be a shame to waste it). "There must be some reason why Matt is Mr Right and all the other guys weren't."

"What do you mean 'all the other guys?'" Matt asks. "I thought I was the only one!"

Katie laughs. "You're cute, but you're not that cute!"

"Well, you know what I think," Emma says, opening a bag of Doritos and emptying it into a bowl. "Mr Right is a load of bollocks."

"A few days ago you were saying you thought Jim was Mr Right," I remind her. She is clearly missing the point here – the point being that I am clinging to the last shred of hope with my bare fingertips.

"Nothing but a brief moment of insanity," she explains casually, biting the end off a Dorito. "There are so many guys out there. Half of them could be right for any one of us."

"I disagree," Matt says. "I think I was meant to find Katie. Look how we met."

"Yes. You were wearing flares and an afro wig. You were lucky I even spoke to you," Katie points out.

"Ah...yes...but you did," he says.

"Yes, but that was Becky's fault."

"Don't be blaming me," I say. "If I'd never started chatting to him and Tony, you could be about to marry some other wally."

"Which is my point exactly," Matt says, clearly choosing to ignore the 'wally' reference. "It's fate."

"No, no," Emma argues. "If she'd not met you then she'd have met someone else who could have been just as right for her. Or she could still be sad and single like me and Becks," she adds as an afterthought.

"Speak for yourself!" I say. "Anyway, Em, if you think Mr Right is a load of bollocks, then you must think my feature is a load of bollocks too? Unwriteable even?"

"No, I don't. I'm really proud of you for getting that commission. It's all you've ever wanted to do and now you've been given the opportunity to do it. I just think if you really do believe in Mr Right, then you might not necessarily find the answer where you think you will."

I have a feeling she's right, though I have no idea why.

KATIE

"What happened after the afro wig night, Katie?" Fiona asks, pulling a piece of mushroom off her slice of pizza and popping it into her mouth.

She's come over to help us celebrate. If I still have anything to celebrate, that is.

Matt has left us to it and gone to the pub with the lads, on the grounds that this definitely qualifies as 'girl talk.'

"He phoned to take me out for dinner the following night, but Becky and I were spending the weekend with our friend Harriet so he had to take both of them out too!"

"Aah. How lovely."

"I know. It cost him a fortune."

"And then what happened?"

"I went back up to Leeds and forgot all about him. Until he phoned, two weeks later and asked if he could come up and see me."

"So she kicked me out of the house for the weekend," I add, and Katie laughs.

"He drove up on the Friday afternoon and when he arrived I opened the door and he was stood there with a huge bunch of tulips – he had remembered me saying they were my favourite flower. He looked really sexy too and I thought, 'oh you're actually quite nice!'

"We went out for dinner and talked all evening. He'd recently

152

been to New York on holiday and was telling me all about it. I'd never been before and he said he'd take me there one day. It sounds dead cheesy, but I knew he meant it. He wasn't being flash – he was being genuine.

"The next day we went to our York – the one up north – because he'd never been there. And I remember on the way home I said I had to nip to Tesco for some washing powder because Becky and I had run out. I apologised because it seemed like such an unromantic thing to do. But later he told me that that was one of the best bits of the weekend, because it was such a couply thing to do and it made him feel like my boyfriend!"

Fiona is mesmerised with the story that Emma and I have heard a thousand times.

"That evening was the first time I kissed him."

Fiona's eyes widen. "Really?"

"Yes. We hadn't kissed yet."

"You mean he'd driven all the way to Leeds to see someone he hadn't even kissed yet?"

Katie nods.

"We went to this bar in York. I went to the loo and when I came back he was talking to this couple and they were laughing. I think that was when I started falling for him.

"We were both quite drunk when we left the bar and I remember thinking I had to kiss him. So I just grabbed him and kissed him. In the middle of the street. Up against a police van!"

Emma snorts. "I still can't believe you did that!"

"Did you really?" Fiona laughs.

"Yeah. I did. And that was it really. He came up most weekends after that – or I'd come down here.

"Then one weekend, after we'd been seeing each other for about two months, we went out with Becky and Alex and our friend Catherine and her boyfriend. And Catherine asked him what his

153

intentions were towards me. You know, just as a joke. She did it all the time. Anyway, right in front of me he looked her in the eye and said: 'I love her and one day I'm going to marry her.'"

"No!"

"Yeah! And it didn't scare me," she adds – as if she's just realised it herself for the first time.

"It creeps up on you. You have to have been through other relationships to know. You learn what you like, what you don't like, what suits you, what you need... By the time I met Matt I knew myself. And I was completely myself when I was with him. There was no pretence. I knew it was right. I never really had a 'wham bam' moment or anything. It just crept up on me. All of a sudden I just realised I was completely in love with this man and I knew that I wanted to be with him forever, that I wanted him to be the father of my children."

Fiona nods in agreement.

"He has the same values as me," Katie continues. "I like the way he treats people. He's decent. He makes an effort. He's not afraid to show his feelings. He's comfortable with who he is. He's not confrontational. But he's not afraid to stand up and say what he believes.

"There are so many things that make up a whole," she says. "But ultimately it's just got to feel right. And you've got to at least believe it will still feel right in years to come. Because it's fine when you are both young, and sexy. But you won't always be. Can you still see yourself with that person when they are old and wrinkly, sitting on a park bench?

"That's the question you have to ask yourself. You have to know that when you're sixty, or seventy, that you'll still want them to be sitting there, next to you, holding your hand."

It's such a touching moment, but I can't help myself. I burst out laughing. Because I suddenly have a picture in my head of Katie and Matt, old and wrinkly – she's wearing Nora Batty stockings, he's got *a pipe in his mouth, sitting on a park bench, sharing a Tupperware box of cheese and pickle sandwiches.*

"That's beautiful," I tell Katie, trying to compose myself. "Just beautiful. But you do realise you're going to have to tell me all over again?"

I wave my empty pad and pen at them all.

"I haven't written any of it down!"

They all roll their eyes at me. And then Emma refills our glasses and we have a toast – to my very first feature.

"How do you know you've met Mr Right?" we all shout.

FIONA

"How did you meet Adrian, Fiona?" I ask, once Katie has told her story all over again – this time with me making copious notes.

"He was a PE teacher at the school where I worked before I left to start The Pink Frog. That's where I met Caroline too. I had just started there and we had a staff meeting – they had one every morning – and Caroline told me how she could predict where everyone would stand – science teachers in one corner, foreign language teachers in another, support staff in another. Nobody ever mixed, apparently. And she was right. When they filed into that meeting, everyone stood exactly where she had said they would. After a couple of weeks I realised I was never going to get to know anyone like that so I moved – went and stood over with the geography staff – right next to the PE teachers. It totally threw everyone. But anyway – I ended up standing next to Adrian this one day and we got chatting. And we just hit it off, I suppose. But I was in a relationship at the time, so nothing happened. Then my boyfriend and I went through a horrible break up and I moved in with my mum for a bit. I was quite upset and about a month later I spoke to Adrian about it. The next day he sent me flowers. We got together after that."

"Did you know he was the one?" I ask.

"I wasn't sure in the early days. Adrian kept saying he knew I was the one, but I wasn't sure. My ex boyfriend really hurt me and

I guess I was scared of getting hurt again. So I cooled things off and Adrian was really upset.

"But then I realised he was nothing like my ex. He was really lovely. He is the most caring person in the whole world. We got back together and soon after that he asked me to go skiing with him and his family. They go every year. So we went. And he was lovely. He taught me to ski and he was so patient. I was absolutely rubbish, but he never moaned. He stayed by my side the whole time. And he did my boots every morning – because I couldn't even do that. And when I complained that my hands were cold he went out and bought me some heat pads for my gloves. He was so wonderful that I just started falling completely in love with him."

If I didn't know better I'd say even cynical Emma is getting a soppy grin on her face at this story. I look at her and smile and she laughs and digs me in the ribs.

"Then one day we were standing on the top of the mountain on our skis, surrounded by this breathtaking scenery. And my nose started to run."

Emma snorts at this.

"I didn't want to take my gloves off because of the heat pads. So he got this little hanky out of his pocket and wiped my nose for me! I knew right then and there that I loved him. When we got home I moved in with him."

"And is he Mr Right?" I ask.

"Yes." She doesn't have to think about it. "I never thought I'd meet someone I would want to spend the rest of my life with. I've had other relationships, and I'd always got bored with people eventually. But with Adrian I just knew I'd never get bored. Like Katie I just knew that further down the line I'd still feel exactly the same."

CHAPTER THIRTY ONE

Next on my hit list is Caroline, who throws her arms around me when I walk into Potty Wotty on Monday afternoon.

"I'm so pleased for you," she says, handing me a box wrapped in bright pink paper.

"This is from Fiona and me."

Fiona is spending the day with her shop fitter, so it's just Caroline and I for the afternoon.

"What's this for?" I ask, putting the box on the edge of the counter while I take my jacket off.

"It's just a little congratulatory gift we made for you."

"I bet Fi picked the paper," I say, tearing it off.

"How did you guess?" she chuckles.

I let the paper drop to the floor and open the box.

It's a plate, with a picture of a girl holding a notepad and pen. It's a stick person – an arty stick person, though, not the kind I'd draw with horizontal arms and a square head. I think it's meant to be me. I *hope* it's meant to be me. It's the only time in my life I will ever have a figure like that.

"Thanks, Caroline, I love it!" I say, holding the plate against my chest with one arm and hugging her with the other.

"You're welcome. And whenever you need time off to do your research or whatever, just let me know. I'm sure Fiona won't mind helping out."

"Thanks. But actually you might be able to do better than that," I grin.

CAROLINE

I think Caroline will be the perfect person to quiz about Mr Right. She's married. She hasn't filed for divorce. Yet. And she still phones her husband several times a day. Just to say hello.

And what's more – she's really excited about being interviewed too.

"I've never been interviewed before, not for a magazine," she tells me later, after we have set up two customers with paints, pots, glasses and a corkscrew. They are adults, by the way. We are not in the business of encouraging five-year-olds to get plastered whilst painting pots.

We open late on Mondays and people can bring their own wine to drink while they paint – with interesting results, I might add – and not always bad. One woman discovered artistic talents she never knew she had after three quarters of a bottle of Chardonnay.

As Caroline pulls the cork out of our own bottle of wine I put some new batteries in my Dictaphone and press record to test it.

It's not one of those trendy digital things that you can buy these days – the ones that are barely bigger than a book of matches. It's one of the ones that records everything on a mini cassette tape. I bought it when I was at university, for the days when I could just about drag myself out of bed after a big night in the student union bar and make it in for my 9am lecture (okay, 11am), but couldn't quite stretch to lifting pen to paper to make any notes.

"Hello, hello, hello," I say into the microphone.

"Testing, testing, testing," Caroline laughs, as I switch it off and press rewind.

"Hello, hello, hello," my voice comes back at me. It doesn't sound anything like my voice. Caroline doesn't seem unusually alarmed by the alien voice coming out of the machine in front of us both though, so I guess it must sound like me to her. Yuck. Horrid. I must get a new voice.

"So," I say, hitting the record button for real this time.

Suddenly Caroline looks nervous.

"It won't hurt. I promise."

Caroline met Dave at the school where she and Fiona worked. It strikes me their school is the perfect place to meet men. Perhaps I ought to think about a future in teaching if this writing thing doesn't take off. They could list it as a selling point, even – benefits: competitive salary, twelve weeks holiday a year, future husband guaranteed.

Dave was married with a young stepson when they met but it was an unhappy marriage. His wife had just ended her third affair. They were trying to make it work for the little boy's sake, but Dave was miserable. Caroline felt sorry for him.

"I wasn't interested," she says. "He was in such a shit situation at home. If anything I pitied him. I feel terrible about that now. He and his wife finally split up and he took some time off work. When he came back everyone started saying we were perfect for each other and kept trying to get us together. But nothing came of it. I was almost running the other way, if anything."

"Why?"

"Because I didn't like him like that. I wasn't interested at all. I felt people were trying to push me into something I didn't want to be pushed into. The next thing I heard he was going out with one of the science teachers."

161

"Were you jealous?" I ask, concluding that it must have been the green-eyed monster that finally got them together.

"No, I was relieved, which is really weird when you think how happy we are now. But anyway, they split up after a while and again, people started pushing us to go out. We went to a few mutual things, and we chatted. But he never approached me. He never asked me out. So it kind of took the pressure off.

"Then one May Bank holiday neither of us had anything on and he asked if I fancied going out for a bike ride. He was so casual about the whole thing, so I said yes. I realised that day that my whole perception of him had been wrong. I had expected him to turn up in tight Lycra shorts and an equally tight t-shirt. But he didn't. He actually looked quite trendy! And he was such a gentleman. He sorted everything out – the route, the picnic. We sat eating lunch by the river and I looked at him. I caught his eye. And in that split second I just knew."

"What? That he was Mr Right?" I ask, excited.

"No, not then. I just knew there was something different about him. Different from anything I'd ever felt. We went back to my parents for a curry party that evening and I kept wanting to touch him – to hold his hand, to put my arm around him. But we were meant to be just friends. It was weird. We went for a long walk and then back to mine to watch a film. And then he went home. He didn't kiss me. He didn't do anything.

"The next time we went out it was to a work do. He had to leave early to pick up his brother from the airport. I could tell he wasn't going to kiss me then either – so I kissed him instead! Later he told me he hadn't wanted to ruin things. We got together after that.

"I always say to Dave I feel like I haven't got a choice in this relationship," she says.

"What do you mean?"

"I know it's right – so there's no point in thinking what the

162

alternative might be. This is my fate. There's no point questioning it or thinking about meeting anyone else because Dave is the person I'm meant to be with. It's weird. I can't really explain it."

"What makes him so special?" I ask. The question comes out a bit sarcastically – unintentionally –and she laughs.

"It's a comfortable feeling. Secure. Maybe it's not wise to feel that but I do. He's my best friend. I can tell him anything. I can do anything when I'm with him.

"He listens to my dreams," she says, as if she's just remembered this crucial detail that explains why Dave is the man for her.

"Every morning, poor guy. And I have some very strange dreams. And I can sit on the loo and have a chat with him." Another key criteria. "Although he probably wishes I wouldn't," she laughs.

"I know he'll love me no matter what. I always want to be with him. And when I'm not with him, I miss him."

"Did you ever think you'd found Mr Right before Dave?" I ask her.

I want to know if you always know for sure, or if you can get it wrong – if you can think someone is Mr Right and then realise at some point – a day later, a year later, a whole lifetime later – that they're not so right after all.

"I was with my first boyfriend, Sean, for ten years," she says. "I thought he was Mr Right. But we were both very young. We had a lot of growing up to do. If he hadn't cheated on me we'd probably have ended up getting married though. I'm glad we didn't. Because I would never have had all the other experiences I've had since I was with him. And we'd probably be divorced by now anyway.

"But I think that's why I get on so well with Dave – because he's so similar to Sean, without the bad bits.

"I was with my second boyfriend for five years. I still miss him in some ways. But he was never Mr Right. With Dave I can be who I am. I can be me. But I never could be with Pete. He got so frustrated with things. He threw a video recorder out of a window once because

163

he couldn't get it to record Match of the Day. He would never have laid a finger on me, but he was so volatile. I was constantly worried about upsetting him.

"I loved him though. I don't regret any of the relationships I've had in my life, because they are all part of what has made me who I am today.

"I remember having lunch with some friends one day just before Dave and I got together, and saying how I wished I could meet someone who had all the best bits of all my previous boyfriends. That's Dave.

"Ooh, wait, I like that," I say, scribbling some extra notes to accompany the recording.

"Do you want to know the best bits?" she asks, with a cheeky glint in her eye.

"Will I have to censor the tape?" I laugh.

"He has Sean's stability, his maturity – apart from the whole cheating thing, obviously.

"He has Pete's adventurous nature, his willingness to try anything. And Mike – the one after Pete," she says, raising her eyebrows, "well that's where you'd need to censor. Let's just say Mike taught me a lot. Most of what I know, in fact!

"And Dave – well he is everything. My wish came true. That's why I'd never look for anyone else. Because he's the best of all things."

CHAPTER THIRTY TWO

It's official. I'm a woman obsessed.

On my way to the café this morning I asked the old lady sitting next to me on the tube whether she believed in Mr Right.

Once I'd explained what I meant by Mr Right she said she 'most definitely' did. She said she had found him, and that they had had fifty wonderful years together, until he died last year.

I said I was sorry. And she patted my knee and said: "Don't be – I'm one of the lucky ones – I found *my* love."

And on my way to class this evening I got chatting to a girl about my age. I told her about my feature and asked her what she thought. She said she thought it was a load of rubbish. Charming!

"So you don't believe in Mr Right?" I asked her.

"Hell, no," she said. "I don't ever intend to get married. Why on earth would I want to spend my whole life with the same man? How boring would that be? No, I love dating too much," she said. "I love the thrill of the chase. And when I've caught them and been out with them a few times, life always starts to get boring, so I move on to the next one! Keeps things interesting," she smiled.

I keep looking at couples and wondering if they'll make it – wondering if they are meant to be together, or whether sooner or later it will all fall apart, because he's not really her Mr Right. Or maybe, she doesn't even believe in Mr Right.

You can't tell just by looking, though, can you?

I saw a couple in A Slice Of Naughty the other day. They looked like they were in love. He fed her pieces of cookie and gently brushed a strand of hair off her face. She laughed at his jokes and kissed him when he wasn't expecting it. Then she left. And he made a phone call. To another girl. Who he asked out for dinner. Maybe she was just a friend, but I don't think so. So I found myself wondering which one of them thought he was her Mr Right. Maybe both of them. They couldn't both be right, though, could they?

As I take my seat in Room 11B I look around at my classmates and wonder which ones, if any, believe in Mr Right. I'll find out soon enough.

I have briefed them all. And just like Sheila told us, I have arranged their interviews in advance – starting with Tara and Georgina – tonight, after the class, in the pub.

But first we have some work to do.

Tonight we are learning about "Writing the Article".

It's a bit inconvenient, to be honest. I'm not ready to write the article yet. I could do with Sheila postponing this week's class, until I have done my research.

Writing an article is like building a house, apparently.

When you build a house you start with the foundations, then add the supporting beams. Next come the walls and then finally the ceiling. When you write an article, you start with your introduction, then add the body, and finish with the conclusion.

Easy.

Shall we go to the pub now?

"There are numerous types of introduction," Sheila tells us, wiping the notes from last night's French lesson off the blackboard. I think it was beginners. They were learning how to count.

Over the next fifteen minutes she proceeds to list all the different types of introduction.

There are loads.

There's the summary, the anecdote, the description, the direct address, the question, the cliché, the quotation. And then there's the combination of any of the above – like a pic 'n' mix, I guess.

Crikey, it's a minefield. How do you choose?

"Your introduction can be one paragraph, or a whole passage. It's up to you to determine which type works best," Sheila says. "And remember, your introduction can make or break your article. It will either grab the interest of your reader," she says, pausing for dramatic effect, "or lose it."

Yes. Thanks for that.

After a bit more chat about the perfect introduction, Sheila hands out some examples of the different types for us to look at.

And I have to say, while it's immensely entertaining tearing apart someone else's work, I do hope my features are not used in the same way in years to come. If I ever do actually write any, obviously...

I'm not impressed with the article Sheila has handed me.

"What is it about the intro that you don't like, Becky?" she asks me. Seven pairs of eyes all turn in my direction.

"It's boring," I say. "It's an article about a woman who halved her body weight in a year, and it starts by telling us about where she grew up. Who cares where she grew up? She lost thirteen stone. That's how much her husband weighs. She lost the weight of her husband. That's the introduction."

Sheila smiles and nods. I think she thinks I've got potential after all.

Next we move on to the body of the article. Apparently this is where you reward your reader for continuing beyond the first paragraph. Better make it good then.

This is where you give all the information you promised in the introduction – also known as 'the information Becky hasn't got yet.'

"This is where a lot of articles lose the reader," Sheila tells us.

"They get distracted by an interesting advert on the telly, or by something their partner says to them, or by something totally mundane – the ironing, for instance."

Break it to us gently won't you, Sheila?

"The central idea of your article should be evident throughout. In every paragraph," she says.

"As you write, stop and ask yourself if this is so. If it's not then the reader will read what you have written and wonder 'what does this have to do with anything?' And you will lose them."

"And finally we come to the conclusion," Sheila tells us, after we have all been completely deflated, dejected and demoralised.

It hardly seems worth bothering with the conclusion now. Not if the chances of the reader actually getting that far are as slim as Sheila would have us believe. We might as well save ourselves the bloody work.

"Although the conclusion is not as important as either the introduction or the body of the article," she tells us, "you do need a strong one. You want to leave something ringing in the reader's mind – you want to make them glad that they read the article."

If they did, that is…

Sheila gets up, chalk in hand.

I feel a list coming on.

"You might want to consider one of these endings," she says.

Don't tell me. Something else to decide.

"Perhaps you have a good quote that you haven't used in the

main body," she says, scratching the chalk on the board, "– something that you could use as a concluding comment."

She's lost me now. I just want to get to the pub. I need to drown my sorrows.

First I have to think of a spectacular introduction – one that will practically hypnotise my reader. Then, if I haven't lost them already, I have to get some information to fill the middle bit. And then, even though the reader has probably pissed off to do their ironing by now, I have to find a bloody good quote that I haven't already used in order to finish the whole thing off.

I wonder if Malcolm has found a replacement yet.

GEORGINA & TARA

"It's quite noisy in here. Will you be able to hear us when you play it back?" Georgina asks half an hour later, in the pub, where our spirits have been lifted somewhat by a glass of Pinot Grigio.

I rewind the tape and press play.

"I'd like the scampi and chips, but no peas, and another glass of wine please," Tara is saying, through the Dictaphone.

Georgina laughs. "I guess that's a yes."

We've ordered food. It's hungry work, learning how to write.

I press record and put the Dictaphone back down on the table.

"Do you believe in Mr Right?" I ask, draining my glass and handing it to the waitress as she puts a replacement down in front of me. She looks a little confused until she realises I'm talking to Georgina and Tara.

"No," Georgina says.

"So you don't think there's one person out there that you're meant to be with?" I ask, for clarification.

"No, I don't think there's one person for everyone. I don't think there is only one person out there for me. I think there are thousands of people in this world who could be right for me."

"Alright, big head!" Tara laughs. "Nothing like a bit of modesty."

"I'm serious! I do believe in soul mates. I believe I could meet someone and fall completely in love with them, think the same way

170

as them, share the same passions, stay up talking all night... I think there is someone out there like that. But there could be five of them. Or ten. Or twenty."

"A minute ago it was thousands," Tara laughs.

"The point is, I think there are lots of people in the world we could be compatible with. You're just not necessarily going to meet all of them – because your paths might not cross.

"There are so many people in the world – there can't possibly be just one love for each of us. If that were the case then my Mr Right could be in China right now. But I'm probably never going to get to meet him. Unless I go to China, that is, which I'm not planning on doing. My Mr Right could be a Chinaman!" she says, suddenly amused by the prospect.

"Ooh I love that Georgina Bennett," Tara says, attempting a Chinese accent. It comes out more like a cross between an Indian and Scouser, and we all laugh.

"But if you believe in fate then you would believe that you will meet that person somehow," I suggest. "Yes, there may be millions of people in the world, but maybe it's your destiny to meet that one person. The Chinaman…"

"So you believe that your whole life is mapped out for you?" Georgina asks.

"Yes, I suppose I do."

"But what if you lose the love of your life? What if they die in a car crash? Or what if you're in a really unhappy relationship with someone who treats you really badly?"

"Then I would say that fate would show you a way out of it.

"I think there is one person for everyone," Tara says.

"Why?" Georgina asks.

We have to wait for the answer as the waitress arrives with our food.

"Thanks," Tara says, unravelling her knife and fork from the *serviette wrapping.*

"Because I look at some of my friends and I get the feeling that they've settled. For second best, I mean. It's a terrible thing to say. And it's not because they're unhappy. They're happy enough. I'm just not sure they're with the right person for them. I think there's someone special out there for us."

"I think you're just a dreamer," Georgina says, sprinkling salt on her chips.

"Oh yes, I'm definitely a dreamer."

"Well I think it's lovely, I just don't agree. These people who are with someone completely right for them – I think they're lucky, but I don't think it has anything to do with fate, or destiny, or because they've found the one person they are meant to be with."

"Maybe you're right," Tara says. "But I like to think someone meant just for me is out there somewhere. It's comforting, I guess."

"So girls, how do you know the person you are with is the right person for you – whatever you think that means?" I ask, keen to steer them away from this mini-debate they seem to have started. That's what Sheila said we have to do, isn't it?

"I'm not sure he is," Tara says.

"Why not?"

"Because I love him but…,"

"But what?"

"I don't know. There's just a but. I really love him, but… Do you know what I mean?"

I nod. Because I do. I know all about the 'but' that you can't explain.

"I'm so happy with him," she says. "And that's why I'm still with him – because I don't look too far into the future. But I don't know if I'll be with him forever."

"What about you Georgina?" Georgina's just bought a house with her boyfriend. She must think he's right for her. "How do you know

Chris is right for you?"

"I don't!" Georgina laughs.

In that case she doesn't worry like I did. She obviously didn't think it mattered that she wasn't sure he was the one when she signed the mortgage papers.

"I question it all the time, if I'm honest. I love him. A lot. But I don't know if he's the one. And that's why I'm not getting married. Not yet."

"But if you don't believe in Mr Right, why can't you just be happy with Chris?" Tara asks.

"Because I'm scared."

"Scared of what?"

"That there's someone out there I might love more than him. I'm thirty now. What if I'm still not sure about Chris when I'm thirty five? I could never marry him while I'm not sure. Or have kids. But then...if I split up with him, if I went home tonight and said I didn't want to be with him anymore then I'd worry that I might never meet another man that makes me feel the way that he does. What if I threw it all away for nothing?

"There are so many good things about my relationship. So many women would be happy with what I've got. They'd get married, have children. But I can't do that – not as long as I'm questioning it.

"I think I've been brought up on too many romantic films," she laughs. "I want real life to be like it is in the movies, but it's just not like that. My mum says you get out of a relationship what you put into it. She says if I wasn't with Chris I'd really miss him. I think she's right. I think if we split up I'd go on nights out looking for someone just like him! That's what's so confusing."

"So isn't that enough for you to believe he is the one?" I ask.

"No. Because I also worry that there might be someone better out there for me! I know, I'm my own worst enemy," she laughs.

"I think people think too much these days," Tara says nonchalantly, *pinching a chip from Georgina's plate.*

"I don't know if Tom is the one, but I don't spend time worrying about it. If you're happy in the moment, then what's the point in questioning everything?"

"Because I'm thirty years old and I want to know that I'm with the guy I'm going to be with forever," Georgina explains. "But I don't know that. And that worries me."

"So you're not sure he's the one – but you're not sure he isn't either, so why not just enjoy yourself?" Tara asks her.

That's what I tried to do. It doesn't work. But I don't say that. Georgina has to realise that for herself.

"Me and Tom are happy right now. That's all I'm bothered about," Tara says. "I believe in fate. So I believe that if me and Tom are not meant to be together in the end, then we won't be. Right now we are, and we're happy. That's all that matters."

"I'm happy," Georgina says. "I am, but there's a but. And if you have a but, then it's a problem."

Now, I don't wish to appear ungrateful or anything, but a fat lot of good this pair has turned out to be.

One doesn't believe in Mr Right. The other isn't sure she's found him yet.

"Tell me this, Tara," I say, clutching at straws. "How do you think you will know when you have found Mr Right?"

"Hmm," she says, stabbing the last piece of scampi with her fork. Then she looks at me, shrugs her shoulders and says "I have no idea," before popping the scampi in to her mouth.

174

CHAPTER THIRTY THREE

To be fair, it's not just Tara and Georgina who are useless.

Everyone else is too.

I meet up with them all over the next week. I ply them all with alcohol and dry roasted peanuts. And what do they give me? Diddly squat, that's what.

JO

Jo tells me all about the speed-dating night she met Mark. She went with three friends, 'just for a laugh.' She didn't think she'd meet someone. She certainly didn't think she'd meet the man she'd end up saying 'yes' to. But she did. On her first date with Mark, she knew he was the one.

"But how do you explain that?" she asks. "How do you put it into words?"

Exactly.

"When you're single, everyone always says you'll know when you've met 'the one,' and you're like 'yeah, right, whatever!' But it really is like that," she says. "You really do just know."

Bollocks.

STEPHANIE

Stephanie met Paolo at university. They went out for two-and-a-half years then after they graduated Paolo went back to Italy and they split up.

A year later Stephanie bought a ticket to Rome and went to see him. She missed him and she needed to know why. When he met her at Rome airport she knew it was because he was the one.

How did she know?

She can't explain it. She just knew.

She has known him for over twelve years now and when she looks at him she still feels the same rush of love. But she can't bloody well explain it.

Arse.

AUDREY

Audrey has been married for thirty six years but she's still not sure Bill is the one for her.

He's handy around the house, though, and he's pretty good in bed, so she's making the best of it.

Euuuggh. Too much information.

CATHY

Cathy is about to get married for the second time.

She met her first husband at seventeen and married him at twenty three. On the day of the wedding she knew it wasn't right, she said, but she felt it was too late to change her mind – everything had been paid for.

Three years later she completed a quiz in a magazine – Is Your Relationship In Trouble? Each question had a choice of answers, each answer a different score – 150 points was the best, 30 was the worst. Cathy's score came out at 32. 'Crap,' it said, 'you really are in trouble.' A year later they divorced.

Another year later she met Richard. They are getting married in November. This time she says it's for keeps.

"Do you believe in Mr Right?" I ask her.

"Yes, I do," she says.

"Why?"

"Because I've found him. I thought I'd found him once before, but I got it wrong.

"So how do you know Richard is Mr Right?"

"Because I know I haven't got it wrong this time."

BEV

And Bev. She's single. She believes in Mr Right. She believes there's a Mr Right out there for everybody. Everyone has a soul mate – it's just a question of finding them.

She thinks there is too much pressure on women today to be with somebody – anybody – so they settle for the first remotely likely person that comes along. And they marry them, even though they are not necessarily the right person for them. They have a nice life with these people. They are stable. They are good to them. And they love them in their own way. But it will never be that 'right arm' kind of love. They won't ever be their soul mate.

I tell her what Georgina said – that there are billions of people in the world, so how are you ever going to meet that one person?

It's all down to fate, Bev says, and the people who question how you are ever going to meet that one person are the ones who don't believe in fate – the ones who have settled with the first person that came along.

That's why there are so many divorces in the world, Bev says. It's a knock on effect of people feeling pressured.

Bev is very black and white. She's the same with her whole life, she says. She doesn't settle for just 'okay.' She doesn't settle for second best in anything – and definitely not in love, because that's the most important thing of all.

180

I like Bev. She's opinionated, a little bolshie even, but she tells it like it is. She knows what she wants. And she's not prepared to settle for anything less. Even if that means waiting a lifetime.

I'm not sure I'm that brave. I'm not sure I'd rather be alone forever than settle for someone I wasn't quite sure about.

I wasn't sure Bev was going to be much use to me, to be honest. I am trying to find out how you know you have met Mr Right, and Bev hasn't met him yet, so how can she help me? I ask her this.

"You're probably more likely to get the truth from people who are single," she says. "The people who have found what they're not looking for – they're the ones who really know what they're looking for."

"So how do you think you will know when you've found what you're looking for?" I ask. "And do you think it's guaranteed that we all will meet that one person?"

"No. It's not guaranteed. Not if you settle for somebody else."

"If you don't though? If you don't settle, do you think you'll meet your Mr Right?"

"Absolutely. One hundred per cent. When the time is right for me. When the time is right for him. Yes, I believe our paths will cross, and we will be together.

"That's why I'm such a positive person," she says. "Because I believe. I don't go 'oh, woe is me, I'm single,' blah, blah, blah. And I don't believe in all this rubbish about 'having to get out there.' People waffle on about how if you want to meet a man then you need to do this and you need to do that. Rubbish. All you need to do is get on with your life. And when the time is right, Mr Right will come along."

"Yes, but if you are stuck in every night, not doing anything, then how are you ever going to meet them?"

"It could be the gasman," she says, dead matter-of-fact – and she knows she's opening my eyes to things I've never even considered before. Although, I do hope it's not the gasman. The gasman came to Katie's flat the other day to read the meter. He had terrible BO. And his trousers were too short. My Mr Right would never wear trousers half way up his ankles. And he'd wear deodorant. I'm sure of that.

"A friend of my sister's met her husband in a car park," she says. "He was paying for his ticket and he turned round and said 'nice car.' A year later they were married. And they are really really happy. In fact, they're just about to renew their wedding vows in Las Vegas! In front of Elvis!"

I laugh. "So how do you think you'll know?" I ask again.

"There'll be no surprises. I'll feel completely comfortable. There'll be none of this 'shall I phone him, shall I not phone him, will I look too keen?' There'll be none of that, because we'll both feel exactly the same.

"My theory is this – if you have to work too hard when you first meet someone, then get out. You're just not meant to be together.

"You have to listen to your heart – and your stomach. Go with your gut instinct. If you feel there's something not quite right, then the chances are there's something not quite right. Maybe you've met before, in a previous life, and it was a complete disaster, and you're about to do it all over again. Maybe he was the king and you were his wife and he ended up chopping your head off!"

We both laugh at this.

"Do I have a scar there?" I ask, rubbing my hand across my throat.

"A lot of misery is caused by thinking too much and not going with their instinct," Bev says. "People go along and conform and then spend their whole relationship thinking 'are they the one?' Well, if you are asking yourself that question, then he's not. Bottom line."

CHAPTER THIRTY FOUR

My family are next, but they're not much help.

I phone Sarah and ask her what it is about my brother that makes him Mr Right. She laughs out loud and says she's still trying to figure that out herself.

I phone nana and she says my granddad bought her an ice cream on Brighton seafront then told her a dirty joke and she was smitten.

And I phone my mum and she says 'I ended up with your father by default.' He gate-crashed her 21st birthday party, apparently. She had her eye on his best friend Keith, but Keith didn't fancy her and dad wouldn't take no for an answer. She gave in eventually.

"Thanks mum, that's a great help," I tell her.

CHAPTER THIRTY FIVE

I've asked Katie to find me a man. To interview, I mean. Don't get excited – like Katie did when she thought I meant I was looking for some man action. She had listed no less than six potential dates before I could tell her she'd misunderstood.

After a minor paddy and an admirable attempt at convincing me that Darren from the graphics department was just my type, she accepted the challenge. And a challenge it proved to be, too. It's just as well I only asked for one, because that's all she's managed – and that came at a price. A four-pack of Stella and a guarantee that his name would be changed, to be precise. I'm surprised he didn't make me sign a contract.

I meet Graham – the man in question – after work one day at A Slice of Naughty. He wanted to meet somewhere he wouldn't be recognised.

"He's being interviewed," I told Katie, "not going out dressed as a drag queen."

He's buying a cappuccino and a muffin when I walk in. At least, I'm assuming that's him. He fits the description Katie gave me – tall, dark, reasonably handsome and dressed in a lilac shirt and pink tie. And he's embarrassed about being interviewed...

"You must be Graham," I say.

"Yep, that's me. And you must be Becky," he laughs nervously.

"Can I get you a coffee?"
"Yes, thanks, I'll have a latte."

GRAHAM

We take our drinks to a table in the corner. The cafe is quite busy, but Graham doesn't seem too worried.

"Do you mind if I record the conversation?" I ask him, pulling the Dictaphone out of my bag and putting it down on the table.

"Aren't journalists supposed to be able to do shorthand?"

I love it that he thinks I'm a real journalist.

"I'm afraid my shorthand is non-existent," I confess. "And my longhand isn't that much better!"

He looks nervously at the recorder.

"It's just for me to use. No-one else will ever hear it. Not even Katie," I joke.

"Okay," he says, albeit reluctantly.

Graham looks around the café – no doubt checking there's no-one in here who knows him.

And then he relaxes. Just like that. As soon as I mention his wife, it's like he's a different person altogether.

"So tell me how you and your wife met." That's all I have to say and his face breaks into this big smile.

"I knew right then that she meant everything to me," he tells me, after explaining how they met – at the climbing club at university eleven years ago, and the moment he asked her to marry him – when she fell down a crevasse climbing Mount Kilimanjaro four years ago and he held onto her safety rope as if both their lives depended on it – not just hers.

"I knew she was okay," he explains. "She was wearing a safety harness. But for a split second I imagined what my life would be like without her and I realised I wasn't just holding onto my gorgeous, bright, energetic, loving girlfriend. I was holding onto my whole world. We want the same things out of life," he says. "We both wanted to travel. We both wanted good jobs and a nice home. We both wanted kids."

He opens his wallet to reveal a picture of two children – a boy of about three and a baby girl.

"That's Sam. And that's Kayleigh," he says.

"They're cute," I smile.

"Everything fits," he continues, snapping his wallet shut and putting in on the table.

"There's no struggle in our relationship. We don't bicker. I had some really stressful relationships when I was younger. It's not like that with Paula.

"There's never any doubt. I don't ever spend time thinking 'what if I wasn't with Paula,' thinking 'what if I was with this girl, or that girl.'

"In eleven years I can't ever remember thinking 'what if I found someone else?' "I think if you analyse why you're in a relationship, then maybe you're in the wrong one. I don't feel the need to analyse my relationship," he says. "I'm happy. There's never a time when I would rather be somewhere else than at home. I'm always excited to go home and see Paula and the kids. I can't imagine being with anyone but her."

"Do you think there's one person out there for everyone and that you're meant to be with that person no matter what?" I ask Graham.

"No," he says. It surprises me. Out of everyone I somehow thought he would.

187

"I used to think like that. But now I'm not so sure."

"What made you change your mind?"

"I don't know really…it's a big old world out there. I do believe in fate. I absolutely believe that people are drawn together. But I don't think there's just one person out there for us."

He pauses, trying to work out why.

"If that was the case then there would be so many incredibly unhappy people out there. How would anyone ever meet that one person? Out of seven billion people on the planet – or whatever it is – my one person might be in Australia somewhere. Or America. How would I ever meet her?"

"But you believe in fate," I remind him. "So wouldn't fate take you to her?"

"I don't know. I guess. I just think that a lot of people have more than one right person for them. My sister, for example. She's been married twice. And I believe that both the men she married were absolutely right for her."

"What happened to the first?" I ask.

"They moved to Holland together, but she wanted to come back, and he didn't, so they split up."

"But how can you say he was absolutely right for her when they wanted such different things?"

"I guess. But when they were together they were so right. I suppose what I'm saying is I'd like to think there's more than one person that's right for us – that if anything ever happened to me, God forbid, then Paula would be able to meet someone else she could be happy with. I wouldn't want her to spend the rest of her life alone."

"She could meet someone else. But that wouldn't have to mean that you weren't her true love."

"Yes, I guess. Or maybe there's only one person in the world who's right for us at any one point in time," Graham says.

"So the person who's right for you at twenty five might not be the person who's right for you at thirty? It just depends when you meet them?"

"Yes. Fate takes you on a path where you meet more than one right person. It just depends on when you're ready to settle down."

"I guess. Any more thoughts?" I ask.

"Yes. What if you met somebody and you didn't get together, but you kept looking back thinking they were the one?"

"What, you mean later in life?" I ask.

"Yes. You spend your life with someone else thinking that this other person was the one you were meant to be with. But surely if you've spent fifty years with a person, then they must be the one you are meant to be with – because you've spent half a century with them. Doesn't time count for anything? Do you know what I mean?"

"Yes, I do. And I'm trying to think of an answer," I laugh.

"Who makes the rules?" Graham asks. "Who defines the person you are meant to be with? What's the definition of the person you are meant to be with?"

"You mean, if you were to look up 'the person you are meant to be with' in a dictionary, what would it say?"

"Yes."

"That's exactly what I'm trying to find out!"

"I think it would say it's a feeling – feeling right, feeling complete…"

"But then what about the fifty years?" I say, throwing it all up in the air again. "If you look back for your whole life thinking someone else might have been the one, then how can that be 'feeling right?'"

And Graham just shrugs. Because he doesn't have any more answers. And neither do I.

CHAPTER THIRTY SIX

When Graham has gone I order another coffee and sit and look through the notes from all my interviews, trying to make some sense of it all.

So, how do you know when you've met Mr Right?

I'm not sure I've found the answer yet.

I look at the scribbles in front of me:

It's a feeling that creeps up on you.

It's meeting up with them after a year apart and realising you still feel the same.

It's looking at them after years together and feeling the same love you've always felt.

It's sharing the same sense of humour.

It's someone you can be yourself with. Someone you want to be with forever.

It's someone with the same values.

It's someone who will listen to your dreams. Someone you can chat to while you're sitting on the loo.

It's someone who will wipe your nose at the top of a mountain when you can't feel your own hands because they are so cold.

It's someone you want to be with all the time. Someone you miss when you're not with them.

It's someone who's all the best bits of all the men you've ever known – all rolled into one. The 'best of all things.'

It's not settling.

It's waiting until it's absolutely right. And when it is, you'll just know.

It's not doubting it. It's never worrying that there might be something better out there.

It's knowing that losing them would be like losing your whole world.

It's knowing that it feels right now, and believing that it will still feel right in years to come – believing that you will still want to be with that person forty years from now, sitting on a park bench, holding their hand.

But how do I know how any of that feels if I haven't found him yet?

"You know what you're going to have to do, don't you?" Katie says when I explain the predicament I'm in.

I do know, yes. But I look at her blankly. I don't want to give her the satisfaction.

"You're going to have to get out there and start dating again."

CHAPTER THIRTY SEVEN

Friendly tip for you...

When a friend sets you up on an Internet dating site, delete your profile immediately. Do not go on any dates. Do not pass go. Do not collect £200.

Oh. My. God.

So I decided – against my better judgement, I might add – to give it a go. Strictly for research purposes, you understand. I figured the worst that could happen was that I'd date a few morons and then cancel my membership. And the best? Well, I could even meet my Mr Right! And then I'd know. How you know you've met Mr Right, I mean. So it will all have been worth it. I'll write the feature. It will be absolutely fantastic. And Jennifer Dutton will be falling over herself to hire me. And we will all live happily ever after. Amen.

What did I say was the worst that could happen again?

On Monday I meet Paul. An investment banker. Lives in Clapham. Works in Canary Wharf. Thirty two. Tall. Medium build, short brown hair. No moustache. No beard. Blue eyes. Likes: golf, cinema, macaroni cheese. Hates: laziness, traffic jams, goat's cheese.

Fairly promising you might say?

It's staggering how far a guy is willing to stretch the truth in order to get a date.

Let's just say I am beginning to think I've been stood up after standing in the entrance to the Pig & Whistle for over half an hour. There is a guy stood at the bar, a few yards away, nursing a pint. But that can't be Paul. Paul falls into the 5'8" – 6'2" bracket. Paul is of athletic build. Paul ticked the 'attractive' box. This guy is 5'4", if that. This guy is not so much athletic as rotund. And if this guy ever ticked the attractive box I'd have to say his pen had slipped.

No, this couldn't be Paul.

Yes, this is Paul. I discover this when the barman, aware that I've been standing here like a lemon for over half an hour, looks over at me and asks if I am okay, and 'Paul' turns round and says "Becky?"

"No," I reply. And promptly leave the bar.

On Wednesday I meet Andy. A chef from Putney. Has just opened his own restaurant.

We are off to a good start when he does actually resemble the picture on his profile. Tall, dark, handsome – ish.

And he is quite interesting too. He knows all about food, and wine, and how to make delicious chocolate desserts – three of my all-time favourite things, in fact.

We spend a lovely evening getting to know each other, at the end of which he asks if he can see me again the following evening.

And I say yes. But then I go to the toilet, and as I am coming back to the table I hear him telling somebody by the name of "darling" that he is really sorry but he is going to have to work late tomorrow evening and that he'll make it up to her when he gets home… So I tell him I pity his poor girlfriend and promptly leave the bar.

And on Thursday I meet Ian. A property developer from

Wimbledon. Divorced six months ago after being married for five years. No children.

Just like his picture. Tall, blond, slim, with bright blue eyes and a smile to make you weak at the knees.

And he sounds just like a Munchkin from the Wizard of Oz. Which just won't do at all.

I stay for one drink and *then* promptly leave the bar (I'm not completely heartless after all).

I miss Alex. I do. I know I made the right decision, but I miss the easiness of it all. I didn't have to go on dates with complete idiots, men who lie about their credentials just to get a woman to at least turn up, men who would happily hurt their girlfriends just to have a bit of fun on a weekday night. I didn't have to spend my evenings weeding out the dross from the guys who might be able to make me happy. I didn't have to put on a show. I didn't have to make sure I always looked my best, because Alex had seen me at my worst and he loved me anyway.

"What about speed dating?" Katie suggests on Friday evening after hearing the latest instalment over a takeaway pizza.

"Or I could have a pre-wedding party? Invite lots of single men? Not that I know that many," she says, mentally flicking through her address book while she licks tomato sauce from her little finger. "Although I'm sure between us Matt and I could come up with a few."

She pokes her husband-to-be.

"What?" he says, his head turned towards Katie, his eyes still fixed on the football on the television. It's a tense match, by all accounts. One-nil with only five minutes to go. Don't ask me who's winning. I don't even know who's playing.

"Men. You and I. We can come up with some."

Totally blank. But at least he's looking at her now.

"For Becky," she says, exasperated.

"Oh, yeah – sure, I know loads of nice blokes."

"See!" Katie says – to me this time, already forming a mental checklist for her impromptu party. *Vodka jelly, plastic beer glasses, sausages on sticks, single men for Becky...*

I know what she's like. She'd stop at nothing. She'd have us playing spin the bottle, truth and dare, and if all else failed she'd just lock me in a cupboard with the nearest available guy and turn the lights off.

"No. Honestly guys," I tell Katie firmly, before she gets carried away and starts petitioning both Cilla Black and ITV for a re-launch of Blind Date.

"But it'd be fun," she argues. "I feel like a bit of a party."

"Have a party if you want one. Just not one designed to find me a man."

"But you need a man, B. It's been ages since you had a good..."

"Don't say it!" I shout, slapping my hand over her mouth, startling Matt, whose nerves are already frayed with the tension of the match.

"Sorry," she says sheepishly when I take my hand away.

"I don't need a man in my life," I tell her.

"I'm not saying you need one, but wouldn't it be nice?"

"No. It wouldn't. I'm happy as I am right now. I don't need a man. I don't want a man. Now, Ben & Jerry's or Häagen Dazs?" I say, picking up the pizza box and heading for the kitchen.

CHAPTER THIRTY EIGHT

When it comes, will it come without warning
Just as I'm picking my nose?
Will it knock on my door in the morning,
Or tread in the bus on my toes?
Will it come like a change in the weather?
Will its greeting be courteous or rough?
Will it alter my life altogether?
O tell me the truth about love

'O Tell Me The Truth About Love', W.H.Auden (1907-1873)

So...

I've met a man.

Yes, I know what I said.

But that was then.

And this is now.

And he's fabulous.

I've met him before actually. Well, sort of. At the gym – when I was all sweaty and about to hyperventilate on the exercise bike, and then again at the *Vod Kerr Baa* – the night Emma locked herself in the loos.

It's him.

He came into Potty Wotty this morning.

He's gorgeous. He's funny. He's sweet. He has all his own hair and all his own teeth. (Okay, so I don't actually know that for sure, but they certainly didn't look false to me.) He has lovely brown eyes that I could look into all day. And a smile that makes me go all funny. And a mouth that…well, you get the idea.

And a wife.

And two children.

Bollocks.

I was emptying the kiln of a set of miniature garden gnomes when he came into my world – well, into the café anyway.

The bell on the door rang as he opened it.

"I'll be right with you," I called out.

"No problem." A male voice. A *sexy*, vaguely familiar, male voice.

Putting a miniature motorcyclist gnome safely onto the worktop alongside a policeman and a cowboy (a birthday gift from a husband to his wife whose two greatest loves are gardening and The Village People – and who's probably hoping for a subscription to Homes & Gardens and tickets to see a tribute band,) I rubbed my hands on my apron and went back into the café.

"Hi," I said, to the owner of said sexy male voice. "Oh, hi," I said when I realised who it was.

"So this time we have met before!" he said, with a big cheesy grin.

"Indeed we have! In the *Vod Kerr Baa*. Just before my friend locked herself in the loos and refused to come out." I decided not to mention the whole gym hyperventilation thing, hoping he had forgotten.

"That doesn't sound like fun!"

"Oh, you know us girls, we take it in turns," I said. "Anyway, how can I help you?"

"Well I'm not sure I've got the right place actually. There's not another Potty Wotty Doodah around here is there?"

"No," I laughed. "Just us. Are you here to collect something?"

As soon as the words were out of my mouth, I was completely crushed. Devastated. Depressed.

If he was here to collect something, it could only be for a child. If he was here to collect something for a child, then he had a child. If he had a child, then there was every chance he also had a wife.

Bollocks.

"Yes. Ella Collins'." Ah, the face-painter. The one with the brother and the custard cream.

"I'm a bit late actually," he said. "I promised her mum I'd pick it up days ago. But I forgot."

"Yes, I remember Ella," I told him. "She painted her face!" I smiled at him. Please note, though, I was smiling on the outside only. On the inside I was scowling – at Ella's mum – who bagged herself this amazing specimen of fabulousness long before I could even get a look in.

"Very creative," I said, still smiling.

He laughed and I noticed he had a really cute dimple in his cheek. I didn't notice that in the *Vod Kerr Baa* – or the little scar above his left eye.

"Well whatever artistic talent she might have, she definitely didn't get it from my side of the family. When I was at school I had trouble drawing stick-men, never mind anything else!"

"Me too," I said.

"So you didn't do any of these then?" He gestured to the crockery around the walls.

"God no! Caroline did those. She's the owner. She's very artistic – used to be an art teacher, in fact. I, on the other hand, am worse than useless."

"That must be tricky, then, when a kid asks you to draw something – like a dog, or a cat…"

198

"Or two spiders holding hands?"

He laughed at this. He had probably heard stranger things, being a dad himself.

Grrr.

"That's what this is for," I confessed, patting a pile of tracing paper on the desk.

"You cheat," he laughed. That dimple again...

I held up my hands. "Guilty!" I said. "I'll go and fetch Ella's plate. I won't be a minute."

"Okay. Thanks."

"I was right wasn't I?" he asked, when I returned with the plate. "We have met before. Before the *Vod Kerr Baa*, I mean?"

I made a feeble attempt at looking like I had no idea what he was talking about.

"At the gym," he said, "when..." - don't say it, please, just don't say it, "you were about to keel over on the exercise bike?"

Damn. He said it. And I couldn't just pretend I was at the end of a ten-mile bike ride because he saw me get on the bloody thing.

"Let's just say exercise bikes aren't my thing," I said instead, and he laughed.

"Nor mine. My brother made me join because he got a discount for a joint membership. Sorry – I didn't mean to embarrass you," he added.

"Don't be silly, I'm not embarrassed," I told him. "Why on earth would I be embarrassed at nearly keeling over on an exercise bike at one mile an hour?"

"Oh I think it was a bit faster than that," he said, out of the goodness of his heart, I suspect, and not because it was in the least bit true. "And you were climbing up a very steep hill." Now that *was* true.

"Anyway – here it is," I said, handing him the plate. I had wrapped it in bubble wrap and put it in a bag so his present wouldn't be spoiled.

"Is it paid for?" he asked.

"Yes, her mum paid before she left."

"Great," he said, putting the box under his arm and walking towards the door.

Just before he left he turned back and smiled at me.

"What a lovely place to work," he said. And then he went. Out of my life. As quickly as he came into it.

Sob.

In the words of Hugh Grant in *Four Weddings*: Bugger. Bugger. Bugger.

All I can say is that it is a cruel world that would put this beautiful man within my grasp, only to yank him away again, blatantly mocking me: *You're too late – this one's taken already.*

It is a cruel, cruel world, I tell you.

CHAPTER THIRTY NINE

Do you think it's a sign? Do you think it's fate's way of telling me that I have given up everything for something that doesn't even exist?

Here was someone who could easily have been my Mr Right, I'm sure. And yet, there was no way he could be. Because he's already someone else's.

So maybe I was wrong about Alex? Maybe he is my Mr Right, after all.

CHAPTER FORTY

Have you ever tried searching for Mr Right on the Internet?

Try it.

Type it into Google.

You won't believe it.

Mr Right. These two words alone generate more than 1.26 billion findings. I kid you not.

It's Saturday night.

I could be out.

No, really, I could. Katie and Matt are out with friends for dinner. They invited me along. But I was too depressed, the love of my life having just passed me by, and all. So I've decided to spend a night in with my laptop, a bottle of wine and a tube of Pringles, researching Mr Right on the Internet.

How sad am I?

On second thoughts, don't answer that. Just don't tell any of my friends.

Scrolling down the results, I feel faintly embarrassed to be a woman (I bet googling 'Mrs Right' doesn't even bring up 125 results, never mind 1.25 billion.)

Do we really need all this help with our love lives?

How to find Mr Right – www.getyourselfanewman.com, *Love & Relationship Advice* – www.findingyourmrright.com, *The Secret to*

finding Mr Right – www.therelationshipdoctor.com/find-mr-right,
Sill Dating jerks – www.reclaimyourheart.com, *Finding Mr Right
Tips* - www.insideamansmind.com...

You couldn't make it up!

And none of it is any use whatsoever. All this expert advice
really does is tell you how to meet a guy – and we all know how
to do that.

Lurk in the frozen food aisle at your local supermarket.

Borrow your neighbour's dog for the day.

Stop a bloke and ask him for a light (it tends to help if you
actually smoke).

Etc.

Etc.

What it doesn't tell you is how to know whether he is Mr
Right or not.

Having said that, I'm intrigued. So I click at random and find
myself on www.getyourselfanewman.com where I am introduced
to the kind of information that is now – literally – at my fingertips.
Just a click away, in fact. And a quick £50, of course.

*The mistakes women make with men; Things women do that
annoy men; When your man has a wandering eye.*

Err... Hang on... How about *The whopping great big mistakes
men make with women; Things men do that drive women totally
insane; When your man is a total prat...*?

*Read on to discover how to find your Mr Right – in eighteen
months or less.*

Eighteen months? You've got to be kidding. I don't have eighteen
weeks, let alone eighteen months. I need to know now.

I scroll down further. Maybe there's a fast track programme...

'*Within six months I met my dream man*', begins a testimony
from Hayley from Derbyshire.

'*Tall, dark, handsome, interesting...the most amazing man I have ever met.'*

Of course you did love. And I'm sure you weren't paid a penny to say so.

'I'd like to say it was all down to me, but it was all down to you,' she goes on to tell the author of *Find Your Mr Right* – *in a book store near you for just £21.99.*

'I have great news,' the same author tells visitors to his site. *'Imagine sharing your life with a man who is not only your best friend, but someone you find physically attractive.'*

Hmm. Sounds nice.

'Picture yourself waking up in his arms, looking at him with love as he smiles and leans towards you to kiss you tenderly.'

And you pass out from his morning breath.

'You relax, knowing that your search is over. Can you picture yourself with him right now?'

Err, no.

'If you could have all this, what would it be worth to you?'

Here we go. Now we're getting somewhere.

'Would it be worth a little time?'

Yes.

'Would it be worth a little effort?'

Yes.

'A little money?'

No. Piss off. I thought love was supposed to be free.

What a load of bollocks, I tut to myself, closing my laptop and reaching for another Pringle.

CHAPTER FORTY ONE

Don't shut love out of your life by saying it's impossible to find.
The quickest way to receive love is to give love.
The fastest way to lose love is to hold it too tightly;
and the best way to keep love is to give it wings.
Don't dismiss your dreams.
To be without dreams is to be without hope;
to be without hope is to be without purpose.

'A Creed to Live By', Nancye Sims

"Where can I find a picture of a ladybird, Becky?" Katie asks me on Monday evening.

Caroline has a hospital appointment and Fiona has taken the afternoon off to do shop stuff so Katie has volunteered to help me with the late opening.

I think she's beginning to regret this act of genuine kindness. Ever since I lost the love of my life I have been under a big black cloud.

I think I'm in mourning.

"What?" I say vacantly, flicking through this month's copy of *Love Life*. There's a very interesting article on how to spot a married man.

"Ladybirds? Pictures?" she says, mildly irritated.

"Try Bugs and Beetles. Bottom shelf," I mutter.

"Snap out of it B," she orders me, reaching for the book. "He was probably a twat anyway."

"He wasn't," I protest, like a stubborn child. Any minute now I'll probably start stamping my foot. "He was lovely."

"Well he's married. So get over it. And put the kettle on," she adds.

I am dropping tea bags into two mugs when I hear the door open.

"I've come to collect Ella Collins' pottery," a woman tells Katie.

"Oh, right, I'll just get the manager," Katie replies. Excellent – I've been promoted.

She opens the door to the kitchen and looks at me, contorting her face as if to say 'that's the wife, isn't it?' We know each other very well, remember.

I scowl at her, dragging my fingers through the air – signifying my desire to scratch the woman's eyes out. I'm guessing this answers her question.

"Hello again," I say sweetly, putting two mugs of tea on the counter. It's incredibly restrained of me given what I'd really like to do is hurl them at her. She did steal my Mr Right, after all. Okay, so technically she didn't steal him, but she did get to him first, which is more or less the same thing if you ask me.

"How can I help? Have you come to paint something yourself this time?"

"I've come to collect Ella's pottery," she says.

"Oh – your husband actually came in on Saturday and collected it," I tell her.

"Yes, I know, but he forgot to pick up the clown money box she painted at her friend's birthday party. You know what men are like!" she laughs. "If you want a job doing properly, you're better

206

off doing it yourself!"

Err, no, I want to tell her, I'd be quite happy for him to do jobs for me…all manner of jobs in fact…

I don't, of course.

"Oh right. I'll just go and have a look for it."

"It's the one with the purple flower in the hat," she calls after me.

When I come back into the café, Katie is leaning against the counter, tea in hand, chatting away with this woman. Or should I say, she is fraternising with the enemy.

"Is this the one?" I ask, holding up a square moneybox with a picture of a clown on the side. I remember the night Caroline stayed up really late drawing the outlines so the children could colour them in at the birthday party. I'm sure she hadn't even been home when I got in the next morning.

"Yes, that looks like it."

When I have wrapped it up she takes it from me and walks to the door.

"By the way," she says, turning round.

"Yes?"

Oh no. Can she tell? Does she know? Did I make eyes at him over the counter? Do I have a neon sign above my head that says 'I fancy the pants off your husband?'

"That wasn't my husband who came in on Saturday."

"Oh?" So, they're living in sin? What's that got to do with me?

"That was my brother."

"Oh."

Oh.

I look at Katie and – I try to stay cool – but I allow myself just a little excited grin and I nudge her with my elbow as if to say 'he's not her husband, what about that!' And she grins too, and nudges me back. And then when it's clear I don't appear to be doing anything else she kicks me under the counter.

"Ow!" I say.

"Ask her for his number," she mutters under her breath.

"No!" I mutter back.

"Why not?"

Yes, why not?

It's obvious really. Just because he isn't this woman's husband, doesn't mean he isn't *somebody's* husband. Or boyfriend. Why wouldn't he be? He's gorgeous. And funny. And he's obviously a great uncle.

And Katie can obviously read my mind, because just as the woman (who is not his wife) opens the door Katie, in her usual subtle style, calls out: "So is he anybody's husband?"

"No," she smiles. "He's not. And he doesn't have a girlfriend at the moment either. At least, not one that he's told any of us about!"

I am mortified, clearly. It is a fair few years since I had my best friend co-ordinate my love life for me (you know the drill – "my friend likes your friend – will you ask him if he'll go to the school disco with her?") But I am also quietly quite excited. The first guy I have felt anything remotely resembling a real attraction for is available.

"Just one more thing…" Katie calls out as the woman is pulling the door behind her.

"What's your brother's name?"

"James," she says. "James Newman."

"This is Becky," Katie helpfully says. "Becky Harper."

CHAPTER FORTY TWO

I'm thinking I must have made it pretty obvious that a) I was pleased when I found out he wasn't her husband and b) I was even more pleased when I found out he was single, because the next day James phones the café.

"Good morning. Potty Wotty Doodah," I say.

"Hi, is that Becky?" he says. "Becky Harper?"

"Yes?"

"This is James… Ella's uncle. The guy from the Vod Kerr Baa. And the exercise bike…"

"Oh, yes!" I say, suddenly realising who I'm speaking to, keen to minimise the embarrassment.

"I understand you met my sister yesterday," he adds.

"Yes, I did," I say feeling ever so slightly stupid. But then, it was an easy mistake to make.

"So, I was wondering if you fancy going out for a drink sometime?" Erm…Yes I do!

"I'd love to," I say.

"Are you free tonight?" he asks. "I could meet you after work."

"Erm…"

Tonight could work. Fiona is covering late opening. But what about getting ready? I do a quick mental calculation to work out how long it would take me to get myself looking vaguely

209

presentable. Hair. Makeup. Outfit deliberation. Not to mention the scrubbing that will inevitably be required to remove the paint I am currently wearing. We're talking a good three hours at least. No, tonight won't work.

And I'm just about to say as much, when it occurs to me that James has already seen me looking like this – worse even, in my scruffiest jeans, dishevelled and covered in paint – and he is still here, on the phone, asking me out on a date.

"Tonight sounds great," I say. "What time?"

"I could pick you up at six. Are you hungry? I know a great Italian restaurant not far from the café where we could get something to eat."

"Yeah, that would be lovely."

"Okay. I'll see you at six then."

"See you then."

Oh my god. I have a date. A first date. It's over six years since I've had a first date (my Internet dates don't count – they were not dates, they were disasters.) The last time I had a first date was with Alex. We caught the No. 6 bus and went to the cinema. We saw *Serendipity* with John Cusack and Kate Beckinsale. It was all about fate and destiny and at the time we both left the cinema thinking it was fate that put Alex next to me at the bar, unable to get served by the bartender, who served me only because I tickled him with my felt antlers. Now I think we were just young. And excited. We bought popcorn – sweet, not salty – and we sat in the back row, as you do on a first date. And then we went to Pizza Hut. It was all very romantic.

I have a date. With someone I really like. Oh my god. I have to tell someone.

"Katie, I have a date. With James. He just phoned! I'm so excited.

What shall I wear? I have an hour after Fiona comes in before I have to get back here, looking like I have just finished work and yet stunningly beautiful at the same time. Help!"

"Slow down, Becks, you'll give yourself a heart attack."

"I know, but I'm just so excited. I really like him Katie!"

"Okay. Right. Here's what we'll do."

I love how she says 'we' – like it's a team effort. That's exactly what it is with best friends. First dates, heartbreak, hangovers, life changing moves from one end of the country to the other. You share them all.

"Matt's working from home this afternoon so I'll get him to drop some stuff over to you. What do you want to wear?"

"I don't know. What do you think? Give me some suggestions. Something that looks casual enough for me to have been wearing it to work at the cafe, but going-outy enough that he doesn't think I'm a right slob."

"What are you wearing now? Jeans?"

"Yes."

"Smart jeans or scruffy jeans?"

"Smart."

"Clean or paint-spattered?"

I scratch at a bit of pink paint on my knee.

"Clean – ish."

"Okay. Something to go with jeans then. What about your red short-sleeved shirt?"

"Too scruffy."

"Okay. What about the green sleeveless top with the sparkly bits in the neckline?"

"No. I wouldn't wear that to work."

"The black and white top?"

"Which one? I have two."

"The stripy one with the three-quarter length sleeves?"

211

"No, I've gone off it."

I have to say, I'd have given up – and hung up – by now. Which just goes to show how desperate Katie is to get me a new boyfriend.

"What about the yellow cardy that you wear with that white vest top underneath with the lacy bit at the top?"

"Ooh yeah, that'll do. And get him to bring that yellow bangle I bought from Accessorize last week. Ooh – and my pendant necklace. They're both in the top drawer in my bedside table."

"Do you need your make-up bag?"

"No. I think I have enough in my handbag."

"Okay. I'll get him to phone you if there's anything he can't find."

"Thanks Katie, you're a star," I say, before hanging up.

I phone her straight back again.

"Yes?"

"Can you get him to bring my black boots. The ones in the hall cupboard. I've got my trainers on at the moment!"

"No problem. Good luck hun. Phone me if you need me."

Two hours later the transformation is complete – and nothing short of a miracle.

There is not a hint of paint on my hands, in my nails, in my hair, or on my face; I have brushed my hair so much it looks like something from a shampoo advert and I am looking smart-yet-casual in my jeans (minus the pink paint,) white vest top and yellow cardigan. With the black boots, pendant necklace and yellow bangle to complete the outfit, I think I might just have pulled off the I-look-like-this-every-day-and-it's-no-effort-whatsoever look, without giving away the fact that I virtually knocked poor Fiona out as she was coming in, ran to the gym across the road and begged them to let me use the shower and had my best friend's fiancé courier me over a complete change of clothes – and accessories – to my place of work. And all with fifteen minutes to spare. Excellent.

"I'm guessing you've got a date?" Fiona grins when I finally stand still long enough to say hello.

"Yes," I confirm, my inane grin back for a visit.

God, I hope he's worth it. What if he's not as fabulous as I remember? What if I just imagined the gorgeous guy with the big brown eyes and the smile that made me go all unnecessary, and the dimple. What if he's actually nothing special at all?

CHAPTER FORTY THREE

From the beginning of my life
I have been looking for your face
But today I have seen it

'Looking for Your Face', Jabal ad-Din ar-Rumi (1207 – 1273)
Translated from the Persian by Fereydoun Kia

He *is* as nice as I remember. Nicer, in fact. And on time, which definitely merits a couple of extra brownie points (which I will distribute as and when I see fit.)

"Hi," he says, when I open the door to let him into the café.

"Hi," I say back, feeling like a love-sick teenager again for the first time in I don't know how long (well, ten years nearly, but who's counting?)

"Are you ready?"

"Yep." I turn and wave at Fiona. She waves back and mouths 'good luck' – when James isn't looking, thankfully.

I am acutely aware of my hand shaking as I pull the door shut. I don't think he notices.

"Are you okay to walk? The restaurant is just a few minutes away?" he asks me.

What a gentleman.

"Of course."

"So, how long have you worked at Potty Wotty Doodah?" he asks as we walk to the restaurant.

"Only a few months. It's a temporary thing while I pursue a new career," I tell him. "Long story."

"It's a great place."

"Isn't it!"

"I hadn't seen it before but my niece loves it. She's there virtually every other week for one birthday party or another. I have a whole cupboard full of her mugs at home."

"She's lovely. How old is she?"

"Four. And she has a brother, Charlie, who's three."

"Yes. I've met him. Your sister brought them both in one day. That's when she painted the plate. Actually, I have a confession to make," I say.

"Oh yeah?"

"I thought she was your wife."

He doesn't say anything, so I carry on – leaving out the bit where I wanted to scratch her eyes out, obviously.

"When you came in to the café to collect Ella's plate, I just assumed you were her dad because that's who your sister – sorry I don't even know her name…"

"Leonie."

"Right – because that's who Leonie said would be picking it up. And so when she came back in on Monday I thought she was your wife!"

"Leonie did tell me actually, and I have to admit – we did have a bit of a laugh."

"Why?" I ask, slightly offended. So I might have been wrong, but it wasn't that funny.

"Because we're twins, Leonie and I. Not identical, obviously, but

215

we look so similar. You can definitely tell we're related."

I look up at him as we're walking.

"God, yeah, I can see it now – you do look alike," I laugh, relieved. "Anyway – that's not the end of my confession."

"Oh yeah? What's the rest then?"

He opens the door to *Ristorante Fiore* and holds it as I walk in.

"Table for two sir?" a smartly dressed man with an Italian accent asks James.

"Yes please."

I wait until we are sat across from each other at a candle-lit table at the back of the restaurant before I answer James' question, thinking back to everything Bev said – '*there'll be none of this, shall I say this, should I not say that…*'

I look at him across the table, this man I think I could very easily fall in love with, and I tell him…

"I was a bit jealous."

CHAPTER FORTY FOUR

I'm in love.

Okay, so I'm not in love. Not really. Not yet, anyway. But there is potential. Definite potential.

Of course, in hindsight, maybe telling him I was jealous of his sister – who I thought was his wife – might have been a bit too much information for a first date, but as it happens he didn't seem to mind at all.

In fact, 'I'm glad,' were, I believe, his exact words.

Oh my god, we had such a lovely evening. One of those perfect evenings you witness when two people get together in films – the sort you don't think actually exist in real life.

But they do. They really do.

We talked and talked. In fact we talked so much that the waiter had to come back three times to take our order. And even then we ended up just taking a cursory glance and choosing the first thing on the menu. Which was a bit unfortunate really, given that I don't actually like ravioli all that much. Good job I had lost my appetite anyway.

Okay, so – you want details. Well, he's thirty three, which I think is the perfect age for a twenty seven-year-old girl/woman (I still have trouble thinking of myself as a grown up) – old enough to have left his male immaturity behind, young enough to still want to get up on the dance floor at your best mate's wedding and make a tit of himself (not that I'm thinking that far ahead, obviously.)

He's a management accountant, whatever one of those is (an accountant that manages?) and he's just been made a partner in his family's sign-writing business.

He has never been married, has had two serious relationships and three not-so-serious.

He owns his own home – a flat, in Wimbledon, his own car – a silver Golf GTI, and yes, his own teeth and his own hair.

He has a twin sister, as we already know – Leonie – and an older brother Dan.

His mum died of cancer when he was in his late twenties and his dad, Jack, is re-married – to Grace, who had given up all hope of ever meeting her prince charming before she met Jack.

And as well as Ella and Charlie, he has another nephew – Dan's son Evan, but no children of his own – though he does want them in the future.

There. How did I do?

Good effort, hey?

Oh, and he loves red wine, which of course means we are bound to get along famously.

We got kicked out of the restaurant at closing time – we were oblivious to the last member of staff drumming his fingers on the table next to us, desperate to get home for a beer and a hot bath – and shared a taxi home. He asked the taxi to wait for him while he walked me to the door, where he kissed me softly on the lips (no tongues yet) and thanked me for a lovely evening.

And there lies the story behind the grin that has been plastered to my face ever since.

I'm seeing him again, of course.

When he asked if I was free, I did think about playing hard to get. For about a second. And then I remembered what Bev said, and I thought, what would be the point? I like the guy. He knows I like him. So why not just say yes.

So I did.

I'm seeing him on Friday night.

CHAPTER FORTY FIVE

Can someone please explain to me why it is that when you really want a moment to last forever – Monday night, for instance – it's over in the blink of an eye, and yet, when you want the day to bugger off and be over – today, for instance – the hours just seem to drag on for an eternity.

The last three days have been bad enough.

I spent the whole of Tuesday with my head in the clouds. I think Fiona would have preferred it if I'd not bothered even getting out of bed, to be honest. I glazed three plates and a bowl with nothing on them. I filled the kiln and forgot to turn it on. I ordered thirty one boxes of blank tiles instead of thirteen.

Oh, and I also discovered that I needn't have suffered a temporary broken heart, after all.

"You didn't tell me it was James Newman you liked," Fiona said on Tuesday morning.

Turns out she knows him. Sort of. His brother Dan is making the sign for her shop.

"If I'd have known it was James you liked, I could have told you he was single," she said.

Now she tells me.

I didn't take a single thing in on Tuesday night when Sheila taught us all about How to Avoid Writer's Block. I spent ninety minutes doodling in my notepad instead, drawing little love hearts and writing "*JN 4 RH*". Seriously, I did. I am a lost cause, clearly.

Wednesday and Thursday were equally unbearable, each hour feeling like ten. Can you believe I was actually going to bed early to make the next day come quicker? Actually, don't answer that…

I'm not sure I remember the last time I went to bed at 8 o'clock. And now Friday has arrived. But it's dragging its bloody heels.

I have scrubbed the tables, wiped the floor, re-filled the paints, washed all the water pots, put all the books in alphabetical order from *Noah's Ark* (fantastic for bizarre animal requests) to *Rainbow* (we have had a recent flood of requests for pictures of Zippy and George following a series re-run on UK Gold), polished the counter, replenished the tracing paper, emptied the kiln, re-filled the kiln…

And it's still only 11:45am, damn it.

I have even mentally planned my outfit for this evening – black floaty skirt, pink strapless top, chunky black necklace, heels – and my getting ready 'time-line' – 18:00: bath, shave legs (no, not because I'm hoping he'll be touching my legs later, but because I'm wearing a skirt, although…), shampoo, deep conditioning treat-ment, 18:30: moisturise, deodorise, sparkle-ise (bronzing powder with lots of tiny bits of glitter in), 18:45: pour glass of wine, drink wine, pour second glass of wine, warn self of dangers of drinking on an empty stomach, eg being pissed before the date has even started and making a complete tit of oneself, 19:00: (yes, I *can* drink two glasses of wine in fifteen minutes if time restrictions so require) makeup, hair, jewellery…

At midday my phone rings, throwing me into an immediate state of panic. What if it's James? What if he's phoning to cancel? What if he's gone off me?

It's not James.

It's Emma.

"Hi Em."

"Hiya."

"How's things?"

"Good. You?" She's walking and talking, I think. I can hear her heels clicking on the pavement. "How's the research going? Any better?"

"Kind of." I want to tell her my research has changed direction a bit. I want to tell her about my date with James. But I decide against it. She's still upset about her latest break-up. She doesn't need to hear how excited I am about the developments in my own love life.

"I decided to give the Internet dating a go," I tell her instead, laughing at myself before she can.

"Oh yeah? How's it going?"

"Completely disastrous, as it happens! But I guess it might help with the overall picture – presumably if I work my way through enough Mr Wrongs, I'll eventually find Mr Right, right?" I laugh.

"Process of elimination," Em agrees. "Anyway, I was just phoning to see if you fancy doing something this evening?"

Bollocks.

I'm seeing James tonight.

I consider my options.

I could tell Emma a little white lie. Or I could postpone my date with James.

Emma is one of my best friends. And I hate fibbing. But James is very lovely. And what if he thinks I'm not interested? I don't want him to think that. I really like him.

"I can't tonight, Em," I say. "I already have plans. I could meet you for a quick coffee?"

"Don't worry. It was just an idea."

"Why don't you phone Katie? I think she might be free tonight,"

I suggest, making a mental note to phone Katie myself and warn her not to put her foot in it.

"Yeah, I might do that. I better go. I'm on playground duty in a bit."

"Okay hun. I'll phone you over the weekend."

"Okay, bye."

It feels like it takes a million years but the afternoon does eventually pass – though not before I have supervised a Noddy and Big Ears birthday party, helped a young mum get green paint out of her eyebrows, and managed to squeeze the words 'day Derek' into a space not much wider than my thumb (his wife got a bit carried away with 'Happy 40th Birth' before she realised she was running out of room). And at 5.30pm I finally lock up and head back to the flat.

Katie and Matt aren't home yet which means I can hog the bathroom without any risk of piss-taking at all the lotions and potions that will no doubt be making an appearance for this most auspicious of occasions.

There'll be no dashing to the gym for a quick shower and a change of clothes couriered to me by my best friend's boyfriend tonight.

Tonight I have time to do things in style. To spend hours pampering and preening myself to perfection. To soak in a candlelit bath with lashings of Molton Brown bubble bath (it's Katie's though so best not mention it). To apply a soothing cucumber face mask...

I'm a bit bored to tell you the truth.

The candle has gone out (I splashed it by accident reaching for the soap), the bubbles have all but disappeared, and I am slowly turning into a giant prune.

Sod this.

After rinsing the conditioner out of my hair I grip the plug chain between my toes and let the water out.

I've never been one of those girls who takes hours to get ready – even if it *is* for a hot date.

I've tried, I really have. But the longest it has ever taken me is sixty four minutes. And that included long overdue attention to my eyebrows and extensive use of hair straighteners.

But you hear about these women who get up in the middle of the night practically, to start getting ready to go out – often just to go to work, when frankly I'd be happy to slum it with my hair tied back and a single coat of mascara if it meant a few extra minutes in bed. They spend hours in front of the mirror. What are they doing exactly? Coating each eyelash individually?

Even being generous I fail to see how it could possibly get anywhere near the hour mark, let alone above it.

But maybe I have been leaving the house looking like a complete dog all these years. Who knows?

After blasting my hair dry – a woman on a mission, head tipped upside down for extra volume, and a bit of extra blood to the head to boot – I sit cross-legged in front of the mirror with my makeup bag perched in my lap and get to work.

I am smearing silver cream eye shadow on my left eye, my lips pursed in concentration, when Katie knocks at the door.

"For Dutch courage," she says, handing me a glass of red wine and sitting on the edge of the bed.

"Thanks. I'm a bag of nerves." I hold out my hand to demonstrate. A slight tremble can be seen.

"I can't remember the last time I liked someone this much," I say. "I'm not sure I ever have even."

"Not even Joe Davidson?"

I fell for Joe in the second year at university – at the Christmas ball. He was gorgeous, with a mop of dark floppy hair and a dress

224

shirt covered in cartoon dinosaurs underneath his tux. I thought he was the cutest guy I'd ever seen.

But I was quite shy in those days and I wouldn't approach him. Until Katie dared me to go up to him and snog him, that is. At which point my shyness miraculously disappeared. I never could resist a dare. There was a drink in it for me, if I did it – and a snog, obviously, if I could get it.

I got the snog. And the drink. Which I shared with Joe. Fair's fair – he did help me win it, after all.

Joe and I dated for two-and-a-half weeks. And it was all going beautifully, until he got drunk one night and lost a game of pool. In a forfeit decided before the game, the loser had to shave his head. And Joe was so drunk he hadn't noticed that his opponent was already a skinhead.

Losing the game was one thing. But losing his mop of dark floppy hair too…well that was just too much. I've never gone for skinheads.

"No. Not even Joe Davidson," I tell Katie.

"Do you want me to straighten your hair for you?"

"Ooh, would you? Thanks Katie. What would I do without you?"

"I really don't know," she says, grinning at me in the mirror and reaching for the straighteners from the basket of hair stuff by my bed.

Half an hour later I'm ready for my big date.

Well, physically I am ready. Mentally I'm still a bag of nerves.

"How do I look?" I ask Katie, who is now cuddled up with Matt on the sofa watching *How To Lose A Man In Ten Days*.

"Have you seen this, Becks? You might be able to pick up a few hints!" Matt says.

"Ignore him! You look gorgeous!"

"She knows I'm only kidding, don't you?"

"Yes...I think so."

Katie's grinning at me now. She has that look in her eye. She's up to something.

"What have you done?" I ask.

"Nothing!"

"What are you about to do then?"

"Nothing! Well...it's just..."

"What?"

"Well, I was just going to say, you *can* bring him back here later. If you want to... If you are getting on well... You know..."

Thankfully I am saved by the bell.

"Shall I get that?" Matt asks, leaping to his feet.

"No! That's okay, I'll go," I say, pushing him back down again. "I'll see you both later."

"Don't do anything we wouldn't do," Matt says.

"Well that gives me plenty of scope then, doesn't it?" I reply, blowing them both a kiss and darting out of the room before either of them can protest.

So. We start the evening off in The Hedge.

James' brother made the signage for it. It's quite impressive. Chunky burgundy lettering against a cream background, a bottle of wine at one end and two glasses tipped towards each other at the other.

James gets a discount.

"It's not why I brought you here," he tells me sheepishly as he hands me my drink – a 1978 Cabernet Sauvignon, apparently. Alex bought me a book on wine for my last birthday. He always used to raise his eyes to the ceiling every time I said "they all taste the same to me" when ordering a glass of wine and decided he'd try to educate me. They still do all taste the same to me. It's just that now I say 'mmm, it tastes fruity,' or 'mmm it tastes woody,' instead,

226

hoping I must get it right at least some of the time.

"It's a great place," I say. "I've been here with my friends."

We take our drinks and find an empty sofa.

"So how did your family get into the sign-writing business?" I ask James.

"My brother studied graphic design at university and had always wanted to own his own business. When he graduated, dad offered to lend him the money. Dan took him up on the offer on the grounds that dad be his partner in the business. He had taken early retirement from the police force and was really bored, so he did.

I sip my wine. "And then you joined them?"

He nods.

"I was never really interested in being a part of the business, but it has grown so much that they really needed the extra help with the financial side. I hated my job so it seemed like the right time to join them."

"And are you glad you have?"

"So far, yes. It's fun working with your family. I wasn't sure it would be. But it is. Dan and I have always been friends as well as brothers, so we thought we'd probably work well together."

"I think it's great that you can work with your family. I couldn't work with my brother. He'd think he could boss me around just because he's older, like he always did when we were kids."

James laughs. "It's not for everyone, I guess. So, when do you hope to hear from these magazines then?" he asks, changing the subject to me.

By the way – I know it's not ideal, telling porky pies this early on in a 'relationship', but I've had to tell James a teensy weensy white lie.

Well, I could hardly tell him I'm researching an article on how you know you've met Mr Right, could I? – *'and by the way, I'm hoping you'll be the one to show me…'*

How to lose a man in ten days, more like...

So I have told him the truth up to the bit just before I got the commission – that I left my horrid job as a hole-punch saleswoman to follow my dream of becoming the next Carrie Bradshaw and that I'm still waiting for some wise editor to snap me up. To which James said "Carrie Bradshaw? She's the one from *Sex & The City* isn't she?" Which impressed me immensely. "The one that writes about sex?" he added, raising his eyebrows. Which embarrassed me immensely.

"I'm not sure when I'll hear back from any of them," I fib. "I only sent the letters off recently, so I guess I'll have to wait a while for any responses. But I'm enjoying working at Potty Wotty Doodah for now. It makes a nice change from stationery!"

"Yeah, I imagine it's probably more fun than paper clips and staplers."

"Definitely. Although, a lot more messy too! I frequently go home covered in paint."

"It's a good look on you, though," he jokes.

An hour later, after a second glass of wine, we leave The Hedge. When we are walking to the restaurant James takes hold of my hand. It feels nice. I like it. I like James. A lot.

"Perhaps we should look at the menu before we do anything else," James laughs as we are shown to our table. "We don't want to keep sending the waiter away again."

James orders a steak and I go for the chicken risotto – one of my favourites this time, although I'm even less hungry tonight than I was on Monday. I make sure I eat it though. We've been drinking a lot of wine and I don't want to end up getting drunk and embarrassing myself.

As the restaurant fills up and then empties around us, we satisfy our need to know more about each other.

We talk about what's important to us, what drives us crazy, our interests, our friends, our childhoods.

Now I know that when James was seven he and Dan were fighting over a metal crook-lock on the back seat of their mum's car. They each had hold of one end, both of them pulling with all their strength. Then Dan let go and it hit James in the face, narrowly missing his left eye. He was rushed to hospital where he had nine stitches.

I lean across the table, kiss my index finger and gently touch it against the tiny faded scar.

For dessert we share profiteroles and tales of past relationships.

It shouldn't matter, should it – who you've been out with and for how long? It's in your past, after all, just as much as the boy you held hands with at the school disco when you were twelve years old. But it holds a strange fascination somehow. Maybe we see a person's romantic history as a sign of how successful our own relationship with them might be.

James tells me he recently split up with his last girlfriend.

"I loved being with her, but I didn't love her," he says. "But I think she did love me, so I knew I had to end it."

"How did she take it?"

"She was upset. Which made me want to say I didn't mean it. But I did. So…well, I think sometimes you have to be cruel to be kind. How did your boyfriend – Alex, wasn't it? – how did he take it when you broke up?"

"Well he had just asked me to marry him, so not great."

"Really? Wow. That must have been hard." He pushes the last profiterole towards me. A consolation prize for the worst break-up maybe? I slice it down the middle with the side of my fork, take one half and then push the plate back towards him.

"Yes. It was. But like you, I knew it was right thing to do. I probably should have done it a long time ago really, but I kept hoping I'd feel differently."

"Why?"

"Because I did love him. And because it's so hard telling someone you love that you just don't love them enough."

"How do you know it wasn't enough?"

"Because I couldn't say yes when he asked me to marry him," I say. "I guess I just knew I could love somebody else more."

Could I love James more than I loved Alex? Eventually? Could I love him enough to say 'yes' one day? If he asked me?

I look at him across the table, stabbing the last bit of profiterole with his fork, his eyes never leaving mine, and for a brief moment I wonder if he isn't asking himself the very same thing.

James won't let me pay. Not even half. It's his treat, he says.

"But it was your treat on Monday," I remind him.

"Yes. And it's my treat again tonight," he smiles, placing his credit card on the saucer with the bill and handing it to the waiter as he passes.

"So when will it get to be my treat?" I ask.

"Oh, I think we've got plenty of time," he says, squeezing my hand across the table.

Wimbledon has come alive by the time we leave the restaurant at 10:30.

"We could just make last orders?" James says.

"Okay."

As we walk along in comfortable silence I hold James hand. We are surrounded by other people, all making their way to their next drink, like us. And yet it feels like it's only us.

With his free hand James presses the button at the pedestrian crossing. As I look across the road, I sense him turning towards me, watching me.

I look down the road at the cars coming towards us, self-conscious, unsure. Eventually I look at him and something happens in the pit of my stomach and he leans towards me and kisses me. Gently at first, so that our lips barely touch, and then firmer, wrapping his arms around my waist and pulling me close, as if our very survival depends on this kiss.

I am only vaguely aware of the beeping that signals the lights are now green, and that the cars are waiting patiently for us to cross.

But they are red again long before we break apart, long before we look at each other and both realise that not only could this be something, but that one day, maybe this could be enough.

CHAPTER FORTY SIX

"Why didn't you tell me you had a date last night?" Emma asks the next morning.

After a coffee at James' (yes, just coffee) I got a taxi home at 2am and found Emma snoring on the sofa bed. She had joined Katie and Matt half way through *How To Lose A Guy In Ten Days*. And I had forgotten to tell Katie not to mention the date.

"It's very early days," I tell her. "I didn't want to make a fuss."

"So tell me everything," she orders, nursing a cup of coffee. They had sent Matt out for a takeaway last night after the film. And three bottles of wine. I pick up the empties from the coffee table before one of us throws up.

"He's lovely," I say, acutely aware of the huge grin that has suddenly appeared on my face.

"We met in the café. He was picking up some pottery that his niece had painted. I thought it was his daughter, though, and that he was married."

"What does he look like?"

"He's cute," Katie says, appearing in the doorway, rubbing her eyes, her hair plastered to her head and her pyjamas inside out. "Very cute. God, did we get through three bottles of wine last night," she says, spotting the bottles in my hands.

"Looks like it."

"God, I feel rough. My mouth feels like the Sahara Desert."

"When did you meet him Katie?" Emma asks.

"Last night when he picked her up."

"You didn't meet him," I say. "You were in the living room. How could you see him?"

"You're right. We didn't meet him. But we did see him. We were spying on you out of the bedroom window!"

"You deserve a hangover for that," I laugh.

"So when are we going to meet him properly?" Emma asks.

"Not yet! I don't want to scare him off. Meeting you lot is like meeting my family. And I am definitely not ready for *that*."

"How did last night go?" Katie says.

"Great," I grin. "It went great."

NATALIE

At work on Monday morning I am like the cat that got the cream —
a whole bowl full of the stuff — so much, in fact, that she got drunk
on it and started tripping over her own paws.

Fiona and Caroline stare at me as I wash a stack of water pots
as if it's the most thrilling job I've ever had to do.

"I take it the date went well," Fi says.

"Whatever gave you that idea?" I grin, rinsing one of the pots
under the tap before shaking it.

"You'll be able to interview yourself soon," Caroline says.

"Oh, I don't know about that!"

Today I'm interviewing Natalie, a teacher friend of Caroline's
who has just got engaged. Her lessons don't start until 11am today
so she's calling in on her way to work.

She arrives at 9:30am and I make us both a coffee.

"You don't mind doing this do you?" I ask, handing her the mug.
"I hope Caroline didn't make you feel like you had to do it?"

"Of course not! I'm happy to help," she laughs. "Though I'm not
entirely sure what it is you want to know."

"Oh, you know, just about you and Carl, how you met, how you
know he's the one..."

They met at college. Carl asked Natalie out — but not for himself, for his friend. So she went out with his friend for two years. And then they split up. But she stayed in touch with Carl. After college she went travelling and when she got back they got together. That was seven years ago.

"So how do you know he's the one?" I ask her.

"It's really hard to say," she tells me.

Now where have I heard that before?

"I don't think it was love at first sight. Well, it couldn't have been because I ended up going out with his friend for two years," she laughs. "It was just something that happened gradually.

"I wasn't sure when we first got together. Carl was so lovely and I wasn't used to having somebody being so nice to me – not having to chase them, not worrying about what they thought. It was all a bit alien to me. So I split up with him and we both started seeing other people. But then I realised I'd made a huge mistake, and thankfully he took me back."

"What was different the second time around then?" I ask.

"I let go of my insecurities, I suppose, and realised that he might not be the obvious person but he was the person I wanted to be with.

"I know he's the one because I'm myself when I'm with him. I can pull silly faces. I can look crap and not worry about it. I can go to parties and not worry if I see him talking to another girl – because I know he loves me.

"I enjoy his company. He makes me laugh. The simplest things are more fun when I'm doing them with him. We're best friends, but I fancy him too.

"He's the one because I love him unconditionally, I suppose.

"But he's not what I imagined my Mr Right would be," she says, as if she's just realised this herself.

"We all have an idea of what our Mr Right might be like, don't we? A shape, a size, an age, an idea of what their interests might be. But actually it can be a surprise sometimes.

"If it did work like that we could all just write our own advertisement for a Mr Right, couldn't we – thirty two, tall, dark, no children, enjoys tennis and gardening…

"But it doesn't. Because you can't define a feeling. You can't always explain why one person makes you feel a certain way, while someone else doesn't. Can you?"

"No," I agree. "You can't."

CHAPTER FORTY SEVEN

When Natalie has left the shop is dead, so Caroline, Fi and I enjoy a rare cup of coffee together. And a whole packet of two-finger Kit Kats.

"How's it going Becky?" Caroline asks. "Did Natalie have anything useful to add?"

I dip a Kit Kat finger in my coffee and suck the melting chocolate, pondering the question.

"Yes. And no," I say eventually, when the chocolate has all but gone and I am left with a soggy bit of wafer.

"She couldn't really tell me why Carl is Mr Right. She couldn't tell me why he, over everyone else, is the right person for her. But," I say, unwrapping another Kit Kat, "I do think I'm beginning to get it."

237

CHAPTER FORTY EIGHT

Then seek not, sweet, the 'If' and 'Why'
I love you now until I die:
For I must love because I live
And life in me is what you give.

'Because She Would Ask Me Why I Loved Her', Christopher Brennan (1870 – 1932)

Shovelling cornflakes into my mouth on Tuesday morning, I squint at a piece of paper, desperately trying to read what it says.

I was inspired during the night. At least, I think I was.

It was clearly inspirational enough to reach for a pen and paper (or an eyeliner and the back of an old envelope) in the dark. Not inspirational enough, however, to turn the light on so I could at least see what it was I was writing.

Something about ropes and park benches…

I miss my mouth and several milky cornflakes slide off the spoon back into the bowl.

'Maybe it's'… scribble scribble… 'why'… scribble… 'held… rope'… scribble scribble…

'Maybe it's not' scribble… 'park bench'… scribble scribble…

This reminds me of university, when, in a hungover state, and without the aid of my trusty Dictaphone, I would scrawl a few notes during a lecture and try to decipher them three weeks later, the night before an essay was due in. It was impossible to make sense of it when I could only read every third word. God knows how I ever got a 2:1.

"Maybe it's not about why Graham held onto the climbing rope," Katie says, coming into the kitchen and peering over my shoulder.

That's how I got my 2:1.

"What does that mean?" she asks.

"Good question. I wrote it in the middle of the night. In the dark. I was feeling inspired, I think. It's for my article."

"Oh, okay." She pulls a chair out, puts her tea down on the table and pulls the paper out of my hand.

"Maybe it's not about why Graham held onto the climbing rope," she reads again. "Maybe it's not about why Katie knows she wants to sit on a park bench with Matt."

She looks at me expectantly.

"Nope. Nothing," I tell her, shaking my head.

She looks at the paper again. "You've underlined the word why, if that's any help?" she says.

"Of course!" I say, snatching the paper back from her.

"Maybe it's not about *why* Graham held onto the rope and felt like he was holding onto his whole world, or *why* you know you want to sit on a park bench with Matt when you're seventy…"

"Is that what I said?" Katie asks, buttering a piece of toast.

"Maybe it's not about why, maybe there is no why," I say, ignoring her question. "Maybe it's about just *knowing*. And if you *don't know*, then it's simple – they are just not Mr Right."

"Absolutely," Katie agrees. "I'm so glad we got that sorted out. Pass me the marmalade will you."

So maybe Emma was right – maybe the answer is out there,

239

but I've just been looking in the wrong place. Like Natalie said – maybe you just can't define a feeling. Maybe you can't explain why someone makes you feel a certain way, or even why someone else doesn't.

CHAPTER FORTY NINE

Everyone who made love the night before
was walking around with flashing red lights
on top of their heads – a white-haired old gentleman,
a red-faced schoolboy, a pregnant woman
who smiled at me from across the street
and gave a little secret shrug,
as if the flashing red light on her head
was a small price to pay for what she knew.

'Saturday Morning', Hugo Williams

Things are going well with James.

We have been dating for two weeks and five days (yes I *am* still at the counting-every-second stage).

We have had dinner – twice, been to the cinema (we saw some romantic comedy with Cameron Diaz, though my memory of the evening is limited to the hand-holding, popcorn-sharing part, and not, it seems, to the name of the film, or any part of the storyline thereof), met for morning coffee – several times, and shared a Chinese takeaway and a tub of Ben & Jerry's Chunky Monkey at James' flat.

His flat is lovely. He took me there again after our cinema

date – and cooked dinner for me (enchiladas and crème caramel – seems I've gone and found myself another excellent cook). It's not a girly flat, but it's not overly boyish either, although it does have its fair share of boys' toys – X Box, sound system, flat screen television the size of a car, big comfy sofa on which to enjoy all of the above (a big comfy sofa big enough for two – stretched out.)

There are a few framed photographs dotted about the place too – his dad and Grace, Leonie and Dan, and their kids. None of any ex-girlfriends – or at least, none I could find in a quick scan of the place while he was serving up the enchiladas.

Yes, we have kissed. A lot. Yes, I have stayed over. No, we have not slept together.

This is only a matter of time, of course.

How much time though? How long is the right amount of time to wait? A few weeks? A month? With my first boyfriend I waited three months. But it's different with your first, isn't it? With Alex I waited six weeks. But even that seems excessive now. I know I want to, so what's the point in waiting? But then again, I don't want him to think I'm some kind of tramp who will drop her knickers for anything in a pair of trousers.

Anyway, I'm seeing him again tonight.

Erm.

Two weeks and five days. The perfect amount of time to wait before sleeping with a new boyfriend is two weeks and five days.

How do I know?

How do you *think* I know?

Now, I'd love to be able to tell you that it's just like it is in the movies. That our eyes meet over a candlelit table. That he carries me up the stairs (forget for a moment that he lives in a flat) and lies me gently on the bed where he caresses every little bit of me – slowly, tenderly. That we make love all night long. And that in the morning there's not a hair on my head out of place and my make-up still looks as perfect as it did when I put it on.

But of course it doesn't happen like that.

It happens like this...

Our eyes meet over a Chinese takeaway on James' living room floor. And he kisses me. And we end up moving on to the sofa (see, I told you it was big enough for two), where mid-kiss I ask him: "Do you have any condoms?"

It just sort of pops out – so to speak – before I can stop myself.

He doesn't, as it happens. Which kind of kills the moment.

Of course, part of me is glad he doesn't have any – because if he had then I would have felt like he'd been assuming I'd be up for it (I know I am, but that's not the point). But the rest of me is bloody frustrated.

"There's a petrol station down the road. We could probably get some there," James says, casually rearranging his trousers into a more comfortable position.

"How romantic," I say. And we both burst out laughing. And he kisses me again. And then we really do need to do something about the whole lack-of-condoms situation.

"I don't mind going if you want to stay here," he tells me.

"Let's both go," I say. "The fresh air would be good. That wine has gone straight to my head."

Have you ever been to buy condoms late at night with your boyfriend? It's worth braving the cool night air and the walk (considerably further than 'down the road', I might add) just to see the look on the cashier's face. Especially when they are kept behind the counter with the painkillers, the batteries and the cigarettes, so that you are not even spared the humiliation of having to say the word 'condoms'.

I'm glad it's not my local garage, that's all I'm saying.

"A pack of Durex please," James bravely tells the cashier, putting a box of cornflakes and a loaf of bread on the counter as he does so. I'm guessing the bread and the cornflakes are intended as a distraction of sorts? Perhaps he thinks they will lessen the embarrassment, somehow.

"For breakfast. Tomorrow morning. After a night of non-stop sex," I want to tell the cashier. I don't, obviously. It would have been fun though.

He looks young. His hair needs a good wash. He's covered in teenage spots, bless him. He can only be about sixteen. Is it legal to sell condoms at sixteen?

Apparently so.

He looks at James. "Three, six, or twelve?"

James looks at me, and I feel a giggle rising in my throat.

"Twelve," James confirms. Probably a wise decision. We won't want to be back here in a hurry. That box of cornflakes will last us a while...

"£10.40 please," he says, looking from James to me and back to James again. He puts the cornflakes and bread – and the condoms – in a carrier bag and hands James his change. And then – it's very subtle, but it's there – a look that says 'get in there mate', or something to that effect.

"Well that wasn't at all embarrassing," I laugh as we leave the garage.

"I'm sure we're not the first couple he's ever sold a packet of condoms to," James says, holding my hand. I like the way he calls us a couple. It feels nice. It feels right.

So, we have the condoms. Now all we have to do is recreate the moment where we actually need them.

This isn't difficult.

As soon as we get back to James' flat we by-pass the living room and head straight for his bedroom.

He sits on the edge of the bed and pulls me towards him. Dizzy from the alcohol and the night air I am powerless to resist.

I don't want to resist.

As I lean down to kiss him my hair brushes his face. He shuffles back on the bed and I climb on to his lap and wrap my legs around him.

He pulls me closer and kisses me hard, his light stubble scratching my face. It feels good. Raw.

He runs his hand down my back until his fingers brush the edge of my lace knickers (Victoria's Secret – bought this morning with matching bra – just in case) just inside my jeans.

Breaking away from his face I lift up his shirt. He has a great body. Toned. Lightly tanned. Just a little chest hair. I have seen it before. I have slept next to it. I resisted it once. This time I can't.

I touch his chest and look at his face. He smiles and I feel his desire underneath me. I reach down with my hand and kiss him hard on the lips.

"I don't know about you but I'm ready for a bowl of cornflakes," he says.

And I laugh so hard I almost fall off his lap.

"Me too," I tell him.

CHAPTER FIFTY

I never imagined house hunting on my own could be so depressing. I have had to start though. I didn't want to get home one day and find copies of the local property guide strategically placed around Katie and Matt's place with 'flat to rent' adverts circled with thick red marker pen, arrows pointing to them for extra emphasis, and 'we'll even help you move,' scribbled on the bottom of each page – just in case I still haven't taken the hint. Not that Katie and Matt would do that, of course. They are far too lovely. Which is why I have to do it instead.

But by the time I have eliminated all the properties that are too far away from Potty Wotty or the offices of *Love Life* (you never know,) all those that are on the top floor of a thirty storey building (I'm not afraid of heights as such, but I do get a bit queasy from time to time) and all those that would require the sale of at least one – if not both – of my kidneys to pay for it – I am down to slim pickings. Very slim pickings. Namely a bed-sit in Clapham Junction with a shared bathroom, a one-bed flat above a brothel in Balham (don't ask how I found that out – it's an experience I'd really rather forget) and a lock-up in Wimbledon – which depressingly is actually looking like my best option so far.

I could always find a house-share of course. But besides Katie and Matt, Fiona, Caroline, Emma – who lives in a one bedroom flat herself, and now James, I don't know anyone in London and I'm really not sure I'm comfortable with the idea of moving in with a bunch of complete strangers. I might find myself living with an insomniac who paces the floorboards in the dead of night... or a secret midnight snacker who eats the fridge bare during the night – the only evidence being a trail of empty wrappers along the kitchen counter and the odd crumb here and there... or a slob who doesn't believe in washing up more than once a month... or worse still a clean freak who whips your plate away before you're halfway through your fish and chips and starts scrubbing at it frantically with a Scotch-Brite and a pair of rubber gloves. A moth collector... A mass murderer...

"You could always move in with me," James says when I have finished telling him the horrors of the brothel story.

"I can't do that," I laugh. Good God, I hope he doesn't think that's why I was telling him.

"Why not?"

"Because we've only known each other a month."

"So?"

"So – people don't move in together after a month."

"Why not?"

Why not? It's a good question. I don't know.

"Because it's only a month," I say, for want of anything better.

"I know. But what an incredible month, hey!" he laughs, pulling me towards him on the sofa and sliding his hand up my top.

"Be serious James," I laugh.

"I am being serious." I believe him. "I never thought I'd meet someone like you," he says. "I can't believe how you've made me feel this past month. I didn't think it was possible to feel like this about someone. You've made me come alive. I want to be with you. I know that. So why not? Move in with me. I'd much rather you did that than live above a brothel in Balham," he laughs. "Or set up camp in a lock-up in Wimbledon. Although," he grins, "that would be handier than Balham as it's just down the road from me!"

"I don't know," I say, cuddling up to him. "I feel the same. After Alex I thought it would be a very long time before I met someone else. And now you've come along. And you make me so happy. But I'm scared. It's so fast. I don't want to do the wrong thing. I don't want to risk what we have right now by rushing things."

He smiles at me.

"I know," he says, pulling me close. "Just say you'll think about it."

"Okay. I'll think about it."

"Great. Now, where were we," he says, sliding his hand back up my shirt.

"Do you think a month is too soon to move in with someone?" I ask Caroline the following week.

"It depends who it is really," she says, shutting the lid of the kiln. We're firing twenty six mugs from a birthday party at the weekend. "I moved in with Dave after three weeks. But we had known each other for a lot longer than that, I suppose. Why? Are you thinking of moving in with James?"

"He's asked me to. But I'm not sure. I don't think he'd planned it or anything. I was just telling him about some of the dives I'd been to look at to rent and he suggested I move in with him."

"I thought you were staying with your friend Katie."

"I am." I programme the kiln while she wraps up some finished plates. "But it was only ever meant to be temporary. Katie and Matt are getting married in September. They don't want me hanging around playing gooseberry."

"Well, if you're looking for somewhere to live, and you're not sure about moving in with James, then what about the flat above this place?"

"What about it?"

"I own it."

"Really?" I had no idea.

"Yes – or rather, Dave and I own it. And it just so happens that I'm looking for a new tenant. Amy, who has lived there since I opened the café, has just moved in with her boyfriend. It's not huge but it's big enough for one – and a regular visitor," she adds, raising her eyebrows.

"Well, it's the perfect location for me, obviously," I say. "But it really depends on what you're asking for it. I'm kind of living off my savings at the moment. I have my job here, obviously, but that's only part time, and I won't get anything from the magazine until my feature is published."

"Well Amy paid us £500 a month, but I wouldn't mind taking a bit less until you find your feet – or decide to move in with James."

"How much less?"

"How does £400 sound, all in?"

"It sounds fantastic, but are you sure you wouldn't rather find someone who can pay you the full £500?"

"No. To be honest I'd rather have someone I know living there. I knew Amy before she moved in; she's been a great tenant, and I'm sure you would be too. In any case, it's not like I'd have far to find you if you weren't!"

"That's true. In that case you're on."

"Great. I could give you a quick tour now if you like?"

CHAPTER FIFTY ONE

I love you, not for what you are, but what I am, when I am
with you.

'Love', Roy Croft

"Have you seen my blue jacket?" I ask Katie on Saturday morning.

"Not since you wore it the night we celebrated your commission," she says, biting into a piece of toast smothered in marmalade. "But I wouldn't worry. It's not like you're going very far. And in the meantime if I find it I can borrow it!" she grins.

I told Katie about the flat as soon as I got home from work on Monday. She tried to persuade me to stay. She even roped Matt in on the effort – though his pleas were far less convincing, I have to say. He probably can't wait to get rid of me. He'll have his bathroom back, for starters. Poor bloke has had his toiletries relegated to the windowsill, to make room in the bathroom cabinet for all mine and Katie's combined lotions and potions. And he must be sick of wearing creased shirts to work ever since we gave up on the canvas wardrobe – when it collapsed for the fifth time – and squashed all my clothes into their wardrobe alongside all of their clothes.

"I've got to get myself sorted," I told her. "I can't live with you and Matt forever. You don't want me hanging around when you're married. Besides – I'm not going far. I'll be round for my tea every night!"

She's come round to the idea now. In fact, I think she's looking forward to it. She's been doing more of the packing that I have. Although, I'm sure half the stuff she's packed isn't even mine. She keeps holding up random items and saying "I think this is yours, B," and chucking it into one of the cardboard boxes currently lining the living room floor, regardless of whether it actually is or not.

I think she may be using my boxes as her own personal skip. I'll probably get to the flat and discover out-of-date takeaway leaflets and freebie newspapers amongst my stuff, her ancient floral pyjamas with the hole in the bum, the bottle of fake CK One that's gone off.

James is helping me move.

He has come around to the idea too now, once I'd explained that I don't have a contract with Caroline – that I can move out whenever I like – whenever we're ready.

He knocks on the door at 11am, just as Katie is climbing off my suitcase. She had to sit on it to get it to shut…

"Hey!" I say, kissing him on the lips. We do that now, you know – whenever we greet each other. It's sad, I know. But I love it.

"James' removals at your service," he says, flexing his muscles.

"Fabulous. Thanks for doing this."

"It's no problem. I want to help. In any case, I'm going to be spending a lot of time at your new place so it's only fair that I help you move in." He looks at me expectantly and I smile my agreement.

Any minute now I'll wake up. Someone will pinch me and I will wake up, on the sofa in Leeds, with a Penand Inc catalogue in my lap and a big sleep dribble working its way down my chin.

"So, what's going?" James asks.

I'm not dreaming. This fantastic guy really is helping me move into my new home. This fantastic guy really is my boyfriend.

I nod towards the boxes stacked up by the door.

"These boxes here and the suitcases in my bedroom. I just need to shove the last of my clothes into a couple of Katie's holdalls."

"You mean your clothes didn't fit into two suitcases?"

"Don't be silly!" Katie laughs. "Hi James," she says, squeezing his arm affectionately.

They've met each other a few times now.

They met for the first time when Katie was helping me out with the Monday evening shift again and James popped in to bring me my shorthand book which I'd left in his flat. Don't ask – it's like a foreign language – or Morse Code – dot dot dash dash. I don't stand a chance. He stayed for a cup of tea – and painted a mug "just to see what all the fuss is about" and then he left, at which point Katie told me she was going to ditch Matt at the altar and marry James instead, describing him as "absolutely scrummy and absolutely lovely". Exactly.

And then they met again when we all went to The Hedge for a drink on Wednesday evening. We asked Emma to come too, but she was going on a date, which was definite progress, we decided, so we didn't push it.

And then James came round for dinner last night. Katie cooked a big lasagne (I helped – I grated the cheese). And we all got drunk and played Monopoly – me and James versus Katie and Matt. Katie and Matt had Mayfair and Park Lane. And Oxford Street. And Bond Street. And Regent Street. James and I had Old Kent Road and Whitechapel. And the Waterworks. But I wouldn't give up – not before I'd sold off all our houses and hotels, re-mortgaged all of our properties and taken out a £10,000 bank loan.

"Remind me that I'm in charge when we buy our first place

together," James said. And I didn't even flinch. Katie did though – she stared at me with big "oh my god" eyes and kicked me under the coffee table. It bloody hurt too.

He didn't stay over. I have a single bed, if you recall, and the one and only time he has ever stayed over I rolled over and pushed him out of it.

"Hey Katie," James says. "How does it feel to have wiped the floor with us last night?"

"Pretty good, as it happens," she grins, flicking the kettle on. "Tea?"

"Yes please. So… what was that you were saying about Becky's clothes?"

Great. Now they're ganging up on me.

"Let's just say the sheer weight broke my wardrobe."

James looks suitably shocked.

"It's a canvas wardrobe," I protest. "It wouldn't hold Barbie's clothes, never mind mine!"

"Now then, girls," James laughs, bringing one of my suitcases out of the bedroom and pretending to keel over from the weight of it.

As he takes it out to the car Katie hands me a gift bag.

"What's this?" I ask.

"It's just a little something to decorate your new home."

I remove a parcel from the bag and tear off the paper.

It's a picture frame from Potty Wotty with an old photograph of Katie, Emma and I at my 21st. There are three stick figures across the top and the word 'friends' in colourful block writing across the bottom.

"I did it myself," she tells me proudly.

"It's great. I don't think I've ever seen that picture."

I show James as he comes back in for the next load.

"Look James, Katie made it for me as a housewarming present."

He glances at it briefly before picking up a box.

"It's lovely."

"I have something for you too," I tell Katie. "To say thanks. I've left it on the coffee table though. Open it when I've gone. I'll probably cry otherwise."

"Okay."

Between us we load the rest of the stuff into James' car and then I hug Katie.

"Thank you so much for everything Katie. You're a great friend."

"You too. Call me if you need anything. A chat. A cup of sugar. Anything."

I laugh at this. "Well, I don't take it in my tea and I'm sure you didn't mean for baking, but thanks!"

I don't know why I'm crying. It's stupid. It's not like I'm going far. Only 3.6 miles, in fact. I made James clock it in the car. Maybe it's living on my own that's worrying me. I've never lived on my own before. What if I hate it?

"You'll be fine," James says, reading my mind. "You've got me now."

And he's right. I do.

CHAPTER FIFTY TWO

Sharing one umbrella
We have to hold each other
Round the waist to keep together.
You ask me why I'm smiling –
It's because I'm thinking
I want it to rain forever.

'Love Poem', Vicki Feaver

It's not a huge flat. In fact, it's a very small flat. But it's mine. And as much as I loved living with Katie and Matt, it's nice to know I can spread my stuff out as much as I like and not have to feel guilty about it.

It's furnished – which is rather handy, given that what I currently own is limited to a flat pack bookcase (bought on the way over here from Argos) and a semi-dilapidated canvas wardrobe (kindly donated to me by Katie – more out of her sense of humour, I'm sure, than any need of mine). And it's spotless – thanks to the feather duster and vat of Domestos that Caroline came over with yesterday.

She insisted. She is a week overdue. She has tried a hot curry, and castor oil, a long walk and several other home remedies that are supposed to induce an overdue baby. Cleaning was the only thing she hadn't tried yet. It didn't work. But on a good note, I do now have the cleanest flat in London.

There's a living room with a throw-covered sofa bed, a coffee table and a television; a small but fairly new fitted kitchen and a bathroom with no bath but a power shower. And it has a small double bedroom with fitted wardrobes and a pine chest of drawers, which until yesterday came complete with free blobs of Blu-Tack and patches of faded wood – presumably where Amy had stuck pictures of her cat/boyfriend/nieces and nephews. The Blu-Tack has gone, but the patches of faded pine remain. I make a mental note to cover them up with pictures of my dog/nephew/friends. I'll leave one free for a piccie of James...

The first thing I do is make the bed. I treated myself to some new bedding yesterday – cream with big pink flowers to brighten the place up a bit.

James is in charge of unpacking boxes.

"What the hell is a 'Thirst Quenching Hydra-Balance Mask'?" he shouts from the lounge. He's found the bathroom box.

I push the quilt into the cover, grab the corners and shake it.

"It's for your face," I shout back, fastening the poppers.

"And 'Exfoliating Skin Polish' – what does that do?"

"It makes your skin all soft and smooth. At least it's meant to!" I take a pillowcase from the top of the chest of drawers.

"Yeah?" he says, appearing in the doorway, with a big grin plastered all over his face.

"I think maybe I ought to check if it's working."

He grabs me around the waist and tickles me. I try to wriggle free and drop the pillow from under my chin. I flick him with the pillowcase.

"Hey. I'm trying to make the bed," I protest.

"Oh yeah? And I'm trying to get you into it," he laughs.

No prizes for guessing who wins this particular battle.

CHAPTER FIFTY THREE

Emma has come over for the night. Katie's come too. And Fiona.

We're all huddled together on my one sofa and a beanbag (a gift from Em which she carried all the way here on the tube.)

It's a proper girly night, with lots of wine, bad food and *Sex & The City*.

I'm a bit embarrassed to admit this, but it's the first night I've spent apart from James in three weeks.

I'm even more embarrassed to say I miss him.

Emma is still moping. Sort of. She's trying. She's been on a few dates. She went out with her colleague's brother. But he was too short, apparently, and he blinked too much. And she went out with a guy who has just moved into the flat below hers. But he told too many jokes, she said, and wasn't serious enough. And she went out with a guy she met in a service station on the M4 on the way home from a teachers' conference. She quite liked him. But he never phoned to ask her out again. I'm sure the fact that she told him all about her ex boyfriend – promptly bursting into tears when she got to the bit where they broke up – had absolutely nothing to do with it. She says she's giving up on men.

She asks me about James.

"I think I might be in love," I say.

Katie and Fiona look up from the DVD player where they are

trying to find the episode where Big buys Carrie that ridiculous duck clutch bag and she tells him she loves him.

"Really?" they all say simultaneously.

"Yes," I say, surprising myself almost as much as I appear to have surprised my friends. Of course, I don't *think* I'm in love. You're either in love or you're not. And I am.

"Wow," Emma says. She drains her glass of wine and pours herself another.

Wow indeed.

"That's fabulous," Katie says. "Shall I invite him to the wedding?"

I think about it for a moment. A fraction of a moment.

"Yes. I think maybe you should. If that's okay?"

"Of course it is!"

And then, as though one of us declaring she thinks she's in love is a normal, everyday occurrence – like saying the post is here, or that the kettle has boiled, Katie and Fiona turn their attention back to the DVD.

"That's great Becks," Emma says. "I'm really happy for you."

And then: "Has he got any nice friends, d'you know?"

"I thought you said you were giving up on men," I laugh.

"I did. But I've changed my mind. I can't stay single forever, can I?" she says, sounding much more like the Emma we know and love.

"In that case I'll ask him. I'm supposed to be meeting some of his friends in the next couple of weeks. I'll find out if there are any single men among them!"

"Excellent. Have you found it yet girls?" she asks Katie and Fiona, just as Katie clicks play on the remote and plonks herself down on the beanbag.

"Pass the Pringles, B."

"I love this episode," I say, taking a handful before putting the lid back on the tube and tossing it to Katie. "I just love that she tells him she loves him after he's given her that ridiculous duck bag."

She fast-forwards through the credits.

"It's such a dilemma, isn't it, when to tell someone you love them?" I say, undeterred by the silence I'm greeted with. I'm dreadful to watch television with. If I'm not chattering away about something completely unrelated, I'm giving a running commentary that's neither necessary nor wanted.

"Is that your way of telling us that you love James?" Fiona says, taking the Pringles from Katie and looking at me, eyebrows raised expectantly.

"Of course not. It's far too early... But say I did? Do I tell him? Or do I wait for him to say it first?"

"I told Matt on our third date," Katie says.

"Oh god, yeah, you did didn't you!"

"Really?" Fiona says.

"Yeah. I was drunk. But I meant it."

"What did he say?" Fiona asks.

"He said he loved me too, of course," Katie says, popping a Pringle into her mouth with a self-satisfied grin.

I told Alex after he told me – which happened after we'd been together for about six months.

We were camping in France in the summer holidays. It had been a really hot day so we lit a barbecue on the beach and cooked ourselves sausages and burgers (we were students remember – we didn't have money for anything more exotic). Alex fed me a hot dog in the moonlight and wiped tomato ketchup from my chin. And then he told me that he loved me. So I said I loved him too. I meant it. I did love him. But it all felt a bit staged, somehow. The beach. The fire. The reflection of the moon glistening on the sea. It didn't feel real. Maybe I knew even back then that it would never be enough?

For the next three hours we watch back-to-back episodes of

Sex & The City and drink our way through three bottles of wine and the dregs of a bottle of Baileys.

When we have finally taken about as much of Carrie, Charlotte, Samantha and Miranda as we can for one night, Fiona gets a taxi home and the rest of us all stagger to bed – Emma and Katie on the sofa bed and me in my bed. Alone. Without James.

It feels empty without him.

I put my hand on his empty pillow. And then I mentally slap myself for being so sad.

But I do grab my phone from the bedside table and send him a quick text: *Night J x*.

I turn off the light and seconds later my phone beeps and lights up the room.

Hey! I was just thinking about you. Did you have fun with the girls?

I text him back in the darkness.

Yes. We watched S&TC and drank lots of wine! Think my head will hurt tomorrow.

I put my phone on silent so the girls won't be kept awake, or, more to the point, won't take the piss in the morning.

A minute later the room lights up again.

Oh dear! I'll have to look after you...

I am in the middle of replying when another message flashes up.

By the way...I miss you x

I delete what I'd written. It wasn't important.

I miss you too x I write instead.

I had arranged to meet James at Victoria station this morning so he could meet Emma before she gets the train home to see her mum.

But we get to the station earlier than we'd thought and there is a train about to leave.

"I might as well get it, B. I'll meet him next time," she says, hugging me and jumping on the train.

"And don't forget to suss out his friends for me will you? I'm not fussy. Just someone tall, dark and handsome, with lots and lots of money!"

"Okay," I laugh, and push the button to close the door.

CHAPTER FIFTY FOUR

It's official. Dinosaurs are not, as we originally suspected, extinct. They are, in fact, still in abundance. They are in Potty Wotty Doodah anyway.

Fiona and I are getting ready for a four-year-old's birthday party. A four-year-old dinosaur fanatic's birthday party. We have dinosaur tablecloths, dinosaur napkins, dinosaur paper cups and plates and dinosaur party hats. We even have a dinosaur cake. And between us we have drawn dinosaur outlines on fourteen plates and fourteen bowls. If I ever see another dinosaur again it will be far too soon.

I haven't seen much of Fiona lately. She has been busy with the shop. I've been busy with James. And between Fiona and I, we have been covering Caroline's shifts at the café. She has finally had the baby. A boy. Benjamin. He was two weeks late in the end. Caroline had practically scrubbed the surface off her entire house before he finally decided to put in an appearance. But he was definitely worth the wait. He's a cutie, and Fiona and I have both fallen in love with him.

"How's the shop coming along, Fi?" I ask, putting two trays of paints out on the table.

"Great, actually. I'm hoping to move the opening forward."

"Really? Wow, you must have been busy."

I go out to the back room and fetch the boxes of plates and bowls to put out on the tables. As I'm coming back through the bell on the door rings, marking the arrival of the birthday boy.

He spots his table straightaway and dives into the first seat he comes to, shrugging his jacket off and flinging it at his poor mum.

"You must be Zack," I say.

He nods, an excited look on his face.

"Well, a little bird told me that you like dinosaurs, Zack. Is that true?" Another nod.

"How would you like to paint a dinosaur plate to take home today?"

Another nod. This'll be easy.

Over the next few minutes Zack is joined by another eight boys and three girls – dropped off by their mums or dads. I recognise one of the girls – it's James' niece Ella.

What a pity these little girls are too young to appreciate the minority they are now in. Ten or twelve years from now they would kill for a boy: girl ratio such as this one.

There's a brief scuffle amongst the last three boys to arrive over who has to sit next to a girl and then we get the party started.

"We thought they could do the painting first and then we'll bring the party food out. Is that okay?" I ask Zack's mum. She has brought three other mums with her to help supervise the children, which makes mine and Fiona's jobs considerably easier. Last week we somehow both became moving targets, replacing the dinner plates as the items to be decorated. Fiona went home with a cat's face on the back of her hand, while I spent the next day scrubbing a pig off my arm.

"Yes. That sounds fine."

"Can I get you all a coffee?" Fiona asks them.

While Fiona makes the drinks, I hand out the dinosaur plates to the party animals.

Before the last plate is even on the table there is paint on body parts and the contents of a pot of water all over the table.

When the kids have finished painting their plates and bowls – each one beautifully defaced with big splodges of colour – we collect them up and replace them with dinosaur table cloths and plates of sandwiches, crisps and sausage rolls.

The food is quickly gobbled down – sandwiches rejected, jammy dodgers and chocolate fingers fought over – the latter not only being eaten but also inserted into nostrils and used as miniature swords.

I do hope my own children, whenever I have them, never insert chocolate fingers into their nostrils, I think to myself, as I resist the urge to nibble at my own childhood favourites and sip my cup of tea instead.

Once the table is cleared the games begin. Musical chairs would be far too costly in a pottery café, so we skip straight to pass the parcel. As usual, there's a layer for each child to tear off, with a dinosaur sticker hidden inside. Ella wins the final prize – a dinosaur yoyo.

I used to love yoyos. I show her how to use it.

The boys do not look happy that a girl has won the game.

At five o'clock the rest of the mums and dads arrive to pick up their little darlings. Much to mine and Fiona's relief.

"Mummy, look what I won," Ella tells Leonie when she walks through the door with Charlie in her arms.

"Hi Becky," she says.

"Hi, how are you?" I ask. I haven't seen her since the day she told me James was her brother, not her husband.

"Good, thanks. And you? I hear things are going well with James."

264

"They are," I smile.

"I hope this one hasn't been too much trouble," she says, ruffling Ella's hair.

"Good as gold. A little artist too. Look what a great job she's made of her plate."

"That's wonderful darling," she tells her.

"I'll just go and say hello to Zack's mummy and then we'd better get you home for a bath," she laughs, surveying her paint-covered daughter.

A few minutes later she opens the door to leave but turns back towards us.

"Have you got a second, Becky," she asks. Oh no. She's going to tell me that she is his wife after all, that she just has a very strange sense of humour.

"Sure."

"I probably shouldn't say anything, but you know me…"

I want to say yes, but that would be rude, so I wait for her to carry on. I remember I'm still wearing my dinosaur party hat and I suddenly feel a little silly. But I leave it on.

"It's just that, well…"

I want to tell her to just spit it out. But that would also be rude. So I don't.

"You know men, they have these grand ideas, but they forget the finer details – the bits that are important to us women," she says.

Now I'm really nervous. She's going to tell me I'm not his only girlfriend. She's going to tell me that he's got another three on the go. He just forgot to tell me. It just slipped his mind.

"Listen – I didn't tell you this okay, but if James offers to take you shopping, make sure you pack your best knickers."

Erm?

I want to ask why I'd need to pack my best knickers for a trip to the shops, but I suspect she's already told me more than she

265

should, so I don't.

Any ideas?

It sounds like he's planning on taking me away for the night, doesn't it? But where? Somewhere where there are shops?

London? Unlikely. We both live in London. Unless the shopping is just an excuse for a night in a swanky hotel.

The south coast? Bournemouth? Brighton? Bognor Regis? I do hope he didn't take me too literally when I told him how much I loved the summers there as a child.

"Right. Okay," I tell Leonie.

"Remember – mum's the word," she says, putting her finger to her lips. "I didn't say a word!"

"Absolutely. Mum's the word. And thanks. I think!"

CHAPTER FIFTY FIVE

...love is the creator of our favourite memories and the foundation of our fondest dreams...

'Love's Hidden Treasure', Anonymous

You will never guess where I am.

Well you might, I suppose. But you probably won't.

Go on, guess. Guess where I am.

New York! Ha! Seriously!

Actually, right now I am on seat C, row 14 of a Boeing 747 somewhere over the Atlantic. But in less an hour I will be in New York.

I am soooooo excited.

It turns out that what I needed to pack my best knickers for was a weekend in New York. Not Brighton. Or Bournemouth. Or Bognor Regis.

James came over last night and asked if I wanted to go shopping at the weekend.

"Silly question," I told him, pulling the cork out of a bottle of wine, whilst mentally rifling through my underwear drawer for my 'best knickers.'

I don't do sexy underwear, if I'm honest. I'm more a comfy

Marks and Sparks pants girl really. Not the big granny ones – I'm not that bad – just the sort that are big enough to cover your bum at the very least.

I do own a couple of thongs, though personally I don't see the attraction in cutting yourself in half with a piece of cheese wire. But then it would be a very boring world if we all felt the same about cheese wire up our bums, now wouldn't it?

I have some very pretty pink silky knickers as well, but they tend only to come out on special occasions. Like Valentine's Day and…well actually just Valentine's Day.

I haven't bought any 'nice' underwear since I was with Alex. In fact, I think the set I own is one he bought me for Christmas last year. I think he was trying to tell me something. It was a good choice, to be fair. Some black lacy knickers from La Senza with a matching bra (padded – I'm not proud, I know where I need help – and so do my boyfriends).

Is it wrong to take underwear bought for me by one boyfriend on a weekend away with another, do you think? On second thoughts, don't answer that. I'll buy some new stuff in New York.

So, anyway…

"Yeah, shopping would be good," I told James. "I don't really know what I want to get Katie and Matt for a wedding present, so it would probably be a good idea to start looking."

"I thought we could go somewhere a bit different," he said.

"Where?" I asked. I was plumping for Brighton. More shops. Better night life – I was assuming the need for underwear indicated an overnight stay. And I love checking out the cakes in Choccywoccydoodah.

"It's a surprise," he said, grinning like the Cheshire Cat. "But we'll be leaving here at six thirty in the morning. Oh, and you'll need an overnight bag."

Six thirty?

It's wasn't Brighton then. With the slowest car in the world we'd still be sitting drinking McDonalds' tea for a good hour before the shops open.

It's ever so difficult packing an overnight bag when you don't know where you're going.

I pulled virtually every item of clothing I own from my wardrobe and flung it on my bed, hoping to be struck by inspiration.

I wasn't.

Jeans? Sparkly black trousers? Denim skirt? Jodhpurs?

Jodhpurs? God, I'd forgotten I even had them. I put them on my Christmas list four years ago after one horse-riding lesson. My parents predicted it would be a five-minute wonder, but I was adamant. I've never worn the bloody things.

I poked my head through my bedroom door at James. He was watching *Deal or No Deal*.

"Is it a jeans and t-shirt sort of place that we're going to or do I need to take something dressier?"

He just shrugged. As if he didn't know.

"Will we be indoors or outdoors?"

Maybe we were going to the Trafford shopping centre. Indoors, and far enough away to require an overnight stay.

"This guy's going to lose the lot if he opens any more boxes," he muttered at the television screen.

"Are we driving there or getting the train?"

"Do you fancy ordering pizza tonight?" he shouted through to me. "I haven't had pizza in ages."

An hour later I figured he only had himself to blame when I appeared from the bedroom with a suitcase big enough for a two-week skiing holiday in the French Alps.

"I had no choice," I told him, when his eyes nearly popped out of his head. "Without knowing where we are going I had to pack for every eventuality."

"What on earth have you got in there?"

"Oh, you know – just stuff," I said, trying to sound all mysterious. Two could play at that game.

"Well it looks heavy," he laughed. "I hope you're feeling strong."

He still wouldn't tell me when we got up in the morning. At five thirty.

Five thirty!

I'm not a morning person. I can't function until I have consumed at least three cups of tea. Preferably at nine o'clock, say, or ten.

"Are you going to tell me where we're going yet?" I asked him, splashing cold water on my face.

It's already hard enough convincing myself I'm not dreaming when I wake to see James lying next to me every morning. It's considerably harder at five thirty.

"Of course not, silly," he said, kissing me on the cheek and ruffling my hair.

What I want to know is how the hell he looks and sounds so wide-awake at five thirty. Make that five forty-five. Another forty five minutes of being kept in the dark.

At twenty-five past six his phone rang.

"Okay, we'll be down in thirty seconds," he told whoever it was on the other end.

"Ready?" he said – to me this time.

"Who was that?" I asked him.

"Dan," he said, as though it was the most normal thing in the world to be talking to his brother at twenty-five past six on a Saturday morning.

"Did I not tell you he was giving us a lift to the airport?"

"The airport?" I said, or rather shrieked, as he bundled me and my giant wheelie suitcase into the back of Dan's car.

"But I don't have my passport," I told him. And then I felt really silly. We were probably flying up to Manchester. Or Scotland. Or Leeds.

"No, but I do," he said. Smug so-and-so.

James' bag was small enough to carry on the plane with us (it is, after all, one of the inherent differences between men and women – men can travel light, women cannot – no matter where it is they are travelling to), so he checked my bag in as his own. That way I wouldn't be able to see where we were going. I had given up trying to break him down.

We sat in the departure lounge at Heathrow and as each and every flight was announced I watched him, waiting for him to stand up.

Edinburgh? Nothing.

Amsterdam? Nothing.

Prague? Nothing.

Madrid? Nothing. Ooh... no... he was just getting his wallet out of his bag. "Do you want a drink, B?"

And then, just after ten o'clock there was an announcement for passengers on flight BA0117 to New York to make their way to Gate 26.

James stood up.

He must be winding me up, I figured, so I stayed in my seat, looked at my magazine and said nothing.

He looked at me.

"Well you can stay here if you want to, but I'm off to New York!" he said with a big grin.

The captain has just turned on the seatbelt sign. We are on our way down.

I can't believe it. I can't believe James is taking me to New York.

I squeeze his arm in excitement and he leans over and kisses me.

"By the way, we're staying until Monday night," he tells me. "Don't worry about the café. Fiona is covering for you. And Caroline knows all about it. She said to tell you to have a great time."

"What did I do to deserve you?" I ask him, genuinely baffled.

"What did I do to deserve you?" he says.

"I asked first."

"You made me believe."

"In what?" I ask him.

"In love."

I have been to New York before. I came with Alex two years ago.

We saw the city from the top of the Empire State Building.

We took the ferry over to Liberty Island, climbed up the Statue of Liberty and looked out at the skyline through her crown.

We saw Times Square – by day and by night. We ate lunch at the Carnegie Deli, a New York landmark where the sandwiches are as big as your arm.

We visited Greenwich Village. And Little Italy. And SoHo.

And I remember thinking, 'this is not how I imagined it would be.' I don't think I meant being in New York. I think I meant being in New York with Alex.

I feel like Carrie Bradshaw, only not as glamorous, obviously. And I'm not a successful sex columnist (ask me again in six months – you never know). And my best friends don't include a nymphomaniac, a lawyer and a hopeless romantic. And I'm not on the side of a bus.

Okay, so I'm nothing like Carrie Bradshaw. But, hey, I'm in New York!

We are staying at the Hilton near Times Square. In room 2812.

On the 28th floor.

As James tips the bellboy I rush over to the window.

"Oh my god, I can see Central Park," I shriek.

The park is dotted with people baking in the June sun. Lying on the grass with friends, roller-blading, sitting side-by-side on park benches.

Alex and I came in the winter. We went ice-skating on the rink in Central Park. I was hopeless. I think Alex was embarrassed to be seen with me. He skated off at top speed, leaving me wobbling like a Weeble every time anyone so much as brushed past me.

Our room is fabulous. It has a king-size bed with crisp white linen and big fat feather pillows that look like they'd be great in a pillow-fight.

The bathroom is white too – with a marble sink and chrome fittings and thick fluffy white towels. And a bath that's definitely big enough for two.

"It's a good job I brought a lot of stuff," I tell James, unzipping my suitcase. "I need to look my best in New York! I could have taken you at your word and packed nothing but my toothbrush and a spare pair of knickers."

"That's impossible. No woman can ever go away anywhere without at least three changes of outfit. I knew you'd be okay."

"Oi, cheeky!"

After I have swapped my jeans and t-shirt for a pair of white cut-off trousers and a floral halter-neck top we take the lift down to the lobby and walk out into the sunshine.

Our first stop is Central Park. I want to sit on a park bench with James. I want to know what it feels like.

It feels good. It feels right. It feels like I've been doing it all my life.

"You okay?" he asks, as we eat sandwiches we picked up from

Starbucks and sip cans of lemonade through straws.

"I'm more than okay," I say.

"And this is what you want to do, is it?" he grins. "Sit here on a park bench, holding my hand?"

"Yes," I say. "I do."

And I could do this forever, I think to myself.

But of course, we're in New York. So we can't spend too long just sitting on a park bench.

"Let's go shop!" James says, tossing the sandwich wrappers and lemonade cans in the bin. He pulls his sunglasses down from his head and grabs my hand.

"If we must," I laugh.

I've never been big on designer labels, but hey, we're in New York, so I drag James to all the best shops. We don't buy anything, we just step inside, breathing in the scent of a different world, before rejoining the rest of the plebs on the city streets. Prada, Armani, Dolce & Gabbana, Manolo Blahnik – 'that's where Carrie buys her shoes,' I tell James, who pretends to be suitably impressed. We go into them all. We look. We touch. We do not buy.

I think I catch one of the sales assistants looking at us with the same disdain with which they look at Julia Roberts in *Pretty Woman* when she turns up with safety pins holding up her boots looking for a new frock.

I'd love to go back, my arms laden with bags, and tell them how they made a 'big mistake – huge'. Sadly the only bags I will be going back with so far are plastic carrier bags from CVS Pharmacy containing sun tan lotion, Twizzlers and souvenir pencils with yellow taxis on the end.

When we have seen everything we can't afford to buy we head to Bloomingdale's, where I buy a wedding card for Katie and Matt, just so I can have one of their 'little brown bags.' And then we go to Macy's – 'The World's Largest Department Store.'

I hold James' hand. If I let go I'm sure to lose him forever. I wouldn't want that. I think I love him.

There are a thousand floors. Okay, not a thousand, but a lot. I lead James straight to women's clothing.

He marvels at how easily a woman can get lost despite following a meticulously marked road map and yet can find the women's clothing section of any department store blindfolded.

"Charlotte did actually attempt to navigate her way around a department store blindfolded in *Sex & The City*," I tell him, with a little grin. "Carrie was supposed to be her guide, but she got distracted by the shoes."

Quite by chance we are right by the shoes as I share this little bit of trivia with him.

"I need some shoes to go with my bridesmaid dress," I tell James, picking up a pair of black knee-high boots.

"You're not thinking of wearing those, I hope?" he laughs. And then he frowns suddenly.

"Will I be coming to the wedding?" he asks me.

I didn't want to mention it. It's in September. I didn't want to scare him off by looking too far ahead.

"Do you want to come?" I say.

I think it would be the first wedding I have ever been to with a guy who isn't Alex.

"Do you want me to come?" He asks.

"I'd love you to come. If you don't mind spending half the day with my friends while I'm on bridesmaid duty, that is."

"In that case I'm going to need a new suit."

"This is just a ploy to get me away from the shoes and into the men's department, isn't it?" I laugh, putting the boot back on its perch.

275

"I can be crafty when I want to be," he grins, wrapping his arm round my waist and pulling me towards him.

It's getting dark when we leave Macy's an hour and a half later with five bags between us. A new suit and tie for James, a pair of shoes for me, toys and clothes for the kids and some silly souvenirs to take home.

On the way home we stop for dinner at a little Italian restaurant, with red and white chequered tablecloths and pictures of old fashioned pasta makers on the walls and a waiter who over-pronounces his s's. He brings us bread and olive oil and runs through the 'ssspecials' – 'sssspaghetti with oyssssters and mussscles, tagliatelli with ssspicy sssausssage and Ssscicilian pizza'.

I tear off a piece of bread and dip it in the olive oil. The waiter returns with our wine and pours a small amount in my glass.

I taste it and nod my approval, though I'd probably nod enthusiastically at any wine. I hope James isn't disappointed.

"Having fun?" he says.

"The best ever." I reach across the table for his hand, bring it to my lips, kiss it.

"I still can't believe you've brought me here. It must have cost you a fortune."

"You're worth it," he says. "And I can afford it. Business is booming! I should know – I'm the accountant!"

"How is Dan getting on with Fiona's sign?"

He bites off a piece of bread and chews it quickly.

"Great. He's been working on some designs. I think they're meeting this weekend to go through them."

"And?"

"And what?"

"What are they like? Tell me! What's the point in being your girlfriend if it doesn't get me a bit of inside info?"

276

"I couldn't possibly," he laughs. "I'm sworn to secrecy! Fiona's orders!"

"Ooh, the sly fox!"

I brush the breadcrumbs into a neat little mound in front of me and stifle a yawn.

James looks at his watch. "It's almost one o'clock in the morning at home. It's been a long day."

"It's been a fabulous day. I'm having such an amazing time."

"Well, I have one more surprise for you yet," he says.

He leans forward and takes his wallet out of his back pocket. He looks really pleased with himself.

He takes two tickets out and places them on the table.

Tickets for the *Sex & The City* tour.

"No way!" I shriek. The couple on the table next to us look over.

"No way!" I whisper. "You are just the best boyfriend in the world!"

"I do my best," he smiles.

It's just all too good to be true. I turn down a marriage proposal, leave my well-paid job and move from one end of the country to the other. I move in with my best friend, get a job where I get to be painted from top to toe every day for free and land a commission with what is currently one of the most popular magazines in the country. And then I just happen to stumble upon the best boyfriend in the world – who not only brings me to New York, to stay in a swanky hotel with fluffy white towels and chocolates on the pillows, but also buys me tickets for the *Sex & The City* tour.

As if.

I pinch myself. It hurts. And James is still sat opposite me, tucking into Ssspaghetti Carbonara.

Yes, it is true.

CHAPTER FIFTY SIX

"Are you ready for sex?"

No, this is not some strange proposition. It's our tour guide greeting us as we board the *Sex & The City* tour bus at 11 o'clock the following morning.

We only just make it. We overslept this morning. We both woke up at nine o'clock English time – five o'clock New York time. We were wide-awake, but it was too early to get up. This wasn't a problem, if you catch my drift. But we were pretty tired by the time we fell asleep again an hour later. And then we didn't wake up until 10:07. This gave us precisely fifty three minutes to shower, dress, wolf down a bagel with cream cheese and a glass of freshly squeezed orange juice then make our way to the On Location Tours tour bus (and fit in another quickie before the shower if I'm being completely honest.)

Our tour guide is Stephanie Borowsky, an aspiring actress funding acting classes with daily three-hour stints on tour buses, sharing Magnolia Bakery cupcakes and Cosmopolitans with maniacs like me who believe that Carrie Bradshaw is a real person – that she really does live in New York, really is on the side of a bus, and really does love a guy called Mr Big...

"I am your sexpert," she grins, from the front of the bus.

I link my arm through James'. He'd probably rather stick pins in his eyes than be sat on this bus with a bunch of *Sex & The City* fans. The fact that he's here despite that makes me love him even more than I think I already might.

"You will be getting off... the bus," Stephanie continues, with a dirty laugh.

I think she's going to be fun. She looks a bit like Carrie actually. She's tiny, with blonde hair tied back in a loose ponytail. Little dress. High heels.

She ticks us all off her list and signals to the driver to get going, telling us as he pulls away that if we look out of the window to our right we will see the Plaza Hotel, where Carrie asks Mr Big why she wasn't 'the one.' Series three, episode three (yes, I know, it's tragic.)

As Stephanie plays a clip on the television that hangs from the roof of the bus it occurs to me that all this time I have been asking the same question that every girl wants the answer to.

"Now, who can tell us one of the bloopers in the opening credits," she says, not expecting any takers, I'm sure.

She's met her match though. Before I can stop myself my hand shoots into the air. Just call me teacher's pet.

"The people on the bus," I shout out.

She looks impressed. So does James. Not that he has a clue what we're talking about.

Just so that the rest of the class can catch up she plays us the clip.

"Watch the people in the bus," she instructs, hitting pause so she can point them out.

Thirty-six pairs of eyes are glued to the television, watching as the people on the bus which splashes Carrie in her pink tutu, disappear in the last few seconds of the credits and it becomes an empty bus.

Stephanie explains how when the programme was launched nobody in the cutting room spotted the mistake.

"It appears in every single episode ever made," she says.

James looks at me and grins. It's hard to tell what he's thinking. Either he's just realised how sad his girlfriend really is, or he's marvelling at my expert observation skills. I'd like to think it's the latter. I am, however, realistic.

We are on our way to the shop where the girls took Charlotte to buy her 'rabbit,' Stephanie tells us. We will be able to get off, apparently, and examine the merchandise.

"For those of you in any doubt, it is *not* a pet shop," she adds with a big grin.

"It's a sex shop," I whisper to James.

"I know," he whispers back and I feel a bit silly.

A few minutes later all thirty six of us pour into The Pleasure Chest. It's only a small shop so it's a bit of a squeeze. The manager looks up from his magazine and nods hello. He's not phased. Twice a day, every day, he has a busload of people pour into his shop, marvel at the size of the vibrators that fill the shelves, take a few photographs and pour back out again. He must get something out of it, I guess, but there doesn't seem to be too many people keen on taking a rabbit back onto the bus with them.

"Do you want to get something?" James whispers in my ear. His breath tickles my neck and I wriggle away from him and laugh.

"Do you?" I whisper back.

"I asked first."

I'm not sure what to say. I'm not sure he's being serious. But then again...

"How about some of this?" I ask, picking up a jar of chocolate body paint.

He licks his lips and raises an eyebrow. "Delicious."

Twenty minutes later I am licking my own lips, which are covered in the frosting of a vanilla cup cake from the Magnolia Bakery where

280

Carrie told Miranda she had a new crush – this time on Aidan.

We are round the corner from Carrie's apartment. It turns out she doesn't live on West 73rd Street, after all. She lives on 9th Avenue and 14th Street. At least, that's where the filming is done. Whatever…

Finishing off our cupcakes as we walk, we all follow Stephanie to the apartment where we queue up to have our picture taken on Carrie's stoop.

"Are you enjoying this?" I ask James as we wait for our turn.

"Absolutely!" he laughs, kissing a bit of frosting off my lips.

We reach the front of the queue and I hand Stephanie my camera on our way up the steps.

The real resident of this apartment (it isn't actually Carrie Bradshaw, you know!) must get sick and tired of people queuing up to have their picture taken on her apartment steps. Thirty-odd *Sex & The City* fans, a couple of mums and a spattering of boyfriends, twice a day, seven days a week. I think I'd go nuts.

It's ridiculous really. I'm standing on a pavement in New York, looking up at a bunch of ordinary concrete steps, which lead up to an ordinary front door. Another thirty four people are doing exactly the same thing. And we are all thinking 'wow, that's Carrie's front door'.

But Carrie doesn't even exist. She is not real. So are we not the saddest bunch of individuals on the planet?

The next stop is SCOUT – Steve and Aidan's bar – where we wash down our cupcakes with Cosmopolitans. The staff at Onieals Speakeasy (I am disappointed to discover the bar isn't really named after Steve's dog) are ready for us – with thirty six pink drinks in cocktail glasses lined up on the bar. James and I have a second one each and are feeling a little bit squiffy when we get back on the bus for the rest of the tour.

As we continue to weave our way through the streets of New

York City Stephanie points out dozens of locations from the series: Aidan's furniture shop, The Little Church Around the Corner where Samantha set her sights on Friar Fuck, the ABC Carpet and Home Store where Charlotte and Trey bought their new bed, The Cowgirl Hall of Fame, where Carrie and Miranda bumped into Steve and Aidan with their new girlfriends…

A debate follows. Mr Big fans versus Aidan fans.

We take a vote and the Mr Bigs have it hands down. My own hand is amongst them. Don't get me wrong, I am a huge Aidan fan, and I will never truly understand how she could ever let him go. But you see, Mr Big is her Mr Right. And that's the point. Why is he? We don't know. He just is.

"What's so special about Aidan anyway?" James asks as we leave the bus at the end of the tour. "Didn't she have lots of other boyfriends?"

"Oh, you know, he was just lovely," I say.

I want to tell him that he reminds me a bit of Aidan. Because he's tall, and incredibly sexy. Because he's kind, and loving, and reliable.

But I don't, because I realise he actually reminds me more of Mr Big. Why? Because he might just be Mr Right. Why? I don't know why.

We spend the rest of the day sightseeing. We go up the Empire State Building and laugh at how the yellow taxis far below us look like toy cars. We go to Times Square and ask a stranger to take a picture of the two of us. We find the best ice cream shop in the world – Cold Stone Creamery – where you pick a flavour and select your fillings and they mix it up for you on cold stone. Or you can choose one of their own concoctions. There are three sizes – 'like it,' 'love it,' 'gotta have it.' I have the Caramel Turtle

Temptation – sweet cream ice cream, pecans, fudge and caramel. James has the Mud Pie Mojo – coffee ice cream with Oreos, peanut butter, roasted almonds, fudge and whipped topping. Our eyes are bigger than our bellies and we both order 'gotta have its.' So it's no surprise when we feel sick on the ferry over to the Statue of Liberty where I buy James a foam crown and make him wear it for a photograph in front of the statue. He looks adorable. And I realise that yes, I do love him.

It's evening by the time we get back to the hotel.

Waiting for the lift James strokes the back of my neck and I shiver. Inside he presses the button for our floor and then kisses me, pinning me to the wall by my hands.

I don't want to go home. I want to stay here forever.

We reach our floor and I can barely move, I'm aching for him so badly.

Back in our room James slips my bag off my shoulder and tosses it on the bed.

He kisses me softly, his lips barely touching mine and tugs gently at the ribbon securing my top around my neck. It falls to my waist and he pushes me towards the wall with his body. I can feel him harden against me.

I lift my arms up and he slides my top up over my head, dropping it to the floor. He says nothing, but his eyes never leave mine. I don't think I have ever wanted someone so badly. Or needed them. He unbuttons his own shirt and I slip my hands inside to slide it off his back.

I tug at his belt. I want to feel him inside me.

I wrap my arms around his neck and pull his face towards mine. And as I kiss him hard on the mouth his hands move down to where I want them. Where I need them.

I want this night to last forever.

I think *this* is how it feels to have found Mr Right.

James is like the missing piece of my jigsaw puzzle. When he makes love to me I lose myself in him. I don't know where I am, what day it is, whether it's night or day. All I know is that I'm where everything is right.

"Are you okay?" he asks softly as he moves inside me against the crisp white sheets, our clothes abandoned across the room with the unopened jar of chocolate body paint. Turns out we didn't need it. We just needed each other.

"Yes," I whisper, the words barely audible, my arms holding him tight against me, scared to let go, scared no moment will ever compare to this one.

I have to tell him.

He has to know.

"I have a present for you," he says, later, tracing the curves of my body as we lie naked on top of the duvet, the air conditioning battling against a hot summer's evening.

"You just gave me one," I smile.

He grins. "Yeah, well, you deserve another one."

"What is it?"

He slips off the bed and I watch him pad across the room.

He returns with a small Macy's bag, lies down next to me on the bed and hands it to me.

There's a box inside. A small box.

I take it out and look at him.

"It's not a ring," he laughs nervously.

He's right, it isn't a ring. It's earrings. And I'm no expert, but they look like diamonds.

"They're beautiful," I say.

"You're beautiful. Becky, I…"

"Wait!" I say, panicking.

He looks hurt.

"There's something I have to tell you," I say.

He sits up on the bed. "What?"

"I lied to you," I tell him. I'm scared, but I have to tell him.

"About what?"

"When I said I hadn't heard from any magazines yet, I lied. I have. I got a commission from one a couple of months ago. Before I met you."

"But that's great. Why would you lie about that?"

I look down at the earrings in my hand.

"Why would you not tell me something like that?" he asks again.

"Because of what it is I'm writing about. I didn't want it to scare you off."

"What is it? How to lose a guy in ten days?" he laughs. "Because I have to tell you, you're not doing very well!"

I smile at him. "No."

"Well? It can't be that bad, whatever it is."

"It's 'How do you know you've found Mr Right?'"

He doesn't say anything. He just looks at me.

He's probably planning his escape. He travelled lightly – he could pack his bags while I'm on the loo. A taxi to the airport. A seat on the next flight home.

I shouldn't have said anything. It's too soon.

It feels like hours before he finally says something. It's a question.

"And have you found him yet?"

"Yes," I say, because I'm guessing the damage is already done, and I've got nothing left to lose.

"Well that makes what *I* was about to tell *you* much easier," he says.

"And what's that?" I ask.

"I love you."

"Just out of interest," James asks an hour later, after we have made a significant dent in the chocolate body paint.

"How *do* you know?"

I dip the flannel into the bath water and squeeze it out over him (well, there's only so much chocolate you can lick off a person...)

"Honestly? I don't know how," I tell him. "I just know."

CHAPTER FIFTY SEVEN

I consider phoning Jennifer Dutton. Telling her that it *is* indefinable after all. That my friends were right. That you do 'just know'. That James isn't my Mr Right because of how he makes my stomach flip over every time I see him, or because he can make me laugh without even trying, or because he's the first guy I have ever truly been myself with. That it's not because of his cute dimple, or the way his hair stands on end when he wakes up in the morning, or the way he touches my face when he kisses me like it's the most precious thing in the world and he's afraid he might break it.

It's none of those things and yet all of them.

But if you do 'just know', then that's still an answer isn't it? It's not the one I was expecting of course, but it is an answer.

CHAPTER FIFTY EIGHT

The problem with finding Mr Right, I'm finding, is that it leaves no time for writing about him.

Since we have been back from New York I have been busy every weekend.

First there was the weekend in Brighton, when James met my parents. And Johnny and Sarah, and Jacob. I didn't need to worry about them liking him. What with Johnny entertaining him with embarrassing childhoods stories about me, Jacob immediately holding his arms out for a cuddle (which was more than I got, the traitor,) and my mum making roast beef for the first time in about three years in his honour, it was like the bloody James Newman Appreciation Society.

He was nervous though, which surprised me.

"Are you always this nervous when you meet a girlfriend's family?" I asked him on the way there.

"You make me sound like a serial dater," he said. "How many girlfriends' families do you think I've met?"

"Ooh thousands, probably!" I said.

But he hadn't. He'd only met the families of two girlfriends. Hannah – his very first girlfriend, and Rachel – his girlfriend from the age of twenty five to twenty eight. They split up because she wanted to get married and have children, and he didn't. Not then.

"It's a big thing, meeting a girlfriend's family," he said. "It's the thing that often means the most to them. It means you've become part of their family in a way. Hannah and Rachel were the only girlfriends I loved enough to want that. And now you."

Then there was the weekend in Watford when I met his dad and Grace. Judging by their reaction to me, he doesn't introduce his girlfriends to them very often either. I felt like a rare specimen indeed. Not that it wasn't lovely to meet them. But I did feel a bit like I was on an interview.

"Where do you live?"

"Where do you come from?"

"Where do you work?"

"What do you do?"

"Do you have any brothers and sisters?"

"How long have you and James been seeing each other?"

"What's your shoe size?"

They didn't really ask me that last question. They might as well have done, though.

"Sorry," James said to me on the way home. "They're not used to meeting my girlfriends!"

"You don't say! I thought they were going to pinch me at one point to make sure I was real!"

"I feel like doing that myself sometimes," James laughed.

And then there was the weekend when I met his friends – when I walked into the pub and found six pairs of eyes all staring up at me expectantly.

"Everybody, this is Becky," James announced, standing up and kissing me on the cheek.

"Becky, this is everybody."

'Everybody' included his brother Dan and his wife Christina, his friend Simon and his girlfriend Anna, and his friend Gary and his girlfriend Beth.

Simon and Gary both went to school with James.

After just a couple of beers they attempted to embarrass him with tales of fashion disasters, romantic mishaps and drunken debauchery.

It was great fun.

"Has he told you about the time he was caught cheating in his history exam?" Simon asked me, getting up to get the drinks in.

"No," I said, grinning at James.

"He had all the answers written on the inside of his arms in secret code. He claimed they were henna tattoos he got on holiday in Rhodes. He was made to stand at the front of the room until the end of the exam, with his sleeves rolled up and his arms in the air."

"They were tattoos!" James protested. "Don't believe a word of it Becky."

"Oh, I will," I said, putting my hand over his mouth.

"So James tells us you want to be a journalist," Anna said.

"Yes. I've just got my first commission," I told them.

James was under strict instructions not to tell them what it was. By the lack of sarcasm that follows I decided he'd kept his word.

"What's it about?" Christina asked.

"You'll have to buy a copy of the magazine in September if you want to know," James said, coming to my rescue. He squeezed my thigh affectionately.

"Which magazine?"

"*Love Life*," I told them proudly.

"Wow! Brilliant! I love that magazine," Anna said. "I'll look out for your name in it! Are you doing anything else in the meantime?"

"I work at Potty Wotty Doodah," I told them. Most of them looked completely bemused.

"It's a ceramics café in Clapham. That's where I met James."

"She thought Leonie was James' wife," Dan said, embarrassing me.

"*And* she was jealous," James added, with a wink.

"Thank you James," I said. And everyone laughed.

So anyway, after all this socialising, I have finally found a bit of time in which to do some work.

I start by transcribing all the interviews that I recorded on my Dictaphone. It takes me hours. I really must learn how to write in shorthand.

I've been through all the letters sent to me from the magazine, separating the pass-the-bucket mush from the ones that are actually worth using – like the one from a girl who got back together with her childhood sweetheart seventeen years after they first dated. "Everyone said we were perfect for each other, we just met when we were too young," she wrote, "so when fate brought us back together seventeen years later, we knew it was meant to be".

I have also borrowed a stack of psychology books from the library. And a book of quotations with a useful section on love.

And now I simply can't put it off any longer. I have a deadline to meet, after all.

James is under strict instructions not to come round until at least 9pm. He knows I have no willpower. He knows I can't resist him.

I look at my watch. It's 7pm. I have at least two hours before he gets here. I could write a lot in two hours.

I turn my laptop on and stare at the empty screen in front of me, wondering how to fill it.

I consult the notes I made in Sheila's writing class.

"Introductions – lots of types. Description, question, quotation…Up to you to find out what works best…"

Hmm. I guess I could start with a question. That is what it's all about, after all.

I start typing.

My boyfriend has got lovely brown eyes that I could look into all day long. My boyfriend has a cute dimple in his right cheek and a tiny scar above his left eye where he fought over a crook-lock with his brother when he was just a boy. My boyfriend makes me laugh – even when I feel like crying.

Is this why he is Mr Right?

No.

I feel like I'm back at university, hunched over a dimly-lit desk at 3am, attempting to write a 4,000-word essay six hours before the deadline. Except it felt like hell back then. And this is fun. I feel Like Carrie Bradshaw, tapping away at her laptop building up to the big question – the point where the camera always zooms in on the cursor.

Although, it seems to come much more easily to Carrie, while I have already re-written the first paragraph seven times and I'm still not happy with it.

I decide to move on and come back to it later.

I work my way through each interview, incorporating the best bits, leaving out the rubbish bits, and highlighting all the in-between bits – just in case I am a few words short, or a few hundred...

It's amazing how the words start flowing once you've started. I'm not sure where it's all coming from, but by the time James arrives I have written. I check the word count on the laptop...two hundred and forty three words.

Two hundred and forty three?!

Bollocks.

I thought I'd written at least a thousand.

Two hundred and forty three out of two thousand. That leaves...

Bollocks.

James brings Chinese takeaway and a bottle of wine with him.

292

I wolf down sweet and sour chicken with egg-fried rice and go back to my laptop, glass of wine in hand. No time to waste. James doesn't mind. He watches telly and makes me cups of tea. I'll put that in the feature. *Mr Right will make you cups of tea when you are too busy to make them for yourself.*

"Can I read it?" he asks me, putting the mug down on the coffee table and leaning over to sneak a look.

I fold the lid down so he can't see it.

"Not yet. Maybe when it's finished."

"When will that be?"

"God knows. I'm barely past the first paragraph!"

"How long have you got to write it?"

"It has to be with the editor by August."

"That's loads of time," he laughs.

"Not when you're doing it for the first time, it isn't."

"Still – it's enough time to take a break," he says, brushing my hair away from my neck and kissing me.

"I guess so," I say, not at all reluctantly.

CHAPTER FIFTY NINE

Today is a fun day. Today Katie and I get to be prodded and poked again.

Today is dress-fitting day.

We meet Emma at *All Things Bride & Beautiful*. She's in a good mood. She's met a new man. He's called Daniel. She met him in a Spanish class she's started.

He's a solicitor. Thirty-two. They've been out on three dates. So far so good. He's meeting us for a drink later. Even better.

"I really like him," she says, as we enter the shop.

"Hello girls," Pippa says, meeting us in the waiting room. "And how are we all?"

"Fine," we say in unison, Emma ever so slightly more enthusiastically, I note with delight.

"So how was New York?" she asks me as Katie disappears behind the curtain with Pippa.

"It was amazing," I say.

"Brilliant. And when do I get to meet the elusive James? I'm beginning to think you've made him up!"

"He might join us tonight actually," I say. "You need to meet him because I'm relying on you to look after him at the wedding while I'm running around after the bride."

"Too right," Katie says, drawing the curtain back.

"Oh Katie, it looks fantastic," Emma says.

"Really?"

"Yes. It's even better now it's the proper size."

"Have you lost weight?" Pippa asks. "I'm sure it was a 12 you tried on but it seems a little loose." She tugs at the dress and Katie's boobs very nearly pop out.

"I don't think I have. Is it a problem?"

"No, we can take it in. The question is are you likely to lose more weight before the wedding, or put it back on?"

"What do you think girls?" Katie says, looking at Emma and me.

"Well, if there was any justice in the world, you'd put three stone on, the amount you eat, but I'm sure you won't," I tell her. "You'll probably stay the same, I'd say."

"I agree," Emma says. "I'd have it taken in a bit. You don't want it falling down while you're saying your vows, do you?"

"Is that okay?" Katie asks Pippa.

"Of course."

While Pippa starts sticking pins in our friend, Emma and I hand her a variety of veils and tiaras to try on.

She's got her back to the mirror, which means we can put all sorts of hideous contraptions on her head and convince her they look fabulous. We settle on an elaborate crown affair. It makes me think of James and his foam crown at the Statue of Liberty and I start laughing.

Pippa pretends to look disapprovingly at us and, when she's finished pinning, lets Katie loose to find her reflection.

The look of horror on her face says it all.

"Are you feeling very Statue of Liberty?" Pippa asks with a little chuckle. And I laugh again.

"How does that feel, love?" she asks, tugging at the dress again. It stays put this time. And so do Katie's boobs.

"Perfect."

"You'll need to come back in a week or so to try it on again. You can make an appointment downstairs."

I'd like to say we have the same problem with my dress when we arrive at *Bridesmaid Revisited* for my fitting. Alas, we don't. It fits perfectly. Except around the boobs, obviously, which, as promised, is rectified with a super-dooper-extra-padding-for-girls-with-no-boobs bra.

I don't tell the girls, but I feel like a princess. And for a brief moment I imagine what it would be like to be going through all this as the bride, not the bridesmaid. If I were marrying James…

I think it would be just lovely.

CHAPTER SIXTY

Love cannot be defined in one single term,
It cannot be taught and cannot be measured.
...
You cannot help who you love,
Nor can you make one love another.

'Love', Reddy Fox

We deserve a drink after all that prodding and poking, we've decided. Not that we need an excuse. Fiona is joining us. I told her she needed a night out. She's been working so hard for the shop opening she hasn't been out in weeks.

Matt is away at a stag do so we're all staying with Katie.

We're already quite merry by the time Fi arrives at nine o'clock – thanks to the glass of wine we had on our way home (okay, two) and the three quarters of a bottle we had with our dinner (spaghetti bolognaise with garlic bread – good job none of us are on the pull.)

I slosh the rest of the bottle into a glass for Fiona and thrust it into her hand as she walks through the door, urging her to catch us up. I'm a bad person. I encourage my friends to drink. Quickly. She does what I tell her – good girl – and then we all pile into a taxi.

"Evening ladies," the driver says. It's probably the only time this evening that we'll be worthy of such a title, I imagine. A few glasses of wine followed by several spirits and finished off with a couple of shots, doesn't generally give rise to particularly lady-like behaviour, I find.

"Evening," we all chime in unison.

"Where to?"

"Tiger Tiger," I say, as Emma lets out a little growl. See what I mean?

"What time is it?" Emma asks as we tumble out of the taxi the other end and join the queue to get into the club.

I look at my watch.

"Ten o'clock."

"What time did you say you'd meet him?" Fiona asks.

We are meeting Emma's new chap tonight.

"He said he'd phone me when he gets here. Ooh, ooh, that could be him," she says, grabbing her phone which is playing 'Is This The Way to Amarillo'. A couple of guys in the queue snigger. I glare at them. So does Katie. And Fiona. (Not Emma, who's too busy whispering sweet nothings down the phone.)

We are on the verge of an out-staring victory when Emma snaps her phone shut dramatically.

"He'll be here in twenty minutes," she says, beaming.

He's started well. He's brought us all drinks. Doubles too. He gets my vote.

"What do you think?" Emma mouths at us as he collects his change at the bar.

We quickly give her the thumbs up before he turns around.

He's cute. Actually, he's very cute. He looks a bit like Jude Law, only a bit shorter. And he's got great dress sense. I think that's a

298

Paul Smith shirt he's wearing. And he's showing an interest in her friends, which is always a good sign.

"Emma tells me you're getting married Katie – congratulations," he says, and "Emma tells me you're opening your own shop Fiona – that must be exciting," and "Emma tells me you're writing a feature for a magazine Becky." Actually, he doesn't say that – he says "Emma tells me you two grew up together Becky – that you used to pretend you were roller-booting champions and made paperweights out of pebbles". Yeah. Thanks, Em.

He'll probably be glad when James gets here and evens things up a bit. I think he's a bit overwhelmed by all the boob tubes and glitter.

He casually slips his arm around Emma's waist and we all drink our drinks.

And then it all goes downhill.

Very downhill.

After dropping our jackets off at the cloakroom we head back to the bar for another round of drinks.

Fiona spots a friend and goes over to say hello. And Emma goes off to the loo, leaving Daniel with Katie and I.

"We should dance," I say, waving my glass at them in time to Club Tropicana.

"Great idea," Katie says. "You up for a dance Danny?"

He laughs. Poor guy – he probably hates Wham. And being called Danny, for that matter.

"Sure."

"That's seddled then," Katie slurs. "As soon as Emma and Fi get back we'll hit the dance floor."

But when Emma gets back she's not really in the mood for a boogie. She's verging on hysterical, actually.

She grabs my arm – very nearly pulling it out of its socket, I might add – and drags me away from the bar. She obviously doesn't want Daniel to hear.

"He's here," she whispers, evidently panic-stricken.

"Who's here?" I ask, sipping my vodka and tonic.

"Jim!" she says, as if I've just asked a really stupid question.

"Where?" I ask, swinging around for a look and nearly falling over, which was a bit pointless anyway given that I have absolutely no idea what he looks like.

"I just saw him going into the men's toilets."

"Did you speak to him?"

"No. He didn't see me. Oh, B, what am I going to do?"

"Do you want to go somewhere else?" I ask.

"Yes. No. I mean don't know. I want to see him. But I don't want to see him. If you know what I mean."

"Maybe we *should* go somewhere else," I say, glancing over at Daniel, who is understandably wondering what the hell is going on.

"No, no, I'll be fine," she says, taking my glass and finishing my drink for me. She gives me back the empty glass. How kind.

"Are you sure?"

"Yes."

I'm not convinced.

"No," she says, changing her mind as two big fat tears wobble just inside her eyes for a moment before spilling out onto her cheeks – first one, and then the other.

She wipes them away with the back of her hand as I pull her just a little further away from the others. It's never a good thing for your new man to see you crying over your old one.

"We're just going to the loos," I shout over to Katie and Daniel, in my brightest nothing-to-worry-about-everything-in-the-garden-is-rosy voice. They don't look in the least bit convinced.

So, where is the toilet woman when you actually need her?

Just when we could really do with a face cloth and a blob of foundation, she's nowhere to be seen. Not to mention some mascara to replace the remnants that are currently rolling down Emma's face.

"You really must invest in some waterproof mascara," I tell her, dabbing at the black smudges under her eyes with a bit of soggy toilet paper.

"Am I getting on your nerves?" she sobs.

"Don't be silly. I just want you to be happy. And I think you are. You've got a really great guy waiting for you out there – who's probably wondering what the hell is going on. He was even willing to dance to Club Tropicana!"

She laughs at this.

"You're just drunk," I say, rubbing at a stubborn blob of mascara that's welded itself to her cheek. "If you were sober you'd probably have walked up to Jim, said hello, and asked how he was."

"I wouldn't."

"Well, no, maybe that was a bit optimistic. But I don't think you'd have got quite so upset. You've been so much happier lately. And now you've met Daniel. He seems lovely. And he's very cute," I add, raising my eyebrows. "Good catch! Although…"

"What?"

"I do wish you'd stop telling your new boyfriends that we pretended we were roller-booting champions and that we gave our Girls Worlds mohicans. It's not really the first impression I want them to have of me!"

She laughs and then turns to look in the mirror.

"God, I look a mess."

"Nothing a quick comb and a bit of lippy won't fix."

"You go," she says, rummaging in her handbag for her lipstick. "I'll be fine. Tell them I feel sick or something. Blame Katie's

301

cooking."

"She'll love that," I laugh, giving her a quick hug before leaving her to it.

When I get back to the bar James has arrived and is talking to Daniel, Katie and Fiona.

I sneak up behind him and wrap my arms around his waist. He turns round, grins and kisses me on the lips. He tastes of lager.

"Hello you," he says. "Do you want a drink?"

"Ooh yes please. A vodka and tonic would be lovely. Emma finished off my last one!"

Katie looks at me and I nod. Translation: Is she okay? Yes, she's fine, she's just sorting her face out.

"Where is she?" James asks.

"She's just in the ladies. She'll be out in a minute. Dicky tummy," I add. "Must have been Katie's spaghetti bolognaise," I laugh, looking at Katie, who scowls at me, because she knows she can't argue.

James gets my drink – and one for everyone else – and then I spot Emma across the bar on her way back over. I wave at her and slide my arm around James. I can't wait to introduce him to her.

But I don't get the chance. Seconds later Emma slaps me across the face. Hard.

"You bitch," she spits.

I'm not sure who's more shocked – Emma that she can slap so hard, or me that I've been slapped at all.

I've never been slapped before. It hurts.

Remember how your mother used to pull your pants down and smack you on the backside when you were really naughty? (I'm assuming I'm not alone here – sometimes in the middle of the supermarket if I was being particularly bad.) Well, imagine that, on your face. It's sharp. It stings. And it hurts that little bit more when you're not expecting it. When you don't know what

302

the hell you've done to deserve it.

Katie rushes forward and grabs Emma to stop her coming in for an encore, while I clutch my cheek, open-mouthed.

Daniel looks horrified. Fiona looks as confused as me. James has his head in his hands...

A crowd quickly forms, people clutching their drinks looking over in our direction. They want to know what's going on. So do I.

A couple of lads in the corner are clearly hoping for a catfight. I'm assuming they won't be getting one.

"What the..." is all I manage before I'm drowned out by Emma.

"How could you do this to me?" she screams.

Do what?

"You're supposed to be my best friend."

What the hell is she on about?

"You had someone who loved you. You had Alex. Why did you have to have Jim?"

"What?"

Jim?

Oh God.

It's Jim.

James – is *Jim*.

CHAPTER SIXTY ONE

"You don't honestly believe I would do that to you Em?" I say. I think I'm almost laughing, despite myself. She can't possibly think that. Can she?

"I had no idea that James was Jim. How could I? He and I met months after you two split up. And I'd never met him before. I'd never even seen any photos of him."

James goes to say something – to confirm what I'm saying, presumably – but Katie holds him back.

"That's rubbish," Emma shouts. "I talked about him all the time. Christ, he was the first person I *did* talk about all the time. I loved him."

At this point Daniel decides he's heard enough. He quietly puts his glass down and slides away from the bar. I think we can safely say we won't be seeing him again in a hurry.

Emma doesn't even try to stop him. She has bigger things to deal with right now.

"You must have seen photos," she continues – trying to convince herself as well as me, perhaps. "You must have known it was him."

"I never saw any photos Emma. You never showed us any – me or Katie." I look at Katie for confirmation, which I get.

"We knew very little about him full stop, other than that you really liked him. But that was no different to anybody else you'd been out with, to be fair. I swear to you Em, I didn't know."

We're both crying now.

"I don't believe you," Emma says. "You just thought you'd have him for yourself. You dumped Alex and moved to London and then you thought, 'I know, Emma's Jim is available. He'll do. I'll have him.'"

I stare at her, stunned.

"Emma, how could you think that? You're my best friend. I've known you my whole life. I would never set out to hurt you deliberately. You know that. You *must* know that," I add, when it's clear she doesn't appear to.

"You're not my friend," she says, angrily brushing the tears from her face with her hand. "A friend would never do this. Never."

I look around the bar. Is anyone going to help me out here, I wonder?

"She didn't know, Emma," Katie says softly. She's holding James' arm. He looks like I feel. He looks crushed. He looks like his whole world has just come crashing down around him. He had no idea, I know that. I know him. He's honest and kind. He would never deliberately hurt someone.

I look at Emma and silently plead with her to believe me. But instead she just looks away. She can't even look at me now. We've been friends our whole lives and she can't even look at me.

I look down and realise I'm still holding my drink. I down it in one before tossing the empty glass on the bar and looking at Jim. James. My James. My Mr Right.

He looks so sad. He wants to come to me, but Katie stops him. It's the right thing to do. She knows how I'm feeling. She knows because Emma is her friend too. And she wouldn't want to make that choice either.

I look at Emma and shake my head, defeated. She doesn't even look up.

"I didn't know, Em," I say. And then I turn and walk away.

CHAPTER SIXTY TWO

The fountains mingle with the river
And the rivers with the ocean,
The winds of heaven mix for ever
With a sweet emotion;
Nothing in the world is single.
All things by a law divine
In one spirit meet and mingle –
Why not I with thine?

'Love's Philosophy', Percy Bysshe Shelley

"James is on the phone," Fiona says, removing a cold cup of tea from my bedside table and replacing it with a fresh one.

It's the third time he's called. The third mug of tea gone cold. Such a waste of tea. Such a waste of a great boyfriend.

My eyes feel like I've been in ten rounds with Mike Tyson. Or Frank Bruno. Who was the better boxer?

No, she didn't punch me – not that I'm sure she wouldn't have done if I'd hung around long enough. But it only takes a few minutes of crying to make your eyes puff up like a frog's. Imagine what a whole night of it can do.

Poor Fiona was on tissue duty last night. There are still a few soggy ones on the floor by my bed where she couldn't keep up.

She followed me out of the club and we caught a taxi back to my flat. She must have drawn the short straw. Although, I guess Katie's straw was pretty short too – having had to console Emma for the night.

I didn't say anything on the way home. I just cried. And they weren't quiet, controlled tears – the sort that slide gently down your cheeks into a waiting handy-sized four-ply pocket Kleenex, barely noticed by your friends and anyone else who happens to be in the vicinity. No, they were the emotional equivalent of a loud guffaw, you might say – sobs that lurch out of you like giant hiccups. At one point I expected the taxi driver to turn around and attempt to make me jump.

But at least the stinging in my eyes has replaced the stinging on my cheek. When I looked in the mirror last night I had a big handprint on my face. I hope it's gone. I'm not sure how I'd explain it to the kids at Potty Wotty Doodah tomorrow. I spend half my time telling them to draw on the pottery, not each other. One argument in a night club and I could have undone all my good work.

"Tell him I'm out," I say to Fiona.

"He knows you're not."

"Then just tell him I can't talk to him." I pull the duvet over my head before she tries to talk me round.

She leaves the room to deliver the news and returns a few minutes later with a plate of toast to go with my tea.

Why do we always try to feed people in times of distress when they couldn't possibly feel less like eating?

"Why won't you speak to him, Becky?" she asks, sitting on the edge of my bed and pulling the duvet off my head.

"I can't, Fi. You heard Emma. She thinks I deliberately set out to steal him. If I see James I'll lose her."

307

"And if you don't, you'll lose *him*. Is that what you want?"

"No. I can't bear the thought of losing him. But I can't have both, can I? Emma will never speak to me again if I stay with James, Fi. She loved him. She probably still does. I think he was the first guy she's *ever* loved."

"But you didn't know it was him. You never set out to hurt her."

"That doesn't matter. As far as Emma's concerned, her best friend is with her ex-boyfriend. And she's hurting. She won't understand if I stay with James."

I sit up and pull my knees up to my chest, wrapping my arms around them. If I make myself really small, maybe all this will just disappear.

"But you shouldn't have to choose. Do you really want to be friends with someone who would make you choose?"

"It isn't that simple, Fi. Emma and I have been friends our whole lives. She means a lot to me."

"But so does James."

"I'll meet someone else. There are plenty of other guys out there."

"But you said he was the one. You said he was Mr Right."

"I know I did. And he was. But he isn't anymore. He can't be."

Fiona stays with me all day. She must be a glutton for punishment.

Katie phones in the afternoon. I make Fiona tell her I'm asleep. When she phones again an hour later, I make her say I'm still asleep.

"Your friends are going to think I'm keeping you hostage," Fiona says, after telling Katie for the third time that I'm still asleep (although, what she actually says is 'she *said* she's still asleep', which is not really the idea.)

"I can't speak to anyone right now," I say.

"But it might help. It might make you feel better."

"I'll be fine," I tell her, pulling the duvet back over my head.

308

Will I be fine?

Do you get two goes at Mr Right, do you think?

I found James, who I love more than I loved Alex. Will there be someone else I can love more than I love James? Or at least as much?

I'm not sure it works like that.

What if I was right? What if there really is just one person out there for each of us? Just one person that we are meant to find and spend the rest of our lives with?

I must eventually fall asleep for real, because at some point later on I wake up to the sound of the telephone ringing again.

I look at the clock. It's half past six. I must have been asleep for hours.

I hear Fiona answer. Poor girl. She's been like my secretary today. But I can't answer it. If I hear James' voice I'll start crying again. And I've run out of tissues. Tesco's have probably run out of tissues with the amount I'm getting through.

She knows the drill by now. After a brief conversation I hear the phone beep. And then her footsteps.

"James again," she sighs.

I bury my head under the pillow. I don't want to see the anguish on her face. It's James' anguish. She's just the messenger. And I can't bear to see how much he's hurting.

"Why don't you stay at home tomorrow?," she says, sitting on my bed and gently prising the pillow out of my hands. "I'll cover your shift at the café."

I probably stink. I've been in my pyjamas all day. She probably thinks I'll scare the kids.

"Thanks."

"But do something for me, will you?"

I look at her, waiting for her to tell me what.

309

"Get out of those pyjamas. Take a shower. It'll make you feel better. And stop listening to this depressing music," she says, grabbing the remote control for my stereo and hitting the 'off' button.

"I like Leona Lewis," I protest.

"Well, if you will insist on listening to *Bleeding Love* then that's your choice, obviously, but not while you're upset, hey Becks?"

I smile at this and she smiles back – relieved I'm still capable.

Why do we do that? Why do we listen to the most depressing music in our CD collection when we are at our absolute lowest?

Because, however much we might wish we did, no-one ever actually does feel like listening to the *Locomotion* or *Girls Just Wanna Have Fun* when all they really just wanna do is lie in bed all day and not shower. That's why.

Not that I'm considering slitting my wrists or anything.

"Okay," I concede. I'll just turn it back on when she leaves the room.

"And Fi…"

"Yes?"

"Thanks."

"Don't be daft. What are friends for?" she says, and plants a kiss on my forehead.

Before she leaves the room, she marches over to my stereo, hits eject and removes my Leona Lewis CD.

"I think I'll keep this for a while," she says.

She's wrong.

I don't feel better after a shower.

I feel cleaner. But I don't feel better.

And now I've not even got any Leona to listen to. Fi has stripped my CD collection bare, leaving me with only Wham and my *Back to the 80's School Disco* compilation to choose from. Is that really the extent of my cheerful music? Now that *is* depressing.

I'm pulling on a t-shirt when I hear the doorbell ring, followed by the sound of Fiona opening the door. Muffled voices.

In spite of myself I open the bedroom door.

It's Mr Right.

It's James.

And as soon as he looks at me I know. Whatever I tell myself, whatever I try to convince myself, however I try to reason it all – he's still the one. He's still my Mr Right.

And the moment I realise that, there's only one thing I can do. Cry. Again.

And as the tears roll down my cheeks and drip off the end of my chin onto my clean t-shirt, he holds me in his arms and promises never to let me go.

"I'll leave you two to it," Fiona says.

I am only vaguely aware of her coming over to us and kissing me on the head before she quietly opens the door and does just that.

CHAPTER SIXTY THREE

I shouldn't have slept with him, obviously. But it just happened. I couldn't stop myself. One minute I'm sobbing in his arms and the next...

I've never had sex like it either. It was urgent. It was raw. It was needy. I needed to feel him inside me. To remember what it felt like when everything was perfect, when everything was right.

Nothing's changed. He's still Mr Right. But he's still my best friend's ex too.

"Jim?" I ask him, afterwards.

"She called me it one day and it just stuck," he says.

"What happened?" I say.

"What do you mean?"

"Why did you split up?"

"I didn't love her. And I knew I never would. It wasn't right. We had a lot of fun together. But that was all it was for me. I knew she wasn't the one. But I had the feeling that it was becoming more for her. So I did what I felt was the right thing and ended it. I didn't want to hurt her, but I would have hurt her a lot more in the long run if I had stayed with her any longer. After a while she phoned me and asked me to give it another go. I was tempted, because I was single, and because we had had fun together, but I knew it would be giving her false hope, so I said no."

I suddenly remember the photograph that Katie gave me when I moved out of the flat. The one of her and me – and Emma.

"I showed you a photograph," I tell him. "You must have recognised her."

"I know. And I thought I did," he says, pulling his jeans on. I've asked him to leave. I'm a terrible person. I've slept with him and now I'm asking him to leave.

"But I looked away before I could be sure."

"Why?"

"Because I didn't want it to be true," he says, sitting next to me on the bed and taking my hand. "Because I knew what it would mean if it was true. And I already loved you by then. I was already in too deep."

"I can't do it to her, James. She's my best friend."

"But you love me, I know you do."

"Yes, I do," I whisper.

"I want to marry you one day Becky. I want to spend the rest of my life with you. I can't bear the thought of not being with you. It's unimaginable. You're my whole life."

As he's saying all of this, all I can think about is a park bench. I can see me. And I can see James. We're sixty, or seventy – it makes no difference – we're just older. And we're together. And I'm holding his hand.

But it just can't be, so I look down and gently pull my hand out of his.

And James knows then that he won't change my mind. So he stands up and kisses me on the mouth – his lips barely touching mine, just like our first kiss. And then he leaves.

CHAPTER SIXTY FOUR

I wake in the morning to fourteen missed calls and a text from Katie, politely informing me that if I have not phoned her at work by 11 o'clock then she is taking the rest of the day off and coming round. When I say politely, I do mean in the loosest sense of the word, obviously.

I look at the clock. It's 10.52am.

Bugger. She's probably left already.

I dial her work number.

"Hello, *Books!* Yvonne speaking."

"Hi Yvonne. It's Katie's friend Becky. Is she there?"

"Hi Becky. No, sorry, she just left. Doctor's appointment."

Damn.

"Okay, thanks, I'll try her on her mobile."

Her mobile is switched off. She's probably on the tube. If she's just left, that means she'll probably be here in less than an hour.

I consider my options.

I could pretend I'm asleep when she rings the doorbell. I could pretend to be in the shower. I could pretend to be out. I could actually *be* out– though I have to admit this is my least favourite option since it does actually involve being out. Which means getting dressed. Which means getting out of bed.

I'm still considering the best course of action when she arrives,

314

forty five minutes later. As the doorbell rings, my phone lights up with a new message.

I'm not leaving until you let me in so there's no point hiding.

Bollocks.

Defeated, I get out of bed and put my dressing gown on. I begin a half-hearted attempt at making my bed, shaking the duvet which sends a mass of soggy tissues flying up in the air and cascading back down again – the remnants of another night's sobbing. I gather them all up and drop them into the bin, on top of the empty Kleenex box.

I go to fluff the pillows a bit before deciding not to bother. I'll be getting back in as soon as I've got rid of her.

The doorbell rings again.

"I'm coming," I shout.

"You look awful," she says, when I open the door.

It's true then. I do look as bad as I feel.

"Thanks," I say.

The concerned look on her face is all it takes to set me off again and she instinctively wraps her arms around me.

"Oh B," she says. "What am I going to do with you?"

We go into the kitchen and Katie puts the kettle on. Make tea – it's always the first thing to do in a crisis isn't it?

"How's Emma?" I ask, tearing off a piece of kitchen roll and blowing my nose. I'm officially all out of tissues. I'm almost out of kitchen roll too. I will have to stop crying or I may have to resort to newspaper before long.

"She's okay. I think I've managed to convince her that you didn't know who James was."

"I can't believe she could have thought I did."

"You know what she's like, B. She's impulsive. She doesn't think things through. She just saw the two of you together and jumped

315

to conclusions."

"I've tried phoning her, but she won't answer my calls."

"Give her time. She'll come round. She's not stupid. You and her have been friends for a long time. She won't want to lose that."

"I hope not."

She gets two mugs out of the cupboard and drops tea bags into them.

"Have you spoken to James?"

"Yes."

"And?"

"And nothing."

"What happened?"

"I slept with him," I admit. "And then I asked him to leave. I am a terrible person."

"Don't, B." She pours in the water and stirs the teabags in the mugs. "Go sit down. I'll bring the drinks through."

She puts the mugs down on the coffee table and sits next to me on the sofa, taking my hand in hers. I feel a speech coming on.

"You love him, right?" she says.

"Yes, but that's not the point."

"It's completely the point."

"And what about Emma?"

"What about Emma?"

"She'll never speak to me again."

"Of course she will. She'll come round eventually. She's not stupid. She knows you haven't done this to hurt her. She's not about to throw away a friendship she's had practically her whole life."

"She was crushed, Katie. You saw her. She loved James. Jim."

"Yes, and she'll meet someone else she loves even more. And who loves her. You know what she's like. She's got men queuing up to date her. Look at Daniel. She met him at a bloody Spanish class, for heaven's sake. And she really liked him too. You heard

316

her say so herself. Though I'm not sure he'll be calling her again in a hurry after Saturday night's performance.

"Anyway, what I'm trying to say is, once she realises what you guys mean to each other, she'll come round. I'm sure of it. It might take a bit of time, but she can't expect you to give him up."

"Wouldn't you?" I ask.

"What do you mean?"

"If you and Matt split up and then I fell in love with him, wouldn't you expect me to give him up? Wouldn't you expect me to choose you over him?"

"That's completely different. You've known Matt for years. You'd never even met Jim. You had no idea it was the same person."

"Yes, but it was," I argue.

You don't go out with your best friend's ex. I thought that was the unwritten rule? Even if you didn't know that's who he was. Even if he *is* Mr Right.

"Can you imagine your life without James?" Katie asks me.

"No. But I'll have to, won't I?"

"Well, it's your choice, but for what it's worth, I think you're crazy."

Lecture over and tea drunk, Katie orders me into the bathroom and instructs me not to come back out until I have doused myself with some very large doses of smelly stuff. She says I smell…

Judging by the person staring back at me in the bathroom mirror she's probably right. I almost frighten myself, never mind anyone else. My hair is plastered to my head in greasy clumps, there are several black streaks down my cheeks where my two-day old mascara has made a run for freedom and the bags under my eyes are beginning to resemble suitcases – the large kind, the expand-able kind with extra pockets and everything. I should invite James round right now. He'd soon come round to my way of thinking.

I sit on the toilet watching the bubbles climb up the bath as it fills with water.

When I was little Johnny and I used to share a bath. We'd cover our faces with bubbles and pretend they were beards. And when they'd all melted away we'd rub shampoo in our hair and give ourselves Mohicans and other weird and wonderful hairstyles until the water went cold and our fingers and toes had turned all wrinkly. And mum or dad would shout 'first out of the bath is the winner.'

Bath time was fun back then. Now it seems to be a time to soak away your aches and pains, your worries, your heartache. It seems to be a place to contemplate how you've monumentally messed your life up yet again.

I miss him.

I've only been without him for a day and a half and I miss him.

Is that completely ridiculous? We were only together a few months.

I can't remember what my life was like without him.

Yes I can. It was lonely. There was just me. On my own.

But it's not being alone than scares me. It's being without James.

"Is this your article?" Katie asks when I finally emerge from the bathroom half an hour later, prune-like, but considerably cleaner.

I shrug. She knows it is.

"It's brilliant, Becky. It's even better than I thought it would be. Why didn't you tell me you'd finished it? Have you sent it to the magazine?"

"No, and I'm not going to," I say, snatching it from her hands. She looks at me crossly.

"I don't even know why I've still got it," I tell her, tossing it into the bin.

Katie stares at me, as if I've just grown an extra head.

318

"What are you doing?"

"It's rubbish."

"It's not rubbish. It's bloody brilliant. What are you doing, Becky? This is your big chance. This is what you wanted. You gave up everything to do this."

"I'll write something else," I say, tipping my head forward and rubbing my hair with the towel.

She takes the article back out of the bin and smoothes out the pages.

"Just because you and James have split up, that doesn't mean every word of this isn't true, Becky."

"Yes it does. What do I know about finding Mr Right? All I know about is finding someone else's Mr Right. And hurting my best friend. And losing the best thing that ever happened to me. I don't think anybody needs advice from me, do you?"

"You didn't lose the best thing that ever happened to you. You threw it away."

She's angry with me now.

"You're being ridiculous," she snaps.

"Well I'm not sending it and that's that," I say, stuffing the pages back in the bin along with the soggy tissues and the empty Kleenex box.

CHAPTER SIXTY FIVE

On Tuesday I manage to drag myself into work.

Fiona probably wishes I hadn't bothered. It's only 10 o'clock and there have been four breakages already. Of course, when I say 'there have been four breakages,' what I actually mean is 'I personally have broken four things.' Fiona doesn't break things. Fiona is not an emotional wreck. Thank god they weren't painted. I think that would have finished me off.

I cried for two hours this morning. Alarming, yes, but a significant improvement on yesterday's six-and-a-half hours.

"Why don't you go home?" Fiona suggests, emptying the last fragments of plate from the dustpan into the bin. "I can cope without you."

What she really means is 'I can't cope *with* you,' she's just too nice to say so.

"I'm fine, honestly," I tell her. "I'm better off being at work."

The dishes aren't though, she wants to say, but doesn't. She takes a pile of plates from my arms instead and puts them safely onto the worktop before taking the top two and handing them to the twin boys who have come in with their grandma to make something for their mum's birthday.

"Okay. Why don't you help me then," Fiona says to me. "I want to make a gift for the guests at the opening."

"Sure. What have you got in mind?"

Caroline is probably paying her to keep me away from the dishes.

"Caroline said I could have some tiles at cost price so I thought if we put felt on the bottom we could make coasters. Paint them with the shop logo and the date of the opening, maybe?"

"That sounds like a good idea."

If she'd told me she wanted to make something out of toilet rolls and aluminium foil, I'd probably have said that was a good idea too, to be honest.

My mind isn't really here. It's with James. It's in his flat, sharing a takeaway. It's at my mum and dad's watching him pull faces at Jacob. It's in New York sitting on a park bench holding his hand.

If only I'd stuck with the Internet for longer. I'm sure I would have met someone vaguely normal sooner or later. But no, I had to let myself fall in love with the first lovely guy to walk into Potty Wotty Doodah.

"What do you think of this?" Fiona asks, pushing a piece of paper under my nose.

It's only a rough drawing, but it looks great. The Pink Frog logo looks great. Dan has done a fantastic job with the design. Underneath the logo, Fiona has drawn a door with an open sign hanging on the door knob, and the date of the opening underneath that.

"That looks fab, Fi," I tell her.

"I've got a stencil of the logo that…," she says, before stopping herself.

"…that Dan gave you?" I say.

She nods reluctantly.

"It's okay, Fi. The world doesn't stop just because my love life's in bits. You *can* mention his brother's name without me breaking

321

down."

She squeezes my hand.

"Shall I draw the doors and you can paint them pink?"

"Sure," I say, grabbing a brush determinedly. "Let's do it."

CHAPTER SIXTY SIX

Emma's coming over.

I think I wore her down eventually with all my messages. She probably ran out of memory on her mobile.

I offered to meet her at the tube station, but she said she'd make her own way here.

I'm scared. I don't want to lose Emma as well. She's in all my memories. She's part of who I am.

Emma's the one who hit the brakes too hard when I was riding on the back of her bike. She's the one who cried all the way to the hospital, even though it was *my* knee that was bleeding.

Emma's the one I ran the three-legged race with every school sports day and always came last with because we laughed so much we fell over every few steps.

Emma's the one who got a badge-maker for her eighth birthday and made 'Best Friend' badges for us both that we wore every single day for a whole year.

You can't replace memories like that.

When I open the door, I know she knows that too.

"I'm sorry," she says. "I know you'd never deliberately hurt me."

I let out the breath that I think I've been holding in for three days and hug my best friend.

I had a whole speech planned. I don't need it now.

"I know you love him, but I'm not sure I can handle it," she says, brushing a tear from her face.

I break away from her. "It's okay, Em. It's over. We've split up."

"Do you hate me?"

"No, I don't hate you. I'm just glad you've realised I didn't know. Because I didn't, Em. I had no idea."

"I know you didn't. I was just upset. It was the first time I'd seen him since we split up. And then I saw you, standing next to him and I just put two and two together and came up with five. I'm sorry."

We don't say much after that. She doesn't ask if I've seen James since. And I don't tell her that I have. We both need to move on. Without James. And Jim.

"What happened with Daniel?" I ask her, as we share a bottle of wine later on.

"God, don't ask," she laughs. "I tried to phone him the next day to apologise, but he ignored my calls. I left a message for him to call me, but he hasn't yet. And who can blame him? We'd only been on three dates. He probably thinks he's had a lucky escape. It's a shame though. He was nice. Still – plenty more fish in the sea," she says, tapping her glass against mine.

For the rest of the evening we don't say much. We sit on the sofa and watch episodes of *Sex & The City* – series four, where Carrie gets a job at Vogue and the editor strips off to his Versace underpants and asks her how he looks.

And we both laugh, and sip red wine, like it's any other evening.

It doesn't feel normal, but it's our attempt at normal.

I look at her and smile. At least I have my friend back.

She reaches down for the tube of Pringles by her feet and shakes it at me. I take a stack of five and stuff them in my mouth all at once.

"What about your article?" she asks.

"I never finished it," I lie. "It wasn't really working. Not enough material. Rubbish interviewees. I'll write something else."

We watch Carrie as she writes her first article for Vogue about handbags and shoes.

"Maybe I could write about fashion," I say to Emma.

She laughs until she realises I might actually be serious. And then she really laughs. And then I laugh. And before long we are both hysterical.

Now, *this* is normal.

CHAPTER SIXTY SEVEN

It's not that easy though is it? I'll probably miss James for the rest of my life.

Would I have been better off if I'd never met him? Part of me wants to say yes. But then I wouldn't have experienced the most amazing feeling in the world, would I?

How do you mend a broken heart? I wish there was a manual you could buy – a step-by-step guide. You could look it up on the Internet, maybe. Print it out. Follow it. There could be footnotes showing the time needed to complete each section.

They say it takes half the time you were with someone to get over them. That means it should take me less than six weeks.

I went out with Thomas Jenkins for two months when I was sixteen. He was a jerk. He smoked, drank and had spitting competitions with his mates. He was rude to his parents and bullied his younger sister. I only went out with him because Emma was going out with his best friend. He dumped me when I wouldn't sleep with him. I told him I'd rather sleep with a toad. According to the theory it should have taken me one month to get over Thomas. It took me one minute, if that.

I don't know if I'll ever get over James.

CHAPTER SIXTY EIGHT

It's the opening of Fiona's shop today.

I'm not really in the mood for a party, but I can't let her down. She has been so good to me. She's phoned me every morning to make sure I've got out of bed; she's brought flowers and Maltesers to cheer me up – and boxes of tissues. And let's face it – she has been doing the lion's share of the work at Potty Wotty.

I broke a plate yesterday. Not a clean, white, unpainted plate. No. I broke a plate that was ready to be collected by its four-year-old designer and her mother. Fiona was brilliant. She pieced it together and then copied it, splodge for splodge, onto a brand new plate. (Fortunately this particular four-year-old artist was no Van Gogh, but still...) Later she apologised to the mother that there had been a backlog in the firing and it would be ready on Monday. And then she made me a cup of tea.

Dan and Christina are going to be there. That's fine. Dan did make the sign, after all. I can't expect contact between the Newmans and the rest of the world to stop just because of me. It won't be easy though. He'll ask how I am. And I'll lie and say 'fine.' Or maybe he won't. Maybe he'll just pretend I no longer exist. And who could blame him, after the way I've treated his brother? I can't expect everyone to understand my logic – *the reason I'm not speaking to your brother is because I love him...*

327

I'm surprised Fiona invited me to be honest. I wouldn't want me at a party right now. I'd turn me away at the door. There will be children at this party. I'll scare them. I'll turn the milk sour. Even the Pink Frog will be depressed after I've finished with him.

Fiona's kitchen is full of party food – enough to make the Mad Hatter's eyes light up. Plates of sandwiches, sausage rolls, cheese straws, mini pizzas. And that's just for the children. For the adults there are quiches, salads, trays of dips with sticks of celery, carrot and cucumber.

I stayed over last night and we made shortbread and fairy cakes. We found an old Ladybird 'Cooking With Mother' book in the cupboard. Fiona did get a bit carried away at one point and suggested making cheese and pineapple hedgehogs. Fortunately she was fresh out of cocktail sticks.

"Do you think it's too much?" Fiona asks, surveying all the food.

Yes, there's enough food here to feed an army.

"No, it's fine," I assure her.

She's really nervous. She doesn't need to be, of course. Her stuff is fantastic. People will be falling over themselves to get into the shop and buy it once it's open.

"Morning ladies," Adrian says, coming into the kitchen with an industrial-sized box of chocolate fingers and kissing me on the cheek. He was out when I arrived last night. Fiona had told him he was getting in the way when he kept dipping his fingers in the cake mix, apparently. He was still out when we finally switched off the oven at midnight and went to bed.

I've met Adrian a couple of times now, and each time I see him, I get this picture in my head of him, wiping Fi's nose at the top of a mountain and I just want to laugh.

"How are you?" he asks. It's not a normal 'how are you?' It's a head-tilted-to-one-side, mouth-slightly-twisted, sympathetic 'how

328

are you?' The kind you don't generally expect an honest answer to.

"I'm fine," I tell him.

He's happy with the response. He's got a car to fill with party food. There's no time for tears.

We load the drinks and packaged foods into the boot and arrange the rest on the back seat next to me.

The wine bottles clink together at every bump in the road, and I glance nervously at the foil plates next to me, relieved they're only sandwiches. I dread to think what state a trifle would arrive in.

There has been brown paper up at the window of The Pink Frog for weeks. Fiona wouldn't let any of us see inside. She wanted us to wait for the full effect.

It was worth the wait. I'm blown away.

The shop-front is simple – white woodwork around the window and double doors in the centre with stainless steel door handles and letterbox. Dan has done a fantastic job with the sign. 'The' and 'Frog' are spelt out in chunky silver letters, the word 'Pink' is just as you would expect – bright pink and bold. There's a pink frog at the far right, sitting on top of the shop's telephone number, ready to leap. It's striking. It makes you want to step inside and look around.

Two giant black and white pictures of babies hang from the ceiling in the windows either side of the doors. And behind them you can see the first of the rails of clothes.

We take the food inside where Fiona has set up trestle tables covered with white linen table cloths.

There are rails filled with baby-grows in every colour of the rainbow; tiny dresses, dungarees, t-shirts… About three-quarters of the stock has been bought in from other designers. The rest is her own. And it's beautiful. It has taken her years to build up the stock. If the shop is successful she'll have to take on staff to

329

help her make more.

It's not just clothes. There are shelves full of soft toys, baby-changing mats and blankets and mobiles hang from the ceiling.

Everything is covered in clear plastic sheets for today. Red wine and children's sticky fingers are a dangerous combination.

"It's amazing, Fi," I tell her as we arrange the food on the tables and unwrap packets of napkins.

"Thanks," she says, proudly.

I think she has invited practically everyone she knows as she's so scared no-one will come.

They do though, of course.

Before the cling film has even been taken off the sandwiches they start arriving. Family and friends, owners and staff of neighbouring businesses, Katie and Emma. And everyone with children has bought them with them. They are what it's all about after all. And we need to get rid of some food.

Potty Wotty Doodah is closed today. There's no-one left to run it. Caroline has brought Benjamin with her. I rush over for a peek, but he's fast asleep in his car seat. Caroline puts him down on the floor next to her and hugs Fiona tightly.

"Congratulations," she says, bending down and sliding a card out from next to Benjamin. He's wearing a Pink Frog baby-grow.

Everyone raves about the shop, especially about The Pink Frog range. Fiona takes well over £200 before she has even finished her first glass of champagne.

"I want to start having babies now, just so that I can dress them in your clothes," Katie tells her.

"Don't let me stop you," Fiona laughs.

"I'm not sure the dress-fitter would be too thrilled if I turned up with a bump."

"The wedding isn't that far away, you probably wouldn't be showing," Emma says, winking.

"Stop it, all of you!" Katie laughs, and the four of us all have our own mini toast.

"To The Pink Frog!" Katie says.

"The Pink Frog," we all echo, clinking our glasses together.

As Fiona leaves us to mingle with her other guests Dan walks in with Christina and Evan.

He comes straight over and kisses me on the cheek as Evan hands me his bunny rabbit. He's wearing a pair of Pink Frog dungarees. Evan, I mean, not the bunny. I hand the toy to Christina and pick Evan up for a cuddle.

"Don't you look handsome," I say, tickling him.

"How are you?" Dan asks.

"Oh, you know…"

I glance nervously at Emma.

I have to ask. I can't *not* ask.

"How's James?"

"Not great," he says, and shrugs, as if to say 'what do you expect?'

Emma looks at Katie, and then back at me. I feel like everyone is waiting to hear what I'm going to say next.

I don't know what I'm going to say next.

"Let's go get a drink, Em," Katie, says, coming to my rescue. "I could use another glass of vino." She steers Emma away from us, towards the back of the shop where Fiona is being interviewed by a reporter from the local newspaper.

"Is that *the* Emma?" Dan asks me. Of course… he hasn't met her before. None of James' family has. I wondered why Emma was looking so confused.

I nod.

"Shall we go find you a drink, darling?" Christina says, taking Evan from me and leaving us to it.

"He's in bits, Becky," Dan says. "He loves you. You're the one, you must know that?"

"I do Dan. And I love him too. More than I've ever loved anyone. More than I ever thought I *could* love someone. But I can't do it to Emma. I've known her my whole life. She's like my family. And I can't be her friend *and* be with James."

I look to the back of the shop.

"I can't do this right now. This is Fiona's day."

I lean forward and kiss him on the cheek.

"Look after him for me."

He nods, as I walk away to join my friends.

Emma looks at me. She bites her top lip and tucks her hair behind her ear, and then looks over at Dan as he picks up his son.

"I never met his family," she says.

"I know," I tell her.

The opening is a huge success. Everyone Fiona invited comes. Passers-by even pop in – hoping to blag a free glass of champagne and find a little treasure trove as well.

A photographer from the paper turns up to get a picture to go with the story. He takes one of Fiona, behind the counter, holding Evan and Benjamin in their Pink Frog outfits. She beams.

We put up a pink ribbon at the door for the official opening and Fiona makes a speech. She thanks everyone for coming, thanks everyone for all their help, thanks Dan for his fabulous sign, thanks Adrian for being her biggest supporter. And then she cuts the ribbon and we all cheer. And we drink champagne and eat cucumber sticks and dips, and fairy cakes with pink icing.

By the end of the afternoon there are just a few sandwiches and a couple of chocolate fingers left.

They look lonely. I put one in my mouth and sweep empty paper plates into a rubbish sack.

"Thanks Becky," Fiona says, wrapping her arm around my waist.

"S'okay," I mumble through a mouthful of chocolate biscuit.

I'll miss Fiona at Potty Wotty. I know she'll only be a few doors away. But it's not the same, is it?

Still, I've got Caroline – and baby Benjamin now.

Besides, I don't want to be there forever, do I?

I want to be a writer.

CHAPTER SIXTY NINE

'*I Can't Be In The Same Room As A Mushroom,*' '*I Have Multiple Orgasms All Day Every Day,*' '*My Boyfriend Left Me For My Brother.*'

These are not statements about my own life, no. They are magazine features. Believe it or not, there's even 'Cheese & Pineapple on a stick, anyone?' – a feature about a 1970s fashion revival, thus proving that there really is nothing you can't write about.

So why can't I come up with another feature idea?

I have been to WH Smith and practically stripped the shelves bare looking for inspiration.

I have bought no less than fourteen magazines (okay, so they're not that bare). And I have read them all from cover to cover.

But the inspiration is distinctly lacking.

How Do You Know You've Met Mr Right? That's all I can come up with. That, and *How To Lose a Mr Right in Three Months*, obviously, which nobody in their right mind would want to read.

I need to come up with something though. I can't work at Potty Wotty forever. That was never the plan.

I have to write to Jennifer Sutton. I have to tell her she won't be getting my feature after all. I guess that's one magazine I can cross off my mailing list.

Well there's no time like the present.

I clear the magazines off the coffee table and plug my laptop in.

Dear Jennifer,

I'll just play a quick game of Patience. And then I'll write the letter.

Dear Jennifer,

I think my bedroom carpet could do with a vacuum.

I am very sorry to let you down, but I've gone and lost yet another wonderful boyfriend, so I really don't think I'm in any position to give your readers advice on their love lives...

Too honest.

I'm terribly sorry, but I won't be able to send you the feature we discussed, after all. You remember? The one I have waited all my life to write...

Too sarcastic.

I am writing to let you know that due to a sudden change in my personal circumstances I will no longer be submitting the feature How Do You Know You've Met Mr Right for inclusion in the September issue of Love Life.

Just right.

Please accept my sincere apologies for any inconvenience this causes you.

Yours sincerely,

Rebecca Harper

"Are you really sure you want to send this?" Katie asks me when I go round to hers. "Your article was so good. It's such a waste."

I didn't want Katie to see the letter. I knew she'd try and change my mind. But I had no choice. I don't own a printer.

"Yes. I was pleased with it, Katie. I really was. But it just doesn't feel right now. I've proved I can do it now though so I'll just have to write something else."

"Okay then," she says, handing me the letter to sign.

I sign it and stuff it into an envelope.

"Can I ask you something though, B?"

I lick the envelope. "Yes."

"Would you want to be with James if Emma was okay with it?"

"Yes." I don't have to think about it. "But she'll never be okay with it. I'll be okay though, Katie. You don't need to worry about me."

CHAPTER SIXTY SEVENTY

Over the next few weeks things slowly start to get back to normal.

I fail to come up with a single viable feature idea and begin to seriously doubt my future as a writer.

James stops phoning. And you can't blame him. I guess there are only so many times you can phone a person who doesn't phone you back. But I wish he hadn't stopped. That's really selfish of me, I know. But I miss him. I miss hearing his voice on my answering machine, telling me he still loves me.

Emma starts dating again. She's currently seeing a dentist. She met him at the opticians. She doesn't think it will work out, though. He's 'too nice,' apparently. But she's sticking with it for now.

And the wedding plans are coming along nicely. It's just a few weeks away now. Katie's running through her checklist. For the zillionth time. The church is booked. And the reception. The table decorations have been bought – simple floating candles and tiny gold hearts to scatter over cream linen tablecloths.

She's made the menus and place cards. Or, should I say – we've made the menus and place cards. And the orders of service. And the table plan. The food has been chosen – salmon en croute with new potatoes, broccoli and green beans with raspberry pavlova for dessert.

I'm told it's to die for. I wouldn't know myself. I've not yet forgiven Katie for not enlisting my help with the food tasting. Wedding dress hunting, invitation assembling, place card manufacture – these things I am invited to participate in. But tasting roast beef with Yorkshire puddings, coq-au-vin with new potatoes, salmon en croute, apple pie and cream, chocolate fudge cake with ice cream, raspberry pavlova – these things I am excluded from? It hardly seems fair.

The flowers have been ordered – posies of cream roses tied with gold ribbon for our bouquets, single roses for the boys' buttonholes, and roses in tall glass vases twisted with gold ribbon for the centrepieces.

The rings have been collected, the photographer booked and the cake ordered. Katie has snubbed tradition in favour of a three-tier cake with a difference. "I don't really like fruit cake," she says. "But everyone loves chocolate cake. And sponge cake. And carrot cake." So they are having one tier of each.

All the dresses and suits are now hanging in Katie's wardrobe.

And Emma has finally chosen a reading. She's not telling us what it is. But we'll love it, apparently.

Which just leaves the hen do.

CHAPTER SEVENTY ONE

As hen dos go, it was not the easiest to arrange, what with all the numerous rules and regulations that were laid down the second Katie got engaged.

"No tiaras, no L-plates, no furry handcuffs," she said. "No devil horns, no edible underwear, no veils – especially no veils with condoms hanging from them. Promise me, Becky."

"I promise."

"No seedy nightclubs, no pole dancing lessons, no strippers. Absolutely no strippers. If you get me a stripper, I will walk out, I swear I will."

"It'll be the tamest hen do in history at this rate," Emma moaned.

"Tame is good," Katie said. "Tame is what I want. Promise me guys."

"I'm not promising anything," Emma said.

"Okay," I relented. "No veils or L-plates, no furry handcuffs and no strippers, but beyond that you leave it up to us."

"And no condoms – don't forget the condoms."

"Fine – no condoms."

"How about lunch at the old folks home down the road?" Emma had suggested.

We settled on an eighties-themed weekend in a cottage in the

Cotswolds. Ten of us. Katie, Emma, me, Fiona, Caroline, Matt's sister Clare and four of Katie's friends from work.

We drove up here this afternoon in a convoy of three cars, packed to the brim with food, drink, party games and toilet rolls – because it was stipulated in the house rules – "you must bring your own toilet paper."

And in any case – we needed it for the first game.

"You're pulling it too hard," Emma shouts at me, as I tear a strip of toilet paper for the third time.

"There's no way we're gonna win this."

This is Fiona's contribution to Katie's hen do – *Here Comes The Bride* – a game she played at her sister-in-law's hen do last year.

She has split us into two teams – Caroline, Emma and me with Yvonne and Louise from Katie's work in the living room and Katie, Fiona and Clare with Shirley and Anna from *Books!* in the dining room.

Each team has a toilet roll. That's it. Just a toilet roll. And we have to dress the bride ready for her big day.

Emma is our bride.

I hope Katie isn't this much trouble to dress.

I loosely tie together the strips of paper that have just broken and continue to wind the roll around Emma's body.

Fiona snorts.

"She looks more like a mummy than a bride!"

"You should be doing this, you're the dressmaker," I laugh.

"I know, but it's much more fun watching you!"

"I'm not sure she's going to be able to walk in this," Yvonne says.

Under the rules of the game each bride has to walk up the stairs and back down again, and the winning team is the one whose bride's dress is still on her.

Yvonne's right. We haven't got a hope in hell.

340

But we won't go down without a fight.

"Keep winding!" I shout, like our very lives depend on it.

Ten seconds later the alarm sounds on Fiona's phone, signalling we are out of time.

I tug the last strip of paper from the roll and tuck the end into Emma's bra, before standing back to survey the damage.

"We might as well just give them the prize now," I laugh, resigning myself to not sharing in a packet of milk chocolate willies.

"It's not that bad," Louise laughs.

"You *are* kidding?" Emma says. "Have you seen the state of me?"

At this, she turns and looks in the mirror above the fireplace and giggles.

"We're coming in," Katie shouts from the dining room.

Yes, we have definitely lost the willies.

Katie's team have created a masterpiece. They have pulled down the straps of her top and her bra and wound the toilet paper around her boobs so it looks like a bodice. And then they have tucked metre-length strips of toilet paper into her jeans, all the way around the waistband. It looks like a grass skirt, but in toilet paper.

They haven't stopped there. They have made her a toilet paper tiara, a toilet paper necklace, and toilet paper earrings. They were just finishing off the toilet paper bracelet when the alarm went off.

This outfit is so good it could be held in reserve for the big day next month. You know – just in case her other dress doesn't fit, or something…

"Off you go girls," Fiona tells Emma and Katie, who begin their intrepid climb up the stairs.

By the third step, Emma's dress is trailing on the floor, while Katie's is holding up as well as you might expect that of a super-model on the catwalk.

By the sixth step Emma's dress is hanging on by a single tuck in her left bra strap, while Katie's is looking more and more like something you might see in the window of a bridal shop.

By the seventh step Emma has decided she has had enough of this game and rips Katie's dress off her as they both fall on to the stairs in a giggling heap.

The cottage is great. Emma and I found it on the Internet.

The website described it as 'a luxury five-bedroom cottage with oodles of charm and no immediate neighbours.' We figured we couldn't go wrong. We can make as much noise as we want and no-one will be forced to phone the police.

There are five bedrooms, all en-suite, a big country kitchen with a huge table and twelve chairs in the middle, a living room, and downstairs toilet, which is currently being used as a storage room for fifteen bottles of wine, a bottle of vodka, a bottle of gin, six bottles of tonic water, three bottles of lemonade, three bottles of coke, six cartons of orange juice, two dozen eggs, six tubes of Pringles, four extra large bags of Doritos, two boxes of bread sticks...

"Do you think we have overdone it on the food and drink?" Katie asks, emerging with a refill of gin and tonic, and removing a stray piece of toilet paper from the pocket of her jeans.

"Probably, but we can always take it home with us," I laugh. I laugh every time I look at Katie, who, in keeping with the eighties theme, we have dressed in luminous pink leg warmers, luminous pink sweat bands, and a luminous pink headband. Oh, and a luminous pink feather boa around her neck – just because we could. She said no L-plates or tiaras, she said nothing about 'no luminous pink leg warmers and matching accessories.'

The rest of the evening passes by in a blur, as we put a significant dent in the supplies, blast eighties music out of the iPod stereo and dance around the living room with toy microphones and inflatable guitars.

It is past three in the morning by the time we pass out in our respective rooms.

I'm sharing with Fiona.

She has warned me she snores.

Fortunately I am asleep even before my head hits the pillow.

In the morning we cook a massive fry up to soak up all the alcohol we consumed last night, and nurse our hangovers with big mugs of tea.

"That's a mean impersonation of Tina Turner you've got there," Yvonne says to me.

"Oh, bloody hell, I didn't did I?" I say, rubbing my eye, just before I remember that I didn't take my mascara off last night.

Fortunately I am not alone. We all did our party tricks last night – including Emma who does a fantastic Victoria Wood and Katie who can hang spoons on the end of her nose.

We spend the day doing our own thing. The girls from Katie's work drive into town to check out a book fair they saw advertised in the house information file. Caroline and Fiona go off to meet a supplier who is interested in selling their produce in Fiona's shop. Which leaves Katie, Clare, Emma and I – who are stopping here, lying on the sofa watching television and working our way through an extra-large tin of Quality Streets.

"Pass us a fudge" Emma says, the other end of the sofa to me. I have the tin wedged firmly between my thighs.

"Is that the pink one?" I mumble, mid chomp through an orange cream.

"Yes."

"None left."

"Yes there are, give me the tin you big fatty!" she laughs.

Clare is reading a magazine.

Katie is asleep.

I only know this because she hasn't yet attempted to raid the tin of all the green triangles.

"How did you get on with that article you were writing Becky?" Clare asks me, looking up from the magazine.

"Oh, it's sort of on the back burner at the moment," I fib. Clare was one of my interviewees. I don't want her to know I wasted her time. And everyone else's time, for that matter.

"I have been really busy at work recently, what with Fiona leaving and it being the school holidays."

"Well make sure you let me know when it's in the magazine, won't you. I can't wait to tell people I know someone who writes for *Love Life*."

"Absolutely," I tell her.

I miss James.

I was fine a minute ago. I was quite happy chomping my way through all the caramels in an extra-large tin of Quality Streets. But it only takes one thing to make you think of someone. A song. A smell. A place you've been together. An article you've written that's all about them…

I hope I meet someone else. I hope I'm not going to be alone for the rest of my life. I hope I meet someone who makes me as happy as he made me.

The sun is shining when the girls arrive back at the cottage so we make some lunch and sit out in the garden chatting.

Fiona shows us some samples from the supplier she and Caroline met. They're good. They are nowhere near as brilliant as hers, but they're good.

"What gave you the idea for The Pink Frog?" Clare asks her.

"I've always wanted to have my own business," she says. "And it had to be something that involved sewing because I loved it so much at school. It was actually my sister's little girl who gave me the idea for the shop. I wanted to buy an outfit for her when she was born, but the clothes in the high street shops were all so boring, so I decided to make her something instead. I made this really cute dress with matching booties and sunhat. Everyone raved about it and said I should make more of them and sell them. After that it just sort of snowballed."

"Oh my god, Fi, you have just given me the best idea," I shout, startling Katie who had nodded off again.

"What?" she asks, excited but not sure why.

"My next feature," I say. "I could write a feature about women who have been inspired by children to start their own business. There's you, Fi. And Caroline," I say, thinking out loud. "She got the idea for the café when Molly was painting one day and put handprints all over one of her mugs. And I'm sure I could find others."

"That's a great idea, B," Katie says, half asleep. "There's a woman at work who has just written a children's book. You could interview her, I'm sure."

And just like that suddenly I feel really excited again. I feel like I can turn this around. I feel like maybe my dream may come true after all. One of them, anyway.

Tonight Katie will be doing no cooking. Tonight we are going to cook Katie a slap up meal. Tonight we are going to wash, peel, chop, sauté, fry, boil and simmer our hearts out. We are going to bowl our friend over with our culinary prowess.

Okay, so tonight we have a chef coming to the cottage to cook us a slap up meal.

Said chef – Gerard Yumi – arrives at 7pm, at which point we are instructed to vacate the kitchen and "Go have fun." Which we do.

Tonight we all have luminous pink leg warmers on, which look pretty fetching with our party frocks. And even better with the pink sparkly boppers that Katie is required to wear for the evening.

She didn't say 'no pink sparkly boppers.' She said 'no L plates or tiaras.' She said nothing about pink sparkly boppers.

Did I mention the bopper bits are willies? Bright pink sparkly ones?

She doesn't even protest. She knows she won't win.

"How do I look?" she asks, giving us all a twirl.

"Take a look," Fiona tells her, pointing to the mirror.

She totters over in her heels, holding on to the boppers to stop them bouncing about on their springs.

"Excellent," she says.

While we are waiting for dinner to be served we play more games. First up is a hen do version of *Pin the Tale on the Donkey* – *Pin the Willy on Matt*, where, blindfolded, we are each spun round three times before sticking our own cut-out Post-It Note willy on a picture of a model with Matt's head stuck on it. Needless to say the poor lad ends up with willies all over his face.

Next up is *How Well Do You Know Your Friend* where Katie is given one fact about each of us and has to guess which fact is about which friend.

She does quite well. She guesses that Fiona met the Queen once when she was a little girl and asked her if she would like to come for tea. And she guesses that Emma once told a guy she had three children, just to get him to stop phoning her.

I try to outwit her. I didn't think she knew that I once sent a homemade Valentine's card to a boy I liked at school, with a cassette recording of Abba's *Take A Chance On Me* inside it. Evidently she did.

At 8pm Gerard calls us into the dining room where we enjoy a starter of melon and parma ham and each give Katie our hen do gift. The rules were; it costs no more than a fiver and is something that would come in handy in her married life. So far she has opened a packet of penis shaped pasta, a pair of furry pink handcuffs and an edible g-string – one with multicoloured sweets like the kind you used to get on necklaces when we were kids – the ones that made your neck all sticky when you bit them off.

Over the main course – stir fried chilli chicken with noodles – we play *Mr and Mrs* to test how well Katie knows the man she is about to marry.

I got the answers from Matt last week so there's no way of cheating.

But Katie doesn't need to cheat.

She knows that Matt has blue eyes, that he lost his virginity at sixteen to his first girlfriend Liz in his mum and dad's bed while they were out shopping at Tesco, that his worst habit is cleaning his football boots on the sofa, that his favourite food is liver and onions, that he's afraid of mould…

We tested Matt too. To check he knows our friend as well as he should.

He does.

He knew she had her first kiss at fifteen on holiday with an Italian waiter who didn't speak a word of English, that her first love was Jason Hart, who she held hands with under their desks and whose name she wrote in love hearts on the front of her geography book, that the worst thing she ever did at school was cheat in a Maths exam and let the girl she copied from take the blame, that her favourite food is Cadbury's chocolate buttons, that she is afraid of tarantulas, even though she's never seen one in real life.

Maybe I was wrong. Maybe finding Mr Right isn't about 'just knowing,' maybe it's about knowing everything about him and loving him for all of those things – because it's endearing that he's afraid of mould and would rather throw away the entire cheese box than remove a mouldy piece and because you can't stand liver

347

and onions but will make it for him because it's his favourite food.

We toast the couple's knowledge of each other with a glass of champagne before finishing off the meal with chocolate tart with mascarpone. Yummy.

CHAPTER SEVENTY TWO

"Was I crying last night?" I ask Fiona the next morning. I don't remember crying, but there are black streaks down my face.

I stare at my reflection in the bathroom mirror, squinting.

"Don't you remember?"

No.

"No. What?"

"It was when we came up to bed. You found a text on your phone from James."

Of course.

I reach for my phone from the floor beside the bed.

B, I know you have moved on now, but I remembered it was Katie's hen do this weekend and I just wanted to say I hope you all have a great time. I still love you. Jx

I look at Fiona.

"He's wrong isn't he? You haven't moved on, have you?"

I shake my head.

"You have to tell him, Becky."

"No. I can't. It'll get better."

"But you're so unhappy."

"I'm not," I lie. "I'm fine. Honestly. I was just drunk. I don't even remember getting upset last night. Things will get easier. I'll meet someone else. Eventually."

I wish I didn't believe in Mr Right. I wish I thought there wasn't just one right person for each of us. I wish I believed there were hundreds of people that could all be right for us, in different ways. That if you meet one of them and it doesn't work out – because they die, or because they leave you, or because they turn out to be your best friend's ex, say – then you could just go on and meet one of the others instead.

If they leave you, then I think that means they weren't right in the first place. Does the same apply if they turn out to be your best friend's ex?

Maybe I got it wrong. Maybe James isn't Mr Right. If he were then we'd be together, wouldn't we? Because that's what I believe – that fate will lead you to your Mr Right. And what's the point in fate leading you to him if it's not going to finish off the job and make sure you stay together?

CHAPTER SEVENTY THREE

"Are you sure you've got everything?" Emma says, looking around my bedroom – which currently looks like the scene of a nuclear disaster. I couldn't decide what to pack.

It's the third time she's asked me.

The first time I realised I'd forgotten to pack my toothbrush.

The second time I realised I'd forgotten my dress. My bridesmaid dress.

A missing toothbrush is not a problem. I'm sure they have toothbrushes in the New Forest. A bridesmaid dress, however, is a different matter entirely.

I scan my mental list of things-to-remember-for-the-wedding (a mental list of things to remember is not a good idea – how the hell are you supposed to remember what's on the bloody list?)

Anyway. In no particular order:

Knickers.

Deodorant.

Bras – including the super-dooper-extra-padding-for-girls-with-no-boobs one that's no doubt going to make me look like I've grown a decent pair of boobs over night (these people know me, remember – they won't be fooled).

Tights.

Perfume.

Shoes – to go with dress. Bought in New York. When I was with James.

Cut off jeans.

Travel jewellery case containing two pairs of earrings, three necklaces and a bracelet.

White gypsy skirt.

Flip-flops – because I'm clearly going to have oodles of time for leisurely strolls around the New Forest.

Makeup.

Two t-shirts and three strappy tops.

"You're going for two nights, not two weeks," Emma tells me, when I've run out of fingers – on her hands and mine – to count off all the things on my mental checklist.

"I know, I know, but better to have too much stuff than not enough," I say, zipping up my case. "Let's go."

Emma is driving us to the New Forest.

Driving with Emma scares me. She drove us to Bournemouth once for a camping weekend after our A levels. We were stuck in traffic on a dual carriageway and she persuaded me to get out of the car and give my telephone number to a cute boy in the car behind us. Then the traffic started moving again and Emma thought it would be hilarious to make me run in my flip-flops to catch up with her. I don't think I've ever quite got over the humiliation – especially since an old codger in the lane next to us started hooting his horn and shouting at us through the window. We thought he was telling us off for being so irresponsible so we just flipped the bird at him and drove off. It was only when we got a bit peckish later on that we realised he was probably just trying to tell us our packet of chocolate chip Tracker bars had fallen out of the car as I'd hurriedly hopped back in. The cute guy never did call either.

I throw the case in the boot and drape my dress across the

back seat before jumping in next to Emma. This is going to be a fab weekend.

"Now, you're absolutely sure you've got everything?"

"Yep," I say, patting my handbag in my lap and glancing back at my dress.

Emma reaches across me and gets her CD holder out of the glove compartment.

"Pick something good," she says, handing it to me, before starting the engine.

"That would imply you have CDs in here that are not good," I laugh, flicking through them and settling on Kelly Clarkson's new album. I insert it in the CD player and turn up the volume, ready to sing my heart out.

"Ready?" she says.

Erm…

When do you think would be a good time to tell her I've forgotten the wedding present?

"We're lost," I say, biting into a Twix.

"We're not lost," Emma says, holding her half in her mouth like a cigar while she does a 17-point turn in the middle of a country lane.

"We are. We're lost."

"We're not."

When the car is finally facing the right direction – or at least in *a* direction, as opposed to one of the hedges on either side of the road – Emma prods the map.

"We're right here," she says. And there was me thinking she was prodding at random.

"How can you tell?"

"I just can."

I think we've reached the New Forest. We're surrounded by

trees. That ought to be a good sign. But quite where we are in relation to the hotel is anybody's guess.

I squint at the map. Map reading has never been my strong point. I tend to phone my dad instead. He's my walking talking map – a bit like Sat Nav but far less expensive and generally doesn't lead you down dead ends. I frequently phone him from the middle of nowhere and say: "Dad I'm lost, I need your help, I've just passed a sign for pick your own strawberries if that's any help." And he always rises to the challenge – fetching his map, phoning me back, and navigating me to exactly where I need to be. Except for the time I found myself going the wrong way around the M25 and he told me: "You need to get off."

"I can't," I had yelled hysterically down the phone at him. "The Dartford tunnel is in front of me. *Right* in front of me," I had added, for clarification." I ended up going through the damn thing, turning round and coming back over the bridge. It wasn't my dad's fault. I had taken my eyes off the road for a second – which I know is naughty, but I'd dropped a Malteser between my legs and on a hot day with no air conditioning, the consequences could have been disastrous – so I ended up getting in the wrong lane.

"Shall I phone my dad?" I ask Emma.

She nods.

It turns out we were just around the corner from the Montagu Arms Hotel.

It's a lovely place. It's an old property with all the original oak beams and antique furniture.

I have a double room. I booked it when I was still with Alex. And then I met James, so I kept it. It's gorgeous. It has a four-poster bed, and fluffy dressing gowns and Molton Brown toiletries. And there's everything you need in case you're too busy to make it down to breakfast the next morning – a kettle and mugs, tea, coffee, cereals, a little fridge with a jug of milk. It was too late to cancel and book a single room. And Emma had already booked her own room.

The ceremony is being held in the village church up the road. Then everyone will come back here for the reception.

Katie takes us to the room where the reception is being held. The hotel staff are busy setting up the tables with cream linen tablecloths, silver cutlery and glasses. The place cards are piled up in the centre of each table, ready to be laid out according to the table plan.

"It's looking good," I tell her.

I feel a hand on my shoulder. A booming voice in my ear.

"Becky, how lovely to see you." It's Katie's dad.

"Hi Roger," I say, kissing him on the cheek.

"Katie told us your news. Barbara and I are delighted for you," he says. Katie pokes him in the side.

"What news?"

"Dad, what do you think so far?" she asks.

"I think it looks smashing love. Absolutely smashing."

We spend the rest of the afternoon at the hotel. Guests who are travelling a long way for the wedding start arriving. Family members, old school friends, uni friends.

Everyone goes up to their rooms to unpack and then a few of us get some dinner in the hotel restaurant, followed by a night cap in the bar.

And then bed.

It's a big day tomorrow.

Katie's getting married.

CHAPTER SEVENTY FOUR

It's raining. And when I say it's raining. I mean absolutely pouring. So much so that it woke Emma, who woke me, who woke Katie – telephoning her room at 7am. I don't feel guilty. She has to get up anyway. She's got a wedding to get ready for.

"I have umbrellas," she informs me sleepily. "White ones."

Is there anything this super calm, super efficient bride has not thought of?

"Besides, it's going to be lovely and sunny later on," she adds, confidently. "The weather girl said so."

"How are you feeling?" I ask.

"Great. I can't wait to get married."

We don't need to be at the hairdresser's for another two hours yet.

"Are you hungry?" I ask. "Do you want to get some breakfast?"

"Yeah. Why don't you and Emma get dressed and come and get me when you're ready."

"Okay."

I phone Emma's room and tell her I'll fetch her on my way to Katie's room and then run myself a bath.

It's strange to think my friend is getting married today. In less than five hours she'll be a 'Mrs.'

I turn on the hot tap and leave it running while I rifle through my suitcase for something to wear.

There's something poking out of one of the side pockets. I pull on it. It's the *Sex & The City* tour leaflet. I'm not going to get upset. Not today. It's Katie's day. She doesn't need me blubbing all day. There'll be enough of that with her mum and dad and her auntie Rose mopping up her tears with her frilly handkerchief.

But just for the record, I do still miss him. I miss him terribly.

I toss the leaflet on the bedside table and continue rifling for clothes.

Cut-off jeans. T-shirt. Bra. Knickers. Shoes.

Bollocks. I have one flip-flop. One. I manage to pack four bras for a two day visit to the New Forest, but I can't even manage to bring footwear for both my feet.

Clutching my phone and keys in one hand and my flip-flop in the other I tap on Emma's door with the edge of the shoe. The door is ajar so I let myself in.

I can hear Emma in the bathroom on the phone.

"It's fine, honestly, I spoke to him last night," she's saying. "No, she hasn't got a clue."

"Em," I call out.

There's a loud clunk – the sound of a mobile phone crashing on to the tiled bathroom floor.

"Hey," she says, coming out, smearing her lips with lip gloss.

"Who was that?" I ask.

"No-one," she says.

"What are you up to?" I ask.

"Nothing," she says, picking an imaginary hair off her sleeve.

She's forgetting how well I know her. That's what she does when she's fibbing. She picks imaginary hairs off her clothes. She did it all the time at school.

"Where's your assignment," Mrs Darnley would ask.

"I'm sorry Miss, I left it at home," she'd say, picking an imaginary hair off her school jumper.

"Who were you talking to?" I ask her.

"Erm. . ." She's usually quicker than this.

"And who hasn't got a clue about what?"

"Katie. About my reading. It's a surprise. I told her which one I was doing, but I've changed my mind."

"Right. So who were you talking to? And who did you speak to this morning?"

"I was talking to Matt's best man. And I was talking to Matt last night."

"What for?"

"To check I could change the reading."

She's fibbing. She's up to something. I know she is. But right now I have more pressing concerns.

"I need to borrow some shoes," I say, waving my flip-flop at her.

"Take your pick," she says, gesturing to six pairs of shoes arranged neatly underneath the dressing table. And she said I brought too much stuff?

Katie opens the door beaming.

"*I'm getting married in the morning,*" she sings.

We go in and sit on her bed while she finishes getting ready.

"*Ding dong the bells are gonna chime.*

"*La la la la, la la la la… so get me to the church on time.*"

I roll my eyes.

"It's not too late to swap, Em," I say. "I'm sure my dress would fit you."

"No way. I'm going to have far too much fun with my reading."

I may be imagining it, but I could have sworn she just gave Katie a 'look.'

"Anyway, come on you two, I've got a wedding to get ready

for," Katie says.

"Mine!" she adds, for clarification.

I don't know where she puts it. Katie is hours away from putting on the most expensive dress she'll ever wear and walking up the aisle in front of all her friends and family and she's scoffing down a full English breakfast. Sausage, bacon, eggs, tomato, hash browns, baked beans and black pudding. You can't even see the plate.

"I probably won't get to eat again all day," she says, seeing the stunned expression on both mine and Emma's faces as we trough *our* way through a bowl of muesli and a slice of toast (wholemeal.)

"I'll probably spend the entire afternoon posing for photographs and listening to all my old rellies witter on about how much I've grown, while you lot trough on salmon en croute and raspberry pavlova."

"That'll serve you right for not taking us with you on the food tasting!" I point out.

She's shovelling another forkful into her mouth when the girl-friend of Matt's friend Marcus walks into the dining room. Anita.

We don't like Anita. She's loud. She talks far too much. She's full of self-importance. She's one of those girlfriends of your boyfriend's mates that you just have to put up with. She tried to wangle an invite to the hen do. We told her we weren't doing anything special. Just close friends and family for dinner.

"Katie!" she shouts, skipping over to our table.

An awkward half-hug follows, where they both try desperately not to dip their elbow in the baked beans.

"I'm so excited for you. How are you feeling? What's your dress like? Where are you going on your honeymoon? Where's Matt? I hope you didn't spend the night together, you naughty girl."

She doesn't even take a breath, let alone give Katie time to answer.

"And you Becky," she says, looking at me. "Congratulations."

"So, Anita, what are you wearing?" Emma asks, rudely interrupting her. Thank God. But what is it with all these congratulations? I may be walking down the aisle, but I'm only the bloody bridesmaid for heaven's sake.

"Well, I was going to wear a white trouser suit, but my sister told me I shouldn't, that it's not the done thing to wear white to someone else's wedding, so anyway..." She trails off mid-sentence when she spots Marcus at the breakfast buffet and slopes off to join him.

"She's the second person to congratulate me," I tell Emma and Katie, draining my glass of juice.

"Anyone would think it was me that was getting married."

"Well it's quite an honour being my bridesmaid, you know," Katie says, looking pointedly at Emma.

"I know, I know," she says. "I'm a terrible person. But," she adds, dramatically, "you are going to love, love, *love* my reading."

"I can't wait," Katie says, grinning.

"Me neither."

It's still pouring when we leave the hotel for the hairdressers. It's a good job that's where we're going because we get drenched just getting to the car.

I did point out the fact that Katie has four brand new umbrellas back in her room.

"They're for the wedding," she said. "I don't want to spoil them."

"A bit of rain won't hurt them," I laughed.

"What if a bird poos on them?"

"What if a bird poos on us?" I asked. "Or, more to the point, what if it rains on our hairdos."

"I told you, it's going to be beautiful later. It'll be sunny by the time we're done," she said.

"Isn't bird poo white anyway?" Emma had asked, still pondering the last part of the conversation.

So, anyway, we get drenched getting into the car and half an hour later we get drenched again getting out of it and into the hairdressers.

I've told Katie I'll have my hair done any way she wants. I may live to regret my flexibility. She might decide she wants me sporting a mohican. Okay, probably not, but you never know.

The three of us sit in a row facing the mirror. Emma, here in her supervisory capacity, flicks through a bridal magazine.

"What about this?" she says, holding up the magazine so that I can see it in the mirror.

I screw up my face.

"She won't want anything too poufy," Kate tells my stylist.

My friend. She knows me well. She knows I am the girl who washes her hair as soon as she gets home from the hairdressers because it looks too 'big'.

"No mousse. No gel. No hairspray," she adds.

My stylist screws her face up this time.

"Well maybe just a bit," I concede.

Before I can change my mind she squirts what is definitely more than 'just a bit' of mousse onto her hand, rubs it between her palms and splats it on top of my head with a grin.

After a brief discussion Katie decides I should wear it half up half down. So that's what the stylist does, weaving in lots of little twisty things with sparkly bits in the middle that we brought with us from Accessorize.

"I like it," Emma says as I swivel round in my chair to show her the finished effect.

"You should wear it like that for your own wedding," she adds. "It really suits you."

"I didn't know you were getting married too," the stylist says. "When's the big day."

"I'm not," I say.

"No, but you will be one day," Emma says, sticking her head back in the magazine.

Half an hour later Katie is done too.

She looks lovely. She normally wears her hair down. Today it's swept off her face in soft curls.

Not only does she look gorgeous, but she looks bloody smug as well. It's stopped raining. And not only has it stopped raining, but the sun is shining.

Whoop whoop!

"Time check," Katie says as we walk out to the car.

I glance at my watch.

"11.13am precisely."

"Just think Katie, in less than two and a half hours you'll be a married woman. Goodbye Katie Roberts, hello Katie Henley."

Becky Newman, I think to myself. I can't help it. These things just pop into your head.

"Hello, I'm Katie Henley, pleased to meet you. Have you met my husband, Matt?" Katie says, grinning.

"Oh my god, my *husband*!" she repeats, as if she has just heard the word for the first time.

Next stop, makeup.

We've decided to do our own makeup. I've never liked other people painting my face – the beauticians at the makeup counters in Boots, for example – tickling my eyelids with their makeup brushes and scrutinising every imperfection. I always end up laughing. And it's not really all that funny, so then I just look really stupid. And why would I want to look stupid when I can just smear the stuff on my own face?

Besides, Katie said she wouldn't feel like her if someone else did her makeup.

"He's marrying me," she explained. "I want it to be me he sees when he's standing at the altar."

She must want to look a bit different to normal though – she has allocated a whole hour and a quarter for makeup.

I could shower, style my hair, put on my makeup and get dressed in that time and still have at least twenty minutes spare for a double vodka and tonic for Dutch courage.

"I'm going to leave you to it," Emma says, as we rifle through our pooled makeup supplies.

I really must update my makeup, I tell myself, removing a loose chunk of eye shadow from the bottom of the bag and examining a dried up lip gloss and a concealer stick with bits of fluff stuck to it.

I pick up one of Katie's Ruby & Millie eye shadows. "You've got ages yet, stay a bit longer."

"I need to get ready. I need to look my best for my reading," she says, winking at Katie.

She's *definitely* up to something.

CHAPTER SEVENTY FIVE

I stare in the mirror at my friend's reflection.

"We did a good job," she says.

"We did," I agree. "You look beautiful Katie. Matt's a very lucky man."

"I love him so much, Becky."

"I know you do. And he loves you too."

"Here. This is for you," she says, handing me a gift bag.

"What is it?"

"It's just something to say thank you for putting up with me over the last nine months. I know people usually give out presents at the reception, but I wanted this to be just me and you."

There are two presents inside the bag. The first is a silver necklace with a tiny glass heart pendant.

"I thought it went with your dress," she says, slipping it around my neck and fastening it.

The second is a framed card bearing a quote about love. It's the same card that Katie and Matt have on their bedroom wall. I told her once how much I loved it.

Love is not finding someone you can live with. It's finding someone you can't live without.

"It's not easy to find," she says, squeezing my hand.

"No."

"You'll find it again, B," she says, and I feel a lump rise in my throat. "You did a very brave thing. A wonderful thing. And for that alone you deserve to be happy."

"Don't make me cry," I tell her. "It's taken me hours to look this good!" And she laughs.

I'm dabbing at a stray tear that's fought its way out of the corner of my eye when Katie's dad puts his head around the door.

"Ready, girls?"

CHAPTER SEVENTY SIX

You are my husband, you are my wife
My feet shall run because of you
My feet shall dance because of you
My heart shall beat because of you
My eyes see because of you
My mind thinks because of you
And I shall love because of you.

Traditional Eskimo Love Song

"Marriage is the union between one man and one woman," the vicar announces, his voice echoing around the church that's packed full of Katie and Matt's friends and family.

There's an impressive assortment of hats among their guests. It's nice. Not many people wear hats these days. It's all that curling and straightening – people are afraid of putting a dent in their hair. There are some lovely outfits too. Lots of fabulous dresses on the ladies, smart trouser suits and colourful tie choices on the men. I spotted Fi and Adrian as we were walking down the aisle. She is wearing a pink dress and he is sporting a pink tie. Very colour co-ordinated. Very Fi.

I'm babbling now, I know, but I'm afraid if I actually stop and think how wonderful this all is, I might cry. And then I'll think about James. And I'll cry some more. And pretty soon I'll be a blubbering wreck and guests in the back rows will be handing me down their tissue supplies. And that won't do at all. Standing next to Matt at the front of the church, I've never seen Katie look so beautiful. Or so happy.

I can't imagine what their lives would be like without each other.

Sitting down, I look behind me and spot Emma. I smile. I wonder if she's nervous. She waves a piece of paper at me with a big grin on her face. I think she'll be okay.

"We have come together in the presence of God," the vicar booms out, making me jump in my seat. These pews aren't the comfiest. My bum's going numb.

"…to witness the marriage of Matthew and Katherine." Matthew and Katherine? Who are they? Oh, yeah…

"…to ask for his blessing on them and to share in their joy."

Matt squeezes Katie's hand.

"But first we have a couple of readings that have been chosen by Katie and Matt's friends and family. First Katie's father Roger Harris will be reading an excerpt from *Captain Corelli's Mandolin*, from a scene where Dr Iannis is speaking to his daughter Pelagia."

Roger steps up to the altar and pulls a piece of paper from his jacket pocket. Placing it gently on the lectern in front of him, he looks out at everyone, clears his throat, and smiles. He looks so proud.

"Love is a temporary madness. It erupts like volcanoes and then subsides. And when it subsides you have to make a decision.

You have to work out whether your roots have so entwined together that it is inconceivable that you should ever part. Because this is what love is. Love is not breathlessness, it is not excitement, it is not the promulgation of promises of eternal passion. That is just being 'in love' which any fool can do. Love itself is what is left over when being in love has burned away, and this is both an art and a fortunate accident.

Your mother and I had it, we had roots that grew towards each other underground, and when all the pretty blossom had fallen from our branches we found that we were one tree and not two."

He smiles at his daughter and future son-in-law and then returns to his place beside Katie's mum.

And then it's Emma's turn.

"And now Katie and Matt's good friend Emma is going to read a piece about love by an unknown author. *I Knew That I Had Been Touched By Love.*"

There's a brief interlude as she shuffles past everyone on her row, followed by the clicking of her heels against the marble floor as she makes her way slowly to the front. The noise echoes softly around the church.

Then, just before she reaches the lectern, she turns and smiles at Katie and Matt. And then at me.

She's carrying an A4 folder. Crikey, how long is this reading?

"Actually, there has been a slight change of plan," she tells her audience.

"I'm going to do two readings, not one.

"You see, I found one that I loved – and that took me a while, I can tell you," she laughs. "But then I found another. And I liked that one even more. Because it described what Katie and Matt have better than anything else I'd found before. And boy have I read a few wedding readings. You should see my library fines! So, well, anyway, what can I say? I'm greedy – so Katie and Matt said I could do both."

She smiles again. The church is silent. You could hear a pin drop. Even the kids have gone quiet. She has every guest in the building hanging off her every word.

And so she starts.

368

"I knew that I had been touched by love the first time I saw you, and I felt your warmth, and I heard your laughter.

"I knew that I had been touched by love when I was hurting from something that happened, and you came along and made the hurt go away.

"I knew that I had been touched by love when I stopped making plans with my friends and started making dreams with you.

"I knew that I had been touched by love when I suddenly stopped thinking in terms of 'me' and started thinking in terms of 'we'.

"I knew that I had been touched by love when suddenly I couldn't make decisions by myself anymore, and I had the strong desire to share everything with you.

"I knew that I had been touched by love the first time we spent alone together, and I knew that I wanted to stay with you forever, because I had never felt this touched by love."

When she has finished, she looks up and smiles.

"And now for the one that beats all the others," she says, opening the folder, "the one that says it like it really is."

I had no idea that Emma had put this much work into it. She obviously felt guilty about the whole three-times-a-bridesmaid thing.

"My boyfriend has got lovely brown eyes," she reads. "My boyfriend has a cute dimple in his right cheek and a tiny scar above his left eye. My boyfriend makes me laugh – even when I feel like crying."

Suddenly my hand flies to my mouth and I gasp. A little louder than I'd intended. Emma stops. Katie looks around. Matt looks around. The best man looks around. The vicar looks over at me. He probably thinks I've just remembered some just cause or impediment why these two persons should not be joined in holy matrimony. "Do be quiet," he probably wants to say, "I haven't got to that bit yet."

As for Emma – well, she just looks at me and smiles. It's a smile that's just for me and a lump catches in my throat. And then she starts again.

"Is this why he is Mr Right?

"No.

"My boyfriend makes me feel loved. When he touches me he makes me feel something that no-one else has ever made me feel. I want to be with my boyfriend all the time, and when I am not with him, I miss him.

"Is this why he is Mr Right?

"No.

"My boyfriend would listen to my dreams every morning if I wanted him to. My boyfriend would chat to me while I was sat on the loo – he wouldn't mind.

"Is this why he is Mr Right?

"No.

"The reason my boyfriend is Mr Right is none of these things and all of them.

"How do any of us know we have met Mr Right?

"The answer is simpler than you would ever imagine. There is no why. There is no how. There is just knowing.

"We just *know*."

I don't understand. It was in the bin. I put it there myself. On top of a pile of soggy tissues. It was the day that Katie came round and dragged me out of bed.

Katie…

Just as I'm identifying the culprit, she turns around and looks at me. Slowly she plants a kiss on her fingertips and blows it over to me. And I breathe again.

"Who is Mr Right?" Emma continues.

"Mr Right is someone you love unconditionally. He's someone you want to be with forever, someone who makes you feel safe and secure...

"He's someone who will wipe your nose when you're on the top of a mountain because your hands are so cold you can't even take your gloves off to do it yourself ...

"He's someone you'll grab and kiss – up against a police riot van if there's one in the way – not because you want to, but because you just can't stop yourself."

Katie looks at Matt at this one and laughs out loud. So does the rest of the church. Even the vicar.

"It can be sudden, or it can creep up on you. And before you know it you are head over heels in love...

"And when you've found him you won't question it. You'll never ask yourself 'is he the one?' Because you'll know that he is...

"You'll never feel like you've settled. You'll look at him and know that he's a part of who you are – and that losing him would be like losing your whole world...

"You'll no doubt have loved before. But this love will be different. This love will be the best of all things...

"There are so many things that make up a whole. But ultimately it's got to feel right. And you've got to at least believe it will still feel right in years to come.

"It's like Captain Corelli said," she adds, looking up from the words in front of her for a brief moment. "It's alright when you are young and fresh-faced and sexy. But you won't always be.

"Can you still see yourself with him when he is old and wrinkly. Sitting on a park bench? Holding your hand?

"You have to know that when you're sixty, or seventy, or eighty, you'll still want him to be sitting there next to you, holding your hand.

"I once asked an old friend of mine how she knew her husband was the one – how I'd know when *I* had found the one. And she looked at me and said 'honestly?'

"I nodded.

"'When you don't need to ask that question', she said."

Then Emma closes her folder, takes a breath and begins her third and final speech. And this one is all her own.

"Some of you who know me might be wondering why I'm up here," she says, "why I'm not down there with Becky, in a bridesmaid dress with a bouquet in my hand and twinkly bits in my hair.

"Katie did ask me. She wanted both of us – Becky and me – as her bridesmaids. But I said no. Because I was superstitious," she laughs. "I believed that a penny on the floor was good luck and that being a bridesmaid three times was bad luck.

"I thought that if I was bridesmaid for the third time then I'd be jinxed – that I might never find someone to marry myself. Not that I ever really believed in Mr Right," she laughs. "Katie and Becky will tell you that. I thought the best I could hope for was to find someone who I could love quite a bit," – everyone laughs at this, "and who wouldn't get on my nerves too much. You know – by leaving their dirty socks all over the bedroom floor and deleting the Eastenders omnibus.

"But I was wrong. Love isn't finding someone you can live with. Love is finding someone you can't live *without*. And when you find that person you can try to live without them – if there is a reason why you think you should, or why someone else thinks you should. But in the end you'll just have to be together. Why? Because. Just because."

I look up at my friend and I smile.

"Someone told me that when I was just a little girl," she smiles.

"I thought it was rubbish. But I know now that it's true. You just have to look at Katie and Matt to see that."

And then she gathers up her papers, steps down from the altar and walks back to her seat, stopping only to hand me the folder.

I open it up and there in front of me, on page 26 of *Love Life* magazine is my very first feature. *How Do You Know You've Found Mr Right? By Rebecca Harper.*

And at the very top of the page there's a note, in Emma's handwriting. *Look behind you.*

So I do. And when I do, I see my Mr Right. And I find myself falling in love with him all over again.

CHAPTER SEVENTY SEVEN

Somewhere there waiteth in this world of ours
For one lone soul, another lonely soul –
Each chasing each through all the weary hours,
And meeting strangely at one sudden goal;
Then blend they – like green leaves with golden flowers,
Into one beautiful and perfect whole –
And life's long night is ended, and the way
Lies open onward to eternal day.

'Somewhere', Sir Edwin Arnold (1832 – 1904)

"Squish in everybody," the photographer instructs all the boys. "There are a lot of you to fit in."

We've had the bride and groom shot. We've had just the bride, just the groom, the groom and his best man, the bride and her bridesmaid, the bride and her bridesmaid and the one who said no. We've had all the family shots, all the kids, all the grandparents.

Now it's Katie with all the boys.

James is there, laughing with them all as they attempt to pick Katie up and hold her horizontally, without completely stripping her of every last shred of dignity.

"Why now?" I ask Emma, as we sip champagne in the gardens

of the Montagu Arms and celebrate our best friend's wedding.

I have so far discovered that Katie rescued my article from the bin. She's clever though – she replaced it with some other pieces of paper so I wouldn't notice. Then she sent it to Jennifer Dutton, who replied saying she loved it and was going to use it in the September issue as planned – only she still had Katie's address, so it was Katie who opened the letter, and Katie who forged my signature in the contract. As for my letter to Jennifer Dutton – the one explaining why I wouldn't be sending my article after all – well she put that one in the bin after offering to post it for me. I did think at the time it was incredibly kind of her, given that she'd more or less told me I was a fool for even writing it. And finally she has been doing her best to stop me from seeing the magazine for the last three days since it appeared on the shelves of every newsagents in the whole of London. She's had a couple of close calls, what with her dad and then Anita…

And she showed it to Emma, of course.

"I didn't get it before," she says. "But I do now. I want what Katie and Matt have got, Becky. And I want you to have that too. But if I don't let Jim – James – go then you'll never have that. He's your Mr Right. No-one else will do."

"Are you sure Em?" I ask. "Are you really sure?"

She sips her champagne.

"Yes. I won't pretend it's easy, because it's not. But I know now that it's right. You're my best friend, B, and I want you to be happy."

"Thank you, Em," I say hugging her tight.

Katie dashes over, looking flushed and laughing.

"Come on, Em," she says. "Come and see the cake. You'll love it."

And then he's there, by my side. My Mr Right.

"Oh, by the way B," Katie shouts, running back over, her dress trailing obediently behind her.

"I think you'll find this is yours," she says, handing me an envelope.

"What is it?"

"Take a look."

I open the envelope and take out the piece of paper inside.

It's a cheque. For £378. And there's a *Love Life* compliment slip attached.

Becky, I am most impressed. Please call my secretary and arrange an appointment to discuss regular freelance work. Regards, Jennifer.

"Oh my god," I say, and they all smile – Katie, Emma and James – my two best friends and the love of my life.

"Great article," James says when Emma and Katie have left to look at the cake.

"That boyfriend… the one with the lovely brown eyes and the scar above his left eye… Anyone I know?"

"Oh him, he's just some guy I met," I say, gently touching his scar.

He takes my hand in his and kisses it.

"I love you Becky. I never want to lose you again."

"I love you too."

"So, about this room of yours," he says, grinning. "It doesn't happen to be a double does it?"

I nod.

"Four poster bed in fact. And do you know what else it's got?" I say.

"What?"

"Cornflakes," I tell him. "Packets and packets of cornflakes…"

There is no remedy for love than to love more.
Henry David Thoreau (1817 – 1862)

AUTHOR NOTE

In The Park Bench Test the heroine Becky needs to find
out how you know you've met Mr Right. As I was single
when I first started writing the novel (I am now married
with two small children!) I was blissfully unaware how you
knew when you'd found "the one"! To give the story a bit
of authenticity, therefore, I interviewed my own friends,
family members and colleagues on this issue. In other
words, the interviews in The Park Bench Test are genuine
– and not a figment of my imagination! Names have been
changed to protect the innocent!